PAT McINTOSH, like Gil Cunningham, is a graduate of Glasgow University. Born and brought up in Lanarkshire, for many years the author lived and worked in Glasgow and is now settled on the West Coast with a husband, three cats and a daughter.

D0595248

The Rough Collier

Pat McIntosh

SOHO
CONSTABLE

ROBINSON
London

Constable & Robinson Ltd
3 The Lanchesters
162 Fulham Palace Road
London W6 9ER
www.constablerobinson.com

First published in the UK by Constable,
an imprint of Constable & Robinson Ltd 2008

This paperback edition published by Robinson,
an imprint of Constable & Robinson Ltd, 2009

First US edition published by SohoConstable,
an imprint of Soho Press, 2008
This paperback edition published by SohoConstable, 2009

Soho Press, Inc.
853 Broadway,
New York, NY 10003
www.sohopress.com

A copy of the British Library Cataloguing in
Publication Data is available from the British Library

UK ISBN: 978-1-84529-900-2

US ISBN: 978-1-56947-581-2

Printed and bound in the UK by CPI Mackays, Chatham ME5 8TD

1 3 5 7 9 10 8 6 4 2

For Ros,
a book about Lanarkshire
John 1:46

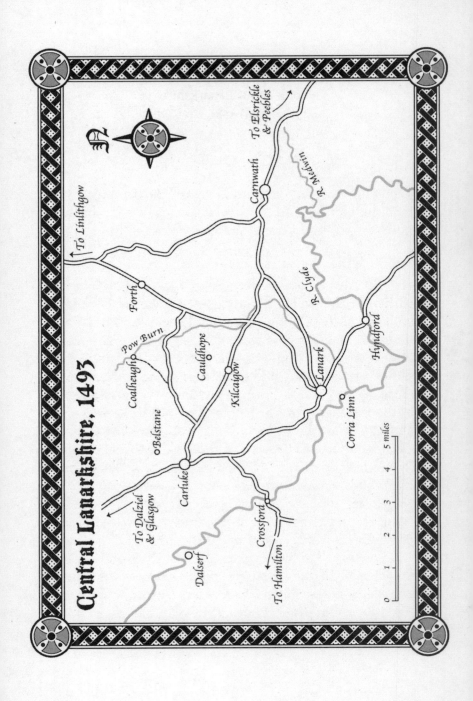

Central Lanarkshire, 1493

To Linlithgow

To Elsrickle & Peebles

Carnwath

R. Medwin

R. Clyde

Forth

Pow Burn

Coalheugh

Cauldhope

Kilcaigow

Belstane

Lanark

Hyndford

Corra Linn

To Dalziel & Glasgow

Carluke

Crossford

Dalserf

To Hamilton

0   1   2   3   4   5 miles

Chapter One

When the peat-cutters came to report the dead man, Gil
Cunningham was up in the roof-space of his mother's
house, teaching his new young wife swordplay.

He and Alys had ridden out from Glasgow to Belstane
earlier in the week, planning to stay for a few days
so that Lady Cunningham could get to know her
daughter-in-law better, and relishing their escape from
his duties about the Consistory court and hers in her
father's house. In fulfilment of a promise he had made
eight months ago, Gil had persuaded Alys into the attics
at the first opportunity, where they had flung wide the
shutters to let the light in along with the wide view of
Carluke town and the hills of south Lanarkshire beyond
it, and cleared an area of the dusty floorboards by shifting the kists and lumber of several generations of Gil's
Muirhead forebears. They had progressed, in three
days, to practising with an old straw target and a pair
of wooden swords out of one of the kists.

'Like this,' Gil said, in the French they used when
they were together. Alys's wide skirts were kilted
above her knees, for freedom of movement; he dragged
his eyes from the slender legs and ankles in their
knitted stockings to demonstrate the grip he wanted

her to take on the polished hilt. 'Keep the point up. Then you can turn it from the elbow –'

'Like turning a key?' suggested Alys.

He reached round her shoulders to put his hand next to hers, and she leaned briefly into his embrace and looked up at him, brown eyes dancing. He bent to kiss her, and remarked, 'It was never this much of a pleasure when old Drew taught these moves to my brothers and me.'

'I should hope not,' said his bride primly. She settled her grip and turned the little stave experimentally. 'Like this?'

'Less slantwise.' Gil tried to recall the old weapon-master's approach. 'You need to find the balance.' He kissed her again, and stepped away. 'Now strike as I showed you – across, and twist the blade, and back. That's it!'

'But surely,' Alys swung the sword again, striking dust and flakes of straw from the target, 'your opponent doesn't wait for you to hit him a second time?'

She checked and turned her head as footsteps sounded on the stairs, and ducked hastily behind the timbers of a dismantled bed, pulling at the folds of wool about her waist. The ankles vanished as Lady Egidia's waiting-woman appeared at the door to the stair-tower.

'Maister Gil,' she said, puffing slightly. 'The mistress said you was up here. There's a fellow at the yett, come from the peat-cuttings up ayont Thorn, wants a word wi' you.'

'With me?' said Gil in surprise. 'I've no authority here – it's my mother holds the land.'

'No, it's you he's wanting.' Nan had got her breath by now. 'It's on Douglas land but wi' Sir James and all of them being from home he came here to tell you. They've found a deid man.'

'A dead man?' Alys emerged from her hide. Nan nodded triumphantly, the ends of her white headdress swinging.

'Aye, and he says he's all turned to leather wi' the peat, but they ken fine who it is, and they want you to see to taking up the woman that did it.'

Egidia Muirhead, Lady Cunningham, had come in from inspecting her horses and was interrogating the messenger in the hall. She sat in her great chair by the fire, straight-backed and commanding in a mended kirtle and a loose furred gown which had belonged to her dead husband. At her back stood her steward, a fair, stocky fellow with a pleasant face and the harried manner any man developed in contact with Lady Egidia, and before her a countryman in muddy boots and worn leather doublet was twisting his bonnet in his hands and answering hesitantly. As Gil stepped in from the stair-tower, Alys at his heels, the wolfhound which was sprawled on the hearth leapt to its feet and bounded forward to greet him. The grey cat on the plate-cupboard hissed, and his mother said over the dog's singing:

'Here's Wat Paton, Gil, with some tale of a corp in the peat-diggings.'

The man ducked his shaggy head.

'Good day to ye, Maister Cunningham,' he said in some confusion, 'and good wishes to yer bonny bride and all.'

Alys thanked him, and curtsied, to his further confusion.

'You're one of my godfather's tenants,' said Gil, studying the man. 'Down, Socrates,' he added to the dog, who dropped obligingly to four paws and took his attentions on to Alys.

'Aye, that's right, sir, I am, I'm one of Sir James's tenants,' agreed Paton. 'In Thorn, over yonder. There's seven of us dwells there, and we all went up to the peat-digging the day morn, and here was this dead man. And when we kent who it was that we'd found, and seen that something had to be done about it, we decided I'd come to get you, and it's right convenient you being here to visit your lady mother the now, sir, what wi' Sir James being away at Stirling, and his depute gone to Edinburgh this week about the case at law, and Maister Michael no closer than Glasgow.'

Gil flicked a glance at his mother, and saw her face tighten briefly at this mention of her godson, offspring of her nearest neighbour Sir James Douglas.

'But how do you ken who it is?' he asked.

'Oh, that's clear enough, and no trouble to discern,' said Paton with an access of confidence. 'See, we came on his head first, and though you wouldny ken his face now, his hair's as red as a tod in summer, and there's the one fellow missing the now, and he's red-headed and all. It's Tammas Murray from the coal-heugh up by the Pow Burn, clear as day, and he's been put there by witchcraft so Sir David said, which must ha' been by the witch that dwells up there and all. So if you'd come wi' us, maister –'

'Hold up here,' said Gil. 'Why do you want me? Has the man been formally identified? Who's bringing the charge of witchcraft?'

'I wouldny ken about that,' said Paton, wringing his bonnet again, 'only that Sir David said we wanted you and I was to come and get you, and we all agreed on that, and the rest of them has went to lift the witch and fetch her to confront the corp.'

'The impertinence of that Davy Fleming!' said Nan, from the doorway where she was listening avidly.

4

'Why should he take Maister Gil away from visiting you, mistress? And from his bride and all?'

'Where is this?' Alys asked. 'Where are the peat-cuttings?'

'It's no far, mem,' said Alan Forrest the steward, and pointed generally eastward. 'They're up yonder, just off our land, no more than a mile or two from here. It's no as if it's asking Maister Gil to go out to the coal-heugh.'

'We'll no keep your man that long, mistress,' Paton assured her.

'I think you must go, Gilbert,' said Lady Cunningham, meeting his eye significantly. Gil gave her a tiny nod.

'Give me time to get my boots on,' he said. 'Did you ride here, man, or are you afoot?'

'I rode the old pony,' said Paton, grinning in relief. 'I'm glad of that, maister, I'd no wish to go back to Sir David saying you wouldny come out.'

Gil nodded, and turned to go back up the spiral stair, Socrates at his knee. Alys hurried after him to the small chamber his mother had allocated to them, and seized her riding-dress from where it hung on a nail behind the door.

'May I come with you?' she said in French, unlacing her blue woollen gown. Gil paused, boot in hand, to watch appreciatively as she squirmed out of the tight bodice. Five months of marriage had altered her, he recognized. Once she would have waited for his answer before she began to change her clothes.

'I may be some time,' he warned her.

'All the more reason.' She was tugging on the leather breeches which went under the garment. 'I've never seen a peat-digging,' she added, tying the waistband. Gil kicked off his shoes and pulled the boot on.

'It's just a hole in the ground.' He tramped down on the heel, wriggling his toes in place, and accepted the

5

second boot from Socrates, who stood waving his stringy tail, ears pricked in anticipation of an outing.

'With a dead man in it.'

'Yes,' he agreed thoughtfully. 'Something I have not heard of before.'

'It's a strange place to dispose of a dead person. After all, if people dig the peat, a body must be found sooner or later, no?'

'You would think so.'

'And if this woman is to be taken as a witch,' she added, her voice muffled by the folds of the skirt. Emerging from the swathes of pale brown wool and smoothing it down over her kirtle she went on, 'someone should be there to support her. Another woman, I mean.'

'It could be nasty.'

'I know.' Her face sobered. 'I once saw a witch taken up. We were in Paris, and I was too young to do anything.'

Gil, digesting this, exchanged the loose short gown he wore in the house for a closer garment with a budge lining. Alys, having laced her bodice, craned to see into the mirror, settled her hat carefully over the linen cap that hid her long honey-coloured hair, and lifted the gloves to match the blue leather trimmings on the riding-dress.

'You're very *bien tenue*, sweetheart. You could be riding out on the King's hunt, not crossing our own lands to the peat-cutting.'

'It's all I have.' She gathered up her skirts to precede him down the stairs. 'Besides,' she added, and glanced over her shoulder at him with her quick smile as Socrates slithered behind them, 'now while I am a bride, I must dress as befits your station. Once I'm known as your lady I may wear what I please.'

* * *

6

One of the Belstane menservants rode out with them across the moorland, a scrawny dark-browed fellow called Henry who had been a stable-boy when Gil was a child and was now one of Lady Egidia's upper stud-grooms. Following him, they could hear the disturbance by the peat-cutting before they saw it, a confusion of the lapwings' plaintive cries blown on the wind with a loud, nasal tenor carrying the lower line on its own.

'That'll be Sir David,' said Paton confidently. 'A good clear voice he's got.'

'That is your priest?' asked Alys, turning in the saddle to look at him where he bobbed along in their wake on the old pony. He grinned at her and nodded.

'That's him right enough, Maister Gil,' pronounced Henry as they rounded the shoulder of the bleak hillside. 'David Fleming. He's a strong man for Sir James's rights,' he added in neutral tones.

'Aye, he is that,' agreed Paton. 'He's chaplain to Sir James, see, and priests for us all when we canny get down to the kirk in Carluke, and takes to do wi' the estate when Jock Douglas the steward's away. That's him in the grey plaid, talking to Rab Simson.'

There were two men in the sharp-edged hollow, one in homespun leaning on a peat-spade, the other stouter and grey-clad, gesticulating at something which lay shrouded by a felt cloak on a hurdle at their feet. A small cart was tilted on end nearby. A hare skipped across the hillside higher up, and the lapwings wheeled and called across the empty sky beyond. Henry halted his horse by the cart, which it inspected suspiciously, and Gil reined in beside him and whistled for his dog. At this the tubby priest looked round, broke off what he was saying and made haste to climb out on to the rough, wind-shaken grass, raising his round felt cap.

7

His wrinkled, mended hose were smudged with peat as if he had been kneeling.

'Maister Cunningham,' he said eagerly, coming to Gil's stirrup. 'So Wat bore his message. My thanks to you for coming out, maister, and you'll ha' Sir James's gratitude for it and all. And madam your wife honours us!' He bowed to Alys, gave her an appraising grin and raised the cap again, exposing a fluffy tonsure surrounded by limp mousy hair. 'I'm David Fleming, maister, madam, chaplain to Sir James and depute to his steward, and they're both away, you ken, which is why –'

'No trouble,' said Gil politely. 'What have you to show us, Sir David?'

'It's this corp we've found in the peat,' explained the priest, 'or I'd never have inconvenienced you, for we've sent to take up the woman that done it, and it all needs to be dealt wi' in due process. Will you dismount, maister, and take a look at him? Henry, take Maister Cunningham's reins,' he ordered sharply as Gil handed his reins to the man. 'It's certain enow who it is, maister,' he went on, 'but it needs an authority to call the quest on him, and carry the charge agin the witch.'

'You've proof, have you?' Gil lifted his wife down from her saddle. 'Some evidence?'

'Oh, she's well kent to ha' quarrelled with the man.' Fleming bowed again to Alys. 'Now you bide here, Mistress Cunningham,' he went on, in a condescending tone which Gil felt was ill advised, 'and Henry can have a care to you, while I show your goodman this –'

'Thank you,' said Alys, smiling sweetly at him, 'but I can get down into the digging.' Fleming looked askance at this, and his expression turned to indignation as she gathered her skirts together and jumped, without waiting for Gil's supporting hand. She looked

8

about her with interest, prodding with her booted toe at the dark surface of last year's cut. Gil followed her.

'It's no a fit sight for a young lassie,' Fleming protested. 'Maister, I think you should bid her stay here. His face is no –'

'My wife makes up her own mind,' said Gil mildly. Socrates appeared at the gallop over the curve of the hill and leapt down beside his master, tongue lolling. 'Get on, Sir David.'

'Aye, but –' Fleming bit his lip, and gave up. 'If you'll come over here, maister, you can get a look at him, and here's Rab Simson that found him, all buried in the peat, and –'

The man by the hurdle touched his blue bonnet as they approached across the springy surface, then bent to draw back the patched felt cloak which covered the corpse. Socrates pricked his ears intently, his nose twitching, but Gil put out a hand.

'Bide a moment. Before I see him,' he said, 'tell me how you found him. Was it you saw him first? What are you doing up here anyway?' he added. 'It's early to be casting peats. Were you setting out this year's portions?'

Simson looked sidelong at Paton, and nodded, muttering agreement.

'We was cleaning up a bit,' volunteered Paton. 'And looking how wet the peat is and clearing the grass off the cut, and the like. It's a good day for it, seeing it's been dry for a week.'

'How many of you? Was it all seven of you from Thorn? Did you all come up here together?'

'Oh, aye,' said Paton. 'We came up here wi' the cart, an hour after Prime, since the oats is sown and the land's no ready for the bere yet. We came all together from Thorn town, Geordie Meikle and his brother Jock, Rab here, William Douglas,' he counted on his fingers,

'Eck Shaw, Adam Livingstone and me. And it's Jock and Geordie's cart,' he added. 'All the rest's gone up to the coal-heugh to take the witch.'

'And then we saw this man staring out of the peat-wall like the Judgement Day,' said Fleming in his nasal tenor.

'What did you do first?' asked Gil, ignoring this.

'Walked the ground,' said Paton promptly.

'Paced off the portions,' agreed Simson, with growing confidence, 'and put the first of the markers down.' He pointed at a bundle of wooden stobs which lay on the grass nearby.

'Then Rab and William Douglas came down into the digging to look how dry the peat was,' went on Paton.

'And there he was!' said Fleming.

'It was you that found him?' Gil asked. Rab Simson admitted to this. 'Show me where.'

The man turned to indicate a cavity in the cut face of the peat. The dark, crumbling layers round it were disturbed, and spade-marks indicated where they had used leverage to get the body out. The dog paced forward from Gil's side to peer into the hollow, snuffling hopefully, and Gil snapped his fingers to recall him.

'His head was here, see,' Simson pointed. 'I seen his hair first, just sticking out a crack in the peat-dyke where it shrunk when it dried out a bit, and I thought first it was maybe a jerkin or the like that someone had left last year.'

Gil nodded, but Fleming declared, 'That was daft, Rab Simson. It would never last the year out in the weather like that.'

'Well, he's lasted,' said Simson argumentatively, indicating the corpse.

'So then you came to look,' prompted Gil.

'Aye, and let out a great skelloch,' said Paton, grinning. 'And we all come running, and when we seen it was a head right enough we tried if it was loose, see, and it wasny.' He demonstrated with a swivelling movement of both hands which was somehow quite unnerving. 'And then –'

'And then,' trumpeted Fleming in Gil's ear, 'they found the rest of the body was there, and sent for me, as was right, and I oversaw getting him out the peat, and identifying him. Will you see him now, maister?'

'This is where he was buried,' repeated Gil. Alys looked up at him and nodded.

'Aye, here and nowhere else,' agreed Simson.

Gil turned, and bent to the cloak which shrouded the body on its hurdle. Fleming was ahead of him, grasping the corner, but paused to warn them again:

'It's no a sight for a young lassie. You take my advice, you'd be better up yonder wi' the horses, mistress.'

'Let me see him,' said Gil. Fleming reluctantly drew back the cloak. Socrates extended his long muzzle, sniffing, and growled faintly. Gil checked him.

The object revealed was not immediately obvious as human. The shock of hair caught the eye, as red as the summer fox Paton had mentioned, but at first glance it was attached to a bundle of sticks wrapped in old leather, damp and dark like the peat which still clung to them. Then Gil recognized a hand, and a foot, and began to see how the body was disposed, lying on its left side with the hands crossed in front of the chest and its knees drawn up into the shrunken belly, the chin tucked in and the face turned down on the left shoulder like someone asleep.

'He's near turned to peat himself,' he said.

'Aye, he is that,' agreed Simson. He and Paton nodded proudly, as if it was their doing.

'You'll want to see his face, maister,' prompted Fleming. Gil stepped round the hurdle, and bent to look. 'You see, he's no to be kent by his features. She's

11

made certain o' that. If it wasny for the hair we'd never ha' kent him, maister.'

Gil nodded. The sight was nowhere near so grisly as Fleming's warnings had implied, but the face was unrecognizable. The corpse's features were flattened, the nose bent sideways and the jaw dislocated so that the blackened teeth showed in a misplaced grin. One eye was closed, the lid shrunk into its socket, but the other eyeball had sprung out and lay withered on the crushed cheekbone like a yellow cherry on a stalk. On the peat-brown skin of the jaw was a bloom of gingery stubble.

'How did he die?' asked Alys.

'How?' Fleming was taken aback, but recovered quickly. 'That's no a matter we need to think on, mistress. He's dead, and that's the meat o't.'

'The law will wish to know how he died,' said Gil. 'And when,' he added, sniffing. 'He's been dead a good time. He smells of the peat and nothing else.'

'I was thinking that,' said Alys. 'How long does it take, for something left out here to become black and shrink like this?'

'A long time, surely,' said Gil.

'No, no,' said Paton argumentatively. 'It might be no more than a pair o' weeks.'

'Havers, Wat!' said Simson. 'He's further gone than our old cow was when we found her, the other side of the moor, and she'd been missing two month.'

'As little as that?' said Gil.

'It must take less than that,' said Fleming with authority, 'for it's certainly Murray by the hair, and he's no been missing as long as two month.'

Gil exchanged a glance with Alys, and then turned back to the cavity in the peat.

'Tell me how he was lying,' he said.

12

'Just the way you see him,' pronounced Fleming, 'for we couldny straighten him, what with the flesh so shrunk on the bones.'

'On that side, or the other?'

'Kind of on his right side,' said Rab Simson, thinking as he spoke, 'but no quite. His face was turned right up,' he added, 'and no even a cloth ower it.'

'And you dug in from here, from the side of the peat-wall?' Gil prompted. 'Not down from the top?'

'Aye, that's right,' agreed Paton. 'We just burrowed in wi' our fleuchters.' He pointed to Simson's peat-spade in illustration. At Gil's elbow, Alys repeated the new word silently. 'We didny want to come down from above him, see, in case . . .' He grinned awkwardly.

'The peat above him has never been cut,' Gil said, and touched the dark caked surface. 'Do you see there where there's a lighter band? It goes right across with never a break. The layers have not been disturbed, not till you came along and cut under them with the fleuchters. They're sagging now, but they've never been cut through.'

'Of course they haveny,' proclaimed Fleming. 'I saw that and all, Maister Cunningham. That's how I kent it for witchcraft, for she's simply slain him and set him under the peat without ever having to dig down. And when you set that with other information I have –'

'More likely,' said Gil, 'he was laid here before the peat grew.'

Simson nodded agreement, but Paton objected: 'The peat never grew! It was aye there! You're daft, Rab Simson.'

'You're daft yerself, Wat Paton,' retorted Simson. 'It must ha' growed, else how did the trees get at the bottom of it, that you find in some of the diggings? Or the old peat-spades, from afore Noy's Flood, maybe? And my grandsire found an elf-bolt under the peat

13

ower by Braidwood. I've seen it when I was wee. So it's all grown since Noy's time, likely.'

'Aye, since Noy's time. A thousand year or more. It never grew in the time the man Murray's been missing,' said Fleming, 'which just goes to prove it's witchcraft.'

'We still do not know how he died,' said Alys. She had turned back to the corpse on its hurdle, and was bending for a closer look. 'He has no clothes on,' she added, pulling off her glove to touch the peat-dark skin. 'Except – is this a belt?'

'It isn't leather,' said Gil. 'It still has the fur on.'

'I said he was no sight for a young lassie!' reiterated Fleming.

The lapwings had begun calling again. A noise of several voices shouting reached Gil, and the dog growled just as Paton looked up the flank of the hill and said, 'Maisters, is this them coming back from the coal-heugh now?'

'Aye, it is,' agreed Fleming with enthusiasm. 'You can confront her wi' her crime, Maister Cunningham, and then we can get on and deal wi' it properly.'

The first heads were surfacing above the curve of the hillside, with gesticulating peat-spades and a loud argument which flew in snatches on the brisk wind. Socrates growled more loudly, and Gil checked him. Five men, clad like Paton and Simson in leather and homespun, were hustling a woman along in their midst. She wore neither plaid nor mantle, and her apron and good woollen gown were muddy from the enforced march across the moorland, her indoor cap askew and her hair blowing in the wind. Her hands were bound before her, but it was clear that her tongue was not restrained.

'And if you hadny lifted me from my stillroom,' she declared as they came closer, 'I'd have completed the oil for your mother's joint-ill, Geordie Meikle, and you could have taken it to her this evening. She tellt me when she asked for more that she was just about out of it –'

'You said that a'ready,' said one of the men round her, shoving her roughly towards Gil. She stumbled forward, and fell over the edge of the peat-cutting, landing awkwardly on hip and elbow. Alys exclaimed indignantly, and sprang to her assistance, while Fleming pronounced:

'Well may you grovel, witch, afore the evidence of your ill deeds! This is the witch, Maister Cunningham, well kent for miles about as a cunning woman wi' herbs and ointments, and seen by me to ha' quarrelled wi' Thomas Murray that lies here slain by witchcraft.'

'Thomas?' the woman said as she stood upright. She gave Alys a shaky word of thanks, looked at Gil, and bowed awkwardly over her bound hands. 'Sir, what's to do here? The men would tell me nothing but that I'm accused of witchcraft and evil-doing, and now – are you saying Thomas is dead?'

'You ken well he's dead, woman,' trumpeted Fleming, 'you that set him here in secret!' Gil turned and fixed the tubby priest with his eye. 'But by God's help and these innocent instruments of justice –' He became aware of Gil's gaze and faltered in his oration. 'Your crime's been uncovered,' he ended lamely, and became silent.

'Aye,' said Gil drily, and turned to the woman. 'What's your name, mistress?'

'That's Beattie Lithgo,' supplied one of the men around her. Gil eyed him, and he too fell silent.

'Beatrice Lithgo,' confirmed the woman, 'relict of Adam Crombie the collier.' Her accent was not local, but came from further east, Gil thought, the Lothians perhaps.

15

'Mistress Lithgo,' he said. 'There's a corp found here, that's been identified as Thomas Murray.' He stepped aside, watching her face. She looked from him to the bundle of bones on the hurdle, and frowned, obviously trying to make it out as a body.

'Is that a man?' she questioned. 'From here it could as well be a calf drowned in the mire.'

Fleming opened his mouth, but Gil caught his eye again and he subsided.

'It's a man,' Gil confirmed. 'Look closer, mistress.'

She gave him a doubtful look, and stepped forward to bend awkwardly over the corpse, flinching as she located its battered countenance.

'Oh, the poor soul. His mother wouldny ken him,' she said. 'Has he been beaten, or did this happen while he lay here, do you suppose, sir?'

'You tell us, woman –' began Fleming.

'Do you recognize the man?' Gil asked without expression. Beatrice Lithgo straightened up and turned to him. She was tall for a woman, taller than Alys though shorter than Gil himself, and behind the blowing wisps of reddish-fair hair her face was plain and bony, with a sharp nose and angular jaw. Light eyes between grey and blue considered him, equally without expression.

'I do not,' she said, 'no being his mother. It could be Thomas, it could just as well be some other poor soul. The hair's lighter than his, but –'

'His hair's bleached wi' lying out in the peat,' pronounced Fleming, unable to contain himself longer, 'and if you beat him past knowing afore you hid him here, small wonder we canny tell him by his face.' The men around them nodded, and one or two muttered agreement.

'Maister Gil!' called Henry from among the horses.

'I think it's no him,' went on Mistress Lithgo, 'but I'd

16

sooner you got Thomas's wife to see him, or one of the men that works by his side.'

'To look for marks on his flesh, you mean?' said Alys, coming forward.

'Maister Gil, look up yonder!'

'Any collier has scars,' agreed Mistress Lithgo, 'and Thomas has a few that I treated, but I'd as soon have some other word for it, and I've no doubt you would and all, sir,' she added, with faint humour.

'Maister Gil!'

The dog rose, hackles up, from his position at Gil's feet, and stared up the hillside. Gil looked over his shoulder, and saw another ragged company appearing over the curve of windswept grass. This was a bigger group, grotesque in pointed hoods and long-tailed sarks of leather, and somehow much more threatening even at first sight, before he took in the style of implements the men carried or the tone of the shouting which broke out as they caught sight of Mistress Lithgo.

'It's the colliers,' said one of the men beside Fleming, 'come to fetch the witch home, maybe.' He took an apprehensive grip of his peat-spade, and looked at the priest, who seized hold of Mistress Lithgo's arm.

'Gather round, lads,' he ordered, gesturing with his free hand. 'They'll no get a hold of her for aught we can do!'

'No just the colliers and their mells,' said another man, making no move to obey Fleming. 'There's lassies wi' them. Two lassies.'

'The whole of the day shift, wi' my older daughter,' said Mistress Lithgo in resigned tones, 'and my good-sister Joanna. Joanna Brownlie, Thomas's wife,' she added to Gil.

'Ah,' said Gil. He caught Alys's eye, and held out his arm. She came forward with one of her flickering smiles, laid her gloved hand on his wrist, and allowed him to lead her across the hollow towards the approaching mob of miners with their heavy short-hafted hammers. There were eight or ten of them, with two very pretty young women in their midst whose white linen and well-dyed red and blue wool contrasted sharply with the blackened faces and muddy leathers of the men.

'Give us back our Beattie!' shouted the man at the front as the group halted on the edge of the peat-cutting, and others echoed him. 'Set her free, or we'll –'

'Mistress Brownlie?' asked Gil formally, raising his felt hat.

The older of the two girls stiffened warily, and a wiry man beside her said, 'Who's asking for her?'

'I'm Gil Cunningham, the Archbishop's Quaestor, and this is my wife Alys Mason.'

Gil bowed, and Alys curtsied. The miners fell silent, staring down at them, except for the one who had asked their names, who said, mell at the ready, 'And what's Blacader's questioner to do wi' Joanna Brownlie? Why can you no free Beattie to us and be done?'

'She's no witch,' put in another voice from the back of the group. 'Our Beattie's a good woman. Who's to physic our hurts if she's ta'en up for a witch?'

'There's a corp been found,' said Gil, still speaking formally to the whole group, 'and some thought that it might be Mistress Brownlie's man, who I understand is missing.' There was a small sound of distress from the girl who had reacted earlier, sweet-faced and graceful in dark red with a married woman's headdress of folded white linen. One hand rose to her mouth. 'We need her to look at the corp if she's willing,' Gil went on, 'to tell us if it is or it isny him.'

'What's that to do wi' my mother?' demanded the other girl, a small slender creature just maturing, her

18

long fair hair well set off by a blue woollen gown and red-and-blue checked plaid. She jerked her head at Mistress Brownlie. 'If it's the wonderful Thomas then *she's* the one to put a name to him and wash him, there was no need to lift my mother wi' such a tirravee about it. And will you set her free now, or do we make you?'

'Speak civilly to Maister Cunningham, Phemie,' directed Fleming from behind Gil. The girl opened her mouth on what was obviously to be a sharp answer.

'Mind your tongue, Phemie,' said her mother. Phemie blushed unbecomingly but fell silent.

'Aye, but we'll make you set her free,' said one of the miners, 'and make someone sorry he ever thought of calling our Beattie a witch, priest or no priest.'

'Will you look at the corp, Mistress Brownlie?' asked Alys. She put her free hand out encouragingly. The girl in the linen headdress looked at the wiry man beside her. He gave her a heartening nod and sprang into the cutting, reaching up to swing her easily down beside him. She came forward from his clasp with obvious reluctance. 'He's not a bonnie sight,' Alys warned her in her accented Scots, and took her hand. 'Come, I will show you.'

The miners, Phemie among them, crowded after her towards the corpse on its hurdle and the guard of peat-cutters. Gil took up a position between the two groups, assessing just what he would do if things turned violent. Over the heads he could see Henry the groom, plainly making similar plans.

'Is that him?' said Joanna Brownlie, checking as they approached. 'No, madam, that's surely never Thomas. His hair's the wrong colour.'

'It's bleached wi' the air, like linen,' said Fleming from his post at Mistress Lithgo's side. Gil saw a flicker of amusement cross Beatrice Lithgo's bony face, but she did not speak. Joanna curtsied distractedly to the priest, but stayed where she was, eyeing the corpse with misgiving, and dug her heels in against Alys's coaxing hand.

'That canny be Thomas,' she said after a moment. 'His hair's away too light, he's thinner than a Death on a monument, he's –'

'The body is shrivelled with lying buried in the peat,' Alys explained.

'Thomas was well when I last saw him,' said Joanna rather desperately. 'I canny think this is him, I see no purpose in my looking closer –'

'Has this woman bewitched you and all?' demanded Fleming, shaking Mistress Lithgo's arm. Joanna looked properly at them both for the first time, and crossed herself.

'Our Lady protect us, Beattie, what have they done to you?' she exclaimed, and turned to Gil, a pleading look in her wide blue eyes. 'I don't understand, maister. What's all this about anyway? Phemie came running into the house no an hour since saying the Thorn men had come and taken her mother for a witch, and we called out the day shift and made haste to follow, but we never heard aught about a corp, or Thomas – what has this to do wi' Beattie? Sir David, why have you bound her like that?'

'It isny Thomas Murray,' said another voice. The man who had been at Joanna's elbow was on one knee beside the hurdle, inspecting the corpse, easing the cramped limbs with a careful touch. 'I'll swear to that, on any relic you can produce,' he added significantly, and turned to look hard at the priest, who snorted indignantly, though Gil could see no reason why.

'How no, Jamesie?' asked someone from the miners' group.

'This lad's never held a mell in his life.' Jamesie indicated the corpse's hands. 'Look here. His arms are

20

shrunk to the bone but his hands and feet have the flesh on them yet, and you can see the skin. It's as soft as a priest's a— it's got no calluses,' he amended, and displayed his own palms, the coal-dust ingrained in their hardened skin. He was a sturdy, well-made fellow, his hair fair where it straggled from under his padded bonnet, his teeth very white in his blackened face when he spoke. 'What's more,' he added, after a moment's thought, 'was Thomas no lacking a couple of joints?' He raised his left hand.

Beatrice Lithgo nodded, and Joanna said, 'You're right, Jamesie. These two are short.' She touched the last two fingers on her left hand. 'From a mishap when he was a sinker in Fife, so he told me.'

What is a sinker? Gil wondered, as some of the colliers agreed behind him.

'Well, this one's got all the fingers he was born wi', and the nails on them and all.' Jamesie jerked his head at the corpse again. 'It's never Thomas Murray, whoever it is.'

'Aye, it is Thomas Murray,' argued one of the peat-cutters. Jamesie turned to look at him. 'If it isny Murray, then where is he, Jamesie, tell me that?'

'I've no the least idea where Thomas is,' said the collier, 'no being his keeper. All I ken is he's no lying here on this hurdle wi' his throat cut. Right, Geordie?' he ended in a threatening tone, and the other man quailed.

'Throat cut?' said Alys quickly. 'Show me!'

'Is there no end to this?' demanded Fleming. Ignoring him, Jamesie turned back to the corpse and eased it over a little so that the cords of the neck were visible where they ran under the misplaced jaw. Gil stayed where he was, alert for sudden movements on the part of either group of supporters, but Alys bent to look closely, and suddenly straightened up, biting at the back of her glove, and met Gil's eye in some distress.

21

'As he says,' she confirmed. 'His throat has been cut.'

'Aye, I tellt you he was no sight for a young lady,' said Fleming in that condescending tone. 'I'm sorry if it grieves you, mistress, but I did warn you.'

'Thomas was well when I last saw him,' said Joanna again, 'he canny be lying here wi' his throat cut, and that's never –'

'And how no? I'll believe it isny Murray when you produce the man alive,' declared Fleming, his grip still tight on Beatrice Lithgo's arm. 'You're all in collusion, is what I say, the same as before.'

'Before? What do you mean by that?' said Mistress Lithgo, turning her head to stare at him down her sharp nose.

'You know very well what I mean. Are you to pay these women any mind at all, Maister Cunningham?'

Gil tightened his lips on the first reply which came to him. After a moment he said, 'Whatever we do, I've no wish to stand out here on a windy hillside much longer. I want the corp taken somewhere I can examine it closer, and I want to hear more about Thomas Murray and when he was last seen –'

'That's easy enough,' said Joanna Brownlie. 'He set out on the round the morrow of St Patrick, after Sir David here had come up and said a Mass for us the evening before, and confessed him and the two that were to ride wi' him. And we looked for him –' She bit her lip, an action which became her well though she seemed unaware of it, and turned to exchange a glance with Mistress Lithgo. 'We looked for him by Pace-tide. Near three weeks since,' she finished.

'Indeed aye,' trumpeted Fleming. 'He never came home to the Good Friday Mass, and that's when I became right concerned, Maister Cunningham.'

'Seventeenth – no, eighteenth of March. A Monday. So he's been gone better than five weeks,' Gil calculated. Joanna nodded. 'Has no one ridden out to look for him?'

'Mistress Arbella willny spare the men,' said the collier Jamesie, getting to his feet. 'There's a delivery more than due to leave, and we've been building up the coal-hill ready for it. As it is, he's away wi' our two best sinkers.'

'You're saying there are three of them missing?' prompted Gil.

'What have you done wi' them, woman?' demanded Fleming, shaking Beatrice Lithgo's arm. She said nothing.

'Three of them,' said Phemie from her post at her mother's other side. 'And whatever coin he's collected. He's not away wi' a string of horse, maister,' she elaborated, 'he's gone to collect the fee for last winter's deliveries.'

'Arbella will have his head when he returns,' whispered Joanna, knotting her hands together at her breast. Jamesie looked down at her, but did not speak.

'Arbella?' queried Gil.

'My grandmother,' said Phemie. 'Who's in charge up yonder. Whatever Thomas bloody Murray thinks.'

'School your tongue, lassie!' declaimed Fleming, and she tossed her head. 'That's no way to talk of your grandam, the devout woman that she is.'

'We'll stand out here no longer,' Gil said firmly. 'We'll have the corp borne somewhere we can clean him up till I get a right look at him. I'll ride out to the coal-heugh after I've done that.' He met Alys's gold-brown gaze. She nodded slightly, and gathered up her skirts with one hand as if prepared for a further journey. 'There's questions I want answered afore I make a decision here.'

'And the witch?' demanded Fleming. 'Will we put her secure and all?'

'Set her free,' said Gil, over a rising hostile rumble from the colliers.

'What?' squawked Fleming. 'Wi' the proof of her misdeeds –'

'Set her free,' repeated Gil. 'Now.'

Chapter Two

The stable-yard at Belstane was not the ideal place to study a corpse, but it was probably the best they were going to get. Accompanying the Meikle brothers' cart in at the gateway, Gil managed to dismiss most of the entourage which had followed it down from the diggings and was now swollen by the addition of his mother's stable-hands, several women from the surrounding cottages, and all their children. They gathered outside the great wooden yett peering in and commenting loudly.

'We'll have him here,' he directed over the noise, pointing to the front of the cart-shed, 'under the pent but in the light. Henry, can you get us a pair of trestles, man, and Alys, would –' He looked round, and discovered her horse standing riderless by the groom's.

'She's away to the house, Maister Gil,' said Henry, taking Gil's bridle as well. 'Likely gone to ease herself,' he offered. 'Give us just a wee bittie, maister, and we'll have your corp laid out where you want him. Is he to be washed?'

'No, no,' said Gil hastily. 'I've no notion what water would do to him.'

'Aye, very wise,' said Fleming, bustling forward from the horse trough, wiping his hands on the paunch of his grey gown, 'get Maister Cunningham his trestles,

Henry, as he ordered you, very wise, maister, we'll no risk losing the traces of the witch's ill deed.'

The tubby priest had argued violently against freeing Beatrice Lithgo, but finally, seeing that Gil was determined and that the farm men were reluctant to press the point against the miners with their heavy mells, he had given in, swallowed his indignation, and accompanied the corpse rather possessively, passing the short journey asking effusively after Gil's sisters in between giving loud directions to the Meikles on the management of their own cart. Gil had ignored most of his discourse, but now, hoping to avert the man's supervision, he said politely:

'I know you'll not want to delay your prayers for him any longer, Sir David, whoever he is, even with neither incense nor holy water. If you stand there,' he indicated the far end of the cart-shed, 'you'll be well placed.'

Much gratified, Fleming hurried to the spot, and watched with his beads over his hand while the hurdle was removed from the cart and set up on a pair of trestles. It was still draped in the felt cloak, and just as Henry removed this Alys reappeared, a sacking apron over her riding-dress and her hands full of brushes of different sizes. Socrates left his inspection of the cart-shed to wave his tail at her, sniffing at the brushes.

'That's a good thought!' Gil said.

'Some are bristle and some are hair,' she said, colouring with pleasure. 'This kind we use at home for dusting the panelling.'

'A good harness-cloth would be as apt for the task, mistress,' said Henry with humour, 'seeing he's all turned to leather.'

It was like Alys, Gil reflected, that after only a day or two under his mother's roof, she was on good enough terms with the household to borrow anything she needed. He smiled at her, and bent over the corpse on its support. It was already beginning to dry out, and here and there the leathery skin was split over the long bones and joints.

'He'll not keep long,' he observed. 'We'll have to bury him soon, named or no, or he'll fall into dust.'

'I suppose it is a man,' Alys said doubtfully.

'Look at the beard.' Gil pushed his dog's long nose away from the bright shock of hair.

'His baggie's well shrunk,' Henry said from the other end of the hurdle, 'but you can see it clear. He's a man grown, right enough.'

'His . . .?' Alys began, and coloured up again as she understood. 'I brought a cloth to cover his face,' she added hastily. 'I thought it would be better.'

'I need to study his head first,' Gil said.

Socrates, finding they were doing nothing interesting, went off about his own affairs, and the two of them worked together to brush away the drying peat which clung to the visible portions of the corpse. This provoked some comment from the near audience, which included the muttering Fleming, the Meikle brothers and Wat Paton as well as Henry and the stable-hands, but nobody offered to help. Under the dark, crumbling stuff, the dreadful face was even more gruesome to look at, but Gil studied it with care, poking with a brush handle behind the stained teeth and feeling cautiously at the nose and cheekbones.

'As I thought,' he said eventually in French.

'Mm?' said Alys.

'For one thing,' he pointed with the brush handle, 'his skin's intact over these injuries, the flattened nose and broken bones in his face. I think they've happened after he was buried, I suppose with the pressure of the peat over him. And for another, there's no sign of scavenging, no insects in the peat, no beetles or maggots, as you get with fox kill or the like.'

'So he has been buried as soon as he was dead,' said Alys. Then, with more confidence, 'But we knew that, surely? He must have been folded up like this before he set. But that doesn't tell us how soon he was buried,' she answered herself before Gil could comment, 'and the beetles do. What about –' She bit her lip. 'Flies will settle on a fresh wound. Is there any sign at his throat?'

'I haven't got there yet.' Gil dislodged a caked lump of peat from behind the corpse's small, neat ear. 'His hair's longer than mine. And –' He felt the side of the head through the damp hair. It gave under his fingers. 'This is strange. See this?' He prodded again. 'My fingers leave a hollow – Sorry, sweetheart!' he exclaimed, as she covered her mouth and turned away. He set down the brush and stepped quickly round the hurdle, to put a supporting hand under her elbow. 'I'm sorry,' he said again, 'I forget that you've never been at the hunt. Do you want to go into the house?'

'No, no,' she protested, but leaned gratefully against him. 'How strange, his face and his poor shrivelled body don't disturb me, but that – urgh!'

'I'm sure you should go in,' he said. 'I find it so enthralling, that all our old huntsman taught me about the study of a kill in the forest can be applied to a dead body, that I forget myself. I can work alone, sweetheart.'

'No, I want to help. Let me – let me go on.'

She drew away and turned back to her task, whisking crumbs of peat from the folded arms and legs of the corpse. He watched her in concern for a moment, then looked up and found Henry grinning knowingly at the far end of the hurdle. Catching Gil's eye, the man winked, but said nothing. It was clear he thought he knew the reason for Alys's squeamishness.

But he's wrong, Gil thought, we know that. There was no reason yet for her to be sick, and that in itself – it was barely five months since their wedding, far too soon to be concerned, Alys kept saying. Nevertheless some of her acquaintance among the merchants' wives of Glasgow had begun to ask arch questions, and raise eyebrows at her answer, and now here was the same attitude showing itself. He shook his head, got another knowing wink, and bent over the corpse again.

It was as if the skull had gone from inside the skin, he decided, prodding again at the leathery scalp. And beneath it – he felt carefully at the hollows his fingers had left already. Beneath it the brains had turned to something which felt very like butter. Why would that happen? And why should the skull-bones vanish and the bones of the face remain?

Abandoning these questions for later, he explored the rest of the scalp, parting the harsh bright hair and brushing flakes of peat and strands of moss away from the skin. On the crown of the head, rather to the right side, the skin was split and drawn back, and the yellowish stuff visible within the wound did resemble butter. The whole corpse smelled of the peat it so much resembled, but here it was underlaid, very faintly, by another scent like old cheese. Peering closely at the gash in the scalp, he decided that its edges were slightly thickened, as if this injury had happened before death.

'This is not a working man,' said Alys. He looked up, to find her studying the corpse's hands where they were tucked against its chest. 'See, there are no calluses on his fingers, as the collier said, and his fingernails are neatly trimmed. And his feet –' She gestured with the brush she was using. 'He has no shoes on, but his feet are as soft as his hands. He has gone well shod.'

'There's none of the gentry missing,' said Henry. 'And none wi' that hair hereabouts anyway. He's maybe a traveller of some kind, lost on the moss, Maister Gil.'

'We should be making notes,' said Gil.

'I left my tablets in our chamber,' said Alys. He laid the cloth she had brought across the distorted face, drew his own set of tablets from his purse, and passed them over when she held out her hand.

'Use Scots,' he requested, 'so I don't have to translate if it's needed for evidence.'

She found a clean leaf and noted her own findings, and he summarized his for her.

'You think he has been struck on the head?' she asked as he finished.

'It looks very like,' he admitted.

'Lost on the moss and attacked,' offered Henry, who had listened with interest.

'And his throat cut as well,' said Alys.

'Someone wanted to be certain,' said Henry.

'No further wounds on the scalp. He's got all his front teeth, though they're loose in the jaw now,' Gil noted in passing, and Alys wrote this down. 'And his throat has been cut.' He eased at the displaced jaw, to scrutinize the leathery recesses under it. 'On the left side, from under the ear to the windpipe. No sign of maggots or flies.'

'On the left only?' said Alys, looking up.

'From in front, maybe,' suggested Henry doubtfully.

'You don't cut a man's throat from the front,' said Gil. 'Not unless you want to be drenched in blood.'

'Like a pig-killing,' agreed Alys, nodding. 'So it would have been a right-handed man who killed him, standing behind him?'

'I'd say so, and the blow to the head was right-handed as well.' Gil peered further into the hollow

30

under the jaw, and identified something fibrous wedged in a fold of the skin. 'What's this?' He poked with one finger, but could get no purchase on the strand. 'Alys, have you a hook or a key or something about you?'

Searching in her purse in her turn, she handed him a buttonhook. Even with this it took him some time to get a purchase on what he had seen, so embedded in the flesh was it, but finally it lodged in the curve of the little implement and he was able to coax it out.

'A cord,' said Alys.

'A cord,' Gil agreed, returning the buttonhook. He took the free end in his fingers, and it came away in his grasp. 'It's near rotted to dust, but I think this may be what's killed him. He's been throttled. Here at the back of his neck where the flesh is so shrunk you can't see any trace of it, I suppose the cord must have crumbled away, but under his jaw it had sunk so deep it was protected from the bog-waters. If his throat was slit after he was dead, the blood would drain more slowly.'

'They were really makin' certain,' said Henry, much impressed. 'That's three ways they slain him – cracked him on the head, throttled him wi' a rope, and slit his throat,' he counted off on his fingers. 'I'd no go so far to put down a horse, save he was a right brute.'

'But when?' Gil wondered. 'When has this happened? Is there any tale of someone going missing on the moor?'

'No that I mind,' said Henry, 'nor that I ever heard tell. You'd maybe want to ask some of the old folk,' he added, 'they've little enough to do but talk over what's past.'

'No need of that, surely,' expostulated Fleming almost in Gil's ear, and he realized that the man had ceased his prayers and had been drawing closer for some time, exclaiming indignantly at what was being said. 'It's the man Murray, for certain, and everything you're saying makes it clearer what the witch has been at! Draining his blood after he was dead, and the like, Our Lady protect us from such wickedness. And what did she plan wi' his blood, Maister Cunningham, tell me that!'

'I've no idea,' said Gil politely. 'I've not studied witchcraft, Sir David. It seems you have.'

'It isny Thomas Murray, Sir David,' said Wat Paton beyond the priest, 'Jamesie Meikle was quite clear on it.'

'I have to protect my flock, maister,' protested Fleming, ignoring this. Across the stable-yard there was a disturbance, as the crowd outside the yett parted reluctantly to allow someone through. Hooves clopped on the cobbles. 'I've never studied it close, I only ken what anyone kens!'

'Aye, I've heard a few tales about that,' said Henry, with humour.

'Gil,' said Alys, putting a hand on his sleeve. 'Is that not Michael Douglas at the yett?'

Just inside the iron-bound leaves a slight young man was dismounting from a tired horse, a groom in blue-grey livery already afoot to take his reins. The newcomer wore the narrow blue belted gown of a student of the University of Glasgow, and untrimmed mouse-coloured hair stuck out below his scholar's cap. Fleming hurried forward with more exclamations, brushing the peat-cutters aside and reaching his master's youngest son just before the Belstane steward, to bow and flourish his felt hat, babbling greetings. Michael Douglas stared at him with some surprise, and as Gil joined the group the plump priest waved imperiously at the steward.

'And here's Alan Forrest to make you welcome, Maister Michael. Alan, bring Maister Douglas a stoup of ale, can you no see he's thirsty?'

'Alan can manage his duties without your advice, Sir David,' Gil observed, as the maidservant behind the steward came forward with a tray with jug and beakers. 'Good day to you, Michael.'

'Good day to you, Maister Gil,' said Michael warily in his deep voice. He accepted the ale the steward poured him with gratitude. 'I'd no notion you were here. Madam your mother's no ill?' he added anxiously. 'Or – or your sisters?'

'No, no, Lady Egidia is well, Maister Michael,' Fleming assured him, 'and all the young ladies and all, by what Maister Cunningham tells me!'

'It's a wedding-visit,' explained Gil, deliberately obtuse.

'But what's brought you out from Glasgow, Maister Michael?' Fleming rushed on. 'I hope it's no bad news from Sir James?'

'He sent Attie here to me,' said Michael, nodding at the groom who was intent on his own beaker, 'bade me ride out to the house about – about something, and I thought I'd call here on the way. Pay my respects to my godmother,' he expanded. 'And, well, anyone else that was here. Mistress Mason,' he added, and bent the knee to Alys as she came to Gil's side. 'You're looking well. Your good health.' He raised the beaker and drank.

'Tib's at the convent in Haddington, Michael,' Alys said. Ale splashed down the front of the blue gown. 'As a guest of Sister Dorothea,' she added hastily.

'But you could make yourself very useful here,' said Gil, 'if you can spare the time.'

Michael swallowed, handed the beaker back to the maidservant, and patted drops from his chest and shoulders.

'I don't know that I can,' he said ungraciously, wiping his chin. 'I've only a few days' leave, and I need to see to this matter of the old man's. What's to do, anyway? Is that no half the men from Thorn hiding by the cart-shed?'

'It's good of you to call by, godson,' said Lady Egidia, with faint malice, 'to brighten an old woman's day.'

'What old woman would that be, Mother?' asked Gil politely, pouring wine in the little glasses set in a sparkling row on the plate-cupboard.

Her mouth twitched, but she went on: 'And what brings you out here away from your studies? I hope you've permission to be out of the college.'

'Oh, aye.' Michael felt at the breast of his gown. 'I'd a letter from my father, that when I showed it to the Principal he agreed I must have leave. I've no notion what's worrying him, but he writes that he canny leave the court, and Jock Douglas is away at Edinburgh, and my brothers both about other business, and he's concerned about that fool Fleming and something up at the coal-heugh.'

'The coal-heugh again,' said Alys, accepting wine in her turn from Gil. 'Is that the same one where a man called Thomas Murray dwells, Michael?'

'Aye, it is,' he said, startled, 'and it's the man Murray my father wants me to speak to. It seems the winter fee's long overdue, and he's had a daft word from David Fleming all about witches or some such, and I've to sort it out.'

'Witches,' repeated Alys. 'His mind seems to run on witches.'

'Of course, the Pow Burn crosses your ground,' said Gil, sitting down beside Alys, across the hall hearth from his mother. 'The coal-heugh is your father's then?'

'Well, it's on our land, we have the mineral rights. He gets a good fee for it.'

'What is this about?' demanded his mother. 'I'd a

long tale from Alan and from Nan the now about you cutting up this corp in our cart-shed, Gil –'

'I did no such thing!' said Gil indignantly.

'We simply examined the body, madame,' Alys assured Lady Egidia, 'to see if we could tell how he died, and how long ago it was. We cut nothing open. It would be interesting to do that,' she added thoughtfully. 'I wish Holy Kirk was not so set against it.'

'What corp is this?' asked Michael, looking at her in alarm.

'I can say who it isn't,' said Gil firmly, 'and that's the man Murray. He seems to be missing, Michael, but it's clear enough that's not him in the cart-shed.'

He summarized the events at the peat-digging, while his mother and Michael listened critically, and Alys nodded agreement.

'This is a bad business,' said Lady Egidia when he had finished.

'Do you know them, Mother?' he asked.

'I've had no dealings wi' the Crombie women, save for Beattie,' admitted Lady Egidia. 'We get coals fetched every quarter, and I sell them ponies from time to time, but I've aye dealt wi' the men for that. Beattie sells me simples for the horses when I run out. Formidable she is, but she has a reputation for a good woman, and a good healer.'

'What, charms and spells and love-potions?' Gil asked. 'Half the lassies in the parish trailing up across the moor?'

'No, dear,' said his mother firmly. 'I said she's a healer. She doesn't use charms, except the kind you say over the mortar to make the ointment more effective.' Alys nodded at this. 'She can heal wounds, she has a receipt for a bottle that mends broken bones once they're set, I believe she has a wash for falling hair that sells well. No spells that I ever heard of.'

35

'Dangerous, just the same,' said Gil.

'So it seems. Gil, you must do something about it. If that fool Fleming has taken it into his head Beattie's a witch, there's no knowing where it will end.'

'This must be what's reached my father,' said Michael. He extracted a small wad of paper from the breast of his gown, and opened it up, fold after fold, into a single sheet. 'He writes that he was already concerned about the winter's fee, so he'd directed Fleming to see about it, and the man's writ him a letter he canny understand. Why he tolerates him I canny tell, what wi' his other habits.' He peered at the page. 'Mind you, I canny –' He stopped short, and handed the letter to Lady Egidia. 'Can you do better than me, madam?'

'How must an accusation of witchcraft proceed in Scotland?' Alys asked.

'The same as anywhere else,' Gil answered, watching his mother's face as she held the letter at arm's length. 'First, if Fleming can show that Mistress Lithgo set that body into the peat, whoever it is, or did some other ill deed by witchcraft, second if he can show that she intended to do harm by it, or third . . .' He paused, trawling his memory.

'He has to show she's made an alliance with the Devil,' supplied Michael, more recently taught by the same master, 'or some other ill spirit.' He grimaced. 'Tommy Forsyth makes all clear, doesn't he?'

'Very,' agreed Gil. 'Any of these is enough for the charge to proceed, and whatever court it comes to must investigate. Likely the Sheriff will try it first.'

'But can he do any of that?' Alys said dubiously. 'The priest, I mean.'

'It's easy enough,' said Gil wryly. 'He was hinting about evidence, and once one accusation's made, others will surface. All it needs is one of the colliers' wives with a grudge at the family, and the wise-woman will find herself with her skirts over her head being pricked for a witch-mark. Then it all goes before the Sheriff, with an assize, and if it's found proven, she'll be hanged.'

'Hanged. I thought Sir David seemed very . . .' Alys paused, reflecting on the word she wanted. 'Vindictive. There may be some reason for his accusation. Beyond the belief that she might be a witch, I mean.'

'James doesny make it clear,' said Lady Egidia disapprovingly. *'Fleming has writ me a rigmarole of witches at the Pow Burn. Go you and prevent him.* Prevent him from what?'

Michael shrugged his shoulders. 'Dear knows. Making a fool of hisself? Making a nuisance of hisself?'

'Too late to prevent either, I should say,' said Gil. 'But I agree, something must be done to prevent a miscarriage of justice.'

'If Murray's missing,' said Michael slowly, 'it would account for the fee being late, and it might account for the daft message about witches. Seems to me,' he looked at Gil, 'the first thing to be done is find Thomas Murray.'

'The very first thing, surely,' Alys corrected him, 'is go out to the Pow Burn to talk to the people there.'

'You'll have never seen a coal-heugh before,' said Phemie Crombie.

'I have not,' said Alys. 'It is not at all the same as a stone-quarry.'

'Nor I,' Gil admitted. 'I've ridden past, but I've never looked closely.'

'A new experience, then,' said Phemie, and waved a disparaging hand at the view through the small, writhing panes of glass. The coalmasters' house, a handsome structure of hall and two wings, was set

37

back at a fastidious distance from the muddle of smaller buildings which sprawled away down the slope to the burn, embedded in dark grey mud and busy as a wasps' nest. 'That's the nether coal-hill in the midst, you see. There's three separate ingoes –'

'Three – what?' said Alys.

'The entries to the mine,' Phemie expanded. 'They're a wee bit up from the low coal-hill, yonder.' She pointed to the left. 'Then the mine office is next the hill, where they keep the records and the tallies, and beyond that's the smithy and the wood shop. Then away up the track there's the hewers' row, and the stables, and the two shaft-houses and the upper coal-hill.'

The row of cottages and the stables could hardly be seen through the glass, but Gil had noticed them as they approached; the two squat ranges were identical, except for the coal-smoke rising through the thatch of the dwellings. The house itself, on the other hand, was a well-built timber-framed edifice, the hall and wings roofed with slates, the smaller pents at either end neatly thatched. A little chapel was carefully oriented beside it. There was a windswept garden and kailyard, and the house had several more glass windows as well as this one before which they were seated, waiting for the promised refreshment. Thirsty from the ride, Gil reflected that Henry was probably already well down his first stoup in the kitchen building they had seen on the other side of the house.

'Where does your mother have her stillroom?' asked Alys, smiling at the girl.

'In the pent yonder, next the chapel.' Phemie jerked her head at the blank wall of the chamber beside them. 'It has a door from the outside, which is how the Thorn men took her away without –' She scowled. 'I'll pay them for it, so I will.'

'You will not,' said her mother in the doorway.

Gil rose, scrutinizing her, and Alys moved forward with her hands out, saying, 'How do you feel, Mistress Lithgo? That was a dreadful thing to happen.'

'I'm well, thank you, mistress.' Beatrice Lithgo, her appearance restored since this morning to the neatness Gil somehow felt was natural to her, came forward to embrace her guests while her daughter muttered rebelliously in the background, then seated herself on the leather-covered backstool Gil set for her, saying firmly, 'That'll do, Phemie.'

'It'll no do at all,' Phemie retorted, 'for if I hadny seen all and fetched the men, where would you be now?'

'Where she is, I hope,' said Gil. 'Fleming had no case to argue, that was clear from the beginning. Do you deal in spells, mistress?' he asked point-blank.

'I do not,' she said, equally direct. 'Nor charms, nor tokens to procure love or hatred. I'm a healer, no more than that.'

'I should think it was clear,' said Phemie roundly. The door opened again behind her, to admit Joanna Brownlie with a jug and a tray of beakers. 'My mother's no witch, and I'll pay that fat hypocrite for saying it!'

'Let me understand,' Gil said. 'It seems there's a man missing, this Thomas Murray, and Fleming thought he kent him in the corp. Tell me about Murray. He's in charge here, is he?'

'Aye,' said Joanna softly, at the same time as mother and daughter said, 'Not him!'

'He's the grieve,' added Beatrice. 'Promoted when my good-brother died.'

'He was a common bearer,' said Phemie in a savage tone which Gil could not account for. 'No even a hewer. But since he can read and reckon, the old woman —'

'That will do, Phemie,' said her mother with more emphasis, and Phemie finally became silent.

'You promoted him?' asked Gil neutrally, looking from one woman to another.

'Arbella promoted him,' agreed Joanna.

'Is that your grandmother?' Alys asked Phemie, who nodded ungraciously. 'It must be difficult,' she offered, 'to be a household of women here on the edge of the coal-heugh.'

Gil, who had reached the same conclusion only a moment ago, admired this approach.

'No, it's difficult to be a household of women wi' Arbella at the head of it.'

'*Phemie!*' said her mother. 'You may leave us!'

Phemie flounced to her feet, long hair and blue woollen skirts swirling round her.

'I was just going,' she retorted, tossing the fair locks back. 'You'll forgive me, madam, sir.' She curtsied briefly, and strode towards the door.

It was flung open as she reached it. She recoiled, and another, younger girl entered, and held the door open for a second figure who paused in the opening, gazing at them.

Gil never forgot his first glimpse of Arbella Weir. Slender, finely made, elegantly gowned, with some trick of the light giving her pink-and-white skin and silver-grey silk their own luminosity, she seemed for a moment lit from within. Near her all the women in the room looked gawky, even the graceful Joanna. Even Alys, he thought for a shocked moment. There was no telling her age; from the springy stance she could have been seventeen.

He scrambled to his feet and bowed, aware of Alys beside him making a deep curtsy. The woman in the doorway stepped forward into the chamber, and it became apparent that she was older than she looked at first sight. Vivid, expressive blue eyes under delicate brows held the attention, but silver-white hair showed

40

at her temples below the fashionable French hood, and there were lines in her sweet face as she smiled at her guests.

'Madam,' he said, moving hastily to lead her to a seat. She leaned a little on his arm, her steps uneven, and he revised his estimate of her age again. Behind him, Phemie slipped out of the door, and the other girl came to help Joanna, who had finally begun to dispense the contents of the jug.

There was a stilted round of introductions and compliments. The refreshment was handed by the younger girl, who it seemed was Phemie's sister Bel, a silent lumpy child of fourteen or so with dark hair and watchful blue eyes, and the smooth hands of a spinner. The beakers proved to contain buttered ale, well spiced but not strong. Gil raised his in a toast to Mistress Weir, and she bowed in reply.

'And is it some errand,' she prompted, her voice gentle, 'that brings us the pleasure of your company?'

'Maister Cunningham's here about this morning's disturbance,' said Beatrice. Gil appreciated the understatement, but Arbella Weir shook her head deprecatingly.

'A bad business, maister,' she said, and crossed herself. 'Our Lady be praised that you were present to argue Beattie's part. What could ha' made Davy Fleming take such a notion into his head? He's aye pleasant wi' you when he's up here, Beattie my dear.'

'Aye, he's civil enough to me,' admitted Beatrice drily.

'And have the two of you rid all this way to ask after my good-daughter?' Arbella continued. 'That's a great kindness.'

'They're asking about Thomas as well, Mother,' said Joanna.

Arbella raised her fine, dark brows. 'Thomas? Why

41

should Thomas concern you, maister? He's well enough, I'll warrant.'

'If Sir David thinks the corp in the peat is your grieve,' Alys explained, 'which was part of his charge against Mistress Lithgo, then to prove him wrong my husband needs to find the man. I think he's overdue?'

'A week or two only,' Arbella said, shaking her head. 'He's young. Likely he saw some new business he could do, and it's taking time. Or maybe he went to deal wi' the salt-boilers, as we'd discussed.'

'It wasny time to meet the salt-boilers. He's been gone five weeks, Mother,' said Joanna, a hint of obstinacy in her soft voice. 'There's matters here for him to attend to.'

'Is it as long as that? I'm dealing wi' everything here, my pet,' said Arbella. 'He's no need to hurry back. Never concern yourself, Joanna.'

'What are his duties?' asked Gil, attempting to reclaim the conversation. 'What does that mean, to be grieve at a coal-heugh?'

'He directs the men,' offered Joanna. 'He tells them where they should work, and when there should be a new shaft put in, and how much coal they need on the hill to fill the orders.'

'He's been a disappointment to me, I'll admit,' observed Arbella sadly. 'I thought him knowledgeable, but he's made a few mistakes since I put him in place.'

Gil caught a quirk of a smile crossing Beatrice's face at this, but she said nothing.

'And he deals with the customers,' he prompted. 'Does he deliver the coal – take the string of ponies out with the coal in baskets? I mind the collier coming to Thinacre when I was a boy, but that was from a nearer coal-heugh, down by the Avon.'

'That would be Will Russell at Laigh Quarter,' agreed

Joanna. 'Their round touches ours at Dalserf, but they hold to that side of the Clyde.'

'That was one of Matthew's agreements,' said Arbella, and covered her eyes with a small plump hand. Joanna nodded, and crossed herself.

'Matthew?' asked Gil.

'Matthew is dead,' said Beatrice flatly. After a moment she went on, 'He was my good-brother, and Joanna's first man. He died near two year since, Christ assoil him, for aught I could do.' Joanna turned her face away, and Gil thought he saw tears glittering on her eyelashes. 'Then Joanna wedded Murray, and Arbella set him in Matthew's place.'

'You have not had to seek for trouble,' said Alys in sympathy.

'It's a hard trade, winning coal,' said Arbella, still behind her hand. 'We get our livelihood from under the earth, and the earth takes lives in return.'

Beatrice and Joanna crossed themselves at this, but neither spoke.

'So it's you that directs matters overall, madam,' Gil said. Arbella lowered the hand, and he felt the impact of her blue gaze as she turned it on him.

'I was reared here, maister. It was my father cut the first pit,' she expanded, in gentle pride of possession, 'more than forty year ago, and brought in Adam Crombie as his grieve. I was sole heir to my father, and Adam wedded me, and he and our sons have worked the Pow Burn coal-heugh ever since.'

'Till they died,' said Beatrice, still in that flat tone.

'And have you sons yourself, mistress?' Alys asked her.

Beatrice's expression softened. 'Just the one living. He's eighteen. His name's Adam and all, though he aye gets called Raffie. He's away at the college in Glasgow.'

'And we've met Phemie, and this is Bel,' Alys prompted. Bright colour washed over the girl's plump face, and she bobbed a curtsy where she stood by her mother, but did not speak.

'Bel's a spinner,' Joanna offered. 'None better for her age in Lanarkshire, I dare say.'

'I'm right fortunate in my grandchildren,' said Arbella, with that same gentle pride in her voice. 'My grandson is the boast of the college, and my lassies are kent for their skill for miles about.'

'Hmf!' said Bel's mother, but did not contradict this.

'So Murray has charge here under you,' Gil persisted, 'and he's been gone for five weeks wi' two of the men, and yet you never sent after him?'

Joanna opened her mouth as if to speak, but Arbella said, 'No. I see no need for it.'

'But are you not concerned for him?' asked Alys.

'No yet,' said Arbella. 'Time enough to worry when eight or ten weeks are past. I can direct the colliers, and oversee the hill and the tallies.'

'Considering what happened to your own man, Mother –' said Joanna in her soft voice. Arbella covered her eyes again, and held up the other hand to stop the words. 'No, I'm sorry, I ken it hurts you to mind it, but think on me, Mother! It's my man that's missing now, and never came home for Pace-tide!'

Gil met Alys's eye, and she asked, 'Was that Maister Adam Crombie? Forgive my asking – what happened to him?'

'That was Auld Adam,' agreed Joanna, in spite of Beatrice's tight-lipped stare. 'He must ha' took ill on the road, and died and was buried afore it was known here.'

'Oh, how sad,' said Alys involuntarily. 'When was that? Where did it happen?'

'Afore I came here,' Joanna admitted. Arbella remained silent, though her lips moved as if in prayer.

'That would be in '77,' said Beatrice harshly, 'for my laddie was just walking when the word came back, his grandsire never saw him on his feet, and Phemie was born that summer.'

'I hope at least you have seen his grave,' said Alys. Arbella shook her head, without lowering her hand.

'It must have been a great shock,' Gil remarked.

'Aye,' said Beatrice. Gil waited, but she added nothing.

'So you tell me Murray and two others left here on the eighteenth of March,' he said at length. 'Afoot, or on horseback? Did he seem just as usual when he left? Nothing was out of the ordinary?'

'No,' said Joanna blankly. 'They rode on three of the ponies as they aye do, and they left at first light, just as they aye do. Why would it be different?'

Beatrice's mouth quirked. Observing this, Gil suggested, 'Was he happy to go out on the road? Did he enjoy the change in his work? Or was it something he disliked doing?'

'I think he liked getting away,' said Joanna reluctantly.

'Men aye like getting away,' said Beatrice. 'Mind that, lassie,' she added to Alys, who smiled.

Gil decided not to comment, but said, 'The two men that went with Murray – the man Meikle said they were sinkers. What does a sinker do?'

'Sinks shafts,' explained Joanna. 'By cutting down through the rock, you see.'

'That must be difficult,' said Alys immediately. 'And dangerous. What do they use to break the stone?'

'A great spike and a hammer,' said Joanna, taking this understanding for granted, 'and the stook and feathers.'

'Wedges of iron,' Beatrice translated. 'You drive them in wi' the hammer, see, and the rock splits. Sometimes it'll fly up in splinters. It's a rare sinker that lives to be an auld man.'

Alys nodded, pulling a face, and Gil said, 'So there's no shaft being cut just now.'

'We put in a new one no that long afore Yule,' said Arbella, raising her head. 'It serves well. So I allowed Thomas to take the two men along wi' him, since there was no work for them the now.'

'It was the same two lads he always took,' supplied Joanna in her soft voice.

'I should like to see inside the mine,' Alys remarked thoughtfully, 'though not in these clothes.'

'Nor in any clothes, my dear,' said Arbella, with her sweet smile. 'We'd have the entire shift out for the rest of the day.'

'My good-mother willny have a woman in the mine,' said Beatrice, 'and the men willny cross her.' Her daughter Bel turned to look intently at her, but said nothing. 'Where I'm from,' she added, 'on the shores of the Forth, the women work as bearers, to drag the creels of coal from the face to the stair, and then up to the hill, but here in Lanarkshire it's all done different.'

'So I should hope, Beattie my dear,' said Arbella, raising those delicate eyebrows. 'Where should the women be but seeing to the men's dinner? I pay my colliers enough to live by, they've no need to set their women to work as well.'

'Women working in the mine,' repeated Alys in astonishment.

'So is there,' said Gil, still trying to keep control of the conversation, 'any record of where Murray was going? What houses he was to call at? Is there a list, a way-sheet, a book of accounts?'

Their hostesses looked at one another.

'I've no doubt of it,' said Arbella.

'He'd have a way-sheet,' agreed Beatrice. 'My man aye kept a list, and so did Matthew.' Joanna nodded. 'Did Thomas? Would you ken where it is?'

'He'd take it with him,' said Joanna in her soft voice.

'What about the last time he went out?' Alys prompted. 'Is there a record from that? Or in the accounts?' She turned to Arbella Weir. 'Perhaps in the order the accounts were paid?'

Arbella nodded gracefully, the velvet fall of her French hood sliding over her grey silk shoulder.

'Aye, for certain,' she agreed. 'Bel, my pet, would you be so good?' The girl came shyly forward from her post at her mother's shoulder. 'The great account book that's lying on my kist. Fetch it here for your granny.'

The great account book was bound in worn buff leather, and bristling with slips of paper tucked between the leaves. Bel bore it in cradled in her arms as if it was a child; her mother set up a small folding table for the volume, and Arbella turned back first the upper board and then half the heavy pages, using both hands, to find the entry she wanted.

'The Martinmas reckoning,' she said, and ran her finger down the page. 'Aye, this would likely be the road he would take. It's the same road my dear Adam aye took, I ken that.' Alys rose and came to look over her shoulder. Arbella looked up at her, the velvet head-dress framing her sweet smile. 'You understand accounts, lassie?'

'My father is a master mason.' Alys drew her tablets from her purse. 'May I make a note of these names? What a fine hand – is it your writing, madam?'

'I was well taught,' said Arbella. 'I've had David Fleming teach my granddaughters the same, though he's been a disappointment to me and all, and after today's work I think I'll not allow him to come back. It was his uncle Sir Arnold Douglas, that was chaplain to Sir James's grandsire, taught me to read and write and reckon. Wi' her letters and a good man, what more does a woman need in this life?'

It was apparent to Gil that several of the younger women in the room could think of answers to that, but none of them spoke.

'We must away, afore the light goes,' he said after a pause. 'I think I've gathered enough to go on with. If you can furnish me wi' a description of the man Murray, and the two others, I can send after him, to see if we can track him down. Then we'll know for certain the corp in the peat is some other fellow.'

They mounted before the door, and were given a ceremonious farewell by Arbella, leaning on her grand-daughter's arm on the threshold.

'We'll see you again, I hope,' she said in that gentle voice.

Joanna nodded, and Gil saw that her hands were clasped at her waist, the knuckles showing white. Behind her good-mother Beatrice studied them, and said suddenly, her eyes on Alys, 'Aye, we'll see you again, won't we no?'

'We must return,' Alys answered, 'if only to report what we have learned about your missing man.'

'You'll be back afore that,' said Beatrice. 'I'll be here, lassie.'

'You've no need to concern yourselves wi' Murray,' said Arbella. 'It's only for putting the lie to Davy Fleming that I'd pay any mind to the matter at all.'

'I think we can do that,' said Gil, and hitched his cloak closer. He gathered up his reins in one hand, bent his head and crossed himself with the other in response to Arbella's offered blessing for the journey, and heeled his horse forward. Alys followed him, and the two grooms fell in behind as they set off up the track, past the bleak garden and over the shoulder of the hill.

Half a mile further on, out of sight of the house and the coal-workings, Gil was unsurprised to see a solitary figure standing by the side of the track waiting for them, red-and-blue plaid over her head against the pervasive wind.

'That's the lass from the coal-heugh,' observed Henry.

'It is,' agreed Alys. 'Good evening to you, Phemie.'

'I must talk wi' you,' said Phemie, without preamble.

'No the now, lass,' objected Henry. 'We want to be back on our own land afore the light goes.'

'Aye, and I've to be back for my supper,' she said scornfully. 'I never meant the now, the owls will be flying afore long. Can one of you come back the morn's morn?' She looked closely at Alys, much as her mother had done. 'You'll be back, won't you, mistress?'

'I could come back in the morning,' Alys admitted, with a glance at Gil.

'Do that,' said Phemie, 'and I'll find a way to get a word wi' you. There's plenty Arbella wouldny tell you, and a few things she doesny ken.'

'That seems unlikely,' Gil observed.

Phemie shook her head. 'She canny be everywhere. I'll see you the morn's morn, mistress.' She stepped back from the edge of the track to let them pass, and set off across the rough grass of the hillside, without looking back.

'Well, that's an ill-schooled lassie,' commented the second groom as they rode on.

'She has a lot to trouble her,' said Alys.

Chapter Three

'What were they hiding, I wonder,' said Gil.

'I don't know that they were hiding anything,' said Alys. 'They were simply reluctant to talk to a stranger. Mistress Weir is very certain there is no need to search for this man Murray.'

Gil considered this. He and Alys were in their chamber, halfway through changing their muddy riding-clothes for something fit to go down to supper in, and now he sat on the edge of the box bed and patted the counterpane beside him.

'I want to find him, as I told her. We have a description,' he said, putting his arm round his wife as she came to join him. 'Of the man and the two fellows with him.'

Alys tilted her head back, gazing at the ceiling, and the soft light from the horn window edged the high narrow bridge of her nose.

'A bare description,' she observed. 'Jock and Tam Paterson, who are brothers. One is taller than the other and both have all their fingers yet. I suppose they are young men.'

'And we have the list of the houses where Murray was to call, and the name of the salt-boiler beyond Blackness.'

'So someone must work his way down the list,' prompted Alys, 'asking if he was there, and when, and if all was well. Gil, if you do that, I am distracted.' She put her hand over his, stilling his fingers. 'Blackness is a port, is it not? I wonder if he has simply taken all the money and gone to the Low Countries or England or somewhere.'

'You had a look at the accounts.'

'Yes, but the old lady was watching me, so I could not look too close. I thought they appeared sound enough. The income I saw would support the size of household they have there, and pay the colliers in coin and kind. If the man was taking anything out before he left on this collecting-round he was doing it very circumspectly.'

'And if he ran, why would he take the other two men with him? Sharing the money?'

'I agree. And also Beatrice said they have kin at the coal-heugh, they might not wish to run off with him. We must speak to the kin.' She turned her head to look up at him. 'Will you go out to the houses on the list?'

'I thought we might persuade Michael to do that. My mother ordered him back here for supper, he should have arrived by now.'

'Gil, it was an invitation!' she protested, giggling. 'And very civil.'

'I heard her issue it. He'll not disobey.'

'He may not be willing to help us,' she warned him. 'He is quite afflicted, I think, not to find your sister Tib here.'

'My heart bleeds at that.'

'So does mine, to tell truth,' she said seriously. 'They have been parted for months, with only a couple of meetings in public, he must wonder whether she still –'

'Hah!' said Gil.

'We have been fortunate,' she pointed out. 'You were

never away for more than a few days before we were married, and since then –'

'I'm still greatly displeased with him,' Gil said firmly. 'Tib apologized to me, for what that was worth, but I don't recall that Michael ever did, and their behaviour was ill judged and ill disciplined.'

'They are much in love.'

'So are we, Alys, and I can't imagine enticing you to my bed like that. Much though I might have wished to,' he added wryly, recalling how long the weeks between the contract and the wedding had seemed.

'Nor I you,' she admitted. 'But we were differently placed. We were acknowledged from the start, Gil. We had no need to act in secret.'

He laughed, thinking of the snatched moments of what they had thought at the time was privacy, and tightened his clasp on her waist. 'I suppose it's my fault. I should have made sure my sister was better guarded. Well, too late now, and if Michael wants me to support his case with his father he'll oblige me and be civil about it.' He glanced at the window, where the sun was warming the greyish-yellow panes. 'They'll blow up for supper soon. We must dress.'

She tucked her hand into his as he rose.

'I suppose,' she said diffidently, 'I wish all women to be as fortunate as I am. I married for love *and* to please my father, and I wish Tib could do the same.'

Gil drew her to her feet and into his arms, looking fondly down into her brown gaze.

'It was the best day of my life when Pierre proposed the match to me,' he said, 'and when he told me you wished it too, I could hardly believe my fortune. It's near a year since then,' he discovered. 'We should hold a feast for the anniversary.'

* * *

52

'I never realized,' said Lady Egidia, spooning green sauce over her boiled mutton, 'that all the Crombie men were dead.'

She was seated at the head of the long board, Alys and Gil at her right hand, her godson at her left, with her steward, his wife Eppie and the rest of the household arrayed below them. At the far end among the grooms Gil could see Henry, by his gestures describing the discovery of the corpse in the peat-digging.

'The youngest still lives,' said Alys. 'Mistress Weir's grandson. Ralph, did his mother call him?'

'That's a by-name, I think,' said Gil. 'Adam, she said. He'd be named for his father, or his grandsire. Is there an Adam Crombie at the university, Michael?'

Michael paused with a second oozing wedge of cold pie halfway to his wooden trencher. Socrates, seated at Gil's elbow, the crown of his rough grey head level with the miniature silver saint on the lid of the salt, watched the pastry crumbs falling on the tablecloth, and his nose twitched.

'Down,' said Gil sternly, and the dog lay down with an ostentatious sigh.

'Aye, he's at the college,' Michael admitted. 'Magistrand.'

'That is a fourth year man,' Alys prompted, 'like you?'

'Aye.'

Gil waited, but no further information emerged. A difficult situation, he reflected, to be in the same year as your tenant's son.

'It was sad how Mistress Weir's husband died,' said Alys, passing Gil the salt with her free hand. 'Did she say it was in '77, Gil?'

'Beatrice said that, aye,' Gil agreed.

'I was still at court, then.' Lady Egidia stared into the distance, her long-chinned face remote. 'Aye, I think I recall, your father must have come over from Thinacre

53

to gather the rents and brought the tale back. Where did it happen? Elsrickle? Douglas?'

'They never said.'

'Elsrickle, I think,' said Alys confidently, 'from the tone in which Mistress Weir read out the name. Where is that?'

'It's a fair way from the Pow Burn,' observed Michael. 'It's in Walston parish, the far end of the county. That way.' He nodded vaguely south-east.

'It was sadder yet what happened to the younger son,' Lady Egidia said. 'If I mind right, he came home maybe two years back with a new young wife on his crupper, having met and married her incontinent at some place where he'd taken a load of coals. That alone would ha' been the speak of the parish for weeks, but then he took sick and was dead within the quarter, for all Beattie could do.'

'Oh!' said Alys in distress. 'Is that Joanna? Oh, poor soul!'

'Beatrice mentioned something of the sort,' said Gil.

'I mind that too,' said Michael surprisingly. 'The old man mentioned it in his letters. He'd found her somewhere by Ashgill, the other side of the Clyde.'

'That isn't on the list, is it?' Gil asked Alys.

She shook her head. 'They said their round stayed on this side of the river. How far is Elsrickle? Is it near there?'

'No. Ashgill's to the west, just across the river in Cadzow parish, Elsrickle is fourteen or fifteen miles east of here. The High House beyond Elsrickle,' said Gil, helping Alys to some of the cold pie, 'which I mind is one of the places on the list, must be the furthest away from the coal-heugh. There are ten names altogether, and they told us Murray would stop a night and a day at each, to gather the fees from the surrounding customers, and then ride on to the next.'

'Maybe two weeks' travelling, then,' said Michael, 'allowing for delays.'

Gil nodded. 'And he's been gone more than five weeks.'

'You think he's run off?' asked Michael.

Gil looked at him across the table. 'That or something else. He might have stayed somewhere to draw up some extra business agreement, as Mistress Weir suggested,' he counted off, tapping his fingers on the linen cloth, 'he might have fallen ill or died suddenly, like the grandsire, though I would have thought word would have got back to the coal-heugh by now. He might have gone to the salt-pans at Blackness and been held up there, or he might have decided to take the money he had collected and run to England or the Low Countries. Or I suppose it might be another reason altogether. *Whither trow this man ha' the way take?* He could be anywhere.'

'Surely not England!' said Lady Egidia.

'But what about the two other men?' Alys reminded him.

'That's one of the puzzling things,' agreed Gil.

'One?' said his mother.

'His wife is young and lovely,' said Alys.

Gil pulled a face. 'Too sweet a mouthful for me. But yes, you'd think he'd be drawn home to a bed with Joanna in it. And there's the way all those women see him differently. The old woman seems disappointed with him, Joanna's his wife and speaks accordingly, but I think Beatrice dislikes him and the daughter who spoke to us was venomous.'

'Maybe the daughter thought he should ha' wed her,' suggested Michael sourly.

'Aye, that might be it. And what about you?' Gil raised his eyebrows at the younger man. 'What did you get from Fleming when you rode him over to

Cauldhope? Has he any true information against Mistress Lithgo?'

Michael shrugged. 'None that I can make out,' he admitted. 'He croaked on about having evidence, and how she's infamous as a witch, and how many folk resort to the coal-heugh to get healing from her, and he wouldny hear of this corp being any other than the man Murray. I asked him what was this evidence, what he'd seen or heard for himself that was proof of witch-craft, but he never answered me other than to say she'd quarrelled wi' the man. He's a fool, I wish my father had never set him in place.'

'So how will you begin, dear?' asked Lady Egidia, before Gil could speak. He looked at Alys, and she smiled back and squeezed his hand briefly under the table.

'Someone has to go out and ask each household when they last saw Thomas Murray,' he said. 'And while they're about it, ask each one if there has ever been anything . . .' He paused. 'Unusual. Aye. Anything unusual about the man or his dealings.'

'An easy enough task,' said Lady Egidia. 'Michael, you may as well do that since you're here.'

'*Me?*' said Michael, his voice rising to a squeak. 'I mean – why me? Why should –?'

'I'm sure you'd like to be a help,' Lady Egidia informed him.

'But I – I mean, I have to get back to the college. There's my – I've to deal wi' Davy Fleming. I canny go riding all over Lanarkshire,' Michael protested, looking round him in faint panic. Gil caught his eye, aware of a degree of sympathy which surprised him.

'It would speed your matter, in fact,' he pointed out, 'since the sooner we find the man the sooner we'll con-vince that fool Fleming, and it would come better from

56

you as your father's son, riding round asking other folk's stewards when they paid the bill to his coal-grieve, than from me. Then I can send to the salt-pan, and take the time to ask about here and all, see if there are any old tales of someone going missing, try to find another name for our corp. He must have a name, after all, poor devil.'

'You'll get more than you bargain for,' his mother observed, 'if you're going to encourage all the old gossips and their tales. So that's settled, Michael. Get a note of what questions Gil wants you to ask, and the list of the houses you must call at, before you go home the night, and you can make an early start in the morning.' Michael nodded, and mumbled something ungracious which might have been assent, and she turned to Alys. 'And what about you, my dear?'

'I am bidden back to the coal-heugh,' Alys admitted.

Lady Egidia's gaze sharpened, but all she said was, 'Then you'd best borrow Henry again.'

'Double-distilled is better for burns,' said Beatrice Lithgo, 'and triple is better yet.'

Alys nodded. 'I keep a small flask of the triple-distilled beside the kitchen salt,' she agreed. She put the stoneware jar of lavender-water back in its place, and gazed round the crowded stillroom shelves. The sight appealed deeply to her; she would have liked to open and look into every one of the jars and bottles and leather sacks. 'You are well stocked, mistress. And well informed. Socrates, heel!' she added.

'I learned a lot from Arbella,' admitted Beatrice as the dog reluctantly left the barrel which had attracted him. 'She was good in her day. You need someone handy wi' the simples about a coal-heugh.'

57

'My father is a stonemason,' said Alys, 'and I know stone-cutting and quarry-work, a little. I should like to learn about hewing coal, how it differs.'

'You want Arbella for that,' said Beatrice. 'Or Joanna. She's got it all at her finger-ends already. My man never liked to have much to do wi' the pit, Our Lady succour him, and my father was a salt-boiler. I can tell you all about that, but no so much about coal.'

'I have never seen a salt-pan. I should like to learn about that too,' said Alys, with truth. 'Your man was the elder son, mistress? When did he die?'

Beatrice's face softened, and she gazed through a glass jar of preserved berries into some distant scene.

'He was the elder son,' she agreed. 'His father's heir, and no so like either Arbella or Auld Adam, either in looks or in temper, though he'd his father's grey eyes. My Bel, poor lassie, will have a look of him when she loses her fat.'

'You are saying he was less interested in the business?' Alys prompted. 'That must have been difficult.'

'Oh, it was. You saw Arbella, when you rode in here the day, down in the tally-house inspecting the records and making up the note of what each man had sent up to the hill yesterday?' Alys nodded. 'Adam never cared for that. A great burden he found it, and even more he disliked directing the men at their work. He hated going into the pit. Music, he liked, and books, and talking learning with old Sir Arnold. He'd planned to sell the heugh, or at least his share in it, and move down to Linlithgow. He quarrelled wi' Arbella over that. But then he died. In the pit, in a roof-fall, nine year since. It was his day-mind in March, just after Thomas rode off on the round,' she added. Both women crossed themselves, and Beatrice turned resolutely to the shelf beside her. 'Do you ever use this? I find it good for skin troubles.'

'And Joanna's man was the younger son,' said Alys, taking the little jar and sniffing the contents. The dog looked up at her, his nose twitching. 'Yes, indeed, I use this often.' She sniffed again. 'Is that rosemary in it as well? A good thought, I must try that. He died not long after they married, I think?'

'He brought her home in May, two year ago,' said Beatrice sadly, 'and fell ill within the week, a wasting illness where his skin was dry and cracked on the hands and feet, his hair fell, the flesh melted off him. He couldny stomach a thing. Nothing helped. His breath smelled of garlic, and I couldny balance it out.'

'I never heard of such an ailment!' said Alys in dismay. 'Could it have been poison?'

'I thought that myself, but who would have poisoned him? We were all fond of Matt, he was a bonnie lad and a good maister, better than his brother, though I say it. No, I think it was some sickness, or maybe bad food or some wild plant got into the kailyard, for two of the colliers' bairns had died of something similar no a week afore he brought Joanna home. Their mother did say they'd been drinking at one of the wells on the hillside, but there was a great smell of wild garlic about them.'

'What a strange thing,' said Alys.

'Aye, strange it was. I tried all the remedies I could think of, and so did Arbella, but he was shriven and shrouded afore Lammas. Joanna, poor lass, truly mourned him, for all he'd courted her no more than a day or two and wed her out of hand.'

'And then she took Murray.'

'And then she took Murray,' agreed Beatrice.

Alys watched her face carefully, but it gave nothing away. After a moment she said, 'Does he beat her?'

The other woman's gaze snapped to meet hers, and she smiled bitterly.

59

'My, but you're quick, lassie. No, not with his fists, but he uses his tongue. Sharp, sarcastic, making her out to be a fool. She'll not complain, nor tell Arbella, but I've heard him.'

'And no sign of that when he courted her, I suppose.'

'Deed, no.' Again the bitter smile. 'Near a year she mourned Matthew, and the men were round her like wasps round a windfall, as bonnie as she is. I thought myself she favoured the lad Meikle, and it aye seemed to me Murray had eyes elsewhere, though that would never have −' She broke off. 'But in the end she took Murray, and wed him a year since in July, wi' Arbella's blessing, and by Martinmas he was treating her like a scullery-lass.'

'And was he coal-grieve already when they married?'

'Oh, yes. It was Matthew raised him to grieve under him, then when he died Arbella put Murray in Matt's place. He was a sinker afore that, and worked as a bearer the way some of them do when they areny cutting a shaft. Matt called him a natural pitman, said he had a great understanding of the coal and where it goes under the ground. As Matt himself did, I think.'

'A bearer − that is the man who carries the coals away,' Alys prompted. Beatrice nodded. 'The hewer is a craftsman, and the bearer is his labourer, am I right? I should like to see more of this − without offending Mistress Weir,' she added hastily, before Beatrice could speak. 'Maybe someone could show me how it all happens.'

'I'll get Phemie to walk you up the hill,' Beatrice offered.

'I should like that, if she has the time,' Alys said ingenuously. 'Tell me, mistress, what do you think has come to Murray?'

Beatrice shrugged, and rearranged two yellow-glazed pipkins on the bench at her side.

'I've no notion. The day they left he mounted up at the door and bade farewell, just as he aye does, never said aught to us about where he was going or who he would meet, nor about when to expect him back, but that's nothing unusual. The two lads wi' him were cheery enough, but Jamesie Meikle tells me both had tellt the folk they lodge wi' that they'd no idea how long they'd be away. Whether Murray said aught to Joanna in private I don't know, but I'd ha' thought she'd ha' brought it out by now if he did.'

Alys nodded in agreement. 'If he had decided to run off,' she said, 'for whatever cause, where would he go, do you think? Where is he from originally?'

'Fife, somewhere,' said Beatrice, with a vagueness to which Alys gave no credence. 'He's a trick of calling folk *neebor* the way they do over that way. He'd likely cross the Forth if he'd no cause to come back here. That's never him in the peat-digging.'

'No, I agree.'

'What's come to him – the man from the digging? Will he get a decent burial?'

'He will,' Alys assured her. 'The Belstane carpenter was to make a coffin for him today. My – my husband would like to give him a name before he's buried, if we can. And maybe find who killed him.'

'No easy task. I'd say he's been there a while.'

'And the man Fleming.' Beatrice looked away at the words, and shivered. Yes, thought Alys, you were more afraid yesterday than you showed us. 'Why would he have such a spite for you?' she said aloud. 'There was venom there.'

'I've never a notion,' said Beatrice firmly.

'Oh, he'd consulted my mother,' said Phemie. She peered into the furthest of the shaft-houses, a squat

61

structure walled with hurdles and thatched with heather, merely intended to keep the worst of the weather off man and pony working it. The winding-gear was silent astride the dark maw of the shaft, the long beam with its dangling harness propped on the heading-bar. 'I noticed him slinking into the stillroom by twilight, when we thought he'd gone home. It's no so easy to get out here to the coaltown unseen,' she added.

'Maister Fleming had consulted your mother?' Alys repeated, standing cautiously in the doorway with a tight grasp of Socrates' collar. 'When was that?'

Phemie walked forward and kicked the timber frame of the winding-gear. Her wooden sole made a loud thump which resonated in the hollow of the shaft, vanished downward and returned to them mixed with the tap and clatter of metal tools. Were there voices too? Alys wondered. I am being fanciful, she told herself firmly. In the shadows over her head something made a ruffling sound, like feathers. She drew the dog closer to her knee, and he put his head up to look at her.

'A month ago, maybe,' Phemie said. 'Aye, that would be right, about Lady Day. I don't know what it was about,' she admitted, 'I stayed within sight, and made sure he kent I was there, but I never got close enough to hear. He went away wi' a wee jar of ointment, and a paper of pills, I could tell that by what was lying to be washed when I went into the stillroom.'

'You assist your mother?' Alys realized.

The girl nodded. 'I've helped her mix simples since I could walk,' she said, with some pride.

'And Bel? Does she help too, or is she always at her spinning?'

Phemie looked curiously at Alys, but answered civilly enough. 'Bel's aye wi' our grandam. Times she sits and spins while the old – old lady rests, times

62

she helps her wi' the accounts, times she fetches green-stuff for her off the hillside.'

'Off the hillside?' Alys repeated in surprise.

'Aye. Water from this or that spring, herbs from some burnside for Arbella or my mother. The old woman's none so spry on her feet now, but time was she could find any plant you could name in the parish, so my mother says, and she can still tell my sister where to seek them.' She peered into the cavity beside her, then lifted a piece of dull black stone from the floor, and dropped it down the shaft. There was a long silence, then a distant rattle and thud, and an angry shout. Phemie grinned. 'That'll learn somebody no to stand under the shaft.'

'How deep is it?' So there were voices, thought Alys.

'Fifteen fathom.'

'Fifteen – that is seven-and-twenty ells,' Alys calcu-lated, and opened her eyes wide. 'I had no idea you could go so deep.'

'There's deeper.'

'But does the roof not fall down?'

'No if the stoops are wide enough.' Phemie stepped out of the hut, and Alys followed her with relief, away from the winding-gear and the black gaping maw of the shaft. 'Look.' She bent, lifted another flake of stone, and drew a square in the gritty mud underfoot. 'That's a pillar. We call it a stoop.' She drew another square a little distance from the first. 'That's another. And another. And between the stoops are what we call the rooms. Each hewer works in a room by his lone, wi' a bearer to carry the coal away as he howks it out. The deeper the coal gets, the bigger the stoops and the nar-rower the rooms has to be.'

'To hold the roof up,' Alys nodded. 'I see. So there must be a point where it is not worth hewing any deeper.'

'Aye,' said Phemie, looking up with grudging admiration. 'Because you canny take out enough coal to justify the work. That was what happened to my da. Arbella made him go into the pit, and someone had took out too much coal and the roof came down while he was viewing it.' Alys made a small sympathetic sound, and Phemie shrugged. 'I was seven, I can scarce mind him,' she said dismissively, and went on, 'And that was where Arbella and Thomas wonderful Murray couldny agree.'

She looked round her, and Alys did likewise. They were well above the house here, high enough to look down at the thatched roofs of stables and dwellings. Children played in the trampled space between the two rows, and a group of women were eyeing them covertly from the door of one cottage. Fifty yards away the winding-gear creaked loudly inside the next shaft-house, and an elderly man was pushing a small rumbling cart back and forward along a wooden roadway, adding huge shining black blocks to the upper coal-hill. Further uphill yet, a row of tethered ponies munched at the tussocky grass, ignoring all distractions.

'Come up here,' said Phemie. 'You can see it all from here.'

They tramped across the rough grass away from the coal-hill. Alys let go of the dog's collar and he loped round them, grinning and sniffing at the wind. Some of the ponies broke off their grazing to stare at him, then decided he was no great threat and returned to more important matters.

'There are the three ingoes,' Phemie pointed. 'There's the one we use now, and there's the mid one, and down there's the very first one that Arbella's sire cut when he first took on the heugh from this Sir James's grandsire. Or maybe from that one's father,' she added, 'I forget, what wi' most of them being called James.'

Alys nodded, identifying the three entries. They were smaller than she had expected, barely five feet high and braced with solid timbers, and from the furthest downhill of the three a channel of grey water spilled away down the slope towards the burn. Making a mental note not to let the dog drink from that stream, she sat on a relatively dry patch of grass and said, 'So the men go in there to work. Do they walk all the way under the earth to the point where the shafts go down? How many men are there working at once?'

'Aye, they walk. Or crawl.' Phemie sat down beside her. 'The roof gets lower further in. Sometimes we've more, times fewer, but for now we've four men at a time hewing and four or so bearing, so that's eight at least in the mine, and two or three at the surface.'

'In two shifts? Do they work by night as well?'

'No the now, though we used to have two shifts.' Phemie gave her another of those admiring looks. 'You've a good understanding of this, mistress. You sure you've never seen a coal-heugh?'

'My father is a mason. And my name is Alys.'

They exchanged shy smiles, and Alys went on hastily, counting on her fingers, 'Eight – eleven men, and the smith and his helper, the saddler, the chandler, a man to see to the ponies, the two who are gone with your missing man. Which reminds me, Phemie, I should like to speak to their kin if I may. I think your mother said they had kin here?'

'The Patersons? Aye, their sister's married on one of the colliers. She works in our kitchen.'

Alys nodded, and looked down at her fingers. 'There must be twenty men here. There are not so many households in that row of cottages.'

'There's ten houses. Five-and-twenty men all told, and a few laddies old enough to work. Then some of the women works in the house like Kate Paterson, and

I think there's one or two of them does some weaving and the like. That's how our Bel learned her spinning, one of the colliers' wives taught her.'

'In those little houses,' Alys marvelled. 'Did the man Murray dwell there before he wedded Joanna?'

'In the end house,' said Phemie indifferently. 'It's got two chambers. Likely he wishes he was still there, the way the old beldam gets after him.'

'Are you saying your grandam disliked Murray? That was not the impression she gave us.'

'I'll wager it wasny.' Phemie grinned. 'Nor to him, at first. I've seen it afore. She's aye sweetie-sweetie, as smooth as honey, wi' guests and strangers, but she has a different voice for the household, I can tell you that. Except wi' Joanna,' she added thoughtfully, 'and my brother.'

'I have known people like that,' Alys said.

'Aye. Well, once Murray had wed Joanna, so he was living in the house, in the north wing, see yonder, wi' the separate door?' She pointed, and Alys nodded. 'Arbella began to argue wi' him, and he wouldny buckle under and do her bidding where the coal was concerned, and the shouting there was! And Joanna weeping, the silly creature, and my brother getting into it and all, when he was home –'

'Which side did he take?' Alys asked.

'The side that would cause most argument. Raffie thinks he should ha' been given the charge of the business. He's two year older than me, he's eighteen now, he thinks he could run a coal-heugh, for all he's been away at school and then at the college since he was ten.'

'I have no brothers,' said Alys thoughtfully.

'They're no worth it, I can tell you. Anyway, Arbella and Murray near came to blows the last time they argued. It seems the coal we're working has about

66

given out, there's a throw showed up at the end of the eastmost road.' She gestured along the hillside.

'Whatever does that mean?'

'Times the coal just stops,' Phemie said impatiently. 'The men cut along so far and then there's a break in the rocks and beyond it there's no coal. They call that a throw.'

'Oh, yes! I have seen the same thing in the side of a quarry! But there you can see where the band of good stone has gone to, whether it has stepped up or down, and underground one must guess, I suppose.'

'Aye, or abandon that working and start again else-where. Murray wants to do that. Arbella wouldny hear of it.'

'I can see that she would be angry,' agreed Alys. 'Tell me, has the man any friends about the coal-heugh? Is there anyone he would talk to?'

'What, him?' said Phemie, startled. 'I've no notion. I think maybe no, but if you ask Jamesie Meikle likely he could tell you. He's a good man, wi' an eye for what's going on. Joanna should have taken him.'

'I suppose he is working just now. Where do you think Murray has gone?'

'I hope he's run off. I hope we never see him again. Or if he's stolen the takings, we can put him to the horn for that and then get him hanged for thieving.' Phemie grinned, without humour. 'I can picture it well, the Sheriff's officer blowing the horn at Lanark Cross and reading him out a wanted man.'

'Why do you dislike him so much, Phemie?'

'He's a toad,' said Phemie roundly.

Alys studied her expression. 'Was he courting you?'

The girl looked down, and then away. Her fair hair blew across her face, and she shook her head angrily, trying to dislodge it.

'Was he?' Alys persisted, recalling Michael's comment at supper. 'Or was it your sister he liked?'

'What, Bel? She's a bairn yet!' objected Phemie. Alys waited. 'Aye, if you have to ken. He was courting me last spring. Full of plans to wed me, he was, and build a house over yonder, across the burn from the workings.' She tugged savagely at a tussock of grass by her side, and scattered the torn stems on the wind. Socrates bounded back to snatch at the nearest, white teeth snapping in his long narrow jaws. 'Then he saw how Joanna was placed, and went after her hell-for-leather.'

'How Joanna was placed?'

'Oh, aye.' Phemie turned to meet her eye. 'She's Matt's widow, right? Arbella has said she's to have Matt's share. Even though he wed her out of hand wi' no contract or agreement drawn up, even though he died afore he'd bairned her, when the old witch goes –' Alys saw the girl's expression flicker as she heard her own words, but the angry voice plunged on. 'When the old witch goes, Joanna gets half the business, and the other half goes to my mother and the three of us. No wonder the wonderful Thomas fancied Joanna to his bed.'

'He ill-treats her,' said Alys softly. 'He holds her in contempt.'

'Aye.' Phemie tore at another handful of grass. 'I tellt Arbella of it, the last time he went for Joanna. She wouldny believe me.' She turned her head away, but her next words were just audible: 'He would never ha' treated me like that.'

'Forgive me, mistress,' said Joanna, dabbing at her eyes with the end of her kerchief. 'When I heard you at the outside door the now I thought for one moment – That's the door Thomas aye uses, rather than come through the house in his muddy boots.'

'It must be very hard for you,' said Alys with a rush of genuine sympathy, 'worrying about your man when nobody else seems concerned.'

'It's that,' agreed Joanna, and turned to the other door of the room. 'Will you come ben, mistress, and be seated? A wee cup of cordial, maybe, if Phemie's had you up the hill in this wind?'

'That would be welcome,' Alys admitted, following her into a neat inner chamber with a high curtained bed against one wall. 'The view is interesting, from so high up, but I admit I prefer to be more sheltered.'

'I found the same, when I moved up here.' Joanna drew a new-fashioned spinning machine, a well-made item with turned legs and a narrow-rimmed wheel, into a corner away from the window and set a back-stool for Alys. 'The wind never ceases.'

'You are not from hereabouts, then?' Alys sat down on the padded leather and shook her skirts round her.

'I was raised on the other side of the Clyde. My father was William Brownlie, and held Auldton, by Ashgill. It paid a good rent. And it's nowhere near so high up as this.'

'My father is a mason,' Alys countered. 'He has charge of the Archbishop's new build at the cathedral in Glasgow.'

'And your man is some kind of a man of law,' Joanna offered. She handed Alys a little glass of something brownish and sticky, and sat down herself. 'Your good health, mistress. It's made wi' elderberries – well, mostly elderberries. The colour was no so good last year, but we put the good spirits to it.'

'And yours.' Alys raised her glass, and sipped cautiously. The cordial was bitter, despite a generous inclusion of honey, but the base was indeed strong spirits. She identified the elderberries, and several distinct herbs, and perhaps ginger.

'Mistress Weir seems not to be concerned at all about Maister Thomas,' she observed.

'No,' Joanna agreed, and looked away, turning her own glass in her fingers.

'Has she said why? It is a long time to be overdue on such a journey.' Joanna shook her head, and Alys went on, with some sympathy, 'I think she governs her household firmly.'

'She's aye been kind to me,' said Joanna. 'Since ever poor Matt brought me across the threshold, two year since.' She took another sip of cordial.

'I heard about that – a sad tale. He came to your father's house, did he? And you loved each other at sight? Tell me about it.'

That appeared to be the gist of it. Alys sat and watched while the girl opposite, brave in her dark red wool and snow-white linen kerchief, described the relentless refashioning of her life in the past two years. Joanna's mother was dead ('Mine too,' said Alys) and her brothers, much older, married and settled; Matt Crombie had appeared at the gate one day, hoping to extend his round, and though he had taken no orders for coal he had given his heart to Joanna on sight. He had spent an evening closeted with her father, and the next day they had sent for the priest from Dalserf and she had packed up her clothes and the gold jewel her mother left her.

'We rode up here, new-wed and happy, in such hopes,' she said bleakly. 'I mind how we halted before the house door,' she gestured at the cobbled area under the window where they sat, 'and Phemie and Bel went in all haste for their grandam, and Beattie came running round from the stillroom, only I never knew it was the stillroom then, you understand.' Alys nodded. 'And they fetched the maidservants, and when Matt lifted me over the threshold they all clapped their hands and cheered, just as Arbella came into the hall and caught sight of us, she was walking much better in those days, and the noise gave her such a turn that she dropped the tray she was carrying on to that stone floor and broke three of the good glasses.' She sighed. 'He took ill within the week, my poor laddie. And d'you ken, Arbella's never so much as mentioned those glasses to me.'

'Oh, that's forbearing,' agreed Alys, and took another sip from her glass.

'And then when – when I wedded Thomas, she would have us dwell here in the house, instead of up in the row with the colliers. To tell truth I was glad of it at first,' she admitted, 'for bare walls and an earthen floor's no what I was ever used to.' Alys made noises of sympathy. 'But she and Thomas make such an argybargy of the least wee thing, shouting and disagreeing over whether black's white, times there's no bearing it, Mistress Mason, if you'll believe me.'

'Does she dislike him, then?'

'No, no, she doesny dislike him! Just, they don't get on,' Joanna said earnestly. Alys nodded encouragingly. 'Thomas aye feels he should know more than she tells him, I think. She said to me when she would have me consent, he was a good bargain, and since Matt had respected him as a cunning pitman –' She bit her lip, and paused a moment. 'No, she gave him a gift as they left that morn, so how could she dislike him? Bel brought it here to him as I was packing his scrip. A wee flask of silver,' she held her hand out flat, fingers together, 'the size of that, but flat, to fit inside your doublet for travelling, and a drop of something in it to drink Arbella's health on her birthday, that's three days after St Patrick, seeing he would be away then. We aye mark folks' birthdays up here,' she confided, 'maybe something good to eat or a new garment for them or

71

the like. It's a friendly notion. So I put it right in his scrip, and no delay.'

Alys, whose father had always marked her birthday, smiled in agreement. Joanna looked down at her empty glass.

'Will you take a drop more, mistress?' She rose and fetched the yellow stoneware pipkin from the cupboard-top. 'It's warming stuff, this. Refreshes the heart.'

'It does indeed,' said Alys. 'Perhaps a drop. Have you any thought of what might have delayed your man?'

Joanna topped up Alys's glass, refilled her own, and sat down again, the little jar by her feet.

'I don't know what to think,' she admitted, looking unseeing at the brown sticky liquid in her glass. 'I canny think that it's anything good, by now. He could ha' taken ill, or met wi' some accident, but we'd surely ha' heard by now, would we no? Or he could ha' heard of a new order someone wanted to give us, though I'm not so certain we could fill it just now. But that would never ha' taken three weeks to deal wi'. I just – I just don't know.'

'Would he have any reason to leave here?' Alys asked gently.

'Oh, no. No that I can see.' Joanna's eyes focused on the glass of cordial, and she raised it. 'It's right kind of you to take such an interest,' she said innocently. 'Here's to your good fortune, Mistress Mason.'

'I never heard such a sad tale,' said Alys, accepting this, 'and every word of it true. What does your father think of your second marriage?'

Joanna looked away again, and crossed herself.

'He died two months after Matt,' she whispered. Alys, dismayed, moved her backstool beside Joanna's, and sat down again, taking the other girl's hand. 'He came up here once a week all that summer, while my poor lad was dying, and then I saw he'd begun to sicken of the same thing himself, and then he took to his bed and died.'

'Oh, my poor lass. That was hard for you.' Alys patted the hand she held. 'Did he make a peaceful end?'

'Oh, aye, just as Matt did, wi' Sir Simon to shrive him, that wedded Matt and me, and take down his will, and my brothers present, and all.' Joanna crossed herself again. 'Christ assoil him, he was concerned for me on his deathbed, that Arbella should have an eye to me. *Mistress Weir*, he said, over and over, *Mistress Weir, care.*'

'And I've had a care to you ever since, my pet, have I no?' said Arbella's sweet voice. Alys looked round, and saw the older woman standing in the doorway which led into the rest of the house, steadying herself with one twisted hand against the doorpost, Bel's round sullen face visible over her shoulder.

'Madam,' she said, and rose to curtsy. I must have been engrossed in Joanna's story, she thought, not to have heard her come in.

'Mistress Mason.' Arbella returned the curtsy, and moved forward into the room. Alys gestured at the backstool she had just vacated, and Arbella smiled, her expressive blue eyes softening. 'You are kind, my dear. And what brings you back to brighten our day?' she asked, seating herself with Bel's help.

To brighten an old woman's day, thought Alys. That was Gil's mother, yesterday evening. Distracted, she accepted a lower seat on the bench Bel drew forward, and gave the first answer that came to her.

'I was curious about the coal-heugh, madam. Phemie has told me a great deal, and I've talked of herbs with Mistress Lithgo as well. I've spent a most interesting time.'

'Have you now?' The old woman was wearing a plainer gown today, of tawny worsted faded almost to the colour of the peaches Alys recalled in the garden in Paris, and a wired headdress of black linen over a white indoor cap; now her exquisite eyebrows rose nearly to the lowest fold where it dipped over her brow. 'And are you herb-wise, too, my dear?'

'Beattie was saying –' began Joanna, and was checked by Arbella's uplifted hand. Alys waited a moment, then answered:

'I have run my father's house these six years. One learns to deal with kitchen-ills.'

'Very true. But you're no Scotswoman, by your speech, I thought that yesterday. Where are you from? From France, you say? Our Lady save us! And how did a Frenchwoman come to be wedded to Lady Cunningham's son?'

The inquisition ranged wide, over the marriage settlement, the contract, the size of her father's household, the nature of his business and Gil's. It was customary, of course, to put a new bride to the question, and Alys had witnessed other girls being subjected to the process as well as having had five months of it herself in Glasgow, but she had never been asked such intrusive questions by a relative stranger before. Parrying with all the politeness she had been taught, she gave away as little as necessary, but it was almost a relief when Joanna said shyly:

'Mother, I'm certain Mistress Mason would rather tell us what a bonnie man she's wedded on than how he earns his bread.'

'Aye, he's a bonnie man,' agreed Arbella, 'and I'll wager he can play the man's part well enough when the candles are out, am I right, my dear?'

'I've no complaints,' said Alys, smiling. It was the reply she had found most useful in the circumstance.

74

'I'll believe that.' Arbella chuckled knowingly, then paused to study Alys. 'But he's no finished his task yet, has he?'

'Time enough, Mother, surely,' said Joanna.

'Not yet,' said Alys, aware of her face burning.

'No, I thought not. You've not the look.' The expressive blue gaze flicked from her face to her waistline and back. 'As you say, Joanna my pet, there's time enough. I've said the same to you a time or two.'

Chapter Four

Gil was finding the women of Thorn a different proposition from the men.

He knew the little settlement slightly, a small fermtoun like so many others where four or five families held a piece of land and worked it in common. The houses in the midst of the four striped fields were low and long, the animals bedded at one end and the people at the other, the thatch supported by the cruck timbers which were the property of the tenant not the landlord.

When he got there the men were all out in the furthest field, visible in a morose group round a heap of stones, but he was welcomed by the women in committee. They gathered from kailyard and drying-green and seated him in state on the bench by the door of Annie Douglas's cottage, nearest the track. A beaker of Maidie Paton's ale, as being the best the township could produce, was put in his hand, and all the women crowded round to stare and talk and listen, their children peering round their skirts giggling. Hens wandered through and round the discussion, with a puppy trying to herd them.

'You've no brought your bride to see us,' complained Mistress Douglas. She was a big brawny woman, widow of a man called Meikle whom Gil recalled as another of his mother's stable-hands. The two brothers with the cart must be her sons, he realized. 'You'll just need to come back another time and bring her. And how's your lady mother? And your sisters? Did I hear good news o' Lady Kate? When's her bairn due?'

These questions and others having been addressed, Gil raised the subject which had brought him. At the mention of the corpse in the peat-cutting, there was a general chorus of disapproval and excitement.

'The men tellt us when they came home,' said Rab Simson's wife, broad red hands on her bony hips. 'What a thing to find in the peat! Killt three times over, was he no? And never a stitch on him? And you cut him up in your mother's cart-shed, is that right?'

'Mind your tongue, Lizzie!' ordered another woman, very like her in build and face. 'Or were you looking for ways to deal wi' your Rab?' They all laughed at this. 'Mind you, he'd got a sore fright when he found the corp, Rab did, by the look of him.'

'Aye, Maggie, he'd got a fright,' said Lizzie sourly. 'He'd need of a drink of usquebae to steady him, and then another to wash that away, and then another, till he was that steady he couldny find his way to his bed.'

'At least he'd more sense than go and take Beattie Lithgo up for a witch,' said Mistress Douglas, 'the way my boys did. I skelped them for that when I heard it, I can tell you. The idea!'

'Beattie's a good woman,' agreed Lizzie. 'It was her cured my boy's sore eyes, and your wean's rotten ear, Maidie, you mind.'

'She is, she's a good woman,' said another voice. 'No like —'

'Let alone she's more sense than bury him in our peat-digging,' said someone else from the background. 'If it was Thomas Murray.'

77

'Aye, but it wasny,' said the woman called Maggie. 'Our Wat tellt me your nephew Jamesie said it wasny him, Annie.'

'So he did, and Jamesie has more wit than my two put together,' agreed Mistress Douglas.

'It was Davy Fleming told them to go and get her,' said another voice. 'Our Adam's no more wit than do as the clerk bid him, neither.'

'No more did our Eck,' said Lizzie. 'Taking that wee fornicator's word for it, and all.'

'Aye, well,' said Mistress Douglas. 'They'll none of them make that mistake again soon. And did ye discern yet what man it is, Maister Gil?'

Here was his opening.

'I did not,' he admitted. 'It's not Thomas Murray, you're right about that, but it seems to me he's been dead a long time, with the peat growing over him.'

'Peat doesny grow!' objected one woman, as the men had done. 'It's aye been!'

'No, for there's trees at the bottom of it,' another reminded her. 'From Noy's Flood, our William says. Was this maybe a man from Noy's time, sir?'

'I think not so long ago as that,' Gil said. 'What I wondered was if he was maybe from our grandsires' time, or a bit before. Do any of you mind any tales of a man missing on the moor?'

'What, slain and buried wi' no a stitch on him?' said Maggie. 'I never heard such a tale.'

There was a general agreement. Gil shook his head, and drained the beaker in his hand.

'He was slain and buried in secret,' he pointed out, wiping his mouth. 'The tale of that would never get out. What's more, though I agree wool and leather would last if they'd been there, he might not have been naked. If he was wearing linen shirt and breeks when he was buried, they would rot down in the peat, I

78

would think, like the other growing stuff. Say he was robbed of his outer clothes and anything else on him, and left in a mire, nobody would know of it. Till now.'

Mistress Douglas folded brawny arms across her bosom and considered this.

'Aye,' she said after a moment. 'So what you want is whether there's any tale of a tinker or a cadger gone missing, or the like. Or maybe,' she said slowly, 'a man from here or further down the hill, in the auld times. For if he was buried in the digging to be secret, it must ha' been afore we dug peat there, or whoever slain him would know he'd be found soon or late.'

Gil nodded agreement.

'We've cut peats there since my grandam's day,' said one of the younger women.

'What about your auld fellow, Jeanie?' said another voice. 'He's sharp enough, would he mind o' such a thing?'

The group shuffled about, and a round-faced woman in a faded blue kirtle was pushed forward and identified as Jeanie Forrest, wife to Adam Livingstone. Bobbing nervously, she admitted that her auld fellow, who claimed he was eighty-one, might well know if such a tale existed.

'Who is he?' Gil asked. 'Where may I speak to him?'

He was her grandsire, William Forrest, and he had been huntsman to Sir James's great-grandsire, and Sir James still sent a purse every hunting season, which came in right handy, seeing the old man had all of his wits but no teeth and needed a wee bit extra to his feeding.

'He's where he aye is, sitting in at the fire in our house,' said another woman beside her, thinner in the face but like enough to be her sister. 'Minding the cradle.'

'Would ye come by our bit the now and speak wi' him, maister?' asked Jeanie, bobbing again.

By the time the procession reached Jeanie's house, a shouting horde of children had preceded them, warned Maister William, who was struggling to his feet beside the peat-fire, and woken the occupant of the cradle, who was roaring in displeasure. Jeanie snatched the baby up, sat down on a bench next the door, pulling at the laces which fastened her bodice and shift, and silenced it by thrusting a brownish, thumb-length dug into its mouth. Gil found himself thinking by comparison of Alys's slight breasts and rosy nipples, and wondered how she was progressing at the coal-heugh. He put the distraction with difficulty from his mind, and turned to Jeanie's grandfather, a gaunt, big-framed old fellow bundled in many layers of homespun woollen, topped by a shapeless knitted cape from which his scrawny neck emerged like a lizard's, and a woollen bonnet with a fringe of white hair sticking out below its checked band.

'Maister William,' Gil said, raising his hat. The old man's face split in a toothless grin at the courtesy, and he ducked shakily in response, groping for his own bonnet. Jeanie's sister steadied him with a practised hand under his elbow. 'Sit down, maister, I'll not keep you standing at your age!'

'Eighty-two next Lanimer Day,' announced Maister William proudly, if indistinctly. 'I was huntsman to Sir James Douglas, that was grandsire to this Douglas, ye ken.'

'Great-grandsire,' corrected Jeanie's sister. 'Sit down, Granda, like the gentleman says. He wants to ask you about this corp in the peat-cutting.'

'I never heard of sic a thing!' declared the old man, subsiding into his chair. 'Where's my cushion, Agnes? I've lost my cushion.'

'It's here, Granda.' Agnes rammed a lumpy pad down at his back. 'You sit nice and talk to the gentleman now.'

'Aye, well, I will if you let him get a word in. And you can bid all these women stay outside, I've no wish to be deaved wi' a gabble of women. Have a seat, sir, just take one of they stools, if you wait for my lassies to offer it you'll wait all day. About the corp ye found, is it? No, I never heard of a corp in a peat-cutting afore.'

This topic had to be explored quite thoroughly, along with the question of how long the old man had served the earlier Sir James and his son and grandson ('Seventy year, if you'll credit that, sir! Seventy year I served the family, and no a day less,' boasted Maister William, while his granddaughter shook her head in denial behind him) and his acquaintance with the man who had been huntsman to Gil's father ('Oh, I mind Billy Meikle. I mind him well. I taught him. And he taught you, did he, young sir?') but eventually the conversation was brought back to the discovery in the peat-cuttings. Jeanie's man Adam had described the find, but not clearly.

'He's no a huntsman, you ken,' said Maister William disparagingly. 'Tellt us how he was lying, so he did, and how his face was all flat wi' the peat, but he never said how he died.'

'Slain three times over, our Rab said,' declared Lizzie from the doorway. Maister William turned his shoulder on her and looked hopefully at Gil, who obediently described his findings, to exclamations of shocked interest from the listening women. The old huntsman nodded approval of his account.

'Aye, Billy's taught you well,' he pronounced. 'You've observed well, young sir. And were his hands and feet bound at all?'

'No,' said Gil positively, 'nor marked.'

'So it's been a sudden death,' said the old man acutely. 'Maybe even taken and slain where you found him.'

'I would say so. Certainly there's no sign he's been held prisoner. Assuming sign like that would last,' he qualified.

'Aye, very true. A good point, young sir, a good point. And you want to know if there's ever been anyone missing in the parish.'

'I do, sir.'

Maister William nodded. He went on nodding for some time, staring into the smoke which rose from the smouldering peats. Gil began to wonder if the old man had fallen asleep, and then realized he was counting. The women at the door were discussing the same subject, but seemed to be more interested in a lassie that had run off from Braidwood ten years since, and turned up wedded to a saddler in Rutherglen, than in the men of the parish. He sat hugging his knees, tasting the various smells of the place, peat-smoke and damp earth, the smells of the cattle-stall at the other end of the house, the savoury odour of the three-footed cauldron simmering among the peats and a sharper overtone which emanated from either Maister William or the baby, who was still sucking happily and noisily. After a while the old huntsman raised his head.

'Five,' he said. 'Aye, five in my time, or that I heard folk tell of, and that takes us back to King Robert's day, afore Thorn cut its peats on that patch. No counting my mother's brother Dandy, but he was barely fourteen.'

'And who were they, maister?' Gil asked. That must be over a hundred years, he realized. His memory and knowledge go back so far. I am in the presence of history.

'Ah. Now you're asking.' The old man raised gnarled fingers and began to count. 'There was Andra Simson, that was our Rab's grandsire's cousin at Kilncaigow, in James Second's time. That's right, write it down in your wee tablets. But he wasny a red-headed man, and he was a carpenter what's more and had the marks on his hands to show for it. Did you no say this fellow's hands and feet were soft?'

'What happened to him?' Gil asked. 'How did he disappear?'

'Andra? He was working down in Lanark, I think it was. Aye, Lanark. Set off for Kilncaigow one night from Eppie Watson's alehouse there and never was seen again. Never seen again,' he repeated. 'They found his lantern, if I recall, on Kilncaigow Muir.'

'The road from Lanark to Kilncaigow wouldny take him up here,' said Gil thoughtfully.

'No, it never would.' Maister William champed his toothless jaws and cackled suddenly. 'No unless he'd a woman up the Pow Burn that his wife never kent of!'

'And did he?'

'No that I heard tell,' said the old man regretfully. 'Then there was Tam Davison, twenty year since. Aye, the year this Sir James's father died.'

With a little coaxing, he recounted the details of the remaining disappearances. None of them seemed promising, all were working men who might be assumed to bear the marks of one trade or another, and he was quite certain that none was red-headed. Moreover, it seemed that the peat-cutting had been in use for most of Maister William's lifetime. The women listened intently, nodding sagely at each of the names, but as he reached the last one Jeanie said, from where she sat nursing the baby on the bench at the wall:

'You've forgot the men up at the coal-heugh, Granda.'

'They've never disappeared,' he retorted. 'You'll no

talk to me like that, you malapert hizzy. I don't forget a thing.'

'There was Davy Fleming's father, so I've heard. Fell down one of their nasty holes, so my da said, and never found.'

'Aye, he was,' objected the old man. 'They found him a week later, I mind hearing o't as if it was yesterday. They tracked him by the stink –'

'And then Mistress Weir's man disappeared,' she said stubbornly. 'He went off and died and never came home.'

'Aye, but she kent where he was buried,' countered the old man.

'Aye, so they say. And Beattie Lithgo's man and all,' she persisted. 'Geordie says Jamesie says they never got him out to bury him decent, just closed up that bit of the working, because the roof wasny safe.'

'Aye, and he walks,' said someone else. 'That's why they'll no work by night.'

'Geordie's talking nonsense, for I was at the burial,' declared Maister William. 'I could never walk so far now, you'll understand, sir, but I still had my strength then. Adam Crombie the elder died away at Elsrickle, Will Fleming fell down a shaft, Adam the younger died under a roof-fall. That's no disappearing. Any road, Beattie would never ha' slain them and hid them in the peat, no like – she'd a great liking for her man, Beattie did. She tellt me that, one time she was here wi' a wee pot of grease for my rheumatics. And I'll tell you,' a gnarled finger jabbed at Gil's doublet, 'whatever she'd put in it, it shifted the pains in my knees. I'm needing a bit more, Agnes, mind that, you'd best get me another wee pot.'

'Best be quick about it, and all,' said one of the women, 'afore David Fleming gets his way and she's hanged for a witch.'

'Hah!' said Maister William witheringly. 'Davy Fleming, indeed! I kent his grandsire from he was the age of Jeanie's wee one here, and he was just the same, all ower the countryside, and none of his get had the sense of a puddock. Whatever Davy's took into his head, maister, you can wager he's as wrong as he can be about it.'

Leaving Thorn, Gil strode down the track in the spring sunshine, deep in thought. He was still in hopes of giving the corpse from the peat-digging a name, and kin who could pray for him, but it began to seem likely he was not a local man. Perhaps down in Lanark, he thought, or eastward in Carnwath, someone might recall a tale like old Forrest's. He could ride out that way tomorrow, and perhaps Alys would go too. The dog could come with them; he had sent him with Alys and Henry today as some protection, and it seemed strange to be out in the open without the lithe grey form loping round him.

Cheered by the idea, he made his way down the hillside, crossed the burn at its foot and climbed the other slope to pick up the way to Cauldhope. He had always felt Sir James's dwelling was well named. It was a draughty and inconvenient tower-house at the back of Kilncaigow Hill, surrounded by considerable outbuildings, stables and barn and storehouses and a huddle of cottages like the ones at Thorn. A straggle of wind-blasted beeches made a sort of shelter to the east, but Gil had chilly memories of formal winter dining there as a boy, waiting on his parents and Michael's and serving out congealing sauces with numb fingers while the candle flames streamed sideways. Today in the sunlight it looked more welcoming, and one of the household had obviously recognized him approaching, for

85

Fleming was waiting at the gate, bowing obsequiously as he came up the track between the low houses.

'Maister Gil! Come away in, come in! You'll take a drop of ale to settle the dust? Bring that ale, Simmie, can you no see Maister Cunningham's thirsty! And how can I help you, Maister Gil? They're all from home, I'm sorry to tell you, Maister Michael rode out this morning, never tellt me where he –'

'Never worry about that,' said Gil, accepting the ale. 'It was yourself I wanted a word with, Sir David.'

'Wi' me?' The plump priest looked alarmed, but bowed again. 'At your service, maister. Ask away, whatever you want to know. Come in, come in out this wind, and get a seat.'

The fire in the hall had burned low, but Fleming bustled into a small chamber behind the screen, where a brazier kept the chill at bay. Two big aumbries and a rack of document-shelves stuffed with papers made the room's purpose obvious. The man Simmie set down the tray with jug and beaker and left reluctantly, and Fleming drew the steward's own chair forward for Gil and lifted the jug.

'Take a seat, maister, take a seat, and ha' some more of that ale. And what's your business wi' me? If it's a matter of my maister's affairs I might no be able to answer, you understand, I'm privy to a lot that's in close confidence –'

'No, no,' said Gil. 'I'll not ask you to break a confidence. It's about yesterday's matter. I need to know what your charge is against Beattie Lithgo, and it would help me if you could say when you last set eyes on Thomas Murray.'

'The charge against the woman Lithgo!' exclaimed Fleming. He drained his own beaker, and set it down on a pile of papers. 'Is it no obvious, maister? She's a notorious witch, widely kent for a cunning woman and dealing in charms and spells all over the countryside.'

'This is not what I have heard,' Gil observed. 'Michael mentioned evidence. Do you have any, or have you heard any other say that she has done this?'

'It's all over the countryside,' Fleming repeated. 'Ask anybody. They'll tell you.'

'Not so far,' said Gil. 'All I've heard is that she healed this or mended that. She's aye spoken of as a good woman.'

'It's no natural for a woman to do such things!'

'Rubbish,' said Gil irritably. 'Any woman in charge of a household has to deal wi' cuts and burns and treat sickness. My own mother and my wife are both herb-wise. Who else would keep the kitchen-hands safe or plaister a trodden foot in the stable-yard?'

'She's ill-natured, which is well known to be the attribute of a witch –'

'This is nonsense, man,' said Gil, his exasperation growing. 'By that token, Sir James himself would be a witch, and you'll not accuse your own maister, I hope.'

'You'll not put words in my mouth, Maister Gil,' said Fleming with anxious haste. 'I never suggested any such thing, and you know it.'

'Well, either tell me what Beatrice Lithgo has done that would warrant a charge of witchcraft, or stop spreading such things about. She could have you for slander, you know, if the charge was brought and proved false.'

'Slander!' repeated Fleming in dismay. 'Are you threatening me wi' the law, maister?'

'No, I am not,' said Gil crisply. 'I am warning you. Now will you tell me what prompted your nonsense about witchcraft, or will you desist from it?'

I should not have let my temper get the better of me there, he thought guiltily. Fleming swallowed hard, his expression suddenly blank, and reached out and poured himself another beaker of ale, which he drank down as if it would provide him with an answer. After a moment it appeared to do so.

'It's like this, Maister Cunningham,' he said. 'What made me suspect her was the deaths. Aye, the deaths,' he repeated. 'It's all in the rent roll, which I keep.' He nodded towards the document rack. 'There was a death up there two year since, and one nine year since, that's a seven-year difference, and another seven year afore that. Now what's that if it's no witchcraft, and the worst sort?'

'Nonsense!' exclaimed Gil. 'Are you claiming Mistress Lithgo caused all three deaths? Who were they, anyway?' He paused, reckoning. 'The young one – Matt – two years ago, he took ill and died, and neither his mother nor Mistress Lithgo could save him.'

'Aye, for she'd cast a spell over him,' Fleming asserted, nodding.

'The one before that was an accident below ground, in the pit. How could she contrive that? Women don't go in the pit, they tell me.'

'They can work evil at a distance –'

'And the first one took ill and died miles from home. And did your own father not die up at the heugh? When was that?'

'My father's death, Christ assoil him,' said Fleming, going red and crossing himself, 'was certainly an accident, for it was long before the woman Lithgo came to the heugh. See, Maister Cunningham, I've a wee bookie I've been reading, that a friend lent to me, tells me all about witches and how to recognize them and all sorts of things they do. And in it –'

'What book is this?' Gil interrupted, with a sinking heart.

88

'It's cried *Malleus Maficarum*,' said Fleming proudly, 'which means *Hammer of Evil Women*, ye ken –'

'That should be *Maleficarum*,' Gil corrected. Sweet St Giles, help me, he thought, if this fool has got hold of a copy of that pernicious work, he'll find witches under every hedge.

'Aye, *Maficarum*,' agreed Fleming. 'Oh, the things witches gets up to, I never kent the half of it afore I read about them in this book. It's but the second part of it, I truly wish I could get the whole of it to read!'

Thank you, St Giles! thought Gil.

'Tell me what Mistress Lithgo has done, then,' he prompted.

'Have you read in this book, maister? I never kent they did more than charms and glamour, but this makes all clear, how they entice innocent maids to join their perfidious company, and take an oath of allegiance to the Devil himself, and fly from place to place by the power of demons and a wee pot of ointment –'

'I've heard of all that,' Gil interrupted. 'I don't believe it, either. What I want to know is what you have seen Mistress Lithgo do yourself. Have you proof of her working witchcraft? Has she injured you, for instance?'

'She spends her time in that lair of wickedness she calls her stillroom,' declared Fleming, 'times I've kent her even refuse to come out to hear Mass because the spells she was working needed to be watched all the time. She's in there burning herbs and mixing poisons, wi' charms and cantrips and curses to say over them – what could that be but witchcraft?'

'Go on,' said Gil.

Fleming opened and shut his mouth a few times, drank another draught of ale, and recalled something else. 'She's stole candles and holy water from the chapel. There's aye less of either than I look to find, every time I'm up there, and I have the one key and Mistress Weir, the devout woman that she is, keeps the other.'

'But not the Host?' prompted Gil.

'No, no,' Fleming crossed himself at the word, 'I bear the Body of Christ away wi' me in a wee pyx, sooner than leave it in an unattended place.'

'You've not convinced me so far,' said Gil. 'Can you show me anyone she has injured?'

'There's folk all about here been injured! Old Forrest up at Thorn, the old soul, has pains like knives in every joint, and so does Annie Douglas next door to him. What could that be but her work? And done wi' a glance, just as it tells in the book!'

'They seemed to feel she had helped them with the simples she gave them.'

'Aye, no doubt, but who should undo the injury but the witch herself?'

Gil sighed. 'Maister Fleming,' he said firmly, 'none of this is proof of anything at all.'

'And she's injured me!'

'How?'

'Well, she – she gave me a pot of ointment, and it never worked. It made matters worse. And she tellt me to boil well-water and drink that instead of ale, when a'body kens ale's better for you. The very thought of drinking water!' Fleming took another pull at his ale in agitation.

'Did you go back when the ointment never worked?' Gil asked.

'Aye, and she refused to help me. That was when I kent her for a witch, for she met me wi' evil words, and I've heard her use the very same words wi' Thomas Murray, and here he is dead in a peat-bank!'

'And what words were those?'

'I'll not defile my mouth wi' repeating them, maister.'

90

'Then they won't stand as evidence.'

There was another pause.

'I clearly heard her say to the man Murray,' said Fleming at length, 'that if he continued in some behaviour she would make sure he regretted it.'

'What behaviour? When was this?'

'It was last summer, in the midst of August three weeks after the quarter-day. As to what he was up to, I have no notion, for she never said in my hearing. And when I threatened to report her to Sir James for a witch, two weeks syne,' announced Fleming indignantly, 'she swore I would regret it in the same tone of voice, maister. And what more proof could you want?'

'But how would he get hold of such a book?' asked Lady Egidia. 'He's no university man, is he? Can he even read?'

'It seems so,' said Gil.

Across the hearth Michael swallowed down the mouthful of bread and meat he was chewing and said, 'No, he's no Master of Arts, but he can read Latin, for old Sir Arnold taught him. That's how he got his post, see, he's Arnold's sister's son, he was left fatherless and Arnold saw to his training, and my father thought the world of Arnold.'

'Aye, and quite right. He was a good man and a good priest,' said Lady Egidia.

'Which is more than the nephew,' said Michael roundly.

They were seated in one of the chambers off the hall at Belstane, where Lady Egidia had summoned her godson as soon as he arrived from his tour of the collier's round. He had admitted to being ravenously hungry, having missed both the midday meal and supper, but his consumption was slowing now he had half cleared the platter.

Beside Gil on the settle Alys leaned forward and said, 'Does he run after the maidservants, Michael?'

Michael, chewing again, nodded and rolled his eyes.

'He'd bairned three afore St John's Eve last year,' he divulged, as soon as he could speak. 'And there was at least two the year afore that. There's been less trouble since then, by what my father tells me,' he admitted, 'but it's getting so decent women willny hire to us, so Jock the steward says. And there's the amount of ale he gets through, I noticed it at Yule. He's no often drunk, I'll give him that, but he's a drouth on him like a tinker. And he aye smells of those candied pears like my mother used to make, and willny admit it. Why can I smell them on your breath, says my father, and Fleming swears he was never near such a thing. He must have a secret store of the stuff.'

'But where did the book come from?' persisted Lady Egidia.

'He was at Linlithgow wi' my father the last time,' Michael offered, eyeing the final wedge of bread and cold meat. 'When the court was there, you ken. It's possible someone there would have such a thing to lend him.'

'*Malleus Maleficarum*,' said Alys thoughtfully. 'The hammer of women who do evil. I've never seen the book.'

'I have,' said Gil, grimacing. 'A copy came my way in Paris. It's written by a Dominican who was an inquisitor in Austria or somewhere of the sort, and became obsessed by witchcraft as a particular heresy. The word in Paris was that the bishop of the place put a stop to his witch-hunting, because of his methods, and he went away and wrote this book in retaliation. It's all allegation and anecdote, *richt pungitive with wordis odious.* You can hear the man frothing at the mouth on every page.'

'It sounds unpleasant,' said Lady Egidia.

'It is.'

'Can you or your father not take the book from Fleming?'

Michael shook his head. 'He'll not listen to me, madam. I'll write to my father, and hope he does something, but, well, seems to me the damage is done.'

'You are right,' agreed Alys, tucking her hand into Gil's. 'The ideas are loose in his head now.'

'At least we know where they came from,' said Gil. 'Michael, for pity's sake, eat that. You must be starved of hunger. Did you learn anything the day?'

'No,' said Michael indistinctly as Lady Egidia rose and went out into the hall. 'Not a lot,' he qualified, swallowing. 'I started at the near end, wi' Lockhart at the Lee. Their steward was from home, but I got a word wi' the under-steward who looked up the accounts for me, and it seems the coal was paid the same day Murray set out from the Pow Burn. As you'd expect,' he added. 'That would be the eighteenth of March, as I recall. One night's hospitality writ down at the same time. Then he went on to Waygateshaw, I suppose on the nineteenth, they paid him and he collected a couple more fees while he was there, and rode off on the twentieth for Jerviswood, his two men wi' him.'

'So far, so good,' said Gil. 'These are all close at hand,' he added to Alys, who nodded.

'Aye. Well, after Jerviswood,' Michael went on, 'the next on the list is Lanark town, two houses. I decided I'd not go into Lanark yet, but went on to pick up the trail at Ravenstruther. Their steward looked up the accounts and said they lay there on the . . .' He paused, reflecting. 'Aye. The twenty-third and -fourth of March. Likely Lanark was more attractive, that they'd stayed longer there in between. I turned for home then, since it was well through the afternoon and I didny fancy my chances pressing on to Carnwath and getting back before dark.'

'And all was as usual?' Gil asked. Michael shrugged. Instead of his narrow scholar's gown, today he was wearing a handsome doublet of soft tawny leather, faced with green velvet at the cuffs and neck, the sleeves and throat of his shirt embroidered in green and tawny thread to match. He seemed five years older and far better looking; Gil suddenly saw what might have attracted his youngest sister.

'This was four or five weeks ago,' he was saying. 'I asked, but nobody minded aught that was out of the ordinary.'

'Just Murray and his two men,' said Alys. Michael nodded, and half rose as Lady Egidia returned.

'Sit still,' she said, crossing the chamber to her own chair. 'Alan will bring more food in a little space. This has been good work, godson, even if you learned nothing. Tomorrow you can go on to the next houses on the list.'

Michael went scarlet with what might have been gratification, and Gil sat back, stretching out his legs.

'So all was well for a good week after they set out,' he summarized. 'And meantime, I'm no nearer finding a name to the corp, nor learning just why Fleming brought such a charge against Mistress Lithgo. What about your day, sweetheart?'

'I found out more than that, I think,' said Alys diffidently. Alan Forrest entered, with a fresh platter of bread and cheese and a bowl of rather withered apples, which he set on the table by Michael's elbow. 'Though none of it may be to the point. Did you say Fleming admitted to having consulted Mistress Lithgo?'

'Under pressure.'

'Ah. Only under pressure. That is interesting. He did not say why?'

'No,' Gil admitted, 'though he mentioned ointment which didn't work. No reason why he should, I suppose, though it might have been more corroboration if he'd told me what way the ointment didn't work.'

'Yes,' said Alys. 'Phemie told me she had seen him slipping into her mother's stillroom after they all thought he had left for the day. But Mistress Lithgo never mentioned it today when I spoke to her, nor yesterday when it might have helped her cause.'

'Ah!' echoed Lady Egidia. The steward paused in the doorway, half-watching the company. 'You think . . .'

Alys exchanged a very woman-to-woman glance with her across Gil.

'It seems possible,' she agreed. 'Some problem he might not wish discussed. She is a good woman, and a good healer, I think she would be discreet as a matter of course.'

'Oh, she would. I wonder what it is? I suppose it could be anything he keeps under his hose. A carbuncle on his hinder end, emerods, trouble with his water. Alan, what are you waiting there for?' demanded his mistress. 'Have you aught to add to this?'

'Aye, well,' admitted the steward, grinning sheepishly. 'In a manner o' speaking. It's Davy Fleming ye're discussing, madam, is it?'

'You ken very well it is,' she said tartly. 'What's the word, then? Have you something Maister Gil should hear?'

'I'm no just certain. For all you're saying Beattie Lithgo can be discreet, mistress, I think there's some word going about among the lassies – the young lassies. The way they laugh when his name's mentioned, there's something they're no telling the men.'

95

Another of those significant glances passed, and both women nodded triumphantly. Gil, catching up with their thought, looked from his mother to his wife, and objected: 'Michael's just told us he's putting it well about – what, three lassies last summer, two the year afore – that doesn't sound like what you're suggesting.'

'But none since then,' said Alys.

'What is it you're suggesting?' Michael asked blankly. The steward grinned again, and made an inelegant gesture. Michael went scarlet. 'Oh! D'you mean he canny get – like some kind of retribution? A judgement on him?'

'It might be,' agreed Alys, 'though I have never heard of it happening so appositely.' Gil looked down at the top of her head where she leaned against his shoulder, wondering yet again at her capacity to surprise him.

'I have,' said Lady Egidia. She paused, considering her household. 'The lassies would tell me what the joke is, but I'd have to press them to it likely. They're by far more like to share it wi' you, Alys. Would you care to have a try at one or two of them?'

'I should be honoured,' said Alys.

'Alan will furnish you wi' likely names. And did you learn anything more at the coal-heugh?'

Alys nodded, her head shifting against Gil's shoulder, and put up a hand to straighten her French hood.

'Much of it was shadows,' she qualified. 'Nuances. The man Murray was much disliked – I think all of the women had some reason to wish him ill – but the most interesting was that Joanna is to have her first husband's share of the inheritance. A half share in the business.'

'Is she, now!' said Gil.

'Is that right?' said Alan, still hovering in the doorway. 'I kent the auld – Mistress Weir was daft for her, but I never heard that.'

'Alan, you may as well be seated,' said his mistress resignedly, 'and tell us what you know about the folk at the coal-heugh and all.'

'Well, it's maybe no that much,' said Alan, seating himself primly on the nearest stool. 'They keep their-sels to theirsels up there.'

This proved to be the case. Few facts emerged, but a picture of a community viewed with suspicion, known to be violent, said to be feckless. The heugh was thought to be haunted, possibly by Mistress Lithgo's husband, which Alan thought must be right, for else why would the colliers not work at night? Mistress Lithgo herself was well known and well liked, her daughters regarded warily – 'They're bonnie lassies, but nobody kens how they'll be placed,' said Alan. Gil recognized the reference to the girls' dowries.

'And the old woman?' he prompted. 'What's said of her?'

'Little enough,' returned Alan. 'I think it's well kent who's in charge up there, whatever man's collecting the fee for the coals. Likely nobody wishes to offend her.'

'Nobody wishes to offend me,' said Lady Egidia, 'and there's plenty said about me by what I hear.'

I'll wager there is, thought Gil, hiding a grin.

'Aye, well,' said Alan awkwardly.

'Maister Forrest!' Hasty feet sounded on the tiled floor of the hall, and the steward turned his head. The kitchen-boy appeared in the doorway, puffing in excite-ment. 'Maister Forrest, you're called for,' he said, duck-ing and touching his wide bonnet as he spoke. 'It's someone at the yett. They're saying it's him from the coal-heugh.'

'From the – who is it?' demanded Gil. 'The man Murray?'

The boy stared at him open-mouthed. He was probably ten or twelve, clad in an oversize homespun doublet and wrinkled hose, the general effect with his broad sagging bonnet very like one of the mushrooms that appeared in the horse-pastures in the dawn.

'Who is it at the yett, Nicol?' repeated Alan Forrest. 'And uncover afore your mistress, you daft laddie.'

Nicol dragged off the bonnet, revealing a shaggy fairish thatch, and ducked again.

'I never seen them, Maister Forrest,' he said in alarm. 'Just they're saying it's a man from the coal-heugh.'

Chapter Five

It was not Thomas Murray.

Adam Crombie the youngest stood in the stable-yard in the dying light of the April evening, loud and proud as Ivy, broad-shouldered in his blue student gown, and glowered at Gil.

'Is it you that's set this nonsense afoot?' he demanded. 'What's it all about, then? Thomas dug out of a peat-bank, and my mother taken up for a witch? It makes no sense.'

'I never said that,' said Jamesie Meikle at his elbow. 'I said it's no Thomas Murray, and Mistress Lithgo was freed. By this fellow here,' he added, 'so you might as well be civil to him, maister.'

'I'm glad you're here,' said Gil mildly. He stepped back, to allow Alan Forrest to offer ale to both men, and nodded to the stable-hand who held the bridles of two sturdy ponies. 'Aye, take those beasts in, Tammas. They'll be hungry, if they've come from Glasgow today.'

'Glad? Why should that be?' said Crombie, emerging from his beaker. 'Did you look for us?'

'There's all sorts I need to know that I'd not wish to ask the women, that one or other of you can surely tell me. Will you come in the house? You'll not ride on tonight, I hope. It must be another hour to the heugh, and the light's going. We can feed you and fit you in a corner somewhere, can't we, Alan?'

'Aye, very like,' admitted the steward with faint reluctance.

'We'll no be looked for till the morn,' said Meikle hopefully, 'and the owls will fly soon.'

Crombie grunted ungraciously, but followed Gil up the stone steps into the house, saying, 'What's going on, then? Jamesie brought me a word from my grandam, but all she says is that I'm needed out at the heugh, and what Jamesie has to add to that's no great benefit, what wi' a dead man in the Thorn peat-cutting and that fool Fleming trying to blame my mother for it.'

'That's the meat of it,' agreed Gil, 'that and the fact your grieve's missing. He went off five weeks since to fetch the dues for last quarter and hasn't come home.'

'Five *weeks*? Have they no sent after him?' demanded Crombie. 'Jamesie, you never said it was as long as that.'

'Mistress Weir won't hear of sending after him yet.' Gil led the way into the hall, just as Michael appeared in the doorway of the small chamber, bowing to those within.

'Servant, madam, Mistress Mason,' he said, and turned to leave. He checked at the sight of Crombie, who was staring at him from the hall threshold. 'What are you doing here?'

'What are you doing?' demanded Crombie in return, equally hostile. Gil looked from one to the other in amusement, thinking of fighting-cocks.

'Leaving,' said Michael curtly. 'I'll carry on down the list the morn,' he added to Gil, replacing his hat, 'and report again.'

'Have you light enough to get home by?' called Lady Egidia. Michael turned in the doorway, raising his eyebrows.

'Two mile on the old Roman road, most of it on our

100

own land,' he said. 'I don't need a light. I'll see you the morn, madam.'

'Good man,' said Gil, clapping him on the shoulder as he went past. Michael grunted a reply, ducked round the glowering Adam Crombie, and left the house. Gil led the two new guests into another of the small chambers, and went to alert his mother to their presence.

Once both men had washed and eaten, Crombie in modest state in the chamber off the hall, Meikle in the kitchen with the maidservants giggling by the hearth, they forgathered in the steward's room with a jug of the twice-brewed. Gil offered a concise account of events so far, to which the young coalmaster listened, frowning.

'It makes no sense,' he complained. 'You say you've no notion who this corp might be.' Gil nodded agreement. 'As for where Thomas might ha' got to – Jamesie, can you say?'

'No,' said Meikle baldly.

'And David Fleming calling my mother for a witch. My mother! What's got into him to do that? That's bad, isn't it, Maister Cunningham?'

'It could be,' Gil said warily. 'Any woman as herbwise as your mother is at risk of being accused like that. Have you yourself aught to add to the situation? I'd hoped you might be able to tell me what's behind Fleming's behaviour.'

Crombie was silent, staring into his cup of ale.

'The corp's nothing to do wi' us,' he said at length.

'I think he's been in the peat a good many years. Maybe even before your time.'

'The clerk was teaching my sisters their letters and a bit Latin,' continued Crombie, 'till – oh, last autumn. Then when I was home at Yule he'd ceased the lessons. There seemed no reason for it, but Arbella wouldny hear of it continuing. Whether he broke them off, and she took exception to that, or whether my mother put

101

a stop to them and he took a strunt, or what, I've no notion. He's never liked us, for all Arbella's done him a good few favours. I've aye took it it's down to his father dying in the Long Shaft, but this –'

'This seems to be aimed at Mistress Lithgo herself,' Gil agreed, 'and she can't have been there when that happened.'

'No, well afore her time,' said Crombie, and took another pull at his ale.

'Was Fleming's father a collier?'

'No that I heard. He clerked for the place, kept accounts and the like, I believe. What's that to the point?'

'Little enough, if that's the case. And Fleming himself, is he a good teacher?'

'Who knows. My sisters wereny enjoying his lessons much, they'd no sorrow that they were ended. I just left it,' he said grandly, 'lassies have no need of reading, Latin or Scots, so long as they can keep the accounts straight.'

'And is he liked by folk round about?' Gil asked, ignoring this statement.

'No as much as Sir Arnold was.'

'My auntie hasny a good word for him,' said Meikle.

'I was up at Thorn and heard some of her words today,' Gil said, glancing at him. The collier grinned. 'What did you mean yesterday, Jamesie, about swearing to something on any relic Sir David could produce?'

Master and man looked at each other.

'Is that still –?' said Crombie. The collier nodded. 'What a piece of nonsense. We've a chapel of St Ninian up by the coal-heugh, maister, and Sir David wants a relic for it. He and Arbella can never agree on what to search for, nor how much to pay for it, nor who should pay. It's been an argument atween them these three year.'

102

'The man's a fool. I wonder that my godfather keeps him on,' said Gil. Neither man rose to this bait. 'Does he have much to do with you up at the heugh as under-steward?'

'It's generally him that collects the quarter's fee,' said Crombie, surprised. 'But it's mostly that he priests for us, seeing he's chaplain at Cauldhope.'

Behind them, hinges grumbled as the door was nudged open. The colliers looked round, and both stared in surprise at the long grey muzzle and single bright eye which appeared round the edge of the heavy planks.

'And what about Murray?' said Gil, snapping his fingers. Socrates pushed the door wider and padded into the room. 'Is there any reason why the man would vanish?'

'A whole quarter's takings would maybe be reason enough,' suggested Meikle sourly.

'Is that so? Would he think so? How much should he gather, all told?'

Crombie shrugged, still eyeing the dog with suspicion. 'Ten merks? Twelve? Depends how much coal he sold last winter.'

'Hardly a fortune to run off with. What does the man earn in a quarter?'

'No that much, I assure you.'

'And there's the other two lads,' Meikle pointed out. 'He could never just ride off and leave them. They'd surely be back to let us know.' He made a chirruping noise, and Socrates cocked his head at him.

'And Joanna,' said Crombie. The collier's face froze. 'He'd be daft to go and leave her, the way my sainted grandam's will stands, unless she's altered it since I've been in Glasgow.'

Socrates left Gil and went to Meikle's side, nudging at the man's hand with his long nose. The collier caressed him, fair head bent over rough grey.

103

'Has there been any difficulty with the business?' Gil asked. 'Has he maybe run off because there's no coin, rather than a lot of it?'

'I see why you wouldny want to ask that of my grandam,' said Crombie with a short laugh. 'She'd let you have your head to play with. No, so far's I'm aware there's naught wrong wi' the business. Coal comes out the ground, we sell the coal, the customers pay us and we pay the colliers. Is that no it, Jamesie?'

'Aye,' said Meikle.

'And Murray himself. How do you find the man?' Gil asked the coalmaster.

'I've no need – he's aye about the house.' Meikle gave his master a swift glance, and bent over the dog again. Gil looked at Crombie without expression, and he amended his answer: 'He's a good enough worker, a good pitman so my uncle Matt aye said, and he would know, but he's a knack for rubbing the men up the wrong way. Comes o' being red-haired, I suppose. By Arbella's way of it, she's forever having to smooth things down.'

Meikle shot him another of those looks, and busied himself with refilling the beakers. Socrates had laid his head down on the man's knee.

'Is he trustworthy?'

'You keep coming back to that,' said Crombie, scowling again. 'Have you any reason why I would find him otherwise?'

'Not so far,' Gil said. 'We're hunting along the track he should have taken, soon or late we'll find whether he left it and where, but I want to consider all the possibilities.'

'Why? It's our man that's missing, if he's missing. What's it to you?'

'I was called in to deal wi' the accusation of witchcraft,' Gil reminded him, 'part of it being Fleming's thought that the corp in the peat-digging was Murray. If I can find Murray that part of the evidence fails.'

'I suppose so,' agreed Crombie grudgingly.

'Do you know where he's from? Does he have kin hereabouts, or friends?'

'No,' said Crombie. 'Jamesie? And I never had any reason to doubt him,' he added, 'but then Arbella keeps me out of the business. Jamesie, has he mentioned kin to you ever?'

'No,' said Meikle. 'He goes drinking in Lanark, times, he might have friends down there. He never talks much to the rest of us at the coaltown, save the Patersons. I've a notion he's from Fife somewhere, like them.' He screwed up his eyes. 'He learned his trade at the sea-coal pits by Culross, I think. That side of the water, at any road.'

What would a sea-coal pit need with a sinker? wondered Gil. 'The salt-boilers must be just this side of the Forth from there,' he said aloud.

Crombie snorted, and took a pull at his ale. 'That was a plan Murray had, and talked Arbella into. Daft idea. We're short enough as it −' He broke off, and took another mouthful of ale.

'It was just the small stuff he wanted to sell them,' said Meikle, and got a glare for his pains. 'We canny shift it up here, maister. He might have gone to talk to them.'

'I know the name,' Gil said, and drained his beaker, 'and where they are. I need to talk to them and all. And now I think we should see you settled for the night. You'll want to be up betimes.'

Out in the stable-yard in the twilight, watching the shadowy dog ranging round checking the scents and adding his own, Gil considered the interview carefully.

105

Magistrand or no, young Crombie did not appear to be a clever thinker, but it seemed as if he was concealing something about his dealings with the missing man. He had claimed nothing was wrong with the business, but he gave an impression of discord among those managing it, and Gil had not missed the last, broken-off remark. If the coal-heugh was not doing well, it might be a reason for the grieve to cut his losses and leave without notice, but what did the salt-boilers have to do with it? And where were the other two men?

Perhaps Alys has gathered more information, he thought hopefully, listening to the quiet sounds from the horses, the rustle of hay in a rack, the clip of shod hoof on cobbled floor. The dog snuffled at a stable door, and its resident snorted in answer. Alys would be waiting in their chamber by candlelight, perhaps reading, or combing down the silken honey-coloured tresses which he loved. He had been dismayed to realize that as a married woman she would have to cover her hair in public.

There were footsteps on the stone stair down from the house door, and he turned to see a dark figure moving towards him. Socrates appeared grinning out of the dark, claws rasping on the cobbles, and bounded towards the newcomer, who paused to greet him and then came forward.

'Jamesie,' Gil said.

'The same,' acknowledged Jamesie Meikle.

'Tell me about the salt-boilers.'

The collier's head moved sharply against the deep blue of the sky, as if he was startled by the request, but after a moment he said quietly, 'What makes you think I ken aught of use, maister?'

'I think you're alert to anything that affects Mistress Brownlie,' said Gil. There was another sharp movement, and he went on in soothing tones, 'I'm not suggesting any ill doing. She's a virtuous woman, I think.'

Meikle relaxed with an audible exhalation.

'She's that,' he acknowledged. 'I've no notion even if she kens what I feel for her, though once I did think – well. Anyway she wedded Murray.'

Poor devil. *Love is to his herte gon, with one spere so kene*, thought Gil.

'And?' he prompted, when no more was said.

'The salt-boilers. When you buy coal, Maister Cunningham, you buy the great coal, am I right? Pieces the size o' your head or greater.'

'I suppose so.' Gil recalled watching deliveries of coal at his uncle's house. 'Aye, indeed, the men bear it in from the cart in huge lumps. Some are so big it takes two to carry them.'

'Aye. Most folk prefer to break up their own coal for burning, that way they can be sure it's all good coal and no rock. It doesny all come out the ground in great pieces, though, and we've trouble shifting the small coal. But it suits the salt-boilers to take it off our hands at a good price, they're no fussy about the quality and it saves them the trouble of breaking it. The fire under the pan burns more even and all.'

'Go on.'

'We've a hill of small coal up at the heugh, waiting to be sold on, and Murray was trying to get an agreement to sell it to Willie Wood down at Blackness, that's all.'

'What was the problem?'

'Problem?'

'What was the delay in getting the agreement?'

'None that I ken. Well, it was maybe that we couldny be sure how often we'd have a load worth taking so far, what wi' the throw at one side the working and the seam running thin at the other.'

'Running thin? How much longer will it hold out?'

'No telling. Could be years, could be months. The first seam lasted thirty year, this one's done twenty now. I'd say it was about done, but I could be wrong.'

'Is that why you've only the one shift working, or is the place haunted as they say?'

'Ha!' said Jamesie, without humour. 'There's aye strange things in a mine. Noises and missing tools, voices in the distance, the folk we call the Knockers, you get used to it. Some of the lads thinks there's more than that at the Pow Burn, but I'd say myself it's these owls, which are all ower the place by night. No, you're right, the auld wife has ordered the work slowed down a bittie till we find a new seam. She put out the order five week since, as soon as Murray was off the place.'

Socrates came back to Gil's side, and nudged his hand. He scratched absently behind the dog's soft ears, and said, 'You don't like Murray.'

'Joanna's feart for him. His sharp tongue, you ken.'

'Is that all?'

'Is it no enough? No,' admitted Meikle. 'It's no all. He's a hard master, demanding, aye looking for a reason to cut a man's pay. He's aye after the women behind – behind *her* back. Nan Tweedie where I lodge says he's aye sportsome, aye making suggestions, aye got a hand for a rump or a titty. And he's no easy to work beside neither. You know the way some folk are just aye in the wrong place? He's like that – forever in the way, and it's never his fault. Mind you,' he added, and Gil could hear the wry smile in the man's voice, 'he's learned that if I see Joanna's been weeping, nothing goes right in the mine for him the next day. Strange, that.'

'Does he drink in Lanark often?'

'Once a week, maybe. One of the men's wives up at the heugh brews a good draught, but he'll no sit in a common collier's house and drink ale wi' the rest of us.' This time he laughed. 'Agnes Brewster would likely put a dead mouse in his cup if he tried it.'

'Does he get on with Fleming?'

'Not so's you'd notice. But there's nobody much he does get on with, maister.'

Gil considered this, and at length said, 'What do you think has happened?'

'I think he's run off,' said Meikle promptly. 'Taken the quarter's money and run. But what he's done wi' the two sinker lads I've no notion. They might go along wi' him, unless he's slit their throats and left them under a bank somewhere. But then, that's what I would hope he's done,' he admitted, 'and leave Joanna free.'

'She'd be freer yet if he's dead,' said Gil deliberately. 'You've not slain him yourself, or paid the sinker lads to do the same?'

'Now I never thought of that,' said Meikle with regret. 'Though I doubt if I could ever afford the sum they'd ask for it. Besides, you'd think if he was dead the word would ha' – Is that an owl?'

A pale shape drifted silently across the yard above their heads. Socrates looked up, and something small rustled in the shadows of the cart-shed. The floating shape alighted on the ridge of the far range, and delivered a familiar *Hu-hu-hoo*.

'An owl,' agreed Gil.

'I'll away in,' said Meikle. He turned and hurried up the steps, ignoring Gil's attempt to question him further.

Alys was at her devotions. When he entered the chamber, leaving the dog sprawled before the embers of the hall fire at the foot of the stairs, she was seated relaxed and upright in the candlelight by the empty

109

hearth, her feet next to a brass box of hot coals, the prayer-book which was her father's wedding gift open on her lap; her eyes were shut. Gil undressed quietly, considering the interview with Meikle. It was strange that a man who could speak hardily of the odd things in the mine – who or what were the Knockers? he wondered – should retreat so promptly from the mere presence of an owl. But the other information the man had provided was certainly interesting, though he could not yet see where it might fit into the puzzle. Nobody had a good word for Thomas Murray, other than his wife, but there still seemed no reason for him to disappear.

He abandoned these thoughts, and settled down to make his own petition before the crucifix on the end wall of the bed. As he drew back the bedclothes to climb in, Alys closed her book and turned her head to smile at him.

'Did you speak to the colliers? Did they have anything useful to tell you?' she asked.

'A little.'

She put the book carefully in its tasselled velvet bag and set it on a shelf by the hearth, then rose and came forward to him. Her hair was loose, falling over the shoulders of her bedgown, and shone in the lamplight. He put his hands on her shoulders and bent his head to kiss her.

'What did they say?'

He slid one hand down across her breast, down to the knot of ribbons which fastened the bedgown.

'Later,' he said.

But later, much later, lying skin against skin, heart against heart, drowsy with loving, he found a deep reluctance to break the mood with rational thought. It seemed Alys felt the same way, but just before she fell asleep she murmured something he failed to catch. He made a questioning noise, and she repeated it.

'Joanna. Joanna is the key, I think.'

'Joanna?' he said in the morning. 'What has she – why Joanna? Why not Beatrice?'

They had exchanged fuller accounts of the previous day while they dressed, Gil describing the interview with old William Forrest as he hooked up Alys's gown for her, she recounting her conversation with Joanna as she laced his doublet in a ritual which had grown up almost immediately after their marriage, and tended to slow the start of the day.

'Because Beatrice is a good woman,' Alys answered him now, intent before the dim greenish mirror as she pinned her indoor cap to her braids. 'And she loved her husband.'

'I thought you said Joanna loved her first husband too. Why would she kill him?'

'I don't think she did. Nevertheless, she is the key.' She turned away from the mirror. 'I spoke to Kate Paterson, Gil.'

'The sinkers' kin.'

'Yes, their sister. She works in the kitchen of the house. She is not concerned for her brothers, she said, because she heard some word that they had gone to Linlithgow. Blackness is the port for Linlithgow, I think? Is that where the salt-boilers are?'

'To Linlithgow?' he repeated. 'Why? Did Murray go with them? How did she hear that? It seems strange.'

'It does,' she agreed. 'I questioned her, but all she knew was that the folk at Forth, is that the right name?' He nodded. 'Had told some of the colliers that her brothers were gone to Linlithgow. She seemed to think they were to meet Murray there.'

'Ah!' said Gil, and then, 'But that means they were not there together.'

'So I thought. She knew nothing more.'

'Forth,' said Gil thoughtfully. 'It's the last place on the round. I suppose they could have got that far, but why would Murray have left them and gone ahead to Linlithgow?'

She nodded, and straightened the velvet cuffs of her red worsted gown. 'Would you say Sir David is well liked?'

'No, I suppose I would not.'

'I wonder why,' she said thoughtfully. 'I did not like him myself, but he is not my priest.'

'He's nobody's priest,' Gil pointed out, 'though it seems he acts for Thorn and the coaltown when John Heriot's busy. I don't think I'd take well to anyone that read the *Malleus Maleficarum* for pleasure, and he's not the world's most powerful logician either.'

'John Heriot? That is the vicar here in Carluke?' Gil nodded in answer, and Alys went on, 'I thought the women at the Pow Burn disliked Fleming particularly. I wonder what . . . I wonder if Murray tried to remonstrate with him, and he killed the man?'

'Over what?'

'Perhaps he made advances to Joanna. Or to Phemie. Or perhaps Murray guessed why he had consulted Mistress Lithgo and proposed to make it public.'

'Murray would hardly step in to defend Phemie, by what you say.'

'I suppose not. Gil, we must find some trace of Murray. Where will you search today?'

'Michael is following the trail for now. I thought to pursue the identity of the man from the peat-digging further afield, but instead I might go up to Forth and find out what they know up there. Will you come with me?'

112

She shook her head. 'If we work separately, we can find the answer sooner. Then you can continue to show me swordplay.' Her faint blush made clear her awareness of the double meaning in her words.

He smiled reluctantly, trying to cover his disappointment. 'What will you do, then?'

'I want to find Joanna's family, if your mother will let me borrow Henry again. I wonder if Jamesie Meikle knows . . .'

There was a scraping at the door. Gil crossed to it and let Socrates in, and the conversation paused while they both acknowledged his greetings. Once the dog had settled down Gil said, 'To ask about the agreement with the collier at Dalserf, you mean?'

'That too.' She nodded. 'And Gil, you must find the other two men, the sinkers. They are also important. I wonder if they really have gone to Linlithgow?'

'You think Murray is dead, don't you?'

'I do,' she said seriously, and crossed herself. 'What worries me is why.'

'I suppose that depends on who killed him, and that's not easy to guess. He isn't much liked, but he seems to be respected, there's no sign he was thieving from the business, his wife says nothing against him – what about young Phemie? I'd believe her capable of riding out to meet him and stabbing him, if he jilted her as you say. The two sinkers might have killed him for the coin, I suppose, but why go openly to Linlithgow if so?'

'Her brother? Would he be capable of it?'

'I'd say so. He's one to want *to have the maistry in londes where he goes*, and I suppose he would take exception to it if Murray was trying to take charge, or make decisions that weren't his to make. But when would he have the chance?'

113

'It's a long ride from Glasgow, but he could do as you suggest for Phemie.'

'True. Not an easy journey to get an exeat for, just the same.' Gil grinned. '*Maister Doby, may I have leave to go and slay my aunt by marriage's second husband?* I think the Principal would find it lacking in the Christian virtues.' Alys giggled. 'I suppose that's why he and Michael dislike one another so much,' he went on. 'I thought there would be daggers out when they set eyes on one another last night.'

'They must be acquainted,' Alys observed. 'Other than both being at the university, I mean. They are much of an age, and they have grown up living within a mile or two, on the same lands. That will make matters worse.' She shook out her skirts, and turned to the door. 'Shall we go down?'

The corpse from the peat bog was not improving with exposure. Peering over the steward's shoulder, Gil was dismayed to note the way the cracks in the skin were extending over the elbows and knees. He stood aside to let the two colliers have a closer look, and saw Crombie flinch at the sight.

'I've got Danny the carpenter to him,' said Alan Forrest anxiously, 'and he says he's been maybe five and a half foot high in life, and he's away to make a box we can put him in. So I thought, Maister Gil, if we had him cried by the bellman the length of the parish, we could show him to anyone that thinks they might put a name to him, and then we could bury him decent.'

'You were right, Jamesie. His own mother couldny put a name to him,' said Adam Crombie. He dragged his appalled gaze from the face and surveyed the rest

114

of the body. 'But I thought you said he had all his fingers?' he added to Gil.

'Oh, the Devil's bollocks!' said Alan with unaccustomed vigour, bending to look at the damage. 'Maister Gil, I'm right sorry! The household has all been after me, kitchen and yard, for a closer look, which is why I had him locked in here,' he waved a hand at the feedstore where they stood, 'and one of the women's been on about a charm against getting lost on the moor. Someone's been in here and got one of his fingers off.' He peered round at the floor, then back at the torn black flesh and exposed brownish bone. 'I ken who's done it, I'll wager.'

'Why should he protect you against getting lost on the moor?' said Gil in exasperation. 'He met with a sorry end himself, poor devil. Get it back, Alan, and make it clear we'll not have him treated like that.'

'There's a thing, though,' said Jamesie Meikle, who was still studying the corpse's face. 'Seems to me, he's no got the look of a man who's met wi' violence, for all the different ways he was slain.'

'How can you tell that, Jamesie?' demanded his master in scornful tones. 'You said to me yourself, his own mother wouldny –'

'Aye, but,' persisted the collier. 'He's a face to fright the weans, I agree, but he's not been feared himself.'

'You're havering, Jamesie,' said Crombie dismissively, but Gil, considering the bundle of bones and peeling skin, began to feel the collier had a point. There was something peaceful about the way the body was disposed, despite its savage death.

'At the rate his skin's drying out,' he said, 'we'll need to bury the fellow soon anyway, but I'd rather he went under the earth wi' a name to call his own. Send to Andro Bellman, Alan, that's a good thought, and get him to publish a description abroad. I suppose you've no idea who he might be, Crombie?'

'None.' The younger man looked round as the horses were led out in the sunshine past the door of the feed-store. 'We'll get away out your road, Maister Cunningham, and my thanks to your lady mother again for our night's lodging. I'm for Kilncaigow first, to confront David Fleming.'

'I'll ride out with you as far as the peat-digging,' said Gil. 'I want another look at where this fellow was found, and then I'm for Forth and Haywood.'

'What, up on the roof of Lanarkshire?' said Crombie. 'What would anyone go there for? The folk walk bent sideways from the wind. Our lads go up there times to get a taste of ale other than Agnes Brewster's, but there's no more attraction than that.'

'I'm still on the trail.' Gil followed the two men out into the yard and snapped his fingers for Socrates, who loped over to him from the horse-trough. 'Alan, you'll need to keep him safe, or he'll be round the parish in more fragments than the True Cross. Crombie, do you ken the name of the clerk up at Forth? Who is it you sell coal to?'

The peat-digging told Gil nothing new. He spent a little while confirming what he had observed on the day he had first seen the place, then mounted up again and rode on up the hill. It was a bright day, and much less windy than yesterday; the sun was warm on his face, there were larks singing high up under the fluffy clouds, and the familiar round-shouldered bulk of Tinto Hill showed away to his right. His discontent began to lift. Socrates galloped in great circles on the rough grass, until Gil saw a small flock of ewes with their lambs and whistled the dog in to take him up on

116

the pommel. Even the air seemed cleaner up here, he thought. At times like this he wondered why he stayed in Glasgow.

As Adam Crombie said, Forth village had an unappealing setting. Perched below its chapel on a bald hillside, surrounded by ribbed fields and bent trees, the little group of houses seemed chilly and exposed. However the welcome a stranger received was warm. Gil and Socrates were noticed first by a rough-coated bitch tethered by a doorway, and when she began to hurl abuse at the intruders a group of the children gathered to stare. Gil dismounted and spoke to them, and they came slowly closer. One of them, taking his eyes reluctantly from Socrates, admitted that Sir Martin dwelt here.

'He's at the plough,' said another.

'My da's at the plough and all,' confided a diminutive person with cropped hair and no front teeth, bare feet firmly planted in the mud, well-worn tunic revealing nothing of gender.

'Is your mammy here?' Gil asked, aware that he was observed from several doorways.

The tethered dog continued to bark. Socrates, ignoring her loftily, sat down at Gil's feet. The child with no front teeth shook its head, but the boy who had spoken first said, 'Her mammy's went to the wash at the Cleugh. My mammy's here, but.' He pointed at one of the low houses.

'My mammy's here and all,' announced someone else. 'Does yer dog bite, maister?'

'Only if you're rough with him,' Gil said. 'If you'll tell your mammy I'd like a wee word with her, you can speak to the dog after.'

The boy he addressed nodded and ran off, leaving behind him a chorus of, 'Can I? Can I? Can we all get clapping yer dog, maister?'

117

'You can take turns,' Gil temporized, wondering how Socrates would cope with the assault. A bigger girl organized them into a line at his words, and by the time his messenger returned with a woman bundled in a vast sacking apron he was showing the first child how to offer a hand to the dog for inspection.

'Our John says you're wanting a word wi' me,' she said, bobbing a curtsy while her hands picked nervously at the apron. 'Are ye from the coal-heugh, maister? Was it about the coin? For it's no here.'

'The coin?' he repeated, straightening up and raising his hat to her. 'That's right, show him the back of your hand. Let him sniff you.'

'It's kittly!' said the candidate, snatching the hand away. 'His whiskers is kittly!'

'The coin the colliers left,' said John's mother. 'Is that no what you want, sir?'

'Let me!' said the messenger, pushing the other child aside. 'He said I could!'

'I came up to ask about the colliers. Do you tell me they've been here and gone again?'

'Oh, aye,' she assured him. 'Near a month since.'

Someone silenced the barking dog along the street, and the women gathered from their doorways, one or two still settling their linen headcoverings in place

'There's nobody here burns coal,' said one. 'They're asking ower much for it when there's peat in plenty up yonder.'

'Forbye there's coal lying on the ground for the gathering, over at Climpy,' said another, and they all laughed.

'What happened, then?' Gil asked. 'Why did they leave the coin here?'

'Who's asking?' countered one of the older women. Gil introduced himself, raising his hat to them all, at which they curtsied and several giggled nervously.

118

'You'll have heard about the corp found in the Thorn peat-cutting,' he said.

'Aye, yestreen,' said one or two.

'I have, I have! He's all dried like leather,' said one of the boys with relish, 'Robbie Wishart tellt us that when he came up to drink ale in our house. He said his face is all thrawn.' He pulled a hideous grimace in demonstration, and the child with no front teeth began to cry.

'Who is it, maister?' asked a thin woman in faded blue. 'They're saying it's the man Murray from the heugh, is that right?'

'Are they?' said another woman. 'And him only here last quarter. Is that no a shame!'

'Last month, surely,' said Gil. Heads were shaken, their folded linen bobbing in the sunlight.

'No, he never came last month,' said John's mother. 'It was just the two Paterson lads, and then they went on their way to Blackness.'

Gil looked round the group.

'You're saying that last month,' he said carefully, 'Thomas Murray was never through Forth on his round.'

'No last month,' agreed a stout woman in homespun, 'though he was here in February, I think it was, him and Tam Paterson but no Jock that time, wi' the ponies and all the empty creels. Shifted the lot, so he had.'

'Is it the coin you're wanting to know about, maister?' demanded John's mother. 'Will we send up the field to Sir Martin to come and let you know what he done wi' it?'

'Aye, do that anyway,' said another woman, 'and you can take a seat, maister, and a wee refreshment, and tell us all the world's doing. Is that right, that Jamie Stewart's looking to wed the King of England's daughter?'

119

Much as had happened at Thorn, he was drawn into one of the little houses, given a seat, and a jug of thin sour ale was brought. All the women crowded in to watch and listen as the housewife and the brewster officiated over the receiving of news, in counterpoint to the renewed barking of the dog tethered before the door. They were surprisingly well informed, for cottars at the far end of a large parish.

'Oh, that's Sir Thomas's doing,' someone assured him, when he commented. 'Sir Thomas Bartholomew, that's vicar at St Mary's down at Carnwath and a man of some importance, so he is. He's aye over at Linlithgow, you see, signing papers and talking to the King, and he aye stops here on the road back, to rest hisself and get a stoup of Ellen's brew, and says a Mass for us while he's here, and tells us all that's new.'

'It was Sir Thomas fetched the Paterson lads from Blackness,' said Ellen the brewster. 'Which is right beside Linlithgow, ye ken,' she explained kindly. 'One time he was in our house drinking ale, and some of the colliers was saying they needed a sinker, for they'd lost one deid in a rock-fall, and Sir Thomas asked about next time he was at Linlithgow. And Jock and Tam was looking for another place, seeing their last one had got flooded wi' the sea, and was glad to come up here. So they said,' she finished, nodding.

'So they are the sinkers, right enough,' said Gil.

'Oh, aye,' agreed several people.

'That's what they are. And mighty big fellows, too,' added someone appreciatively.

'You need to watch your tongue, Maidie,' said the woman of the house slyly. 'You'll no speak like that in front of your Eck, will you?'

'When were they here?' Gil asked.

This gave rise to a brisk argument. By the time the tethered dog outside stopped barking they had reached

120

the conclusion that the men had left Forth village at the end of March. One of the boys, leaping up and down, kept trying to interrupt and finally broke in with, 'I ken! I ken, maister! It was the day afore Hunt-the-gowk! I mind, for I'd a good gowk to play on them, I was going to tell them the wrong way to Linlithgow, but then they left afore I could play it.'

'That was just daft,' said another boy. 'You're a gowk yersel, Andro Johnston.'

'Am no!'

'Aye ye ur!'

John's mother, with practised ease, evicted the pair as they struggled, and stood aside to let a thin, balding, muddy man over the doorstep through a group of giggling children.

'Here's Martin Clerk,' she announced. 'He'll tell you all about the Paterson lads, maister. It's a man to hear about the coin from the coal-heugh, Martin.'

'I didny ken what to do wi' it,' said the clerk defensively. 'They never said what to do if Murray didny come for it, maister, and he's never appeared.'

Patient questioning extracted a little more detail. The Paterson brothers had arrived on the morning of the second last day of March, spent the evening drinking ale in Ellen's house and slept before the fire there. The next day they had spoken to Martin the clerk.

'They'd all this coin,' he explained, 'said it was the fees for the quarter from all the folks they sold coal to, and they'd been expecting to meet Thomas Murray long afore that. So they said they'd go on to Blackness in case they'd missed him.'

'Daft, I call it,' said John's mother. 'How would he have got to Blackness except by going through Forth? We'd ha' seen him.'

'So we counted the coin, and all marked a paper of how much it was, and they left it wi' me for safety,' said the clerk anxiously, 'but I couldny think to keep it in my house, nor in the kirk,' he gestured in the direction of the little chapel, 'nor to ask any of the colliers to take it home, the state they mostly leave here in, so I took it to the Cleugh and asked Somerville to put it in his big kist for me. And it's still there, maister, and safe enough, I'll warrant you.'

'That was well done,' Gil assured him. 'Very sensible of you. Did the Patersons say where they last saw Murray?'

The man shook his head, relaxing a little. 'They never said, just that they'd parted on the road, and looked to meet up again afore ever they reached here.'

'First they were for going down to the heugh to see if he was there,' said Ellen, 'but there was a couple of the colliers up the night afore, and they were saying Murray was still away. They'd been surprised no to find him here. So when I tellt them that, they saw it wasny worth the ride down the hill and back up.'

'So where did the Patersons go?' Gil asked, disentangling the various *they* in the statement.

'Why, they went on to Blackness, like I tellt you, maister,' said Martin the clerk.

'Why Blackness? Are they leaving their employment at the Pow Burn?'

'Well, that's no what they said,' said the man. 'By their conversation, they were still expecting to meet up with Thomas Murray, and they were all to go and talk to some salt-boilers down there.'

The two boys who had been put out sidled back into the house with embarrassed grins, and one of them made his way to the side of the woman who was seated opposite Gil.

'Mammy,' he said, in what he clearly imagined to be a whisper, 'see that man's big dog?'

'What's he doing?' asked Gil, suddenly aware of the laughter outside in the road. The boy cast him an alarmed glance, and addressed his mother again.

'He's been tupping our Fly, Mammy, and she was letting him. Mammy, can I have one of their pups? Can I?'

Chapter Six

'Dalserf?' said Lady Cunningham. She waved a hand westward. 'A mile or two that way, just across the Clyde, but why would you want to go there?'

'Do you know it?' Alys asked.

'It's on the road between here and Thinacre. It's Hamilton land, always has been.'

'Ah.' Alys digested the fact of a faux pas. She knew that the lands Gil's father had held, Plotcock and Thinacre, lost to the Cunninghams after the uprising of 1488, were now held by the Hamiltons. This sounded, to judge from her mother-in-law's tone of voice, as if the two families had been at odds for longer than that. 'I should like to find out more about Joanna Brownlie,' she admitted. 'Her father held Auldton, I think she called it, by Dalserf. He died not long after she was married.'

'Brownlie.' Her mother-in-law paused to consider this. 'In Auldton. It's a common enough surname in these parts. Who holds it now? No a Brownlie, I think, it's another name.'

'That's likely, I think. Joanna has older brothers, but they were already settled elsewhere when she wedded Matt Crombie,' Alys supplied. 'Would any of your household know? Alan, perhaps?'

'Oh, more than likely. I wonder if they're kin to the Brownlies over by Thinacre? It's the same parish, after all.'

Alan Forrest, when summoned, confirmed this idea.

'Second cousins, they were, mistress, Will Brownlie in Auldton and Tammas at Broomelton just by our bit.' He paused to consider. 'Will wedded a Lockhart from this side the river, but she died when her lassie was young. They'd only the three bairns – two boys first, a Tammas again, and Hob, and then the lassie a good while later. A late-come, as they say.'

'Where are Joanna's brothers now?' Alys asked.

'Now that I couldny say, but likely my wife could,' suggested Alan, 'seeing as she's gossips wi' Jess Lockhart that dwells by St Andrew's kirk in the town. Will I send out for her, mistress?'

'Aye, do that, Alan,' agreed Lady Cunningham, 'and then tell Nan I want her, till I get my boots on. I must be off to the horses afore it gets any later.'

Alan's wife Eppie, drifting across the outer yard with two children in tow and one in her arms, did not appear as a likely source of good information, but when she had settled the two little girls to play house in a corner of the hall, she sat down at Alys's invitation with her son on her knee and paid more attention to the enquiry than her vague appearance portended.

'Lockhart,' she said. 'Oh, aye, madam, I think Jess mentioned it when the lassie was wedded. What a tale that was! A speak for the whole countryside, it was.' She pushed a stray lock of waving yellow hair back under her linen kerchief, and bounced the baby. 'Let me see, what was it Jess said? Joanna Brownlie's mother's name was Marion, I think. Aye, Marion Lockhart, and she was a second cousin to Jess's father and forbye . . .' She paused, frowning, and the baby burbled something and tugged at the ends of her kerchief. 'First cousin to her mother's good-sister,' she produced triumphantly.

'No, baba, leave Mammy's kerchief alone. Here, chew on a bonnie crust. Num-num-num!' She produced a baked crust from the pocket of her apron and gave it to her son, who waved it at Alys, burbling again.

'Would your friend know when this Marion died?' Alys asked, smiling at the baby.

'Ten year ago last autumn,' said Eppie promptly. Her son leaned over and thrust the dried bread at Alys's mouth. 'I mind that, for I think Joanna Brownlie's of an age wi' me, and I worked it out that she was twelve when she lost her mammy, a sad time for a lassie. Forgive me, madam, he'll no rest till you take a bite at that. Just pretend, mind.'

Alys obediently pretended to nibble the proffered crust, and the baby beamed at her, received it back and stuffed it into his own mouth.

'He's a bonnie fellow. What is his name?' Alys asked. 'How old is he?'

'That's John. After Alan's father, you ken. He'll be a year old in two weeks' time. You've none of your own yet, madam?'

'I was married only in November.' Alys managed to ignore the swift glance at her waist. 'John is a good name. My father has a foster-child who is now a year and a half, and I have care of him. He is also called John.'

'He's in Glasgow, is he? You'll miss him.'

'I do,' Alys admitted, and realized it was true. 'He is just beginning to talk. He says my name already, and his nurse's, but he had some new words just last week before we came away.'

'He'll have more when you get back. Mind you, boys is often late talking,' said Eppie sagely. She pushed another straggling lock back under her kerchief, and adjusted her clasp on her son. 'Then they make up for it later.'

126

'They do,' agreed Alys, thinking of the way Gil and her father could talk when they were together. 'It's strange, here you are with three lovely bairns, and yet Joanna Brownlie is of an age with you and twice married, and has none.'

'Aye, poor soul. Mind, her first man could never ha' done her any good, the way he sickened as soon's he brought her home, but this one that's been murdered in the peat-cutting is a different matter, you'd think.' Eppie glanced round the hall, checked that her daughters were engrossed, and lowered her voice. 'He's near as bad as that Fleming that's sub-steward at Cauldhope. Free wi' his hands, and full of bold talk. I'll wager he's one to insist on his rights.'

'Mind you, I have heard otherwise about Fleming now.'

'Oh, aye, *now.*' A giggle, a sideways glance, an upward flick of the eyebrows. 'His culter's rusted away, all right. That's three lassies they say he's persuaded to his bed since St John's Day last, and then found he couldny stand to do his part. What a judgement on him!' Another gurgling laugh which made the baby chuckle in sympathy.

'A judgement?'

'Well, Agnes Paton in Cauldhope kitchens never had a penny piece for the bairn he gied her last year, that was born at Yule, and he did no better by any of the other lassies. Deserves him right, that's what I say, and a pity it doesny happen to others.'

'It's no way to behave,' agreed Alys, 'and him a priest too. And Murray? Is he the same, then? Does he go after other women?'

'I've never heard it,' admitted Eppie with regret. 'But you can aye tell, the way he talks, he'd like to. My man says it's no him that was got out of the peat-digging,' she recalled. 'Maybe that's where he's vanished away

127

to, he's gone off to somebody else. Poor Mistress Brownlie.'

'I wonder what she will do now. Does she have kin? Can she go to them?'

'Oh, I think she's well placed up at the coal-heugh, by what you hear,' said Eppie. 'She's got two brothers, I think Jess tellt me at the time, but they're a good piece older. One of them's got bairns near her age. They'd maybe no want to take her in.'

'Two brothers,' Alys repeated. 'Where are they, then? I'd have thought they would be here to help her in this trouble.'

'Oh, not them.' Eppie looked down at her son, who was lying against her breast chewing drowsily on his crust. 'The way I heard it,' she said happily, 'they never had much time for her. I suppose they were no too pleased when she was born, they must ha' thought all their father's gear would be theirs and here was another to share it wi', and they both got themselves wedded and settled elsewhere as soon as they might. And that, said Jess to me, just made it worse, for there was the lassie still at home to be made a pet of, and after her mother died she kept her father's house and he bought her jewels and all sorts, and then made sure she'd a good tocher when she was wedded, and all that was so much less to divide amongst the three of them at his death.'

'It's a sad tale,' said Alys, privately wondering if Eppie's last statement was correct. Her own considerable dowry, she knew, had been by way of an advance against whatever she might inherit when – when – but then, there was no brother or sister to share it with. 'No wonder Mistress Brownlie prefers to stay up at the coal-heugh. Where did you say her brothers were settled?'

128

'Let me see now.' Eppie adjusted the weight of the sleeping baby and considered, staring into the distance with vague blue eyes. 'Is one of them in Draffan, maybe? I know who would tell you,' she suggested, 'and that's Sir Simon over at St Mary's in Dalserf. Or maybe Sir John here in the town.'

Sir John Heriot and his clerk were singing Sext in the chancel of St Andrew's kirk. There were a few old women in the nave, murmuring over their beads in a soft organum to the chant which floated out under the double chancel arch. Alys sat down on the ledge at the wall and looked about, and the maidservant who had walked down with her, a young girl quite overcome by the responsibility of accompanying Maister Gil's lady, retreated to the other side of the door and drew her own beads from their place in her girdle.

The stonework of the little building was good, though the carving at the head of the chancel pillar was simple; the windows were neatly constructed and carefully set, and the swallow's-nest pulpit on the south wall was well done. The church was too old, she thought, for Gil's father to have been the original donor, but whoever had built it had summoned experienced masons. The paintings on the plastered walls were clumsy, but the saints they depicted were clear enough: St James the pilgrim, St Roch, St Anne teaching the Virgin to read, a gruesome and comical Doom on the west wall. St Andrew presided as a small, brightly coloured statue on an altar beside the double chancel arch.

The Office was ended. The final Amen, drawn out on enough notes to stuff a cushion, faded into the rafters, and the sounds of tidying began with the heavy slither and flap of pages turning as the book was set up for

Nones. Alys rose, shaking out her skirts, and watched the arches for the appearance of Sir John.

She had considered her appearance with care; her wired headdress and good wool gown set her aside from the country women, but she had deliberately chosen a plaid rather than a mantle to put round her shoulders. No point in alarming her quarry. She had also considered her story on the walk in from Belstane, quite relieved that the girl with her was too shy to chatter. With regret, she had discarded various constructions based on the romances she loved; it seemed improbable that anyone would believe her to be a long-lost scion of the Lockharts, or the daughter of a nobleman stolen by pirates. Besides, she thought, and laughed at herself, she had no convenient birthmark to support such a fiction.

Sir John emerged from the dim chancel, a big fair man with a broad face, and his clerk slipped past as the priest was pounced on by two of the old women with a complicated tale of wrongdoing by a neighbour. Alys waited, watching how he dealt with them, and at length he noticed her and drew her into the conversation.

'You're a stranger here, daughter?' he said. His accent was not local, though Alys could not place it. She curtsied, and introduced herself, at which all three exclaimed, blessed themselves, blessed her, offered good wishes on her marriage. It was clear that Lady Cunningham was well regarded in the town.

'And is it no Belstane where the man's came up out the peat all uncorrupted?' said the larger and stouter of the women. 'Who is he, do they ken yet?'

Alys explained the situation, and they discussed it with interest, Sir John concerned, the two women offering various wild guesses about the identity of the corpse. This took a while, but eventually the second

130

woman, a small withered person with claw-like hands and sharp eyes, said, 'So you came in to hear the Office, mistress?'

'Yes, indeed,' Alys agreed, 'and to admire this kirk, which my good-mother told me was worth the walk. She was certainly right in that.'

This was well received. The best features of the building had to be pointed out and described as if she was unable to see them, and the donors identified. Lady Egidia had given the candlesticks to the Lady-altar.

'And Sir James Douglas sees to St James's altar,' said the first woman, 'and Lockhart at the Lee gave us that St Roch, o' course.'

'Naturally,' said Sir John. 'Indeed.'

'Lockhart,' said Alys, seizing the chance. 'I wonder, could you tell me something. Is there a Marion Lockhart lives here in Carluke town?'

'Marion?' said the small woman. 'No a Marion. There's Mysie, and Eppie, and Jess.' She counted on her fingers. 'Aye, and Maggie and Nan.'

'Eppie Lockhart's youngest is a Marion,' said the other woman, and sucked noisily on her remaining teeth.

'No, but the lassie's name's no Lockhart, it's Robertson,' objected her companion.

'There's many Lockharts in the town,' Sir John explained. 'It's a common name in this parish, madam. Indeed. I confess I canny place a Marion.'

'This would be an older woman,' said Alys. 'She'd be near sixty, I think, if she still lives.'

'Oh, Marion Lockhart!' said the small woman. 'Marion that was daughter to Robin Lockhart the sawyer, Mally. No, she's dead, ten year since. Afore you came here, that would be, Sir John. Was she kin of yours, lassie?'

'No, no,' Alys said. 'But a friend of mine in Glasgow bade me, if she still lived, to say she was asking for her.'

'Glasgow?' said the stout woman suspiciously. 'I mind Robin Lockhart's Marion, but I never heard her mention a friend at Glasgow. Did she ever say such a thing to you, Isa?'

'No, never, Mally,' said Isa, shaking her head. 'What friend was that?'

'Hardly a friend, I think,' said Alys, 'merely that Mistress Lockhart did her a good turn once and she minds her kindly. She'll be sorry to hear she has died. What came to her?'

The two heads turned, and a portentous glance passed.

'I'll away about my business,' said Sir John hastily. Alys curtsied, but the old women hardly noticed him go.

'Women's trouble,' said Mally, lowering her voice. Alys made the appropriate response, the indrawn breath and tilted head, and Mally nodded in satisfaction, sucked her teeth, and folded brawny arms under her large bosom. 'See,' she pronounced, 'she'd the two boys no long after she was wedded.'

'That was to Will Brownlie across the river,' supplied Isa, clasping her claw hands at her narrow waist.

Her friend sucked her teeth again. 'Aye, and she was never the same after the second one. Terrible, it was, so her mammy tellt me.'

'A big bairn,' said Isa, nodding in turn, 'a gey big bairn. Three days crying wi' him, she was, and then he tore her.'

Alys flinched, and Mally put a hand on her arm.

'They're no all like that,' she said encouragingly, 'she'd an easy time of it wi' her first, likely you'll no have trouble. You're no . . .?'

'No,' said Alys.

'Plenty time, lassie,' said Isa. 'Enjoy yer man while you can, it's never the same after the bairns come.'

132

'But was that how Mistress Lockhart died?' asked Alys, thinking that this comment was more acceptable than others she had had.

'No, no. She lived another twenty year,' said Mally.

'Five-and-twenty,' corrected Isa, 'for she was buried the year after my George. But she was never no more use to her man, she tellt me that herself once. Troubled her the rest of her life, that did. She would aye see blood, ye ken,' she confided in a whisper.

'She'd the lassie, mind you,' said Mally. 'When her boys was near grown. Fifteen, the oldest one was, and Marion turned up here on a visit at her mammy's yett wi' a lassie bairn in her plaid.'

'Aye,' said Isa drily. Alys looked quickly at her, and met the sharp dark eyes under the folded linen headdress.

'Had she an easier time with the lassie?' she asked.

'I never heard,' said Mally regretfully. 'Her mammy said it wasny long, the bairn slipped out like a calf, but I never got to ask her myself.'

'I did,' said Isa, and looked surprised at her own words. 'She said the same to me. You mind, her mammy was bad at the time wi' that spring cough that was in the town, and her at the Pow Burn, that was a great friend of Marion's mammy, was away and no help to be got there, so I went in to see to the house for her and get her man's supper, and there was Marion sitting wi' the bairn, and a lassie from Dalserf wi' her to nurse it. Easy time or no, she'd nothing to nurse it wi' herself. No milk. The bairn must ha' been four week old by then, old enough to ha' lost the look of its daddy that they all have when they're newborn. No great look of Marion it had neither,' she added. 'Strange, how it happens.'

Mally shook her head, tut-tutting in sympathy.

133

'What help could the Pow Burn folk have been?' Alys asked. 'Surely you'd never burn coal with a cough in the house, the smoke makes a bad chest worse.'

'Oh, aye,' agreed Mally. 'Coals is the worst thing there is for a bad chest. You can't beat a good mustard plaister, I always say.'

'No, it was that Mistress Weir,' said Isa. Both women crossed themselves. 'She was awful handy wi' a pill or a bottle at the time, if you went up the Pow Burn to ask, but she was away, you ken.'

'Now is that no a strange thing,' said Mally, sucking her teeth.

'What?' demanded Isa.

'The bairn we're speaking of – Marion Lockhart's lassie – that's Mistress Weir's good-daughter now. No the one that does the healing, the other one, Mistress Brownlie.'

'Oh, aye,' said Isa. 'I ken that. For her new man, him that's missing, was asking me the exact same questions, just after Candlemas.'

'Do you tell me!' exclaimed Alys, in genuine astonishment. 'Now if I'd realized, I could have asked about her mother when I saw her yesterday, and saved myself the walk into Carluke. But then I'd never have met either of you ladies,' she said gracefully, and they nodded and smiled, much gratified.

'Nor you'd no ha' seen St Andrew's kirk,' added Mally, 'and that's worth a longer walk than here to Belstane.'

'Was there aught else you wanted to learn, lassie?' asked Isa.

Alys met her sharp gaze again.

'Mistress Lockhart's sons might recall my friend,' she said. 'Where did you say they are now? I think neither of them has their father's land?'

'Aye, that's right,' agreed Mally, 'for they were both

134

wedded and away to their own place long afore Will Brownlie died. Barely saw his lassie wedded, he did, but at least he lasted so long, thanks be to Our Lady.'

'I'd ha' looked for him to last a while longer,' said Isa. 'Fine upstanding man he was. But there you are, you never can tell when you'll meet your end, and at least he made a good death, so I heard.' She crossed herself, and her friend nodded and did likewise. 'Where did Marion's boys go, Mally? There's one of them in Draffan, is there no?'

'Draffan,' agreed Mally. 'That would be Tammas, I'd say. And Hob's in . . .' She paused, and sucked her teeth again. 'Is it Canderside? Both of them went into Lesmahagow,' she explained to Alys, who understood her to mean the next parish.

'Too far for me,' she said.

'Depends on why you're wanting to go there,' said Isa acutely.

Lady Cunningham was in the stable-yard, seated on the mounting-block watching a young horse being led round, oblivious to the light drizzle which had started. She was booted and spurred, clad in a muddy riding-dress and crowned by a battered felt hat shaped like a sugar-loaf, and drew the eye as she always did.

'Trot him out, Dod,' she said, and turned her head as Alys came in at the gate. The young maidservant bobbed nervously to her mistress, then hurried by and into the house. 'There you are, my dear. You've missed Gil.' She turned back to scrutinize the horse's action. 'Aye, he's still going a wee thing short on that leg, isn't he? Another hot soak, Henry, I think. Now let me see the piebald.'

'I have missed Gil?' said Alys. 'I thought he had gone out with the colliers, before I left. And he has not taken

135

Socrates,' she added, as the wolfhound commanded her attention from the end of the cart-shed with one deep imperious remark. 'Why is he chained up?'

'The brute's to get washed,' said Henry resignedly from his post at Lady Cunningham's elbow. 'A bath.'

'A bath? Has he rolled in something?'

'Gil came back,' said his mother, 'lifted a clean shirt and a bannock, and left again half an hour since for Linlithgow or somewhere of the sort, saying he might not be back tonight. He's not alone, he took that fool Patey with him.'

'Oh,' said Alys blankly, over the sudden lurching feeling in her stomach.

'I have a kiss for you,' continued Lady Cunningham. 'I will say, it's a long time since he kissed me like that. He'll be back the morn's night, I should think. Then maybe Patey can get on with his work here.'

He would not wish to delay by waiting for me, thought Alys. How far is it to Linlithgow? Can he be there in daylight?

'And the dog?' she said, to distract herself. Socrates sat down as she spoke and scratched vigorously at his ribs with a narrow grey hind foot.

'That's why the bath,' said Henry. 'Maister Gil said he's been after a strange bitch up at Forth, and likely picked up all sorts off her. I'd as soon wait till he gets back, but I suppose it had best be done the day.'

Alys looked at the dog again. He grinned at her and thumped his tail; there was a self-satisfied air about him which it occurred to her she had seen on his master at times.

'I can help,' she said. 'He will mind me. What do you put in the wash for fleas or lice?'

The piebald clopped out across the yard as Henry began to enumerate the herbs he preferred for the purpose. Lady Cunningham rose and went forward to feel the horse's legs. The animal tossed his head, taking the groom by surprise, and she seized the halter-rope with calming words as hoofbeats sounded outside the high gate, one horse, approaching fast. Henry moved quickly to the gate, peered through the judas-hole, and visibly relaxed.

'It's young Douglas,' he said, swinging one heavy leaf wide as Michael slowed to a halt and dismounted before the gateway. 'We never looked for you till this evening, Maister Michael. Was it himself you wanted, or her ladyship?'

'Is Maister Cunningham here?' demanded Michael, leading his horse into the yard. Finding first Alys and then his godmother present, he stopped, stammering a greeting, and bowed to both.

'My son has gone to Linlithgow,' said Lady Cunningham, still by the piebald's side.

'Linlithgow?' repeated Michael incredulously. 'Why? I – I mean, I thought we were looking for the man Murray.'

'I think this is about Murray,' said Alys. 'The sister of the two sinkers had heard they had gone there. I suppose he got confirmation of that at Forth, and he has followed them.'

'Aye, but,' said Michael, replacing his hat, 'Murray never got as far as Forth. That's what I've learned this morning. The trail's crossed – our man never got beyond Lanark.'

'I thought you said he had collected the money further on,' Alys said.

'Aye, at Ravenstruther,' agreed Michael. He accepted a second beaker of ale from Alan Forrest, and sat down opposite Alys by the great fireplace in the hall. 'Alan, that's gey welcome. I'm as dry as a tinker. That's what

137

I thought too, Mistress Mason. Turns out I had the wrong questions. I asked, had the money for the coal been uplifted, and their steward answered me, Aye it had. I asked him when, and he checked the accounts and told me what days. I never asked him who had been there, or named any names to him yesterday.'

'Ah,' said Alys. Alan set the tray of ale and bannocks on a stool at Michael's elbow, and withdrew to the side of the hall, listening with interest.

'So today I rode on to Carlindean, that's by Carnwath, you ken ...' Alys nodded encouragement, though neither name meant anything to her. 'Jackie Somerville that stays there's a friend of mine. He was from home, but I'd a word wi' his mother, and she called their steward for me, and he turned up the accounts. The colliers lay there just the one night, but even so, there was only the one mess of food written down for their dole. When I said I wondered at that, that they must have eaten frugally for three working men, the steward said, Oh, there was but the two of them.'

'*Two?*' repeated Alys. 'So we have lost only one? Is it Murray?'

'Aye. There was just these brothers, Paterson, or whatever their name is. Murray was never there.'

'So where have you lost the trail, Michael?' asked Lady Cunningham. She swept in from the stair, restored to her indoor garments, and her grey cat sprang down from a shelf of the plate-cupboard and paraded across the floor to meet her.

'Murray was at Jerviswood, before they went to Lanark, but not at Carlindean after it,' supplied Michael. 'And I went round by Ravenstruther the now and asked them, and he wasny there when the fee was uplifted, and he's not been there since, either. That's close by Lanark town, mistress,' he elaborated, and Alys nodded.

'Somewhere in Lanark, then.' Lady Cunningham lifted the cat, which turned its smug yellow gaze on Alys. 'Do you suppose he's still there?'

'Well, if he's elsewhere, I've no notion where it might be.' Michael sat down again as his godmother settled herself in her great chair. 'Your good health, madam.'

'Gil told me Murray goes drinking in Lanark. How big a place is it?' asked Alys.

'Big enough,' said Michael gloomily. 'It's a burgh, maybe the size of the lower town at Glasgow. It's got no cathedral or college to draw folk, but there's good merchants and tradesmen in the place. I suppose there are five or six streets of houses, and all the vennels and back-lands.'

'It should be simple enough, I suppose. You must search the taverns,' said Lady Cunningham, 'until you find some trace of the man. Someone must have seen him. Do we know who he sells coal to? Whatever house-holders he called on might have information for you.'

'Aye,' said Michael.

'I could come with you,' suggested Alys. 'I have never seen Lanark.'

'No, I don't think –' began Michael.

'An excellent idea,' pronounced Lady Cunningham, making room for the cat inside her loose furred gown. 'You'll not be in any taverns yourself, of course,' she continued. 'I can trust you to take care of Mistress Mason, I know, Michael.'

'Oh,' said Michael, and then, as this penetrated, 'You can? I mean, aye, you can!'

Alys, with a vivid remembrance of the occasion when she and Gil's sister Kate had visited a tavern off Glasgow's Gallowgait, simply nodded.

'But why has Gil gone to Linlithgow?' she wondered. 'He did not say exactly what he had learned this morning?'

'At Forth? No, he said little but what he thought of the dog's exploits, and when he would be back.' Lady Cunningham looked from Michael to Alys. 'I suppose, if those two men got as far as Carlindean as you say, Michael, they might have completed the round, which I think would take them to Forth, do I remember right?' Alys nodded. 'So he might have found word of them there after all.'

'And word that took him to Linlithgow. I wonder what it was.'

'If they were to take one or two of the men, mistress,' suggested Alan from the wall where he was still listening avidly, 'they would make a faster job of it. Is there much doing in the stable-yard the day?'

'Nothing that won't wait, apart from the young horse's leg,' admitted his mistress. 'Aye, that would make sense.' She cast a glance at the windows. 'You'd best go, then. The day's wearing on. And you can get on wi' your work, Alan, rather than stand about with your ears flapping like a gander's wings.'

The rain was getting heavier.

'Good for the oats, I suppose,' said Michael, as they rode past the fields of Carluke town, one of the Belstane grooms ahead of them and one bringing up the rear. The fine turned earth of the strips showed dark between the narrow lines of rushes in the intervening ditches, and the boy who was supposed to be scaring the crows was sheltering under a white-blossomed apple tree. 'So long as it doesny get too heavy.'

'Is that a coney running on the plough-land?' said Alys. 'Surely it's too big. Oh, and there is another. What are they doing? Do look, they are dancing!'

'That's hares,' said Michael, peering under his hand at the brown creatures skipping across the near field.

'You can tell by the black tips to the ears.' He smiled, watching the animals' antics. 'They do that all the spring. Some folk says they're gone mad, but it's just how they choose their mates, so our huntsman tellt me.'

'Good eating, a bawd is, if they wereny such unchancy beasts,' commented the man riding behind them, a fair-haired leather-visaged fellow in his thirties called Steenie, a name Alys knew to be the Scots pet-name for Stephen. 'You get them up on the grazing land and all.'

'I saw them when we went to the peat-cutting,' Alys recalled. 'When Sir David was so sure they had dug up Thomas Murray. Do you think we will find the man today?'

'I'm past caring,' admitted Michael, 'save for the need to silence Davy Fleming. He was on at me again this morning before I'd broke my fast, about all the misdeeds witches gets up to, according to his wee book. If I ever learn who lent it to him, I'll cram it down his throat.'

'I never thought to hear Gil abuse a book the way he did that one,' said Alys.

'I've not looked in it myself, but the things Fleming was telling me made my gorge rise.' Michael rode in silence for a short space. Alys was looking about her despite the rain, admiring the blossom on the fruit trees for which Gil had told her the neighbourhood was famous, when he suddenly said, 'Mistress Mason!'

She opened her mouth to tell him to use her first name, but he hurried on.

'Have you – did you see my Tib? Before she was sent to Haddington, I mean?'

She was aware of a great rush of sympathy. No need of birthmarks or stolen children, here was a tale out of the romances, riding beside her under the wet blossom.

'No, but I assure you she went to Haddington voluntarily – is that the right word?' He stared at her. 'I had a letter two weeks since. She said she was bored with her imprisonment, and weary for you, and her sister – Sister Dorothea – had invited her to visit.'

'Weary for me,' he repeated, his sharp features softening. Were those tears? 'And I for her, mistress. Was – were they ill-treating her? My godmother, and the rest?'

'Only by keeping her close, I think, and watching her.'

'She'd take that ill out,' he said, with a loving smile.

'She did.' He had turned in the saddle to look at her more closely, one hand on the cantle, and she met his eye. 'I think, by what she said just now, my goodmother is less angry than she was. What of your father?'

He shrugged. 'I've heard little enough from him since Yule, till I had this letter about Fleming. I suppose, if he's trusting me to see to this business, he's calmed down a bit and all. Would you say there's any hope for us?'

'I do not know,' she admitted. 'I will do what I can for you.'

He dropped his gaze, going scarlet, and muttered something genuinely grateful. Alys was about to answer him when the groom behind them exclaimed in warning, and another big brown hare zigzagged across the path, immediately under the horses' muzzles.

The next few moments seemed to pass very slowly. Michael, riding slack-reined, was taken by surprise as his beast shied, half-reared, plunged backwards into Alys's dapple grey. The grey, also startled, kicked out, lurched aside and pecked on something. Alys, with a better grip on her reins, was just gaining control when the dappled shoulders in front of her vanished and she

142

found herself, with a slow and dreadful inevitability, soaring over her horse's head.

The ground hit her with a thump. For a moment things went far away. Then she heard Michael's voice, exclaiming in alarm.

'Alys – Mistress Mason! Are you hurt? Steenie, get that horse. Willie, come back, man, give me a hand here!' His face appeared close to hers, staring anxiously. 'Are you hurt, mistress?' he asked again. 'Can you move? Are you –?'

'I fell off,' she said foolishly. The world righted itself, and she realized she was lying sprawled on the wet grass, petticoats everywhere, hat askew, one hand trapped under her.

'Can you move?' repeated Michael. 'Does aught pain you? Say you're no hurt, mistress!'

'It was a great jill-bawd,' declared Steenie, appearing beyond his shoulder. 'Sprung out the dyke under their feet, it did, no wonder they was startled.'

She contrived to sit up, and straightened her skirts.

'I am unhurt, I think,' she said cautiously, experimenting with hands and arms. 'Is my horse –?'

'He's right enough,' Steenie assured her. 'I've got him here, mistress. He's took no harm, the great gowk.' He patted the animal's neck.

'Our Lady be thanked!' said Alys. 'What my goodmother would say if I harmed one of her beasts I do not know.'

'No, and you don't want to hear it neither,' said Steenie forthrightly. 'But yourself, mistress? Can she rise, Maister Michael?'

'Should you sit here on the bank a wee while?' Michael asked anxiously. 'Can you rise? Do you want to rest somewhere?' He looked about him. 'Cauldhope's nearer than Belstane from here, you could come back to our place and sit for a bit.'

'There's a house yonder,' said the other groom. 'Stinking Dod's, no half a mile away. Him that's married on Wat Paton's sister. They might give her a seat there, and maybe a drink of well-water or the like. Mind you, it's maybe no suitable.'

She rose, with Michael's assistance, and stood for a moment, feeling quite strange and unsteady. Shock, she thought. What did Mère Isabelle order for shock? She tested her limbs again. Hip and shoulder hurt where they had made contact with the ground, and would be bruised black by the morning, but everything seemed to be working.

'I am embarrassed,' she confessed. 'I have not fallen off since I was a child. Are you certain the horse is safe, Steenie?'

'Never mind the horse,' said Michael, 'what madam my godmother would say if I'd let you come to harm I never want to hear. And it was my fault,' he added, though she had not tried to argue. 'If I'd been looking where we were going I'd ha' seen that coming.'

'No, no,' she said, 'the creature startled the horses. Perhaps I would like to sit down for a little while. Could we see if there is anyone at home in that house?'

The dapple-grey horse seemed slightly puzzled by her sudden descent and all the fuss, but when Steenie put her expertly back in the saddle it moved forward willingly with an even stride. Michael's relief was almost comical, despite his claim to be more concerned for Alys than the horse. One of the men rode ahead, and by the time they reached the house had roused out a thin flustered woman in homespun, with a baby on her hip. An older child peeped round the corner of the house at them and vanished.

'Oh, the Bad Man fly away wi' all bawds, the evil things. A wee seat?' the woman was saying. 'For certain, aye, and no trouble. Will I bring a plaid out to soften the bench a bit maybe, and keep the wet off your bonnie gown, mistress? Or would ye step inside? Only it's a bit smoky, and there's the grandam and all –'

A shrill, unintelligible voice from within the dark little dwelling confirmed this.

'And were ye here for the clerk?' she continued, as Alys dismounted stiffly. 'I was going to send one of the men to Cauldhope about it as soon as they all come back from Lanark at the market, only I'm here my lone –' Another screech from inside the house. '– wi' the grandam and the bairns, and I canny – aye, that's right, mem, you sit there and get your breath. Would ye take a drop of ale, maybe?' There was another shrill comment. 'Or a wee tait spirits? I've a drop o' cordial put by where Dod canny find it. Just let me see the wee one safe, and I'll –'

'No, no, ale or water would be good,' Alys assured her, seating herself cautiously on the bench by the door. She would certainly have bruises by the morning, she recognized.

'Clerk?' said Michael. 'What clerk's this, Mistress Paton?'

The woman turned from tethering her child to the leg of the bench. 'Why, Sir David,' she said. 'Your own sub-steward. I'm right troubled about him, maister, for he's no roused nor stirred since I put him to bed. He'll no be easy to move like that, save if you put him in a cart or the like.'

'Sir David?' said Alys in disbelief. 'What is he doing here? Is he injured, or ill?'

'Aye, Sir David. Him that's sub-steward to Douglas,' she said again, and looked from Alys to Michael. 'He came stackering in off the fields, no long after the rest went off to Lanark, and fell in a dwam in front of the cart-shed yonder. I washed the worst of the blood off

145

him, and got him in the house and put him in our bed, but being here my lone I couldny do more about it.'

'But what's come to him?' said Michael. 'He was well enough when I left Cauldhope this morning. Blood? And what's he about down here?'

'He never said,' said the woman. The piercing voice from indoors said something Alys did not catch. 'I'd say he'd been fighting, if it wasny a clerk, or else he's maybe taken a beating.'

Michael turned to Alys, spread his hands, and then followed their hostess into the house, ducking under the low lintel. She sat still, thinking that she should follow him, listening to him asking for a light, and then to the scrape of a flint. The grandam shrieked, and beside her the child announced something as unintelligibly as the old woman.

Alys looked at it, and drew a sharp, involuntary breath; the little face was marred by a split upper lip like the hare's. No wonder its mother cursed the beasts, she thought, and smiled at the baby. It grinned back, showing several teeth, ducked beneath the seat and emerged with a wooden spoon, which it began to bang vigorously on the bench.

'Mistress Mason?' Michael was saying, and she realized he had spoken to her already. 'Would you come and look at Sir David? I don't like the look of him either.'

The house lived up to its occupant's by-name, and the inside was very dark. This was hardly a surprise, she told herself, since there was no window, the peat on the hearth was smouldering rather than burning, and the light Michael had asked for was provided by a single tiny flame. As her eyes adjusted, she made out two box beds built into the wall at her left. The bundle of rags in the nearest stirred, shaded its eyes against the

146

flame, and produced another shrill comment. She smiled, curtsied, and passed on to the further bed.

'You see,' said Michael. 'He doesny answer, and his breathing's no right. And he keeps twitching.' The man in the reeking bed shuddered as he spoke, and she bent closer.

'Is it truly Sir David?' she asked, looking at the battered, swollen features in the dim light.

'Oh, it's him, all right, poor devil, and I'd say Mistress Paton was right, he's been fighting, or been beaten. Likely some lassie's brothers have caught up wi' him,' he added sourly. 'But what are we to do wi' him, and what's best to do for him first?'

Alys touched the steward's damaged face. His skin was cool rather than hot, and clammy to the touch. The man's breathing was alarmingly shallow, and as she watched another small convulsion shook him. She straightened up, gathering her thoughts.

'Is he fit to be moved, do you think?' asked Michael. 'What should we do wi' him?'

'You'll no leave him here?' said Mistress Paton, on a sharp note very like the old woman's. 'That's our bed. Where are we to sleep?'

'I think we must move him,' said Alys. 'He should be in his own house, and his hurts tended.' Something sweet for strength, she was thinking, trying to recall the words of the Infirmarer at Saint-Croix. The convent's infirmary had possessed several books, of which Alys had had free run, but Mère Isabelle had also her own ideas on the treatment of the injured and sick. 'Mistress Paton, have you given him anything?' she asked.

'Deed, no, excepting a drink of ale when he first got here,' said the woman. 'And it's the same jug my man was drinking from this morning,' she added, 'so it's no anything I gave him that's done this to him.'

'No, no, I never thought it,' said Alys. 'You've taken good care of him already. Have you anything sweet in the house? And is there fresh water?' A foolish question, she told herself, as Mistress Paton stared at her in the dim light. Outside the child was still battering the bench with the spoon. The old woman screeched something, and Mistress Paton started, and nodded.

'Aye, she's right, for once. I've a wee drop honey in a piggin on the shelf. Would that do ye? It's last year's, mind, it's set like glue.' Another piercing remark. 'Aye, by the fire, if the fire was putting out any heat. I canny be everywhere, you auld –' She bit off her comment, and moved to the other side of the house, reaching up to the wall-head to lift from among the objects stowed there a small pottery jar with a scrap of flat stone serving as a lid.

'Honey?' said Michael blankly. 'What will that do?' He watched as Alys set the little jar next to the peat-glow to warm it. One of the men appeared, seized the bellows which lay by the fire and plied them expertly; Michael suddenly moved to the door, and had a word with the other man still outside.

By the time the cart appeared before the house, Alys had contrived a small tisane of thyme and mint from the kailyard with a generous amount of honey in it, and was perched rather painfully on the wooden bar at the outer edge of the bed, dripping her concoction slowly into the clerk's bruised mouth. The first drops had an immediate effect; Fleming drew a deep breath, and the shuddering convulsions ceased.

'Honey is wonderful stuff,' she said, watching this.

The old woman asked a shrill question, and Mistress Paton looked up sharply from the hearth, where she was stirring the iron pot which stood over the revived fire.

'I never thought o' that,' she said. 'Are you her from the Pow Burn? The auld collier's widow? For if ye are –'

'No,' said Alys, startled.

'That's the lady's good-daughter from Belstane,' supplied Steenie.

'Our Lady be thanked,' said the woman. 'If our Dod found I'd let that one over the threshold he'd break a stob across my back.'

'Do you mean Mistress Lithgo?' said Alys. 'What has she done to you?'

'Lithgo? Who's she?'

'Mistress Mason?' said Michael, coming into the house. 'Is he fit to be moved, do you think? We've a cart here.'

Alys looked down at her patient. He was beginning to stir, and now uttered a heart-rending groan. His eyes opened.

'Fleming?' said Michael. He bent over his servant in the gloom. 'What came to you, man? You're in a bad way here.'

There was a pause, in which Fleming opened and closed his swollen mouth. The old woman screeched suddenly, and he flinched, croaked something, swallowed, tried again.

'. . . t'ss Li'hgo,' he said.

Chapter Seven

Riding back up towards Forth in the drizzle, to pick up the road to Linlithgow and Blackness, Gil found he had selected one of the more garrulous stable-hands to accompany him. He was quite unable to concentrate on his thoughts for the questions Patey fired at him. Where were they going, how long would it take, where would they lie this night? He answered patiently at first, then said sharply, 'Hold your peace and let me think, man. I've matters to ponder.'

'And would that be this business of the corp in the peat-cutting?' asked Patey. 'Or is it the man Murray?'

'Hold your peace,' Gil repeated.

'Just I was going to say,' persisted Patey in injured tones, 'there's one of the collier lassies yonder, watching us.'

Gil looked where the man pointed, and saw a small plump figure standing knee-deep in yellow flowers, under a group of bent hawthorn trees in the hollow of a burn below the track. Plaid over her head against the rain, she was still identifiable: not Phemie but her sister. What was the girl's name? Bel, that was it. The one who never spoke.

'The one that doesny speak,' said Patey helpfully. 'Tongue-tied, she is. She isny daft, mind you, and they say she's a grand spinner. No a bad thing in a lassie, to be tongue-tied.'

'What, and never ask you what you want for your supper?' Gil dismounted. 'Bide here and hold my horse. I want a word wi' her.'

'You can have a' the words you want,' said Patey, 'but she'll never have a word for you, maister.' He guffawed at his own wit, then finally became silent under Gil's glare, and took the reins.

Bel was still watching them warily, and when Gil climbed down from the track she looked around as if judging her chances of escape. He stopped at a little distance from her, the yellow flowers round his boots. She must be thirteen or fourteen, he thought, surveying her, plainer than her sister and still covered in puppy-fat. Tib had been much the same at that age, less anxious but with the same sulky expression. If this girl was tongue-tied, that would explain a lot.

'You're Bel Crombie, aren't you?' he asked. She nodded. 'Do you mind me? I'm Gil Cunningham.' She nodded again, and bobbed in a brief, apprehensive curtsy. 'Should you be out here your lone, Bel?'

She shrugged, bent to pick another handful of wet flowers, showed them to him and pushed them into a linen sack at her belt. Gathering something for the still-room, he surmised.

'And it's raining,' he added. She looked at him, then at the sky, and shrugged again. This was not going to be easy, he recognized, and there was a strange quality to the girl which made him uncomfortable about questioning her. Still, one had to try. 'Bel, could I ask you a few things?'

She straightened up to look directly at him, with a withering stare rather like those his mother's cat turned on Socrates, and waited.

'Have you any idea where Thomas Murray might be?' he asked. She shook her head firmly. 'Or what's come to him?' Another eloquent shrug. He paused to consider, trying to frame the question so it could be answered *Yes* or *No*. 'Do you like him?' An innocent enough question. Bel screwed up her face and shook her head. 'Does he ever try to kiss you?'

She shook her head again, looked down at her person and carefully lifted away an invisible something that clung about her hips.

'He's free with his hands,' Gil supplied. She nodded. 'And yet he's never followed it up?' A puzzled look. This is a young lassie, he reminded himself. 'He's never tried kissing you.' Another shake of the head, with an impatient glance: *I told you that*. 'The day he left,' he said, and she frowned, still watching him carefully, 'did anything unusual happen? Anything at all?'

After a moment she nodded. He smiled encouragingly.

'Who did it happen to? Who was involved?' he asked. 'If I name everyone, can you tell me when I say the right names?'

She nodded, and by enumerating the household he learned that Mistress Weir and Joanna had been involved, as well as Murray.

'Was that when Mistress Weir sent you with a gift for Murray?' he asked. Her blue eyes widened, and she nodded. 'Mistress Brownlie told my wife of it. Was that so unusual, for your grandmother to give him something?'

She nodded vehemently, and mimed an angry quarrel, wagging a finger at the rain.

'They're usually at odds,' he interpreted, and she suddenly gave him a shy smile. 'And then he rode off as usual with the Paterson men?' Another nod. 'Do you know why she gave him the gift?'

Bel raised an imaginary glass to drink his health, and counted off one, two, three with the other hand.

'It was to drink her health on her birthday,' he

152

recalled, and she nodded. 'Are you saying that was three days after they left?' Another nod. 'That was a friendly gesture.'

She stared at him, her expression changing slowly back to the withering cat look. Then she shrugged and turned away, bending to the yellow marsh-marigolds round her feet.

'Can you tell me anything else?' Gil asked. Another shrug. 'Why does your grandam dislike Murray?' She gave him a pitying glance. 'Is it simply that he won't do as she bids him?'

She straightened up, pushing another handful of flowers into the linen sack, and placed one hand flat in the air, a little higher than her own height. She gestured round her face, nimble fingers describing the long ends of a linen headdress. A woman, taller than herself but shorter than her mother.

'Joanna – Mistress Brownlie?' he said. Bel nodded. She held up one hand, fingers opening and shutting. Someone talking? She indicated the invisible Joanna, and cowered in fear. 'Threats to Joanna? Who threatens her? Your grandmother?'

This got him an exasperated stare. She squared her shoulders and stuck out her plump chest and her elbows. A man, and a conceited man.

'Your brother? Murray? Murray threatens Joanna?' Another nod. 'It's a man's prerogative to chastise his wife,' he said on a venture. 'I'd have thought Mistress Weir would see little wrong in that.' And that's hypocrisy, he thought, for if I ever raised my hand to Alys I think I would cut my throat afterwards.

Whether she detected the hypocrisy or not, Bel's expression would have parched grain. She sighed ostentatiously, established Joanna again with the same deft movements, and then straightened her back, raised her chin and outlined a wired cap on her head. He nodded, and she assumed an expression of simpering affection, and held her hands out to the invisible Joanna.

'Mistress Weir dotes on Joanna?'

Bel confirmed this. Then she sketched a row of women to her left, and identified them: herself, her sister, her mother. When he named them aloud, she nodded again.

'Is this how you talk to your family?' he asked, fascinated. She threw him an irritated look and, stepping into the role of her grandmother again, swept the row of invisible figures aside with one hand while she drew the equally invisible Joanna closer with the other, still simpering with exaggerated affection.

'So Mistress Weir would place Joanna over all the rest of you,' he said. Bel nodded encouragingly. 'Even your brother?'

She had not thought of that. She considered the question briefly while the rain pattered on the hawthorn leaves, then spread her hands.

'And yet she sent you with the gift for Murray.'

She shrugged, and turned her head away, unmoving for a moment. Then, obviously coming to a decision, she began again. The wired headdress, the elegant stance: Arbella. She steadied a mortar with one hand and worked the pestle with the other, pausing to add a pinch of this and a careful drop of that, and looked expectantly at him.

'Mistress Weir helps your mother in the stillroom,' he offered. 'I thought it was your sister did that.' She frowned, shook her head, stirred the imaginary mortar again, her lips moving busily as if she was speaking. 'Mistress Weir taught your mother.' Bel flicked him a glance, nodded, continued to work the pestle. 'What are you telling me, Bel?'

She sighed, abandoned the mortar, and pulled up the

154

skirt of her gown to reach the purse that hung at her knee between gown and kirtle. From it she drew out a much-scored piece of grey slaty stone and a slate-pencil, bent to lean the slate on her knee and took a careful grasp of the pencil to write. She was no clerk: she formed each letter laboriously, with the use of elbow, tongue and head. Standing in the rain watching her, he appreciated that she would find all her dumb-show (yes, that was exactly the word) much easier than scribing anything at all.

It took her some time, but at last she handed him the stone, with an air which made him feel what it said was very important. He studied it carefully. The wet surface was much-marked already, with earlier inscriptions partly excised, and the uneven letters were hard to make out. Her spelling was imaginative and there were no breaks in the staggering sequence, but after a moment he decided that RBEL probably meant Arbella. But what did the rest mean? It appeared to read PYSH-NUW. After a moment enlightenment dawned, along with surprise that a girl from such a family would use this sort of coarseness.

'You're telling me Arbella dislikes me too? Holds me in contempt?' And yet she was civil enough to my face, he thought. Bel stared at him, open-mouthed, and suddenly shook her head, snatched the slate out of his hand and stuffed it back into her purse, then turned, her back radiating fury, and marched away through the flowers.

'Bel!' he called after her. 'Come back, lassie, I'll take you home out of the rain.'

She went on, ignoring him.

'Bel! Are you safe out here on your lone?'

She swung round, stared at him, then rotated one finger by her temple in a universal sign and continued on her way. Reluctant to pursue her across the hillside,

155

he gathered his wits and prepared to go back up to the waiting horses. The road to Blackness beckoned.

A gleam in the grass caught his eye from where the girl had been standing. He made his way towards it, and found her slate, lodged in a clump of flowers and shining in the light. It must have missed her purse in her haste. He bent to pick it up and turned it in his hand. None of the other inscriptions was clear enough to read more than a letter or two; only the comment about Arbella stood out.

With a feeling of having missed something important, he put the object into his purse and made his way up to the track, where man and beasts waited for him, heads down against the increasing rain.

'Can we get on now, Maister Gil?' asked Patey. 'Just it's ower cold to be standing about like this.'

'We'll go by the Pow Burn,' said Gil, reclaiming his reins and mounting. 'I must let them know where that lassie is. I should have left my plaid over this saddle,' he added, as the damp leather struck cold through his hose.

'What was she doing wi' all the waving her arms?' asked Patey curiously. He demonstrated, causing Gil's horse to shy.

'Watch what you're about, man! That's how she talks. She was telling me about her grandam and Murray.'

'I see. She canny wag her tongue, so she wags her arms instead.' Patey grinned at his own joke. 'What did you say to her then, maister, that she lost her temper wi' you? Maybe I can guess!'

Gil stared at him in revulsion, and he fell silent and after a moment mumbled an apology of sorts.

'So I should think,' Gil said. 'If there's another word like that out of you, I'll be having a talk with Henry when we get back to Belstane.' Patey muttered something else. 'Well, hold your tongue then.'

He spurred his horse forward along the track towards the colliery, without looking back to see if the groom followed him.

The surfacemen were just breaking off for their midday bite when he came over the hillside. Eight or ten men were gathering in the shelter of the smithy, round the fire. On the path which led down from the thatched row of cottages was a procession of children, bareheaded despite the rain, each bearing a father's or brother's meal: a wooden bowl with a kale-leaf over it, a plate covered by a cloth, a small package wrapped in dock-leaves. The men underground must take their food in with them and eat it cold, he conjectured.

He dismounted on the cobbled area before the house and looked about, hoping to find one of the family. It seemed likely that the household would be sitting down to eat as well, and he had no wish to interrupt the meal. To his relief, Mistress Lithgo appeared at the door of her stillroom, and came to meet him.

'Maister Cunningham,' she said, and nodded in answer to his greeting. 'What brings you here? Can we do aught for you? Will you stay for a bite?'

'No, no, I won't stay,' he said. 'I want to get to Blackness today. I met your daughter Bel all on her own over the hill yonder, and thought I should let you know where she was.'

'On her own,' she said, sounding annoyed. 'She will go off like that on her grandam's errands, and I canny teach her it's no safe at her age. My thanks, sir. I'll send her brother after her. And my thanks to your lady mother,' she added, 'for his bed and dole last night. He came in an hour or two since.'

'My dear, you needny trouble about Bel,' said Arbella's sweet voice. Gil turned, to see her emerging from the building Phemie had identified as the mine office. 'I sent her to gather what we need for the spring tonic. She'll not go far, she'll be quite safe.' She approached, leaning on a stick and moving carefully on her high wooden pattens. Her plaid, hitched up over her wired headdress against the rain, hung down in dark folds to her knees, and under it her other hand held her petticoats up out of the grey-black mud. She looked like a mourner at a funeral. 'But it was right kind of you to let us know,' she added, smiling at Gil. 'Was that all that brought you here? I hope you've not rid out of your way for my wee lassie?'

'I was concerned for her,' he explained. 'I stopped to speak to her, and something I said annoyed her and she marched off down the burn towards the low shielings.'

Bel's mother gave him a raking glance, then visibly relaxed.

'Aye, times she's like that,' she admitted. 'She angers easily, with not being able to say what she wants.'

'We'd managed fine up to that. She told me clearly how you'd sent her with a gift for Murray just before he left here, madam.'

Arbella's finely drawn eyebrows rose. 'Did she so? You're perceptive, Maister Cunningham, if you grasped that from her. And are you any nearer finding Thomas for us? To tell truth, since my dear Joanna's out of hearing, I'm beginning to be a wee bit concerned that we've heard nothing.'

'I don't know,' he admitted. 'I'm on my way to Blackness now, to track down your two sinkers. The word in Forth is that they've gone over there to their kin –'

'Aye, William Wood that would be,' agreed Beatrice, nodding.

'To Blackness?' said Arbella. 'In all this rain? You're going to a deal of trouble for my household, maister. Can we do anything for you while you're here? We're about to sit down to dinner – will you join us?'

'No, no, I want to get on my road, I'll not disturb your meal,' he assured her, and then, as a memory surfaced, 'I'd like a look inside your chapel, if I might. Fleming said something about it.'

'Fleming!' Arbella said witheringly, and reached for the bunch of keys at her belt. 'I'm greatly disappointed in that man, you know, sir. After all I did for him, to turn and accuse my good-daughter in such a way.' She began moving towards the little wattle-and-daub building. Beatrice nodded to Gil and retreated into her stillroom again.

'You did him a favour?'

'I did. I knew his father well, sir, a good man and a clever, and died here, Our Lady save him.' She crossed herself, her keys clinking. 'And so Davy was left without sponsor. It was I persuaded Douglas to give him his uncle's place.' She unlocked the door of the chapel and stepped inside. 'And well he's repaid me for it, too, one way and another.' She bowed stiffly to the crucified Christ on the altar, and again to a brightly painted figure of St Ninian with his broken chain, perched on a shelf behind it. 'Forever trying to direct me in the manage of this place and my family. Would you believe, sir, he tried to tell me my grandson would never make a scholar, and I should give him charge here instead of Murray!'

'Did he?' said Gil, in what he hoped was a sympathetic tone.

'Indeed he did, and here's my laddie with tales of how his teachers admire his every word. And the man canny even find me a decent relic for this kirk, to keep the colliers and their women here instead of trailing down into Carluke or Lanark wi' their petitions.'

And how should they bring their prayers here if it's kept locked? Gil wondered, and looked about him. The little space held only the furnished altar, an aumbry on legs for the Mass-vessels, and three benches round the walls. The altar-linen must be shut in the aumbry, and a shelf below the closed portion held an obvious candle-box, its corners gnawed by hopeful rats. A pewter holy-water stoup hung from a nail by the door. Linked ideas made him glance downward, to find the floor made of neatly fitted slabs of grey-blue stone much like Bel's slate, which was still in his purse. No hope of returning that just now, he thought; I can hardly hand it to Arbella with that inscription, and get the lassie into trouble.

'You keep the key?' he asked.

'I have all the keys, maister,' said Arbella simply. 'There's another lives on a nail by the kitchen door,' she added. 'We keep it locked because there's no priest here, but our folk can aye get in if they wish.'

Beyond Linlithgow, the way out to Blackness was a well-made and well-used road, with heaps of stones at intervals to fill in potholes.

'Likely the merchants that use the port keep it up,' said Gil when Patey commented. 'Or it's paid out of the port dues. There's only the one way up from the shore.'

'And is it the shore we're making for, maister?' said Patey. His chastened mood had not lasted long, and Gil had become resigned to the man's chatter. 'Did you say you wanted the salt-boilers? I suppose that would be them yonder where the smoke is.'

'More than likely,' Gil agreed, eyeing the dark column leaning downwind from the distant point, across the bay from the square outline of the castle. 'Since it seems they burn coal. I wonder what it's like in the castle when the wind's in the west?'

They rode down off the low hills which separated Linlithgow from the Forth, through the settlement of

160

Blackness itself where the smells of supper drifted on the wind, and on to the shore. Two merchant vessels were drawn up on the shingle, one loading, one unloading, and another lay at anchor out in the bay. Round the three legs of the crane a stack of barrels waited to be swung on board, several men were handling bales of wool out of a barn, and a handful of carts stood by, the carters shouting directions to the shore porters about their loads. The custumar in a long belted gown of black trimmed with squirrel bustled importantly through the activity, followed by his clerk with ink-pot and parchment at the ready.

'Where do we lie tonight, Maister Gil?' asked Patey, assessing the distance out to the tower of smoke.

'Tonight? I hadn't thought,' Gil confessed.

'Aye, I thought not,' said Patey with a faint resentment, turning to look back at the way they had come. 'Just if we're to go back to Linlithgow to seek a bed, we'll no need to be held up here. The light willny last, ye ken, and it's turned cloudy again, we'll ha' no good of the moon.'

Accosting the custumar got them the information that there were two inns in Blackness, but they didny want to patronize the Blue Bell where all the common mariners lay, they would do better to ask at the Ship.

'Or you might get a bed at the castle,' offered the functionary, studying Gil's horse and clothing, setting it against his lack of a retinue and obviously coming down on the side of his being likely kin or acquaintance of Ross of Hawkhead who held the castle for the Crown.

'We'll try the Ship first,' Gil decided, at which Patey brightened noticeably.

Leaving the horses safely stabled and his man sampling the ale in the inn's public room, Gil walked on along the curving shore and out towards the point on the western side of the bay. The scene round the salt-pans came into view as he approached, a chaos of heaps of coal, heaps of ash, wooden sheds with baskets of salt visible in their shelter. The wide pans of rust-coated iron stood in a row under a long thatched roof, the red glow of the fires beneath them, with dark figures moving to and fro in the drifting smoke and steam. Seagulls swirled screaming over their heads. It made Gil think of a vision of hell by that mad Flemish painter Bosch. Almost he expected to encounter half a dozen devils with lolling tongues and extra faces, prodding a fat bishop into the boiling sea-water.

Instead, he found two weather-beaten men and a woman, armed with bleached wooden rakes and long scoops, trudging back and forward along the pans of bubbling white liquor, plying first rake and then scoop in each. Gulls swooped and mewed and pounced on what was spooned out of the pans and there was a tang of rotting fish in the smoke.

'Aye, you get a' things in the pans,' agreed the eldest salt-boiler, a gnarled man with one red-rimmed eye, leaning on his rake. 'A' thing but coin,' he added, and laughed at his own joke. 'Crabs, o' course, and whelks and that. A glove or a shoe, often enough.'

'Never in pairs, but,' said the woman, who appeared to be his wife. 'Are they, Wullie?'

'I found a drowned bairn,' said the younger man. 'Din't I no, Mammy, I found a –'

'It wasny a bairn, Jock,' said his mother repressively. 'The gentleman doesny want to hear about it.'

'Aye, but it was,' said Jock. 'It was a' green –'

'Jock! Get back to the pans!'

'Can I help you, maister, or was ye just wanting to see the salt-boiling?' asked the older man. 'There's many folk likes to see where their salt comes from. Ye see here,' he said, without waiting for an answer, 'we gather the water here wi' the tide, in yonder tank in the rock, and lift it wi' the bucket-gang and the auld pony, into the pans. We've a great system wi' sluices to let the water run the length o' the pans, and then we shut it off and set the fires.'

'Two days, it takes, to come through the boil, doesn't it no, Wullie?' said his wife. 'These was the first pans on the Forth to have sluices,' she added proudly. 'Ye're looking at the best salt-pans in the Lothians, maister.'

'I never knew there was so much involved,' confessed Gil, looking round him. 'Do you live down here on the shore? Is that your house?'

'That? That's no but a shelter for when the weather's bad. We dwell up yonder.' Wullie pointed to a cottage crouched some yards back from the shore. His wife turned back to the pans, and he continued to show Gil the process with a fluency which made it clear he was used to visitors. Gil heard him out, fascinated and appalled, peered into the shed at the straw skeps of dry salt waiting to be sold on, learned about creech and bittern and the use of bullocks' blood to clarify the brine. 'Swine's blood's no good,' the man informed him, leaning on his rake, 'the reason being, swine's flesh has a natural affinity with salt, ye see, so the blood takes up the salt out the brine instead of drawing up the lees. Or so Peter Nicholson our clerk tells me. Ye need to let the blood stand till it turns rotten, o' course, it's no use when it's fresh.'

'Of course,' echoed Gil, wondering if he could ever put salt on his food again.

'I've heard there's salt-pans at Ayr,' conceded Wullie, 'but the best sea salt comes from the shores of the Forth, maister, mind that. The coal's handy, the sea-water's good, and we get rock salt in from the Low Countries to strengthen the brine.'

163

'How many salt-boilers are there along this shore?' Gil asked. 'I heard of a fellow called Lithgo one time.'

'Simon Lithgo? Aye, that was a bad business.' Wullie shook his head, and Gil made a questioning noise. 'Oh, a bad business. Died at the pans, didn't he. Found in his own Number Two pan, boiled to a turn. Coffined burial,' he added with relish.

'How did that happen?' Gil asked, his thoughts racing. Surely the trouble at the Pow Burn couldn't reach this far, he told himself, but –

'Peter Nicholson reckoned his heart gave out. He should never ha' been tending the pans on his own. And the worst o' it was,' Wullie added, 'he'd no long got his last daughter wedded, he was working for hisself at last. More than ten year syne, that was. I'd no recalled Simon Lithgo in a many year. A bad business,' he said again.

'I never thought of it being a dangerous trade.'

'That's a good one!' Wullie guffawed. 'A dangerous trade! That's a good one! Aye, you're right, maister, it's a dangerous trade. Now, I need to get back to my pans,' he announced, scanning the line with his red-rimmed eye. 'Number Fower's about ready for skimming, I'd say. Ye're welcome to take a dander about, maister, afore ye go.'

'Thanks, I will,' said Gil. 'Are the Paterson lads here, by the way? Jock and Tam, I mean, the two sinkers. I was hoping to get a word wi' them.'

'Jock and Tam.' The man stared at him, and rubbed at his closed eye-socket. 'Aye, they're here wi' me. Jess's nephews, they are. What was ye wanting them for? They're up at the house, but they're likely asleep the now. Here, is it you they're looking for these last two week or more, to talk about the small coal from Lanarkshire? They've been right concerned for ye, maister.'

'No, that's not me, but I'm looking for the same fellow. I want to ask Jock and Tam about him. I'm hoping they can tell me where they parted from him.'

'I wouldny know about that,' said Wullie doubtfully. 'They've never said.'

'You're telling me they're asleep? How long before they're stirring?'

'No long.' Wullie glanced at the sky. 'They've been watching the nights for me while they're here, since our Jock's no to be depended on, poor laddie. Will I rouse them, or will ye wait, maister?'

Gil elected to wait, and strolled on along the shore a little in the evening light, leaving the man to get on with his work. Once he rounded the point the shouts of the men by the ships dwindled, and all he could hear was the bleating of sheep and lambs in the pastures inland, and the cries of the seabirds, and the steady swish of the tide beyond the expanse of mud. The east wind blew in briskly from the German Sea, and across the firth the salt-pans of Fife flew similar plumes of smoke.

He sat down on a bank of rough grass to consider what he should ask the Paterson men. He was still not sure whether he was investigating a murder. On previous occasions there had been a body to identify, or at least in one case a head; here he had a body which was not Murray, and Murray whose body was not to be found, whether the man was alive or dead. Perhaps he has been spirited away, he thought, grinning to himself. Maybe Fleming is right about witchcraft. But Alys had seen no sign of such a thing up at the Pow Burn.

And what had taken Alys into Carluke this morning? She had discovered a great deal for him, one way and another. He found himself smiling again at the thought of her, her endless capacity for surprising him, her incisive mind and astonishing competence. And the warmth of her skin under his hands, the way her lips clung to his. As always, he marvelled at his good fortune. *An hendy hap ich habbe yhent*, he thought. I wonder if she learned anything in the town?

The light was beginning to fail, and the tide was coming in across the wide stretch of mud before him. He rose, stretched, rubbed at the seat of his hose. The grass was not as dry as he had thought, and he must have been sitting here for quite some time.

Wullie and his wife and son had vanished, presumably into their house, and been replaced by two men who were on their knees checking the fires below the row of pans, raking at the hot coals with clanging iron implements. One of them noticed Gil walking in along the tide-line, and spoke to the other; they rose and came forward to meet him, big broad-shouldered men with the same economical walk he had noticed in the colliers.

'Aye, neebor. Is that you that's looking for Tam Murray?' demanded the taller, as soon as he was within earshot. 'Have you any word of him at all?'

'None,' said Gil frankly. 'I was hoping you could tell me more. Where did you see him last? I think you parted from him somewhere on the round before you reached Forth.'

'Oh, long afore that,' said the other man. 'Lanark. We left him in Lanark.'

'Lanark?' repeated Gil incredulously. 'But – Do you mean he left it to you to collect the whole of the fees?'

'Oh, aye,' agreed the taller brother. 'He mostly does. Meets us outside Forth town.'

'Sweet St Giles!' He looked from one man to the other. 'I take it Mistress Weir doesny know of it.'

'What do you think?' said the taller man, the light catching his teeth as he grinned.

'So where does he go? Does he simply stay in Lanark

drinking?' Gil looked about at the twilight. 'Will we sit down and you can tell me what you know about the man.'

There were three stumps of driftwood drawn up in the mouth of one of the sheds, an unlit wood fire set and the ashes of many more fires scattered on the shore around them. Seated here, the Patersons answered his questions, slowly at first, then more confidently. The taller brother, it seemed, was Jock, and it had been his idea originally to take up Sir Thomas Bartholomew's suggestion and seek work in Lanarkshire.

'Lanark folks is all right,' he said dismissively. 'A bit soft, especial in the head, but they're kind enough.'

'Lanark lassies is more than all right,' observed Tam, smacking his lips.

His brother kicked his ankle. 'Och, see you? Anyway, we get there, maister, and find Tammas Murray, that was at the sang-schule in Kincardine wi' our brother Davy, set in authority in the place. He was right pleased to see us and all.'

'Took us on like a maid embracing her lover, so he did,' supplied Tam. 'Treated us well, too. Choice of lodging, bed to oursels, laddie to carry our gear whenever we was working, fetch our sister to mind the house – though that never lasted, she up and wedded Attie Logan.'

'And we hadny been in our place six month afore he sends for us one morning and he says to us, private like –'

'I've a proposition, he says.'

'Aye, a proposition. D'ye think, he says, ye can find your way about Lanarkshire and back here with a bag of coin.'

'What's in it for us, says I.'

'And he says, ye'll get paid extra for it if ye can keep your mouths shut, says he. So we agreed a fee, and he sets out wi' us, and in Lanark he leaves us wi' a list of where we've to call, and the names of who to ask for at each place, and what's owed, and we do the whole round and then meet him in Forth.'

'And we've done it every quarter since,' contributed Tam.

'And no a word to anyone, till now.'

'Well!' said Gil. 'And where was Murray while you were collecting the coin?'

'Now that,' said Jock with deep regret, 'we've never jaloused. It's aye the same place he leaves us, in the midst of Lanark.'

'We took it he was wi' a lassie, but we never found out where.'

'A pity, that, seeing what like his wife is at the Pow Burn,' said Jock thoughtfully. 'If I'd that Joanna in my bed, I'd no feel the need to keep another in secret.'

'No accounting for tastes.'

'You never asked him?'

'We did not. He's no one for idle chat, Tammas Murray.'

'And how long has this been going on?'

The brothers looked at one another in the firelight.

'Two year?' said Tam.

'No as long,' said Jock. 'It was after Matt Crombie died, no the first quarter's reckoning but the next. A year past at Martinmas, I'd say.'

'A year and a half, then. Since before he wedded Joanna,' Gil said.

'Aye, but it went on after.'

'But where does he go? Do you think he stays in the town, or does he venture out elsewhere?' Gil asked.

'I followed him one time,' said Tam, 'but I lost him afore the top of the town. It was market-day, ye see, and he just vanished in the crowd. Must ha' jouked up a vennel.'

'What, you lost a red-haired man?' said Gil in faint disbelief.

'Aye, red-haired, wi' a great blue bonnet on like a'body else's.'

'So how come you're asking for him, maister?' asked Jock. Tam, looking along the row of salt-pans, rose and went to poke at one of the fires.

'The men from Thorn found a red-haired corp in their peat-cutting,' Gil explained.

'A corp? St Peter's bones, what's that doing in a peat-cutting?' exclaimed Jock. 'Is it Tammas Murray, then? Is he dead right enough, and you never said?'

'It isn't Murray,' Gil said carefully, 'but I'm beginning to fear he's dead right enough, for he's never turned up yet. David Fleming was convinced that the corp was Murray, and that Mistress Lithgo had set it there by means of witchcraft.'

'Beattie? No Beattie!' said Tam, sitting back on his heels, the fire-glow lighting his face. 'She'd no do a thing like that. Davy Fleming's no done her any harm, has he?'

'Phemie called out the day shift and rescued her.'

'She would,' said Jock, grinning in the firelight. 'That's a fechtie lass, that Phemie. And did that sort it? He's no laid charges against Beattie, has he? He'll have the whole of the colliers to reckon wi' if he has.'

'He'll have Adam Crombie to reckon with,' Gil said. 'The young man came home yestreen, and was for Cauldhope this morning to confront Fleming.'

'Oh, well. Raffie should sort him. But where has Tammas Murray got to?' said Tam Paterson. He rose and returned to his log, bringing a lighted stick with him which he set to the fire at their feet. 'You say he's no turned up at the Pow Burn either, maister? That's . . . that's . . .' He paused, reckoning on the free hand. Flames sprang in the tinder under the driftwood.

169

'Aye, five week or more since we parted from him in Lanark town.'

'We've been right concerned,' said his brother, 'but you'll see it's no just a matter of going back to the Pow Burn to ask for him. The auld wife would ha' questions for us, and the first would be, Where did he part from you?'

'And where does he part from you?' Gil asked. 'Can you recall anything that might help me track him down?'

'The Nicholas,' said Jock promptly. 'Hard by St Nicholas' kirk. Juggling Nick's they call it.' Gil nodded, familiar with the inn and its sign where the mitred saint stared up the market-place in half-length, his three purses floating round his halo. Its landlady was feared by drinkers in four parishes. 'We aye light down there for a drink after we've rid in from Jerviswood, he collects from the two accounts we've got in the town, and then he takes off.'

'On foot?'

'On foot.'

'So not far, then.' Gil considered. 'Somewhere in the town, or not far outside it. If it was in the town, I'd ha' thought he'd ha' turned up by now, the word about the corp in the peat-cutting should be all over the Middle Ward. Does he leave his horse at Juggling Nick's?'

'Aye, that's right. Then he rides up to meet us when we get to Forth. He'll get a week wi' his woman, I suppose,' reckoned Jock. 'She must be a patient soul, to put up wi' that. A week wi' your man once a quarter doesny seem like a lot.'

'Joanna Brownlie might think it was enough,' said Tam darkly.

'Did he never let anything slip, then? Nothing that might give us a direction?'

The two men considered, and Jock shook his head.

'He'd a sprig of yew in his hat one time he joined us,' offered Tam. 'Tucked behind his St Andrew. Had berries on it.'

'There's yew grows everywhere,' objected his brother. 'That's no use.'

'No, but it might mean the lassie dwells by a yew tree.'

'It's still no use, you daft lump.'

'It might help. Is Juggling Nick's the same place he goes drinking, do you know? I'm told he goes down into Lanark once a week or so.'

'You don't think he takes us wi' him,' said Jock.

'Just the same,' said his brother, 'I'd say it might be. He's a kent face there, aye joking wi' the lassies and taking snash from the ostlers he'd never take from us.'

'It sounds like it,' Gil agreed. He rose, and stretched his back. 'I had best get back to the Ship afore they bar the doors. My thanks to the both of you for all this. If you think of anything else I'll be glad to hear it, though I'll be away back into Lanarkshire at first light.'

'Aye well, here's a thing,' said Jock. 'Just talking of it now, it comes into my mind. Could his lassie maybe work at Juggling Nick's? They've two or three lassies about the place, to see to the chambers and the kitchen and that.'

'No yew trees in the midst of Lanark town, but,' said his brother.

'Aye there is,' retorted Jock, 'there's a great yew tree in St Nicholas' kirkyard leans ower the wall.'

'I think I need to head for Lanark the first chance I get,' said Gil.

Chapter Eight

'Michael was to start for Lanark at first light,' said Alys, from her place in the circle of Gil's arm, 'so he has had most of the day now to search Lanark. He reckoned he could more easily spare half a dozen men for the day than Madame Mère,' she explained, with a quick smile at his mother. 'But I hoped he might send word of my patient.'

Gil drew her closer, relishing her solid warmth. It had been, somehow, a longer ride home than the one out to Blackness, and the thought of her welcome had greatly cheered the journey. He used his other hand to scratch the ears of the rather damp wolfhound who leaned against his knee, making the dog groan ecstatically.

'Maybe I should have gone on to Lanark to find him myself. I'm reluctant to ride further, to be honest . . .'

'Well you might be,' said his mother, with a wry glance at the cushion of the bench he had chosen to sit on. 'I can spare Steenie that long, I suppose. Indeed, he should be back soon. And I bade him ask after Fleming while he was about it, my dear,' she added to Alys.

'Yes, Fleming,' said Gil. 'You say it was Crombie beat him?'

'So he told us,' Alys agreed. 'He made better sense later, once we had got him back to Cauldhope, and washed his hurts and put him to bed. He said he was out in the fields, on his way to wherever it was Michael had sent him, and Crombie and his men found him, and set about him with sticks.'

'Crombie had one man and no sticks when he left here,' Gil said.

'No, I thought that, and I would have said from his bruises they rather used their fists and feet.'

'*Gaif him an outragious blaw, and great boist blew,*' suggested Gil.

Her quick smile flickered as she placed the quotation, but she went on, 'I suppose Crombie wished to threaten him about the charge against Mistress Lithgo. But Gil, I am still puzzled by his lying in a swoon half the day like that, and by the convulsions. I could find no blow to the head that would account for it. I wonder if Mistress Lithgo would tell me ...' Her voice trailed off.

'So you think,' said Lady Egidia, 'that the man Murray has a mistress in or near Lanark, and visits her once a quarter while these two brothers collect the money for him.'

'It looks very like it,' Gil said. Socrates nudged his hand, and he scratched behind the dog's ears again. A waft of the animal's fishy breath reached him.

'It's odd, mind you,' persisted his mother, 'if that's so, that word's never got round. It's a small enough neighbourhood, after all. Carluke folk go down to the market at Lanark, and a juicy bit of gossip like that would travel, you'd think.'

'He might visit her under another name,' said Alys.

'He'd be recognized by someone as he came or went, I'm sure of that.'

'He goes in disguise,' said Gil. 'A turban and a false beard from the Corpus Christi costume kist.'

'*Corpus Christi costume kist.* Now yon's a tongue-trap!' said his mother, half laughing.

'Perhaps she lives secluded,' suggested Alys. 'In a green desert, with one faithful hound for company.' She reached across Gil to stroke their own faithful hound's head, and the dog licked her wrist with a long tongue.

'The yew tree wouldn't fit with that,' said Gil. 'They mostly grow in a kirkyard or at least by a chapel.'

'She is the guardian of the chapel, of course.'

'What, and a man's mistress these two years as well?'

'Temptation can strike anyone,' Alys responded seriously.

'The yew tree might be on the road to her home,' said Lady Egidia.

'Can you think of anywhere that might fit, Mother? You know this side the river better than I do.'

'If it's so much out of the way,' said Alys, 'surely nobody can know of it.'

'You get the odd dwelling down by the Clyde itself,' said Lady Egidia, nodding in acknowledgement of this point, 'even in the gorge below Lanark. But I've a notion I've seen something elsewhere. A solitary place in the cut of one of the rivers, on the way to nowhere. Now where was it and why was I going that way?'

'Exercising the horses?' suggested Alys.

'Maybe Michael will have learned something of use,' said Gil doubtfully. 'I'd like to find Murray, and get this whole matter dealt with. And what about the corp we do have? Has anyone claimed to know him yet?'

'No, and it seems there has been a great stream of folk to inspect him,' Alys said. 'Henry was kept too busy to wash the dog on his own yesterday. I suppose the whole parish must have heard how he was found, no doubt they want to tell their grandchildren they saw him. Most of those who looked have prayed for him, Henry says, so at least he benefits by that.'

Gil nodded. 'I've been wondering,' he said, 'if his death could be much older than we first thought.

174

Maybe as far back as Wallace's time, or even beyond it. Old Forrest the huntsman had no knowledge of him, and his recollection goes back over a hundred years.'

'Could he be from even longer ago, from before the Flood?' asked Alys. 'The men who were cutting the peat talked of tree-roots and elf-bolts that they found under it, from Noah's time, so why not this man as well? He's well enough preserved, I would have thought, he could have lasted so long.'

'He wasn't under the peat,' Gil objected, 'he was in its midst.'

'Then he must be from halfway back to the Flood,' offered Alys. 'Gil!' She sat up straight, turning to stare at him, brown eyes round. 'Gil, do you suppose he could be from the time when Our Lord was born? That he might have seen the star that led the kings?'

'I suppose he could. There's no way of telling,' Gil said cautiously, reluctant to contradict such a notion. Socrates raised his head from his master's knee to stare at the door. 'But surely he wouldn't have seen the star even so. It led the kings out of the east, not the west.'

'But he might have heard the angels in the sky.' Alys's eyes were shining. 'Perhaps he went to Bethlehem. I would have done.'

'So would we all. That's a bonnie thought,' said Lady Cunningham, abandoning her reflections. 'What is it, Alan?'

In the doorway of the chamber, the steward ducked in an apologetic bow.

'Right apposite to what ye were just saying, mistress,' he said. 'It's Jackie Heriot walked out from Carluke asking for a word about the man out of the peat-digging. Will ye see him, or no?'

'Sir John?' Lady Cunningham raised her brows, and rose to her feet. 'Aye, send him in, Alan. Good day to you, Sir John. What can we do for you the day?'

Sir John Heriot, bowing low over his round black hat, had to ask after his parishioner's health, exclaim over encountering Alys again, congratulate Gil on his marriage, admire the wolfhound, who beat his tail on the floor a couple of times in acknowledgement. Eventually the priest was persuaded to sit down, saying, 'It's in a good hour I meet Mistress Mason again. Indeed. I think I have a message for you. You mind you were asking for a Marion Lockhart of this parish, madam?'

'Who's that?' Gil asked. 'The place is full of Lockharts.'

'Joanna's mother,' Alys supplied. 'Go on, sir.'

'Well, after you left St Andrew's kirk yesterday, Isobel Douglas – Isa –'

'Oh, yes.' Alys nodded, smiling. 'A good woman, I think.'

A faint grimace crossed Sir John's broad fair-skinned face. 'Oh, aye, indeed. A valued member of my flock, Isa is. Aye busy about the kirk or my house. Indeed. And yestreen afore Vespers Isa came to me to say she feared she'd sent you on a fool's errand. I think she tellt you Mistress Lockhart's sons were across the river in Lesmahagow?' Alys nodded again. 'Indeed. It seems now she's recalled different. One of them went away into Ayrshire some years ago, and the other moved to Glasgow last Lammas-tide.'

'To Glasgow?' repeated Alys.

'Why ever would he do that?' Gil asked. 'If he'd land to farm in Lesmahagow, what's to take him to Glasgow?'

'He gave up the farm,' said Sir John. 'Isa gave me no sensible idea why, though she said something about birds. Maybe they ate the seed-corn and his crop failed. Indeed. Nor she never said which of the two it was, nor how he would support himself in Glasgow.'

'There's ways enough,' said Gil, 'but he'd need some skill or other.'

'You've contacts in plenty in Glasgow,' said his mother, 'and the burgh's no that big. You should be able to find the man. What was his surname? Brownlie? Do you know his own name?'

'Either Hob or Tammas,' Alys said. 'If I send to my father, he can put that in motion, I suppose. Sir John, I'm grateful for this. I hope you'll pass my thanks to Dame Isa too. Did you come all the way out here just for that? It was most kind of you.'

Sir John blushed like a youth, but admitted, 'No, no, I canny claim it. Indeed. I wished to hear more of this man in the peat-digging, and maybe to get a keek at him if he's yet above ground.'

'Oh, he's above ground,' said Lady Cunningham sardonically. 'Lying coffined in my feed-store wi' half the parish waiting in line to inspect him. You're welcome to a look at him, Sir John.'

The corpse in the feed-store had deteriorated further, though it still smelled only of peat. Preserved far beyond corruption, Gil thought. He could see cracks in the shrunken flesh now, and the skin was beginning to dry out and peel away in places.

'Did you get his finger back, Alan?' he asked. 'And I hope he's lost no more oddments.'

'Aye, it's there.' Alan, standing by with the keys, nodded to a small object folded in linen by the corpse's elbow as if it was a saint's relic. 'I wrapped it up decent.'

Sir John bent over the coffin and uncovered, crossing himself, then laid his free hand cautiously on the shock of red hair and snatched it away.

177

'It's like horsehair,' he said. 'Aye, poor soul. What a death he's met. Slain three times over, as your man said. And have you no idea who he might be?'

'There's a many folk seen him that's offered one name or another,' said Alan, 'but none of them seems to fit, and no two has come up wi' the same name. By rights we ought to have someone at their beads by him,' he admitted, 'and maybe a couple o' candles, but Henry willny have candles in here.'

'Oh, no,' agreed Sir John, with a glance at the sacks of feed. 'Indeed no.'

'My husband thinks he may be a man from an earlier time,' Alys offered.

'Earlier?' The priest looked round at Gil. 'How much earlier, would you say?'

Gil explained his thoughts, aware of the interest of the stable-hands gathered round the door. Sir John replaced his felt hat and listened with care.

'You tell me the peat grows,' he said. 'I never thought of that. I just thought it was aye there. No, I suppose, I've heard the old folk talk of where there was a drowning pool in the moss aforetime, where there's only peat now.'

'That's right,' agreed Gil. 'I've heard the same.'

'And at the bottom of the peat you find logs and the like,' continued Sir John. 'Aye, I agree, now I think on it that could easy be from the time of the Flood.'

'And this man was halfway down the peat,' said Alys.

Gil watched the priest's expression change slowly as his thoughts followed Alys's. He could see the moment when enlightenment struck; the man crossed himself hastily, dragging off his hat again, and bent the knee to the indifferent corpse.

'I must away back to the town,' he said. 'I need to go

178

through the kirk records. There may be something . . .
Indeed.'

He turned to the doorway, and the stable-hands scattered, but the light was cut off. Lady Cunningham paused on the threshold, glanced briefly at the corpse, crossed herself, and held out a set of tablets tied with tape.

'Steenie's returned, Gilbert, with word from Michael. He will be here for supper, and it seems they may have located Murray's bolt-hole. '

'You wrote,' said Gil, handing the little glasses of cordial, 'that you'd a name for one of Murray's drinking friends, and directions to find the fellow.'

'I did,' agreed Michael. He raised his glass in a toast to his godmother, and she smiled and responded. 'Your man reached me at a good moment. I'd found Murray's horse, left standing at Juggling Nick's for weeks, I was just fending off Bessie Dickson's demands for five weeks' livery – which is sheer impudence,' he added, 'for the beast's plainly been working for its keep! Then Steenie arrived wi' your word, and I was able to turn the argument, why had Bessie no sent to his friends, passed the word round those he drinks wi'. But,' he concluded, and took another taste of the bright glassful, 'she claims she couldny.'

'Why not?' asked Alys.

'Seems he mainly drinks wi' this one fellow, name of Andro Syme, fellow much his age that's a forester to Bonnington, and he's not been seen in the town for a few weeks either. I got a description of sorts – ordinary height, ordinary coloured hair, grey eyes. One of the lassies said he was gey handsome but she thought he'd a woman already, he never looked her way.' Michael grinned. 'Bessie had a word or two to say about that.

So I've got the directions to Syme's cottage, down in the gorge below St Kentigern's, but it was too late in the day by then to be starting out after him, let alone waiting for you to catch up with us, Maister Gil.'

'You're telling me this drinking companion hasn't been seen either?' persisted Gil.

'That's right,' Michael agreed. 'Maybe the two of them have gone off together. Gone to sea, gone to England, gone to the Low Countries. Maybe they've both got a lassie in Edinburgh or somewhere.'

'Why would they leave now? Did they leave Juggling Nick's together?'

'Not that Bessie said.' Michael sounded startled. 'I got the idea Murray had simply left his horse wi' her and gone off alone. Syme wasny there.'

'And that was when Bessie last saw Murray? Did you check that?'

'Do you know, I did,' said Michael, with an air of triumph. 'He was back there no so long after he'd been in wi' the two other colliers, looked in and asked for his friend, and went away again. Bessie's not seen him since. And that I'll believe,' he went on, 'for she'd have had the money for his horse's keep off him if he showed his bonnet round the door.'

'You've done well,' said Lady Cunningham in approving tones. Michael glanced at her, his colour deepening in the candlelight, and she smiled at him again. 'And tomorrow you can go to the forester's house.'

'David Fleming does that, Mother,' said Gil. She raised her eyebrows at him. 'Instructs folk to do what they were about to do anyway.'

'Oh, I ask your pardon, dear,' she said with irony.

He grinned at her affectionately, and Alys said, 'How is Sir David, Michael? I think Steenie forgot to ask.'

'Crabbit as a drunkard,' said Michael crisply. 'Flies

into a rage for nothing. Threw his shoes at the laddie that brought his porridge, began abusing me when I wouldny fetch him his pestilent book. Otherwise, I suppose, he's going on well enough. The fever's left him, he's had no more of those twitching fits.'

'I assume your notion of first light is later than mine, Michael,' said Lady Cunningham, 'if the man had his porridge afore you left.'

'I wonder why the rages?' said Alys.

'They're often like that when they're recovering from something,' said her mother-in-law.

'Yes, but this is very soon. It was a severe beating he had.'

'Aye, they're saying that,' said Alan Forrest in the doorway. He bowed to his mistress, who said rather sharply:

'What do you want, man? Is it to the point?'

'Near enough, mistress. I've heard from two folk the day how your man was taken up for dead, Maister Michael,' he said, grinning, 'and one of them tellt me when the funeral was to be. But since they said and all that the young mistress was lying at death's door after she fell from her horse,' he nodded politely at Alys, who stared at him in amazement, 'I wasny concerned.'

'Get to the point, man,' said Lady Egidia.

'Aye, well. It was for Maister Gil. About the mannie in the feed-store.'

'Have you a name for him yet?' Michael asked.

'Not yet,' said Gil. 'John Heriot was here asking the same thing. What is it, Alan?'

'You ken that finger you're so keen to keep by the corp?' Gil nodded. 'Well, I think Jackie Heriot's away wi' it, and its wee bit cloth and all. It's no in the coffin now, and I've threatened the household wi' all sorts since supper and none of them will admit to lifting it.'

* * *

181

'The house should be up this burn somewhere,' said Michael over the rumble of the nearby falls, 'though it wasny clear how far.' He paused in picking his way up the slope among the trees. Behind them his men spread out to trample through the young bracken. 'I'm right glad Mistress Mason stayed behind.'

'She was reluctant,' said Gil, 'but I pressed her to it. We're surely close to finding Murray, and it may be unpleasant. She's ridden up to the Pow Burn instead, to talk about Fleming with Mistress Lithgo.'

He paused to look about him, considering the ground.

They were in a deep hollow of the banks of the Clyde. Not far away the huge waterfall called Corra Linn roared and thundered, but here it was still and somehow oppressive, the trees tall and well-grown but dripping with moss, knee-deep in bracken and ferns just uncurling round the green-and-brown trunks. The spring was well advanced in this sheltered spot; primroses and violets hid among the tree-roots, the hawthorn was in full bloom, the beech trees were leafing out. At the bottom of the hollow a small burn rattled down to join the Clyde. Butterflies flitted, an early bumblebee blundered through a shaft of sunlight. One of the men tripped in a rabbit-hole and cursed, and away above the edge of the valley crows cawed over their nest-building in a stand of elm. *Lef and gras and blosme springes in Averil, I wene*, Gil thought, and gazed round, wondering what was missing. The back of his neck crawled as if he was being watched.

'Fleming!' said Michael as they moved on. 'He's still in a rage this morning. It's not like the man. He's aye full of orders and directions to his inferiors, but in general he crawls like a spaniel with the family – wi' my father and brothers and me – and there he was,

182

frothing like a mad dog because his porridge was over-salted, shouting at me and all.'

'Strange,' said Gil, almost at random. 'I wonder if the beating shook something loose in his head?'

'Seems like it. I hope Mistress Lithgo can help.'

'Are we on the right track here?' Gil asked. He halted again, and waved at the Cauldhope men to stand where they were. 'Bide here,' he said, giving in to his rising sense of unease. 'Let me go ahead. There's too many of us for stealth.'

'You think we need to creep up on him?' Michael turned back to look at him. 'Wi' the linn roaring like that? And no birds to startle?'

That was the missing thing, he acknowledged. There was no birdsong, no flitting wings from tree to tree as one would expect in woodland at this time of year, only the distant crows. He had smelled a fox trail, noted badger droppings, seen more rabbit-holes, so the four-legged creatures were about as well as the insects, but there were no birds where there should be birds in plenty.

'I'm not happy,' he said. 'Something's not right. Bide here, all of you. I'll bark like a dog fox, twice, if I want to call you forward, and come softly.'

Working his way quietly up the hollow on his own, moving from thicket to thicket, senses alert, he turned over Michael's information in his head. If neither Murray nor his drinking-companion had been seen for five weeks, where were they? What would take two young men, one of them wedded to a lovely girl like Joanna, out of their habitual paths for that length of time?

The little valley climbed round to the right. The rumble of the great waterfall was less overwhelming here, but there was still no birdsong in the dappled shade. He paused under an ash tree whose sooty buds

183

were just breaking into green feathers, drew a deep breath, and extended his senses in the way Billy Meikle his father's huntsman had taught him. The place was quiet and still; the crows argued in the distance, the little burn gurgled, the tops of the trees stirred. Scents on the air told him of damp earth and growing things, of the fox again, of the different trees around him. There was an elder tree somewhere, its rank odour unmistakable, and a yew among the hawthorn blossom. The fox had hidden a kill somewhere and forgotten it; he could smell carrion. There was no smell of smoke, or of a human habitation.

Up the valley, something rustled. Unmoving, he stared towards the sound, muscles taut as bowstrings, ears stretched. Another rustle, and the bushes stirred: it sounded like a large creature. Then a branch was pushed aside, a horned head peered out of a thicket, yellow slotted eyes studied him disdainfully. A goat.

It stepped delicately out of the bushes, and another one followed, then a third with a kid at its heels. They inspected him, decided unanimously he was of no use, the first one bleated eloquently and they all turned and made their way up the side of the hollow. He watched them go, and then moved on with caution, thinking hard.

The valley bent again, to the left, and opened out a little. Rounding the curve, he stopped to assess the ground again, and after a moment made out the cottage. It was not in the open by the burn but set back and up a little under the trees, clinging to the slope, the usual low structure of drystone and wattle-and-daub, its thatch of bracken and heather sagging on the beams, its door ajar. Nothing moved. He could smell old peat fires, the midden, the goats, but no smoke rose through the thatch. As he watched, the goats themselves reappeared, tittuped in single file down the valley side and up the other, paused to stare superciliously at him and processed into the house. Behind the door, something scurried.

Another whiff of carrion reached him.

He braced himself, and moved forward carefully, alert for any sign he could read. He did not seem to be on the approach the forester used to his cottage; there had been no trodden way up the little valley, no sign of regular passage, and the track the goats had just followed, down from his right, was broader than their little cloven hooves required and must be the usual access. The yew tree stood beside it, a dark ominous shape in the sunlight.

He crossed the burn where it spread out gurgling into a shallow ford, and stepped on to a cobbled path which led up to the house door. More than one patch of hen-feathers on the stones spoke of the fox's depredations, and the carrion smell was stronger here.

The forester's gear stood around. A handcart, tilted on to its handles, with a rusting pruning-hook leaning across the flat bed. On the ground beside it a ladder and a tangle of hemp rope, a leather helmet, and a long canvas holdall, damp and red-stained. Gil moved cautiously over to look at it. The stains on the bag were dark, rust-red, smelled like rust. He unfastened the buckle and gingerly drew open the mouth of the bag, to find a set of knives and saws, the handles polished by use, the blades patched and pitted and spoiling. One of the saws had fragments of bark caught in its teeth. Andro Syme's tools, lying out in the rain where he had dropped them when he came back from the day's work.

He straightened up, trying to visualize the scene. The forester would have come up the cobbled way from the burn, perhaps manhandling his cart. Or had he gone out without cart and ladder that day? He had reached this point, and something had caused him to drop everything he held and . . .

And what? What had made him leave his tools and prevented him returning to them? Was it fear, surprise, joy? Had he run to meet someone, run to fetch a weapon? Not a weapon, Gil thought, looking down at the rusting blades at his feet. The man had weapons enough to hand. So not fear, then, but surprise: something or someone he had not expected to see. Or perhaps something to do with the goats – the birth of the kid he had seen, or another such crisis. But why had he left his trade here ever since, to be ruined by the rain?

Gil turned and stepped reluctantly up to the house door. Rustling and scurrying sounds greeted him, not all of them due to the goats. There was a tirling-pin set on the wooden jamb. He rattled the ring up and down its twisted iron bar, and said, 'Is anyone at home?'

More sharp scuttlings. Inside the house, one of the goats bleated.

There was a loud, inhuman screech, horrifyingly close. He caught at the door-frame for support as something white sailed over the house roof and down, passed within a handspan of his head and soared up into the trees across the burn.

Heart still hammering, whinger in hand, he swung round to watch it as it furled pale wings, hiding the white inner coverts, and became a familiar gold-brown shape. Round eyes blinked from a shadowed hollow in the branches of the yew tree.

A screech-owl, by daylight.

The smell of carrion was stronger than ever. He waited a moment longer while his heart steadied, then pushed the door wider and stepped into the dark interior of the cottage.

* * *

When Michael and his men appeared in answer to the signal, Gil was sitting on the bench by the house door, beads in hand, watching the goats stripping the leaves on a young beech. He looked up as they rounded the turn of the valley, and Michael's first words died on his lips.

'What is it, man?' he said, staring. 'You look as if you'd been to Hell and back.'

'Near enough,' said Gil. He rose and stowed his beads in his purse, and the newcomers splashed across the ford, the men exclaiming in disgust as the smell reached them. 'It's not a bonnie sight. The most of you can wait outside, but I want someone to study it along wi' me, in case I miss sign that might tell us what happened, for it's not very clear. Whoever he is he'll need a strong stomach.'

Michael shrugged. 'I'll not ask the lads to do aught I'd not do myself. Will I . . .?'

'He's still in there, is he?' asked one of the Cauldhope men, the back of his hand across his nose. 'Or is the pig dead? It stinks like the Devil's midden.'

'No pig,' said Gil. 'One of the goats has died, likely while it was kidding, but that's not the worst of it.' Another of the men bent and threw a stone as he spoke, and something rustled off into the undergrowth at the gable of the house. 'There are rats.'

'Should we no raise the hue and cry?' asked the man who had spoken already.

'Whoever did this is long out of reach,' said Gil. The owl in the tree screeched as if in mockery, and several of the men glanced up and crossed themselves. 'I want a look at the scene with another witness first. We can go up to Bonnington after that.'

Michael swallowed hard and braced his shoulders.

'Well,' he said. 'Shall we . . .?'

187

He followed Gil across the doorsill and stepped aside to let the light in. Gil watched his face as he stared round, seeing him take in the detail he himself had noted. By the cold hearth in the centre of the room lay an iron cooking-pot, on its side and empty. Beyond the hearth a carved chair and a stool were set to a small table, on which lay empty dishes, two knives and spoons, an overturned beaker. The light gleamed on a flat silver flask. Another beaker lay on the chair as if it had rolled there, and a glazed pottery bottle was overturned on the floor beside a muddle of small bones.

'A meal,' said Michael. 'For two. So has Murray been here?'

'He came here,' agreed Gil. 'Where's the food? The scraps, the food in the pot?'

'The rats must have got it.' Michael looked round again. 'And everything else they could get into. Butter dish, cheese crock, the flitch over the fire. Filthy creatures.'

'So I thought,' agreed Gil. 'What else can you see?'

'Where's our man?' Michael peered into the shadows. 'Is he in here? Along the end wi' the goat?'

'Not so far as that.' Gil looked deliberately at the solid box of the bed which separated the living end of the house from the animals' quarters. Michael stepped forward cautiously, and recoiled with an exclamation of horror as he made out what lay there.

'Christ aid!' he said, crossing himself. And then, looking closer, 'Oh, Christ and Our Lady save us, there's two of them.' He turned to Gil, sudden tears glittering at his eyes in the dim light. 'Is it Murray and his leman, dead in the one moment? Has Syme slain them and run to Edinburgh?'

'I don't think so,' said Gil in sympathy. His first reaction had also been pity, though it had not moved him quite to tears. 'Look closer, would you, if you can bear it.'

Michael took a hesitant step nearer, wadding his handkerchief over his nose, and studied what was visible. After a moment he drew back.

'It needs a light of some sort,' he said. 'That's Murray in at the wall, right enough, is it no? You can see the red hair still clinging to . . . to . . .'

'Yes,' agreed Gil. 'I think that's our man, right enough.' He came to stand beside Michael and looked at the bed, the back of his hand to his nose.

Over a month had passed since the two bodies there were warm and live; what the rats, the insects, the fox and time itself had left, tattered and shrunken flesh and naked bones, was still recognizable as human, but little more than that. Two skulls with a little skin still attached, the eye sockets dark and empty, stared into the shadows. As Michael had said, one was identifiable by the hanks of red hair still attached to the taut yellow scalp, though neither Joanna nor anyone else would recognize the face. Two sets of shoulder-bones, two ribcages were tilted inwards as if the lovers had been talking, or as if, Gil thought with another surge of pity, they had realized what was happening and turned to each other for reassurance in the last moments. A linen sheet was under them, and another was drawn over them nearly to waist level, both stained beyond redemption. Brownish skin and drying sinews clung over the joints, keeping the limbs articulated, and though the rats had made off with the fingers and part of the hand, one could still make out the tenderness in the gesture with which the red-haired corpse had laid one arm over the broad shoulders of his bedfellow.

'But this one,' said Michael. 'This is a man and all. The hair's shorter than mine, look at those shoulders.

189

It's got no paps. It's a man!' He turned to Gil in astonishment and horror. 'It's two men. Maister Gil, is that his leman? The forester?'

'I think it must be,' agreed Gil.

'You mean we've gone through all this for a pair of kything kitterel –' He broke off, still staring at Gil over the wadded handkerchief. 'And him a married man, too!'

'Every one of us deserves time for amendment of life,' said Gil, noting this reaction with interest. So there's still innocence abroad, he thought. Or did I simply learn far more in Paris than I was sent for? 'Not to mention,' he added, 'that we need to work out what happened here. How do you read it, Michael?'

'Some things there's no amending,' said Michael. He drew back from the bed, and gazed round again. 'They've died in the same moment,' he hazarded, 'or near it.'

'We canny tell that,' said Gil. 'Near it, I'll allow.'

'And which of them was the catamite?' wondered Michael. 'A collier and a forester – how could either one of them . . .?'

'No way to tell,' said Gil.

'Perhaps they took it in turns,' speculated Michael with distaste.

It was, Gil felt, a matter for the priests to worry about; there was no way to guess from the way the bodies were disposed which man had played the woman's part, endangering his immortal soul and inviting the opprobrium which few would apply to his partner. His concern was more practical: how had the two men died?

'Start at the beginning. Did you have time to discern aught outside, afore I dragged you in here?'

Michael paused to consider. 'The forester's cart's

standing there. Likely he came home from his day's work to find this one here.'

'So I thought,' agreed Gil. 'His knives are lying out there in his scrip, rusting with the rain where he dropped them.'

Michael shut his eyes, apparently to visualize something the better.

'He came home, and his nancy was here waiting for him. They came into the house, and had a meal. They went into the bed – where's their clothes?' he asked, opening his eyes.

'Yonder by the bed-foot, all in the one tangle.' Gil nodded at the shadows. 'I think the goats have been at them. You know the way they'll eat linen.'

'St Peter's bones! Where are the brutes, anyway? I canny abide goats, the way they leer at you.'

As if on a cue, small hooves clipped on the cobbles and the leader of the little flock peered in at the open door. Michael waved his arms and shouted, and the creature gave him a look of ineffable contempt, turned and pattered away. Her companions followed her, the kid bleating anxiously for its mother.

'Then what?' prompted Gil.

Michael, recalled to his task, clamped his handkerchief over his nose, closed his eyes again, and offered indistinctly, 'Then they died. Both together, or one after the other, as you please.'

'O lusty gallands gay,' Gil quoted, 'full laichly thus sall ly thy lusty heid. But why? Why would two grown men fall dead in an afternoon?'

'Afternoon?'

'I'd say they bedded well before nightfall,' Gil observed. 'If it was near dark Syme would have seen to his beasts, surely, milked the goats and shut the hens in, rather than have to rise and fetch them in later.'

191

'I see what you mean.' Michael opened his eyes and looked longingly at the door. 'Can we go outside? I canny breathe in here. You must have a right strong stomach, Maister Gil.'

'We'll stand by the doorway. There's still things to learn here. Can you jalouse why two men should meet their end in the one moment?'

'A judgement on their unnatural ways.'

'What, to *caus all men fra wicket vycis fle*. Aye, possibly, but I'm no so sure it works like that,' Gil said wryly. 'Come on, you're an educated man, and you learned the hunt the same as I did. What can you see, or not see?'

'Was it maybe some sickness? Christ aid, it's foul enough in here now to infect the Host of Scotland. I hope we're no dead by morning ourselves.'

'Do you see sign of sickness? Has either man's belly been afflicted, would you say? The jordan's there below the bed,' he pointed into the shadows, 'but it hadny been used.'

'No, there's no sign, but the rats might have got the traces.'

'If one of them sickened first, the other would have got him to bed. I see only that they bedded together. I think when they went into the bed they were hale.'

'It's a judgement, then, like I said.'

'Think, Michael. Two men, hale when they ate their supper, both dead or too far gone to rise afore it was dark. What does that suggest to you?'

'If it's no a judgement from Heaven, is it poison?'

'So I think.' Gil relaxed. 'I think they were poisoned.'

'Poisoned.' Michael gazed round the sparse, shadowy interior of the cottage, as if looking for a culprit. 'Who by, then? Was it deliberate, or was the supper bad? Is there any ill going about that would slay two men in that time? Or was it maybe a pact atween them two?'

'What, a pact to die together? I'll admit I never thought of that.' Gil frowned, staring into the shadows beyond the bed. 'If it was, it was a sudden idea, for Murray gave no sign at the coaltown or to the two sinkers that he'd not return from this trip. I suppose it could have been solely Syme's doing, a way to keep his leman with him for ever.'

'What a wickedness!' said Michael through the handkerchief. 'Though I'd believe anything of such an unnatural –'

'Wickedness? More than the sin it involves?'

'It's selfish. It's thinking more of yourself than your leman. Would you slay Alys – Mistress Mason – if you couldny dwell wi' her as you wished?'

'No,' admitted Gil, 'and I take nor would you. But the circumstances are different. I've no notion what I'd do if I'd stood in Murray's place, or Syme's.'

'Mine are no so different,' said Michael quietly. 'Nobody's like to be disgusted that Tib and I love one another, but we're kept apart by our families, wi' no great hopes of reunion. Just the same, I'd never look for her to die wi' me, like folk in a silly romance.'

Gil paused for a moment to take in this statement, and gripped the younger man's shoulder with a sympathetic hand. Michael threw him a startled, hesitant smile from behind the handkerchief, and Gil in some embarrassment returned to the subject at issue.

'Whether it was a pact or no, we need to determine what slew them. Then we might learn whose doing it was. Can you see aught to the purpose?'

They both surveyed the scene before them. Outside the men gossiped uneasily beyond the gurgling burn, the crows croaked in the treetops, a goat bleated. Here in the shadows nothing stirred, but something seemed to nudge at Gil's mind, a movement just out of sight, a whisper just below hearing. What was it telling him?

'There's the dead rats,' Michael said suddenly. 'What slew that pair of kitterels maybe slew the rats as well. Could that be it?'

'The rats.' Yes, that was it. Gil stepped carefully round the cold peats on the hearth and looked down at the scatter of little bones. There were two, no, three rat skulls, a powder of tiny teeth, some tatters of skin. 'And the flask. I admit the flask has been worrying me. It's a thing out of place.'

'I've heard you say that sort of thing afore,' observed Michael. 'You think it was poison in the flask that slew the rats? Or maybe in that wee jug, where the bones are? Why is it on the floor, anyway?'

'Circumstantial,' said Gil, 'but persuasive.' Michael blinked at the long words. 'Aye, it looks very much as if flask and bottle fell over, the bottle rolled on to the floor, and the rats drank whatever spilled. But was it that they died of, and which was it in, flask or bottle? Or was it something in the food on the table?'

'Is there a way to find out?' Michael asked.

Gil shrugged. 'Prayer,' he offered. The younger man grunted, with what Gil felt to be a healthy show of scepticism. 'And questioning folk, I suppose. Alys might know something to the purpose.'

'Does she know everything?' asked Michael, in genuine enquiry.

Gil smiled, but said only, 'The flask must be the one Murray was given just before he left the Pow Burn.'

'I wondered about that. It's a valuable thing for either of these two to have owned. Who gave him it? What was in it?'

'Mistress Weir, according to Joanna.' Gil gazed down at the object. 'There was cordial in it, to drink her health on her birthday, so Joanna told my wife.'

'St Peter's bones! So what was really in it, do you suppose? Was it the old woman who poisoned them, then?'

'Or Joanna, who must have handled the thing, or young Bel when she brought it to Joanna, or even her sister, or certainly her grandam – it could have been any of the folk up there save young Crombie, who was in Glasgow at the time. Or, I suppose, anyone who knew the flask was there, at the places they called on the way, or at Juggling Nick's.'

Michael whistled.

'All the folk at the heugh had reason enough, by what we've learned so far,' he admitted. 'Could it have been a conspiracy, then? All of them plotting together?'

'It could. There are many possibilities.'

'Or maybe someone at Nick's was jealous. What do you suppose they used?'

'I've no notion what it was, or what it was in either.' Gil stirred the small bones with his toe. 'And I hope Alys can help me, for we can hardly ask the likeliest to know hereabouts.'

Michael made a questioning noise. Gil bent to lift flask and bottle, and sniffed cautiously at each. The bottle had clearly held usquebae, but on the flask there was a faint smell of old grape spirits, a bitter whiff of something like his mother's cough syrup, a herbal smell. Had Alys mentioned elderberries? He reached for the stopper of the flask where it lay on the table, flakes of wax still clinging to it, and stowed all three items in his purse with care.

'Mistress Lithgo, that everyone calls a good woman,' he said as he fastened the strings, 'is as likely as any of them to have done it, and if she didny, she likely supplied the stuff.'

Chapter Nine

The Hamiltons' steward at Bonnington, a Hamilton himself, was quite unable to take it all in.

'Two dead, you say?' he repeated anxiously, as if the number might have changed since they first told him. 'And lying as long amid the wild beasts – dreadful, dreadful. I canny credit it. You'll take another stoup of this ale, sirs, it's good to clear the throat and settle an uneasy wame.' He poured generously, and Michael leaned forward to take his. He was still a pearly green-ish colour, and had hardly spoken since they left the forester's cottage and its dismal lodgers.

'Two dead,' Gil confirmed.

John Hamilton shook his head. 'And to learn such a thing of Andro, the bonnie lad, the good worker he's aye been. Oh, maister, it's hard to credit, so it is. And taking a collier lad for his catamite and all – dreadful, dreadful! Are ye certain it's Andro?'

'It seems most likely,' said Gil. 'The body's well past knowing, as you'll imagine, but the height and the colour of the hair are right and it's hard to see who else it might be, in the man's own house. When did you see him last?'

'Likely at the quarter-day,' said Hamilton, shaking his head again. 'I canny think. For such a thing to happen on our land, and me not know it! But he's aye been a fellow that kept himself away from the house,' he

196

added. 'Good at his work, he is, for all he's no from hereabouts. Came to us from Ayrshire, he did. So what wi' having no kin in the neighbourhood, and the way his work takes him all across the place, you'll understand, maister, we seldom set eyes on him, and times we lend him out to other landholders forbye. Sir James your father was asking me afore he went to Stirling, Maister Michael, about getting a laddie taught his craft by working wi' Andro. And he's aye preferred to go home to his own roof-tree and get his own supper, rather than come up to eat wi' the household.'

'Well, it's a good couple of mile from here to the cottage, which is reason enough for that,' said Gil. 'So you think you saw him at the quarter-day. That would be just over four weeks since. Did he collect his quarter's fee? What was it?'

'A wee bit coin and a sack of meal,' supplied the steward promptly. 'I can check the accounts, maister, if you'd wish it. I still canny credit this. Such a bonnie lad, all the lassies about the house has a notion to him. And poisoned, ye said? Was it an accident? A bad mushroom, maybe? These workers on the land often have a liking for mushrooms, the unchancy things, and it would be a judgement on the two of them –'

'I don't know,' said Gil. 'The rats and the beasts had cleared the cooking-pot and never suffered from it, though it's a good thought, Maister Hamilton. I'd say it's been a deliberate poisoning, and in something they drank, though it's possible it was meant for the other man rather than Syme.'

'For the collier? Oh, what a wickedness!' Hamilton crossed himself. 'Who would do such a thing, to slay a man in that way and never care who else it took wi' him?'

Gil nodded, and took another pull at his ale. 'A wicked deed, maister. Can you tell me if the forester had enemies? Any of the lassies feel slighted, or their men maybe jealous?'

'What, you think it was my household? Why would anyone here wish to slay the collier? He doesny come to this house, we get our coals across the river in Cadzow parish, from my maister's own coal-heugh.'

'I agree, if it was meant for the collier, it's no more likely to be anyone here than elsewhere,' agreed Gil in placating tones, 'but if it was meant for Syme, it could well have been one of your household.'

'Oh.' Hamilton threw him an uncertain look, and peered into the ale-jug. 'I've no a notion. I wouldny say any of our folk would poison a man. They're no saints,' he qualified, 'we get squabbles and fists thrown and hair-pullings same as any household ye ever kent, but to procure poison and minister it in secret like that, well, I wouldny say so, maister.' He set the jug back on the table before him, where it clunked emptily. 'Now, I've bidden the men get a couple hurdles and a bolt of canvas, and lay them on the big cart, but how we get that down to the forester's house is more than I can tell. We'll maybe need to use his own handcart to bring him out. And then I suppose the Provost or the Sheriff will want to call a quest on them and raise the hue and cry, and all. Oh, my, what a thing to happen on my maister's lands!'

'It might be wiser to coffin them afore you move them,' said Gil doubtfully. 'If you've the stomach for it, you'd best come down yourself and look at the state they're in.'

'Oh, I'll do that, sir.' Hamilton rose. 'Syme's our man whatever his sins, I'll see to his needs.'

'And the accounts,' Gil prompted. 'Maybe you could check those afore we leave, make certain of whether Syme collected his fee at the quarter.'

'Oh, aye, indeed!' The steward bustled to the door of

his chamber and opened it. 'Will! Where's Will Thomson? Send to him I want the last quarter's account.'

Someone answered distantly, and he plunged out into the next chamber with a brief word of apology. Michael finished his beaker of ale and said, 'Will you need me back at the cottage?'

'We left two of your men there,' Gil reminded him. 'No need to enter the place. Or you could ride into Lanark for me and get a word with the Provost. I think my mother said Archie Hamilton the Sheriff was away just now, so it goes rightly to the Provost as his depute.'

'I'll do that, and wait for you at Juggling Nick's. I'd as soon not go back to the forester's place. The whole clearing was fit to turn your wame,' Michael admitted. 'What wi' that great owl sitting in the yew tree watching the house. I was near enough taking a stone to it, save that my head was whirling by the time we came away.' He paused, and grimaced resignedly. 'Then I'll need to get up to the Pow Burn, to break it to them. I take it you'd wish to be present?'

'I do,' agreed Gil, once more aware of being favourably impressed by his sister's seducer. 'I have things to ask them.'

Maister Hamilton hurried back into the chamber, a stout black-gowned clerk following him with a leather-bound roll of parchment open in his hands.

'Here's a thing, Maister Cunningham!' the steward exclaimed. 'Syme never came for his fee at Lady Day. Will here has it all writ down clear as day, he can show you in a moment.'

'All writ down,' confirmed his clerk in a squeaky voice. 'All but four of the outside men had their fee on the quarter-day itself, and the remaining three we paid out on the Tuesday following, when maister steward here came back from Edinburgh. But Andro Syme's never been up to the house.' He ran his finger down the lines of crabbed writing. 'And to tell truth, sir, it had slipped my mind, or I'd ha' been out to his place to mind him o't myself. It makes the accounts untidy, you'll understand, sir, when a man's fee gets left lying like that.'

'It does,' agreed Gil. 'But in this case I think we'll have to forgive Syme. I think he was dead afore Lady Day.' Both the Bonnington men stared at him, open-mouthed. 'The last time the other fellow was seen alive was March twentieth. I think they were both dead by sunset that day.'

'They were no further help at Juggling Nick's?' said Michael.

'Only in the negative,' said Gil. 'So far as Bessie or any other could recall, Murray was just as usual the last time they saw him. He left his horse and said nothing to the stableman or anyone else that suggested he wouldn't be back for it in a week as usual.'

'That's much what she said to me when I first tracked the beast there,' agreed Michael. He looked about him, and turned his horse off the road on to a narrow stony track. Gil followed, and the two Cauldhope men at their backs clattered after them. 'This will take us to the Pow Burn. Maister Lockhart the Provost was no great help either. I had to be firm about it being murder before he'd agree to call a quest. Seemed to feel it was either Bonnington's problem or Carluke's, and none of his.'

Gil grunted. They rode in silence for a while, the pee-wits calling above them, a lark's song carrying in shreds on the wind. Gil found himself thinking of the way Beatrice Lithgo had appeared over the flank of this same hillside among the cottars of Thorn, her hands bound, cap askew, bearing herself with dignity and composure. And there were the other Crombie women: Joanna, sweet and lovely, troubled and fearful; Phemie full of angry intelligence, her sister overflowing with words she could not speak. And Arbella Weir, as dignified as her daughter-in-law, her transcendent pride in the coal-heugh glowing in her blue eyes. One of these, most likely, had poisoned Thomas Murray. But why?

'I still don't see why he was killed,' said Michael suddenly. Gil recalled himself to his surroundings, and made a questioning sound. 'Murray,' Michael qualified unnecessarily. 'He was good at his trade, he brought money in to the coal-heugh, he was no worse a husband than many you hear about, he –'

'He quarrelled with Mistress Weir,' Gil pointed out. 'He was difficult to work with, kept himself superior to the men. Joanna feared his sharp tongue, it seems he's free with his hands among the women, he had slighted Phemie and made fun of the younger one.'

'Are those reasons to kill someone?'

'I'm learning,' Gil said, 'that people will kill for very strange reasons.'

'But does anyone gain by his death?' Michael persisted. 'I've felt angry enough to slay someone if I'd only had a knife in my hand, who hasny? But cold poison, ministered in secret like this, that's a different matter altogether, and you'd surely need to be sure of a great gain to plan and carry out such a thing. Or was it vengeance? Did his wife – Joanna – did she guess what he was?'

'Those are things I'll have to find out.' Gil nodded at the muddle of buildings coming into view over the flank of the hill. 'I've learned a lot about the coal-heugh folk and their business, I may already have the answer in my hand, but I'll have to ask more questions before I can be sure.'

'They've seen us,' said Michael after a moment.

'They have,' Gil agreed, studying the group of women gathering at the near corner of the house by the stillroom pent. He had picked out Alys immediately, in her light-coloured riding-dress. Beside her Beatrice Lithgo and her elder daughter were easily identified; Joanna's white apron was conspicuous, the household servants were just joining them from the outlying kitchen building. The kitchen must be empty, he thought. I hope the supper doesn't burn.

'This will be difficult,' Michael said grimly.

'I think they know already,' said Gil. 'Alys must have said something.'

Under the gaze of many eyes, they rode down the track to the house, and dismounted. Michael handed his reins to one of his men, stepped forward, removed his hat, swallowed once, and said, 'Is Crombie no here?'

'He rode out to Forth this morning,' said Beatrice Lithgo. 'He's no back yet. Have you aught to tell us, Maister Michael?'

Michael nodded. 'Mistress Brownlie?' he said. Round the corner of the house Jamesie Meikle appeared at a run, then checked on the edge of the group and stood tensely, his gaze fixed on Joanna, who floated forward almost as if she was sleepwalking.

'What is it?' she said, on a gasp. 'What do you have to tell me?'

'Mistress Brownlie, I believe we've found your husband,' said Michael awkwardly.

She stared at him, all the colour leaving her face. 'Is he – is he –?'

'I believe Thomas Murray is dead,' he said, more gently. 'We've found the corp of a red-haired man, dead since about the quarter-day.'

She made a little whimpering noise, and put her hands up as if to push the words away. Gil looked

202

beyond her and caught Alys's eye; they both started towards her, but it was Jamesie Meikle's arms which were just in time to receive her slender form as she wilted and fell, boneless as a hank of wool.

'You wee fool!' he spat at Michael. 'To break it that way!' He gathered her up, and swung away from them towards the exclaiming women.

'Aye, bring her in the house, Jamesie,' said Beatrice Lithgo from among the group. 'You'll come within, maisters, I hope,' she added with her usual faint irony, and turned to lead the way round the corner of the building. Alys touched Gil's hand, gave him a quick smile, and hurried after the others. Phemie, left behind, looked from Gil to Michael.

'Is he really dead?' she demanded. 'You're sure of it?'

'As sure as you can be of a five-week-old corp,' said Gil.

'His clothes? His knife? What about his hand?' She demonstrated the shortened fingers.

'All the evidence we've got suggests it's Thomas Murray.'

She drew a deep breath, and stared at the sky, her eyes glittering.

'I'm glad,' she declared. 'I'm right glad of it!'

'Might we go in the house, as your mother bade us?'

Phemie turned that suspiciously bright stare on him.

'Oh – I suppose,' she said grudgingly after a moment. 'Come round to the door. And your men, and the horses.'

Within Joanna's own apartment there was disorder and confusion. Joanna herself was laid on the bed, Jamesie Meikle standing grimly by her pillow. Beatrice was bent over her, and Alys was directing several women who ran to and fro exclaiming, their wooden-soled shoes clattering on the floorboards. As Gil entered behind Phemie, two of the younger maid-servants began a ritual-sounding wailing in a corner. Phemie dealt with this sharply, ordering them to move the cushioned bench from the bed-foot to the window and then be off to the kitchen, to fetch some refreshment for the guests and see to the two Cauldhope men.

'You might as well be seated, maisters,' she said, pointing to the bench. 'There'll be nobody but me to talk to you till Joanna's back in her right mind, seeing my dear brother's no returned from whatever mischief he's got up to.'

'I'll be happy to talk to you,' said Gil, while Michael stared anxiously at Joanna. 'But where is your grandmother?'

'Resting, most like,' said Phemie indifferently. 'She rests a lot now. She's spent a lot of time sleeping this past week. Bel's set by her wi' her spinning, I've no doubt.' She sat down, looking from one to the other of them. 'Is he really dead? Where? How? What happened? And why,' she added, the idea obviously only now occurring to her, 'has it taken this long to find him, if he's near five week dead? He must ha' been well hid.'

'I'll go over all that when Joanna can hear me,' said Gil. She looked at Michael, whose expression was giving away more than he realized, and nodded reluctantly. 'But I need to ask all of you more questions about the last time you saw the man. Can you mind what order things happened the day he left here?'

'What, after this time? Why d'you need to know?' Her gaze sharpened. 'Was it no a natural death, then?'

'Try,' said Gil, ignoring this. 'Cast your mind back.'

She considered him briefly, then shrugged. 'We broke our fast as usual, I suppose, him and Joanna in here, the rest of us in the other great chamber, the one where we sat the first time you were in this house.' Gil nodded. 'There would be porridge and bannocks and small ale, the way there always is. Then the horses were brought round, and the Paterson lads wi' them.' She paused, thinking. 'Then Murray would have come through the house and spoke to Arbella, looking for any last instruction she had for him. Aye, that's right. And she bade him mind her birthday.'

'What did he say to that?'

Phemie curled her lip. 'He said something like, *Oh, I'll not forget, madam. It would be a great feast wherever I was.*'

'Did you see the flask she gave him?'

'Flask?' said Phemie blankly. 'She wouldny give him the time of day, save it was in his contract of labour.'

'Did she have any other instructions for him?'

'None that I recall. Then he said farewell to Joanna, and we all went out to the horses, and Arbella gave them her blessing the way she does, and they rode off.'

'And all this was just as usual?'

'It was. Even the way he said farewell to her.' Phemie jerked her head at the bed, where Joanna was beginning to stir.

'How was that? What was usual about it?'

Phemie hesitated, apparently at a loss.

'Just the way he spoke. And the way she backed off as if he'd struck her. She's a poor thing,' she said quietly, but her mother looked round at the words.

'Phemie, if Maister Cunningham's finished with you, you may go and tell your grandmother what's to do here.'

'I suppose,' she said ungraciously. 'Since she's clearly no jaloused it for herself.'

'Phemie!'

By the time Arbella Weir entered the chamber, supported by a granddaughter at each elbow, Joanna was sitting up, sobbing quietly and sipping at the omnipresent cordial, her beads clutched in her other hand. *A woman sate weeping, with favour in her face far passing*

205

my reson, Gil thought, looking at her across the chamber. Beatrice was still at her side, but the women had been dismissed to the kitchen, and had gone with some regret, until one of them had recalled that Michael's men would be there with all the information one could wish for. Jamesie Meikle stood by the head of the bed, as still as a stone evangelist in a niche, and stared at Joanna. Alys had come to sit at Gil's side; he found her very presence comforting, and the warm pressure of her arm tucked into his seemed to clear his head.

'Oh, my poor lassie,' said Arbella in the doorway. She paused, took her stick from Bel and made her way to the bedside. 'The troubles we women have. And what an end to all your waiting, my wee pet.'

'Oh, Mother!' Joanna wailed, and dropped the beads to reach out to her. 'I never thought he was dead!'

'My poor lassie,' said Arbella again. She gathered Joanna into a loving embrace, and said over her bent head, 'And what are you about, Jamesie Meikle, here in Mistress Brownlie's chamber?'

'I'm here to watch over her interest,' he said quietly. Neither his stance nor his expression altered, but it was very clear he would not be moved. Arbella looked at him narrowly, but making no further attempt to discuss the matter she let go of Joanna, patted her hand and turned away to address the guests where they stood waiting for her.

'It's a great courtesy, Maister Cunningham, Maister Michael, to come up here to break the word to us. I take it right kindly, sirs. Phemie, have they never been offered a refreshment?' Phemie's sharp, defensive reply did not obscure Michael's stammered answer. He hastily set a backstool for her as she made her way towards them, but she paused and gestured at the door. 'Will you come into the other chamber and tell me how the man met his end? I hope he was cared for and shriven?'

'They said they found – they found his corp,' said Joanna from the bed, and sniffled again. Beatrice put a comforting hand on her shoulder, but Jamesie Meikle stood unmoving beside her pillow. 'Does that mean he's never buried yet?'

'I'd sooner we stayed here,' said Gil firmly. 'Mistress Brownlie needs to hear it, and I have questions for all of you.'

'My good-daughter would be best left wi' her grief,' Arbella countered.

'No, Mother,' said Joanna, composing herself with difficulty. 'I must hear it. I must hear what's come to Thomas. I'll not be easy till I know.'

She may not be very easy once she does know, thought Gil, and then, wryly, But not knowing is always worse. Beside him Alys looked anxiously up at his face.

'Very well,' said Arbella, and seated herself. They all sat down likewise, and she studied their faces, turning her head to look from Michael to Gil and back. 'Tell us, then. What's come to my grieve? How did he die, and where?'

Michael swallowed hard again.

'We tracked him,' he said, 'to the house of the man he drinks wi' when he's in Lanark, and when we came there we found the two of them dead.'

'Two of them?' repeated Alys.

'Humph!' said Arbella. 'The man he drinks wi'? Was he no about my business, then?'

'No at his death, madam.' Michael glanced at Gil, and went on hesitantly, 'It's likely they've been dead these five weeks. We're no certain yet how they died, but it seems as if it was quick, as if they'd barely time to guess what was coming.'

207

'So there was none witnessed it?' said Beatrice Lithgo, seated now by Joanna's bedside, Bel standing at her shoulder.

'None witnessed it,' Gil confirmed.

'But what took him to this man's house?' asked Joanna wonderingly. 'He was about his round, he had the fees to gather. Why was he drinking in Lanark?' She turned her numbed gaze on Alys. 'What did you say earlier, mistress? Just that they'd found a man that might ken where Thomas was gone?'

'That was all I knew then. This is the first I've heard of the two deaths,' said Alys gently.

Beatrice studied her for a moment, then nodded. 'And it wasn't a fight between them two?' she said to Gil. 'Was it some sickness? Had they vomited, purged, bled at the mouth? How were they lying? Where were they found?'

'Beatrice, my dear,' said Arbella, turning to her daughter-in-law, 'not in front of your lassies.'

'My lassies are herb-wise already,' said Beatrice. 'They have to learn. What can you tell us, sir?'

Arbella considered her briefly, then looked at Michael, who had fallen silent.

'Aye, sir, what can you tell us? In particular, as my poor daughter says, what took him to this man's house? In Lanark, is it? Had he fetched the fees from the town afore he was struck down? Lockhart the Provost, four merks for the quarter, and George Wishart two merks and five groats. It should be wi' his corp, Maister Michael.'

Michael stared at her, taken aback, and turned to Gil.

'It may be with the rest of the coin,' Gil suggested. 'When that comes back from Forth you can find out.'

'Raffie went to fetch it this morning,' Beatrice observed.

'Aye, and he's no back yet,' said Phemie tartly from her place by the window.

Michael spread his hands. 'I've no knowledge of the coin, madam, other than what we've already told you.'

'Very well.' Arbella struck the floor with her stick. 'Proceed, sir. Tell us what you came to let us know. What were these two doing when they were stricken? Were they at a meal, or an evening's drinking?'

'They were abed,' blurted Michael, going scarlet.

'Lying quite easy,' Gil interposed. He felt Alys tense at his side, and wondered what she had detected from his attitude. 'Whatever came to your man, it was quick. As to your questions,' he went on, looking at Beatrice, 'we saw no evidence that they had bled or purged, or suffered in any way.'

'So he was taken in the night, and quickly,' said Joanna, as if it gave her some comfort.

'M'hm,' said Beatrice.

'But why was he never found till now?' demanded Arbella, a crackle in her voice. 'Did this other fellow's kin or friends not go near him?'

'Aye,' said Phemie. 'If they were lying in the midst of Lanark town five weeks, you'd think someone would have noticed them afore this.'

Arbella turned her head and glanced sharply at her, the blue eyes bright under the wired peak of her black veil.

'You put yourself forward too much, Phemie my pet. Just the same she's right, maisters. How were they not noticed?'

'Syme – the other fellow – dwelt apart,' Michael said. 'Not in Lanark at all. His house is down by the river away from anywhere else.'

'But what was Thomas doing there?' asked Joanna. 'I don't understand!'

'We know he drank with Syme,' said Gil. 'I assume he'd gone there to see his friend, and they were both struck down at the one time.'

He was aware that Beatrice Lithgo considered him thoughtfully at this statement, without speaking. Beside him, Alys sat alert, watching the faces. He looked round at them all himself. It felt like a game of Tarocco, in which he was not entirely certain how many of the people in the room were in the game or even what cards were in his own hand.

'Will you come away ben now, maisters?' said Arbella decisively, preparing to get to her feet. 'My dear lassie has learned enough for this present, we should leave her alone for a wee space and I need to hear what's to do next.'

'No, Mother, that's my part,' said Joanna, with another flash of that independence. 'I'm his wife. His widow, Our Lady protect him,' she corrected herself, her pretty mouth twisting, and crossed herself. 'It's my place to see to his burial.' She drew a deep breath, and said to Gil, 'Is there a joiner in Lanark town would coffin him, maister?'

'Never forget,' said Jamesie Meikle, breaking a long silence, 'never forget you've friends who'll support you in that.'

She turned her head to meet his gaze. Gil could not see her expression, for the disordered folds of her headdress, but he saw Jamesie's face, and thought that for the span of two breaths or three there might as well have been nobody else in the chamber.

'Someone's coming,' said Phemie, staring out of the window. 'There's three – no, four horses coming down the track.'

'This is no hour for visitors,' said Beatrice decisively. She rose and made for the door. 'I'll take them aside, will I, madam?'

'It's no visitors,' reported Phemie, still staring. They could all hear the hoofbeats now. 'It's that fool Fleming and three more of your men, Maister Michael.'

'Fleming?' repeated Michael in disbelief. He twisted to peer through the wriggling glass panes. Sweet St Giles, thought Gil, and I had the trap near laid. 'It is, too. St Peter's bones, what brings him here? He was lying sick, the last I saw of him.'

There was a sudden movement, and a door banged. Gil looked round, to find that Jamesie Meikle had vanished, and the door at the far side of the chamber, its latch not caught, was swinging open again.

'He must have gone to call out the men,' said Alys softly in French. 'I think it wise.'

Gil nodded, and rose to his feet, saying to Arbella, 'Madam, I think you should receive Fleming in the other chamber, if you receive him at all.'

'Surely he's come here as our priest?' said Joanna. She was recovering rapidly from her swooning-fit, and now got cautiously off the bed and began fumbling at the laces of her gown which Beatrice had loosened to revive her. Bel, still at the bedside, turned to help her. 'That's kind in him. I'd be right glad to speak wi' a priest.'

'I'm no so certain,' said Michael, who had risen when Gil did. He bowed briefly to Arbella. 'I'll go out and forestall him, madam, if you'll permit it.'

'You're all full of directions to me,' said Arbella in a caustic tone she had not used before. 'I'll order matters in my own house, maisters, and if Sir David has come here wi' spiritual comfort for us, I'll receive him in here if I —'

There were raised voices, out on the cobbled area before the door. Michael turned on his heel with an apologetic glance at Arbella, and slipped out of the room. Looking through the glass, Gil saw him emerge

211

from the house to confront Jamesie Meikle and a group of muddy men armed with mells and other implements. He appeared to be reasoning with them.

'Stay with Joanna,' he said to Alys in French, and went out to join the argument, passing Beatrice Lithgo who stood quietly in the hall. She smiled thinly at him, but did not speak. As he reached the outer doorway, Michael was saying:

'I'll speak to Fleming first, Meikle. He's my man, he must answer to me.'

'Then you'd best go up and meet him, for he'll no get near this door, maister,' said a brawny man in a smith's leather apron.

'What do you fear, Jamesie?' Gil asked, over a loud chorus of agreement. Meikle glanced at him, and indicated the approaching horsemen. Grey light gleamed on helm and breastplate of all four.

'He comes up here on foot most times. Why's he on horseback now, wi' three of Douglas's men at his back? And going armed like this?'

'I agree, but what do you fear? What do you think he wants?'

'They're after our Beattie again,' said the smith.

'And they'll no get her,' said another man, brandishing a reeking stable-fork.

'It isn't Mistress Lithgo they're after, is it?' said Gil as the horsemen came to a halt at the edge of the cobbled area.

Meikle shot him another glance, and shook his head. 'No this time.' He took a tighter grip of the mell in his hand. 'Maister Michael, if you're wishing to try and reason wi' the priest, now's your chance.'

'Then who –?' said Michael. He met Gil's eye as understanding dawned. 'St Peter's bones, the man's a fool!'

He squared his shoulders and strode forward, slight

and commanding. His men looked at him guiltily, still in their saddles, but Sir David dismounted to meet him and ducked in a clumsy bow, touching his helm with a gloved hand.

'I'm right glad to see you here, Maister Michael. If you'll lead me to where this wicked woman is, we'll take her up now –'

Uproar broke out again among the colliers, and several moved threateningly towards the priest. He straightened up, and raised a peremptory hand.

'Peace!' he shouted, and was ignored. Jamesie Meikle shouted something, but it was Michael, turning to face the group, who stilled them briefly.

'I'll hear what Fleming has to say,' he announced. 'There's no man can say he went unheard on Douglas lands. So be silent and let me hear him, and then I'll hear you.' He turned to Fleming again. 'What woman is it you want, Sir David?'

'Why, the woman Brownlie. That's four men she's poisoned, clear as day, and –'

'Joanna?' repeated one of the colliers incredulously. 'What's he saying?'

'Mistress Brownlie?' said Michael, as the rumbling discontent spread again. Within the house Gil heard quick footsteps, and a sudden short scream. 'How do you make that out, man?'

'That's her two husbands,' the priest ticked them off on his fingers, 'her own father, and the forester of Bonnington, all slain by poison. I discerned that as soon as Wat Currie brought the word home to Cauldhope. She'll be found guilty of their deaths, that's for certain, so we need to take her up now and bring her before the Sheriff, to be held in Lanark jail till the justice-ayre.'

'We need nothing of the sort,' said Michael. 'If you'd keep to the tasks afore you, Sir David, namely stewarding my father's estate and acting as his chaplain, and leave the law and its business to those that's called to it, we'd all get on a sight better.'

'Ah, Maister Michael,' protested Fleming, with an ingratiating smile. 'You're young yet, you can take the advice of wiser folk –'

'Wiser, aye,' said Michael. 'I've yet to see that that includes you, man! Now get back on that horse and get back to Cauldhope.'

'No without the poisoner –'

'David Fleming,' said Arbella Weir from the house door. 'Sir David, I'm right disappointed in you, and so would your mother be. As for you men,' she went on, with that crackle of ice in her voice again, 'you may get back to your work, or I'll dock a day's wages off the whole crowd of you.'

'They're wanting to lift Beattie again,' someone told her loudly.

'No, man, it's Joanna they're after!' said another voice.

'They're saying it was pyson,' said the smith. 'That she used pyson on her man and all those others. They'll no say that about a collier's wife, even if she is a farm-lassie.'

'I thank you for your support, George Russell,' said Arbella, in a tone that made the man quail, 'but I can deal wi' Davy Fleming myself, I think, seeing I kent his father and his grandsire and they're both of them, dead and buried though they are, better men now than he'll ever be.' She leaned on her stick and stared between the muddy shoulders and upheld hammers and pickaxes at Fleming. 'Come here, man, where I can see you properly. I'm sure Maister Michael will give you leave to obey my direction afore you follow his,' she added, raising her delicate eyebrows at Michael. Gil watched, fascinated, as Fleming approached. He was impressed to see that the colliers had withdrawn, though only to

214

the next corner of the building, out of Mistress Weir's sight and very convenient for the side door into Joanna's lodging which Jamesie Meikle must have used earlier.

'Uncover afore me, man,' said Arbella as Fleming approached. He gave her another of those ingratiating smiles, and reached up to unbuckle his helm. 'Now what in Our Lady's name are you about here? Riding to my door wi' armed men –'

'And I'll have a word to say to them on that count, madam, I can tell you,' interposed Michael hotly. 'They're here by none of my wish or command.'

'I ken that, maister,' she assured him, with another lift of her eyebrows. 'You and your house has aye treated us here at the heugh wi' courtesy. Well, Davy? What's it about, then?'

'Arbella my daughter,' he began. Ill-advised, Gil thought, watching appreciatively. Beyond Arbella's apricot wool shoulder he could see movement in the hall: Beatrice? There was no sign of Joanna, and he hoped Alys had remained with her.

'I'm no daughter of yourn, Davy, and your actions these past few days leave you no right to be our confessor here,' said Arbella pointedly.

'Madam,' he corrected himself. 'Mistress Weir. You're a good woman, and devout, but nevertheless you're no but a weak woman, it's no wonder you're imposed on as you are. It's clear to me Joanna your good-daughter's long immersed in wickedness. That's four men dead in the time since she came here, and her well established in your favour and placed to gain from all her misdeeds.'

Out of Arbella's sight, beyond the house corner, Jamesie Meikle snarled soundlessly and took a firmer grip on the heavy wooden mell. Catching the man's eye, Gil shook his head infinitesimally, and the collier gave him a savage grin.

'Go on,' said Arbella levelly. 'How do you make all that out, man?'

'It's clear as day!'

'No to me, Davy. I held Joanna in my arms after my poor Matt breathed his last, and I thought myself she would be dead of her grief afore morning. Beattie and I had our work cut out to bring her back into her right mind. I helped her watch her father's deathbed, I saw her only now after she received the news that Thomas is dead, God shrive him.' She crossed herself and closed her eyes briefly. 'No, Davy Fleming, if that's all you can say I'll no hear another word of this. Maister Michael,' she turned the blue gaze on him, 'I'd be obliged if your men would see this fellow off the land I hold from your house, and I'd be the more obliged if you'd make sure he doesny return while I dwell here.'

I love you verily at my toe, thought Gil. And one can scarce blame her.

'You heard Mistress Weir, Fleming,' said Michael curtly. 'Mount up, man, as I bade you, and be off home to Cauldhope. And hope you're back there afore I am.'

'Will none of you see reason?' demanded Fleming. He turned to look from Michael to Gil, then at the staring men-at-arms still on horseback by the edge of the cobbled patch. 'It's plain as day! Here's Murray, struck dead in the very midst of his wickedness, and his catamite wi' him, and it's clear they've been poisoned in their drink –'

'Not to me,' said Gil. Confound the man's tongue, he thought, it goes like a fiddlestick. 'I was there, Sir David, and you wereny. Poison it may be, but there's no evidence to say how they took it –'

'Catamite?' said Arbella, the blue eyes opening wide. 'Pyson?' said Beatrice Lithgo, appearing at her

216

mother-in-law's back in the doorway. 'What pyson? You said . . .' She fell silent, looking hard at Gil. 'No, you never said what killed them,' she acknowledged.

'What in Our Lady's name's going on here?' demanded a loud voice. Gil looked round, and saw Adam Crombie striding round the corner of the house, booted and spurred and well pleased with himself, clearly just come down from the stable-row. 'What's this Jamesie says? Thomas dead, and Joanna taken up for his murder?'

'No, my dear,' said Arbella, her voice like the cooing of wood-pigeons. 'I've shown Sir David the error of his thoughts –'

'You, Adam Crombie!' said Fleming. 'I wonder you've the gall to show yourself afore me, you that raised your hand to an anointed clerk –'

'Aye, and I'll raise it again!' Crombie's gaze fell on Michael. 'Can you Douglases no control your servants? Here's Fleming running all about the countryside, doing all he can to harm our women, and never a hand raised at Cauldhope to prevent it. Get him off our land, will you, afore I hunt him off it mysel!'

'Raffie, my dear,' said Arbella chidingly.

'Raffie,' said Beatrice from the doorway. He exchanged a long look with his mother. She relaxed slightly, but his chin went up.

'I mean it,' he said. 'If I catch him on our land again, I'll see him off it wi' a lash.'

Chapter Ten

'There is no owl in the chamber,' said Alys. 'It was only a dream.'

He could hear her fumbling with the tinderbox. Sweating, gasping for breath, he stared into the darkness of the box bed, trying to throw off the image and the swamping fear it had generated.

Light flowered, making him blink, showing her face and the sweet curve of her breasts as she bent over the candle to set the tiny glow to it. The candle caught, and she used it to light the two on the pricket-stand and turned to look at him in the brightening room. He devoured the reassuring sight of her, standing there like Eve in the candlelight, holding her hair back with her free hand, and his breathing steadied.

'Only a dream,' she repeated. 'Here, this will help.' She came to lift his beads from the stool where the candle had lain, and handed them to him. The familiar texture of the carved wood steadied him further, and the prayers that rose to his mind at the touch drew his scattered thoughts together. Alys padded back across the room to the window, the bruises on hip and shoulder showing dark on her white skin, and bent to the cupboard in the panelling below the sill. 'Catherine always gives me something to eat if I wake in the night like this. What has Nan left in the dole-cupboard?'

The little cupboard proved to hold a dish of small

cakes, two glasses and a flask of the German wine his father had favoured. They sat side by side on the edge of the bed, the coverlet drawn round their shoulders, and feasted on these, and Alys said, 'Do you want to talk about it? Sometimes it helps to tell someone.'

'No,' he said, shuddering. He could still feel the claws scraping at his skin, the hooked beak tearing at his belly; there were silent wings in the shadows outside the corners of vision. Describing it would give it power, make it real in some way.

'Tell me about what you found in the forester's cottage, then.'

'Not that, not now. We'll talk about something else. What did Mistress Lithgo have to say about Fleming? I saw the two of you confer after Michael took him away.'

'Ah, now, that was interesting.' She turned within his arm to look at him. 'I had a long talk with her earlier, before you came. She preserved great discretion, until I told her of the rages Michael reported, and what I suspect. Then we were agreed immediately.'

'On what?'

'The man has his death on him, Gil. His water is sweet – sweet as honey, Mistress Lithgo says. He has lost flesh lately on his arms and legs though not his belly, you have only to look at the way his hose hang on him to see how much, and now he has these rages – and it would account for the way he lay in a swound all the day after he was beaten. The complaint has a name in Greek that doctors use,' she added, seeing his questioning look, 'but she called it honey-piss. After he left with Michael, she told me she feels it is progressing faster. We discussed whether we should tell him.'

'Oh,' said Gil, his mind racing. 'Oh, I've heard of that. It's caused by excess of cold moist food, isn't it?'

'So the doctors say,' agreed Alys drily. 'I'm less certain. You would think every man who drank more ale than is good for him would catch it, if so.'

'But why not tell him? He needs to know – to set his life in order, make a will if he has aught to leave.'

'Mistress Lithgo says she tried, when she first recognized it, but he wouldn't listen. She thinks perhaps that's where his thoughts of witchcraft have come from – that he's decided she was threatening him rather than warning him of his death.'

'That would make sense,' Gil said, still thinking hard.

'But Phemie admitted,' she hesitated, then went on, 'that he became familiar with her and with Bel. Pawing at them, attempting to kiss them. This was last autumn, when he was teaching them Latin.' She smiled. 'Phemie and the little Morison girl would get on well. She told me she reckoned she could deal with him herself, but when he started on her sister she went to their grandam about it, and the lessons ended.'

'Ah!' Gil looked at the light through the golden wine in his glass, and grinned, thinking of his sister Kate and her younger stepdaughter. 'And yet he consulted their mother about his ills this spring.'

'Many men take it for granted they can behave like that.'

'Murray seems to have done the same.'

'No, I think not,' she said seriously. 'He was courting Phemie, until they all learned how Joanna would be placed in Mistress Weir's will, I think I told you that.' He nodded. 'But I cannot learn that he did other than kiss her on the lips. I asked Kate Paterson about him, too, when I told her that her brothers are well. She seemed unconcerned about them, but she told me that Murray jokes – joked a lot with the lassies in the miners' row, but no more than talk, and pinching cheeks, and the like, whereas they warn one another not to be alone with David Fleming. It seems his father was the same, by what one of the older women said.'

'Jamesie Meikle said much the same about Murray – that the women say he's free with his hands. That would make sense, as a defence of sorts.'

'A defence? Putting up a false face, you mean? To prevent anyone suspecting he was – Italian in his preferences.' He nodded again, and she went on, 'You know, Gil, I find that extraordinary. I have known – I have seen men in Paris, who were said to be like that, but that was in a great city. How would someone out here in the countryside learn such practices?'

'It isn't like that,' said Gil awkwardly. It was not a subject he found easy to discuss with his wife; he suddenly understood why the songmen of the cathedral took refuge in coarse jokes about it. 'Anywhere young men are gathered together, it happens between some of them.' She glanced sharply at him, but said nothing. 'Most grow out of it, but a few . . .'

'I see,' she said after a moment. 'I still find it strange. And he managed to conceal it well. Joanna, who was wedded to him, seems to have had no idea of it. He was her second man, after all, she must have known what to expect of him, and today I managed to lead the talk to – to how people are expected to go with child within weeks of the wedding. We found we think alike on the subject, and, and . . .' She paused, apparently having difficulty completing the sentence.

'And you'd think,' he supplied, 'that if he wasn't doing his part she might have let on.'

'Between the two of us like that, yes,' she agreed gratefully. 'And I repeated something one of the women in Carluke kirk said to me about the same thing, and she agreed with it.'

221

'Alys, have a care,' he warned her. 'I believe some-one poisoned Thomas Murray, of deliberate malice, and until we know who –'

'Yes, yes, I know,' she said. 'I am very careful what I say to any of them. But we may still learn something from one or another, and I keep hoping for a look at the accounts. It could tell us a lot about the business, and I think that may be important.'

'There's more than that, sweetheart. Remember I have still to go back and question them all. Justice doesn't allow for friendships.'

'I know,' she said again. 'I can be dispassionate too, Gil.'

He smiled down at the top of her head where the candlelight shone on her hair, and sipped his wine. It was dry, with a sharp taste of flowers about it, a sur-prising thing in the middle of the night.

'But has she admitted she feared Murray? Perhaps she simply doesn't want to gossip about her own affairs. I believe some women don't.'

'No,' she said, and was silent for a little. He sat still, relishing the feel of her against his flank, drank some more wine and considered what she had just said. He had warned her against getting involved with the Crombie women on a protective reflex, but if she could discuss such a subject, one which she found difficult herself, and analyse Joanna's part in the conversation like this, then she was quite right, she could be dispas-sionate too.

'Did you learn anything else?' he asked after a space.

'I talked with Phemie for a while, about how coal is hewn. Gil, it is astonishing. One puts coal on the fire and never thinks of how it's won, of the difficulties working under the ground in the dark, and the dan-gers, and the way the coal behaves. Sometimes it simply vanishes, thins down and disappears into the rock, and other times it starts small and suddenly becomes thick enough for a man to stand up in the working. And she showed me – did you know they find fishes and shells in it? And pieces of tree-trunk, and flattened leaves, all wrought in coal?'

'I've heard of that too. Surely they're not real? The colliers make them in their spare time to show to the credulous.'

'She showed me one,' Alys said, 'a little fish, with all its fins and scales, and a man who could work anything like that, so fine and exact, should be earning more than a collier gets. No, truly I think it is God's own handiwork, set in the coal. I asked if I might have one to keep, and she said she would speak to the colliers.' She stretched, and set her wineglass down on the stool by the bed. 'And we talked of Murray and how he ran the heugh. It seems as if he has been an honest grieve enough, Gil, though with a knack for angering folk.'

'Did you encounter young Crombie?'

'He rode out while I was talking to Mistress Lithgo. He came in to take leave, and was civil, but I had no conversation with him. I think from what they said to one another he had been trying to persuade his grandam to let him leave the college and run the place instead of Murray.'

'Instead of Murray? Do you think they knew already he was dead?'

'Oh!' She turned to look at him, considering. 'I need to think about that. It might only be the young man snatching his opportunity. He seems like that sort to me.'

'A chancer,' said Gil in Scots.

She nodded. 'What will you do tomorrow?'

'Michael spoke to the Provost today, but I had best have a word with him before the quest on the two men, which I suppose means spending at least the morning in Lanark. He has to know about the – the circumstances in which we found the –'

'Yes.' She looked anxiously at him, and he managed a reassuring smile.

'I'm fine now. And then I must go up to the coaltown and ask more questions. Yesterday was not the best time for that, though I will say I learned a lot. What will you do while I'm in Lanark? You could come down with me and look at the market. There are some fine warehouses, since it's so close to Edinburgh.' He reached for another of the little cakes. The coverlet slid down his back and he hitched it up and drew it closer round the two of them.

'I want to go to Dalserf,' she said thoughtfully. 'I could ride round by Lanark to meet you. Is it far?'

'Dalserf? Oh, to find out more about Joanna?'

'And her family, yes. I cannot get used to that part of being out here in the country. It's so much further to go to talk to the neighbours, not at all like being able to put my plaid on and step up the High Street.' She rubbed her eyes. 'Gil, it is still the middle of the night, and I am getting cold. Have you recovered a little? Could you sleep now, do you think?'

'Not yet,' he said, and kissed the bridge of her nose, 'but I can think of something else we could do. *A swete kos of thy mouth mighte be my leche.*' He moved on to her chin, and then the soft curve of her neck.

'Ah,' she said softly, and turned towards him, smiling within his embrace. 'Perhaps we should put the candles out first.'

'So it is murder,' said Lady Egidia.

'Almost certainly,' agreed Gil, putting almond butter on his porridge.

'What happens next?' asked Alys. 'I know there is to

224

be a quest. Are the procedures different, this far from Glasgow?'

'Not in principle,' said Lady Egidia, and placed her wooden porringer on the plate-cupboard for the grey cat to lick. Socrates looked up at it, his long nose twitching; the cat hissed and he flattened his ears and wagged his tail placatingly.

'Provost Lockhart will likely report all to the Sheriff,' said Gil. He set the horn spoon down in his bowl in order to count off the points with one hand. 'That's Archie Hamilton in Lanark. Lockhart will call the quest soon, I hope, since the deaths must be determined in some way, and take evidence, and if the assize brings it in murder and names anyone he'll imprison the party or put them to the horn, just as in Glasgow. The difference is the distances involved, as you were saying last night.' Alys glanced up, and they exchanged a look and a quick, reminiscent smile. 'At least Bonnington is in the same parish as Lanark town, there's only that and Carluke involved.'

'And what will you report to Archie?' His mother moved over to the hearth, and looked in disapproval at the slender logs on the firedogs. 'Alan must send the men out for firewood soon, if that's the best he can produce.'

'Ah.' Gil spooned porridge, thinking. 'What do we know, you mean?'

'Of the man himself,' said Alys, 'we know a certain amount. Thomas Murray, aged six-and-twenty, red-haired, medium height, well-set and missing the last joint of these fingers.' She held up her left hand, two fingers extended. 'Wedded to Joanna Brownlie and grieve at the coal-heugh, last seen there on the morrow of St Patrick's and last seen alive by any we've spoken to so far on the twentieth of March, was that right, Gil?'

'That's right.' He helped himself to more porridge from the pot on the plate-cupboard. The cat stared at him indignantly. 'So far as we can discern, he was honest in his employment, but I suppose we have reason enough to get a look at the accounts now to check that.' He looked across the room at Alys again. 'Maybe you could do that for me, sweetheart.'

'And as to finding the corp,' said his mother, and crossed herself, 'you told us more than I wish to know of that last night. A gruesome sight it must have been. You looked as though you'd been through a millwheel when you came home, my dear. And you've told Mistress Brownlie?'

'That was why we went by the coaltown first,' said Gil. 'Michael wished to go up there straight and take them the word, as his father's depute. I'm well impressed by Michael in this, Mother. He knows his duty in the world, and he acts as it demands.'

'Aye, well.' Lady Egidia tightened her mouth briefly, contemplating the thought of her godson. Alys put her own bowl on the floor, and Socrates paced over to investigate, his claws clicking on the tiles. The cat seized the opportunity to jump down and make for its mistress's lap. 'And you think the man was poisoned,' Lady Egidia went on, holding her loose gown open for her pet to creep inside. 'Could it have been anything else? Any other cause? If it was poison, how do you know it was for Murray and not for the other fellow?'

Gil nodded. 'You're quite right, we don't know enough there. I'm hoping the Provost will send someone else out to question the folk at Bonnington, though whether I can rely on the findings from that ... Anyway, I've my own observations and Michael's.' He finished his second helping of porridge, and put the bowl down for the dog. 'Assuming it was poison, and was meant for Murray, and was added to the flask of cordial, I need to find out what it might have been that would be available here in Lanarkshire and would act so quickly.'

Alys and Lady Egidia exchanged a look.

'And would not be noticed in a cup of the cordial,' said Lady Egidia. 'What does it taste of, the cordial, do you know?'

'I didn't taste what we found, believe me. It smells like your cough syrup,' said Gil, pulling a face.

'Elderberries,' said Alys, 'and honey, and perhaps ginger, if it was the same brew that Joanna gave me.'

'Enough to disguise most things,' said Lady Egidia. 'Particularly with another spoonful of honey in it. How big is this flask?'

'I can show you it. Bide a moment.'

Going quickly up the stair to their chamber, he lifted his outer clothes from the kist where he had flung them down the previous evening. The big purse he had carried was with them, a commodious object of worn leather with half the trim missing. Reflecting that he could now afford a new one, he went back down to the hall, extracting the flask and the pottery bottle as he went. He handed both to Alys, who took them to her mother-in-law, sniffing at one and then the other as she did so.

'I think the cordial is the same,' she said, and looked back at Gil. 'What have you there, Gil? A piece of stone? Is it one of the little fishes from the coal?'

'No,' he said, turning the flat slab over. 'It's Bel's slate, that she dropped. I put it in my purse to give back to her, but I haven't seen the lassie on her own. I'd forgotten it was there.' He put the stone on the plate-cupboard, and nodded at the flask and bottle in his mother's hand. 'Do those tell us anything?'

227

'The flask is quite dry,' said Alys, 'but if we rinsed it out with a very little water, we might learn what was in it.'

'A good thought.' Lady Egidia held the silver flask to her nose again, then turned it in her hand, admiring it. 'It's a valuable gift. German work, to judge by the pattern. I wonder how Mistress Weir came by it?'

'And why she gave it to Murray. She demanded it back, yesterday before we left, as being now Mistress Brownlie's property.'

'What did you say?' his mother asked.

'Oh, I denied all knowledge. The Provost will want it for the quest.'

'True. I'll keep it close for you. And given that you think you know how this man died,' Lady Egidia went on, 'who might have brought about his death? Do you know enough to name anyone to Provost Lockhart?'

'No.' Gil sighed. 'Any of the women at the coal-heugh, I suppose. Much depends on what was in the flask and who put it there.' He brightened. 'I suppose it would be wiser to leave questioning them further till I know more about that.'

Alys caught his eye and nodded agreement.

'True,' said his mother, and indicated the two bowls on the floor. 'You may as well pick those up, if the dog's finished, and save Nan bending for them. And then you'd best be off to Lanark and talk to the Provost, afore the day gets any older.'

Lanark town was significantly bigger than Carluke, and now before Sext its long, curving market-place was bustling with folk, on foot, on horse, even in a couple of tilt-carts with their passengers peering out from under the oiled canvas hoods at the displays on booths and counters. Leaving the garrulous Patey at the

228

Nicholas Inn and the horses tied up in the yard, Gil made his way up the hill to the handsome stone house belonging to the Provost, and gave his name to the maidservant who answered the door.

Provost Lockhart was a pink self-consequential man in a magnificent gown of tawny velvet lined with fur. Torn between a desire to oblige the Archbishop's man and the need to preserve his own pre-eminence in the burgh, he took a little persuading to see Gil's viewpoint. He sat by the neat coal fire in his private closet and frowned across the hearth at his guest, shaking his head.

'Only the facts, Maister Cunningham,' he repeated dubiously, and hitched the furred gown further on to his shoulders. 'I'm no so sure about that. Is it within the law, now? I was always tellt it was my duty to find a name for the man responsible. Or woman, I suppose,' he added.

'You can postpone the end of the quest,' Gil prompted him. 'If you gather all the facts we have, and get them writ down clearly, then you can dismiss the assize for the time being, and reconvene when we've more idea who to name. Then we can let the two sets of kin deal with the burials, and –'

'Aye, well.' Maister Lockhart seized on that point. 'That would be a good thing, and put an end to a pair of six-week-old carcasses cluttering up the town. I've no notion how the assize will react, mind you, they're that used to being allowed to name names and get someone put to the horn or clapped in the jail, but I can see how it might be a good thing to get rid of the cadavers.' He nodded, pursing his lips anxiously. 'I've been hearing already how it's bad for trade up that end of the town, for they're making their presence public, as you might say, everywhere the wind blows from St Mungo's kirk. And who do you think was responsible anyway, maister? Is it someone we'd ken here in Lanark? Someone out at Bonnington? Was it because they were – ye ken, wicked sinners? That's a terrible thing to be found in Lanark, and them ordinary folk, no lords or foreigners.'

'I'm nowhere near naming anyone,' Gil parried. 'Did you send a man out to question the folk at Bonnington, Maister Lockhart?'

'I did that.' Rising, the Provost went to his tall desk and searched among the papers on its sloping front. 'John Mathieson went, and a clerk wi' him to write it all down, and a right pig's dinner they've made of it, no sort of order to the questions and the answers writ down all anyhow.' He extracted a folded leaf from the slithering mass, and peered at it. 'This man, the forester – Syme, his name is – was never seen since well afore the quarter-day, so far as I can make out, but his goats have been wandering everywhere and there's two folk had complained to the steward's clerk about that. Why nobody went down to his house instead of making a note to tell him when they saw him . . .' He turned the page over and perused the back carefully. 'The man Murray never seen about the policies at all. Get their coal from – aye, aye. And the forester lad no close friends on the estate.' He held the page nearer, then at arm's length, and suddenly thrust it at Gil. 'You can read it for yourself, Maister Cunningham, for what good it does. Just let me have it back afore the quest, which is cried for the morn's morn after Sext.'

'Thank you, maister.' Gil tucked the paper in the breast of his doublet before the man could change his mind. 'Who will you call for the quest?'

'Oh, aye.' Maister Lockhart came to sit down, his anxious expression returning. 'I've to give that some thought and all. Yourself and young Douglas, o' course.' Gil nodded agreement. 'John Hamilton the steward at

Bonnington, I suppose, for the forester, as well as for the place they were found. Seems the poor laddie has no kin closer than Ayrshire. The other fellow's maister and kin, though, I've a difficulty there, seeing it's Mistress Weir from the coal-heugh, or else his wife, Our Lady guard her, poor soul, and I'd no want to ask a woman to view the corp. Either one can testify to when he left his work, and the like, but –'

'One of the colliers might take it on, or even young Crombie,' Gil offered.

The Provost considered. 'Aye, that might do. I'll send John Mathieson wi' the summons, after we're done here. He canny question a witness properly, but he can arrange such a matter as that.'

Gil nodded, and rose to take his leave. As he reached the door something Arbella Weir had said came back to him, and he paused.

'Maister Lockhart, did you set eyes on Murray yourself, that day he was in the town?'

Lockhart stared at him, frozen in the act of hitching up his furred gown again.

'Do you know, maister, I did. I did that.' He settled the tawny velvet round his shoulders, and contemplated the fact, pursing his lips. 'For when he asked for the quarter's payment, my steward found there wasny enough in his kist, having paid out on another account just the day afore it, and came to me to get it made up, and the man Murray on his heels.'

'And was he just as usual?'

'Oh, aye. Just as usual. He's – he'd aye an air about him, of all being right wi' his world, and the hell wi' anyone else's.'

'And what time of day would that be?'

'Just afore the noon bite,' said Lockhart positively. 'I was in here, d'ye see, putting the answers together to a

231

couple letters, and a clerk to scrieve them. The same clerk that went wi' John constable yesterday, indeed.'

'That's valuable,' said Gil, considering. 'You've no notion where he went after he left here?'

'I can tell you that and all, and d'ye ken how? I was at my window,' he gestured towards it, a splendid glazed aperture with a painted blaze of arms at its centre, 'and spied him and his two men going down the High Street. I stood and watched them go down past where poor Andro Bothwell's pothecary shop used to be and into the tavern, Juggling Nick's as they cry it, and remarked to Dandy clerk that I hoped he'd no spend the whole of his takings in there, and the daft loon writ it down.' He guffawed. 'Right put out he was, when he'd to scrape it all out and scrieve it again, but I tellt him, I said, that's no going in a letter to my partner in a venture. So that's how I mind that, Maister Cunningham!'

Following Murray's footsteps, Gil went back down the wide street, past the shuttered shop with the wooden mortar and pestle above the door, and paused under the inn sign to admire it again. He had always appreciated the way St Nicholas' right hand, raised in blessing over the market-place, also appeared to be ready to catch the first of the three fat purses which floated round his head. The bishop was due a coat of paint; his colours were fading, his mitre reduced to an indeterminate grey. Hoping the next painter would do the image justice, he put a hand on the taproom door; then, on a sudden impulse, he turned away and stepped into the saint's small chapel next to the inn.

There was a hum of conversation in the nave, where perhaps two dozen townsfolk were standing about to hear the Mass. He found a quiet spot by St Giles's altar, folded his hat and knelt on it to go over the shreds of the midnight dream which still troubled him, to ask for help in putting it from his mind and in reading the puzzle before him. Or did the dream have some bearing on the puzzle? He shivered slightly, as it returned to him in vivid detail.

He had thought he was standing in the clearing by Syme's house, looking in at the door. In the trees to one side a naked man approached, and inside the house something stirred in the shadows, who or what he did not know but suddenly he had been certain that he must not set eyes on it. As he turned to flee the owl had swooped down over the roof, its wings huge and over-shadowing, and seized him in its claws, tearing with its beak at his bare flesh. His back still crawled with the feeling that he was threatened. St Giles, preserve me from all ill, he thought. Perhaps I should go down to the forester's house again.

After a while he rose from his knees, with no feeling of having been answered, and went to sit near St Roch on the stone bench at the wall-foot, half listening to the singing from beyond the chancel arch and turning matters over in his mind.

His mother and Alys had proposed some experiment, involving one of a nest of young rats which Henry had been saving to teach some terrier pups their business. But whether or not the creature died from drinking the water which had rinsed out the flask, what would that tell him? The man Murray was dead, and Andrew Syme with him, that was inarguable, and it seemed almost certain that their deaths were murder. But if I'm wrong, he thought, if it was an accidental poisoning or even a double suicide, what then? He had studied too much law to have any illusions about the judicial process; if he named someone to Maister Lockhart, or to his master the Archbishop, that person would suffer the penalty for murder as likely as not, whether innocent or guilty. And in this case . . .

In this case, the guilty person was most probably someone he had had civil dealings with in the past few days. Someone from the coaltown, or just possibly one of the two fellows he had left at the saltworks on the shores of the Forth. Or David Fleming, or one of the customers whose fees Murray had collected – the list got longer and longer, though he could probably rule out the people of Forth – or someone from the Nicholas Inn. And I must go in there and ask questions, he told himself. But suppose I name the wrong person to the Archbishop?

He opened his eyes and stared at St Roch's dog, a splendid black-and-white creature gazing adoringly up at his master. The man who carved the statue was better at dogs than at people, he thought irrelevantly.

But what if Murray's death was an accident, and the intended victim was Syme? Or perhaps the two of them had been killed deliberately by someone who knew one of the men, knew he had a lover. Now that would work whether the lover was known to be a man or thought to be a woman, but was the poisoner a friend or a would-be lover of Murray or of Syme? Or a friend of Joanna Brownlie, he thought, which takes me back to the coal-heugh and its household.

For the first time since the corpse had come up out of the peat-digging, he wished Alys's father was present. Pierre was good at this sort of exploration of the wider possibilities, and as he had found last night, it was not an easy subject for a man to discuss with his wife. Even Alys. He thought for a moment about her warm sympathy and the matter-of-fact way she had dealt with his dream, and wondered if perhaps she would find the subject less awkward than he did. Her capacity to surprise him really did seem to be endless.

The townspeople round about him were moving, leaving the little chapel. The Mass must be over. He stretched his back, then drew the paper with the report from Bonnington out of his doublet, and tilted it to the light from the nearest window.

Maister Lockhart's strictures on the two men who had compiled it were well deserved. The document was simply a list of answers, in no particular order, with few notes of who had supplied each fact. The spelling was eclectic, but the writing was clear enough. He worked his way down the page, trying to fit the short statements into some kind of narrative. Syme had not been seen since before the quarter-day; the fact of his not having been paid was noted again. None of those asked had known of any reason to kill the man, he seemed to have no quarrel with any of his fellows, the lassies liked him but he favoured none of them. One woman apparently had *aye suspicioned him*, but even the interrogators thought this was hindsight speaking. The tale about the goats occupied half the page, the fact that Murray was unknown to the Bonnington household was dismissed in one line. Sighing, Gil turned the sheet over and studied the other side. Here they had apparently turned to the question of poison, without success. It was surely a bad mushroom, it was a judgement, it was pestilence or witchcraft. *Nane here is abil to mak use o pyshn*, had written the clerk, in simple trust.

Further questioning might uncover something, but at the moment it was plain that no strong trail led from the forester's cottage to Bonnington. The clearest scent led back towards the Pow Burn, and all his training at the hunt told him that was what he should be following. Metaphor, he thought, and grinned as he thought once more of Pierre and his dislike of figures of speech.

He rose and shook the creases out of his hat, and made for the door, pausing again before St Giles. Are the goats your creatures? he asked the oblivious figure.

You made a pet of a deer, perhaps goats appeal to you too. Their master was poisoned. Help me win justice for him, whatever sort of sinner he was. The saint made no reply, but a gleam of light lay on the white hind couched at his feet.

In the busy taproom of the inn, there was no sign of Patey, but Bessie Dickson was supervising the distribution of ale of two different strengths from a pair of large barrels by the further door. She greeted him with disapproval.

'I've no notion why you should think I've any more time for you,' she announced. 'Is it still this man Murray and his horse you're after? I'll sit down and talk wi' you if you'll sweep the draff out the brewhouse for me when we're done.'

'I'll not take up your time,' he said, without answering this offer. 'I wondered if you or any of your folk had a notion of what Murray and his friend talked about when he was in here.'

'Talked about?' She stared at him. She was a big woman with a broad red face; muscular forearms showed below the rolled-up sleeves of kirtle and shift, and the ends of her kerchief, knotted up on top of her head, were threatening to come untied. 'What would they talk about? The same as any that sits in here drinking, I've no doubt. How they could run the world better than them that's set in authority, what lassie's willing for a walk round the kirkyard by night, a'things like that.'

'You've never overheard them?'

'I've more to do than stand about all day listening to my customers.' Bessie pushed her rolled sleeves higher up her arms. 'Like sweeping up that draff out there. If you'll no do it, I'll ha' to find someone that will.'

'Mistress?' The man at the other barrel was looking at Gil. 'Should he maybe get a word wi' Girzie? She's

236

been on about what she heard all day, it might shut her mouth if someone heard her out. The twice-brewed, Annie?' He half-turned to the spigot and drew brown ale foaming into a fat yellow-glazed jug for a maid-servant in a drab homespun gown, who bobbed a curtsy in thanks. 'There you are, lass. On your maister's slate, is it?'

Bessie snorted.

'Her? I've no wish to encourage her. She's barely done a hand's turn since the word came back the man was dead.'

'What did she hear?' Gil asked, in no great hopes. 'Was it Murray?'

'Aye,' said the tapster, 'him or the other fellow. She's out in the yard the now, mistress, I could fetch her in.'

'I'll go out there,' said Gil hastily. 'I'll not keep her long from her work.'

'Hah!' said Bessie bitterly, but did not prevent him from going out through the rear door of the taproom.

The first thing he saw as he stepped into the yard was Socrates, who looked up from his inspection of a storehouse door and hurried across to meet him, tail waving. Acknowledging the dog's greeting, he looked about and found Patey, deep in conversation with another of the Belstane grooms. Two empty beakers were on the ground at their feet, and four of his mother's horses stood tethered beside them.

'The mistress is yonder, Maister Gil,' the second man called, pulling off his bonnet. 'The young mistress,' he added. 'In the kitchen yard, ayont the brewhouse, talk-ing to some weeping lassie.'

Chapter Eleven

'She was very glad to tell someone of it,' said Alys in French, and urged her horse past a milestone. 'I think the other folk at the inn were not sympathetic, though at least they told Steenie about her when he asked if anyone knew anything.'

'And she had heard one of the two speak of mortal sin?' said Gil. 'When was that?'

They were making their way back from Lanark to Carluke yet again, the two Belstane grooms behind them talking about the ploughing. Familiar as Gil was with the trackways and lanes of the district, he was beginning to feel he could take this road in his sleep. It was starting to rain.

'I couldn't make that out,' said Alys in apologetic tones, 'but it was one evening when Syme and Murray were in the place together. I suppose that would be on one of Murray's trips down to Lanark to go drinking.' Gil nodded agreement, and whistled to the dog, who was standing up, one paw on a dyke, peering at a small flock of sheep. 'She told me they would spend the evening talking now with the company in the place, now with one another. Do you suppose they found it hard,' she added thoughtfully, 'to dissemble in such a way?'

Gil turned to smile at her, recognizing the same compassion she brought to running her father's household, and she looked seriously back at him.

'We never had to,' she pointed out, 'as you said when we talked of Michael and your sister. We were always acknowledged.'

'True. What did this Girzie hear?'

'Ah. It seems on this occasion they were sitting in the corner by the hearth, talking with their heads together, and Girzie passed them with a tray for someone else, just as Murray said something about mortal sin.'

'It's hardly a surprise.'

'So,' Alys persisted, 'she took her time going by them on her return to the kitchen, and heard the forester speak of slitting his throat.'

'Oh,' said Gil, and turned to meet her eyes again. 'That could alter matters.'

'Yes. I coaxed her as far as I could, but I'm not sure how much of their talk she really heard. She heard one of them say, *What's done's done*, and then there was something about *Tell the old beldam what I know*, but she recalled nothing more that made sense. She thinks they said also that the old woman was away.'

'Which old woman did they mean?' Gil contemplated this. 'Arbella hasn't left the coaltown this spring, so far as I've learned.'

'They never mentioned a name.' Her smile flickered. 'A good worker, this Girzie, I should think, but rather a silly woman. She kept coming back to the idea of the forester slitting his throat. It seems she had a liking for him, and the thought of him doing such a deed has overset her. I had quite a task to persuade her that he'd done no such thing.'

'But I wonder,' said Gil slowly, 'if that means we need look no further – if it was Murray or Syme supplied the poison, whether the other knew it was there or not.'

'I think not,' she said after a moment. 'It would simplify matters, but –'

239

'It's too simple, isn't it?' he agreed, drawing his plaid up round his neck against the rain.

'There's no hint that they'd been recognized or suspected, no threat to separate them. No pursuit that would be a cause to take poison and be together forever.' He recognized the influence of the romances which were Alys's favourite reading in this pronouncement. 'For all Girzie was so sure the forester had killed himself, she had no notion why he might have done so, and the two men you saw at Blackness gave no hint either, I think?'

'None. And Syme's maister was astounded to hear of it.' Gil's thoughts had run off at a tangent. 'Alys, was it poison indeed? Did you test what was dried into the flask?'

'That was why I rode down to Lanark to find you. We did, and I thought you might need to know.' Again that serious look. 'We rinsed both the flask and the bottle with well-water, and gave the water to two of the beasts Henry brought us. Whatever was in the bottle, it was just as it left the brewer, the ratling that drank that portion came to no harm, but the other one . . .'

'Well?'

Alys pulled a face. 'It died. It seemed quite normal for a while, and then began to stagger, and turned round as if it was dizzy, and then it fell over and after a time it died.' She bit her lip, and stared into the distance. 'I suppose, if the two men died like that, then we know it was quick, and most probably painless.'

'We do,' agreed Gil. 'And we know that whatever it was, there was some in the flask. Have you or my mother any idea what it was?'

She shook her head, scattering raindrops from the brim of her hat.

'I don't know,' she said. 'Poisons are not something I – and all the ones I've heard about would induce

240

purging, or vomiting, before death. And your mother has said she does not know this one either.'

'I thought you knew everything,' said Gil, amused and faintly relieved to find a gap in her astonishing medical knowledge. She blushed pink, and shook her head again.

'I need a book,' she said, 'but I don't know who would have such a one, except . . .'

'Mistress Lithgo,' Gil finished for her.

'Except Mistress Lithgo.' She reached out her hand, and when he took it her fingers clung to his. 'And how can I ask her when we – Oh, Gil, how can we do this? The truth must be served, but the accidents it brings about are fearful.'

'The truth must be served,' he agreed, keeping a grip of her hand.

They rode up into Carluke town, and along its deep-worn main street between the two rows of cottages facing one another across it. As they passed St Andrew's kirk at the far end of the town, Sir John Heriot popped out of his house like a figure in a child's toy, his clerk behind him, and hurried towards them, hand out, exclaiming, 'Maister Cunningham! In a good hour, indeed! I have great news, sir!'

'News?' Gil said blankly, letting go of Alys's hand to bend down and clasp the priest's.

'Indeed, sir. I have a name for our man. I ken who he is.'

The clerk nodded agreement, grinning, and crossed himself energetically. Gil looked from one to the other. Beside him, Alys's horse laid back its ears at a scavenging pig, and she tightened her reins. Steenie dismounted hastily and went to the grey's head.

'A name for . . .' Gil repeated.

241

'For the man out of the peat-digging. The corp in your feed-store, sir. And we must have him out of there as soon as may be, it's no right now that I've discerned who he could only be.' Above the worn and dusty black gown Sir John's face glowed with pride and triumph. His clerk beamed and nodded again. 'I went through the kirk records, sir, and read over all our documents, and only just now between Sext and Nones I found it! It's clear to me that he can be no other than the parish's own saint, the man that first brought the gospel of Christ and Our Lady in this place. Why would Carluke town's other name be "Ecclesmalesoch" but to signify the kirk of the holy Malessock?'

'What, that dusty old corp out the peat-cutting?' said Steenie.

Gil stared at the priest in disbelief. 'Sweet St Giles,' he said after a moment. 'But Sir John, you've no proof –'

Sir John braced himself with a complex movement of his elbows, and settled down to expound on his case, oblivious of the rain beating on his shoulders. 'No, only consider, maister. He's clearly been martyred for his faith, you canny deny that, by the injuries you showed to me, and one of the old tales in a roll out of the Parish Kist tells us how Malessock preached the gospel in the wilderness among the thorns.'

'I never heard that,' said Patey.

And if it doesn't tell it now, thought Gil, it will by the time Sir John gets to his bed tonight. *Who koude ryme in Englysshe proprely His martirdom? for sothe it am nat I,* is clearly not a permissible standpoint here.

'Thorn, you see, *Thorn*, maister,' persisted the priest. 'It can be none other!' He clapped his hands together like a child, smiling radiantly. 'Oh, Maister Cunningham, I'm so joyful I could dance like King David, here in the Worn Way. Indeed! And we'll get him out of madam your mother's feed-store as soon as maybe and brought down here to the kirk, and lay him up properly. What a great thing for my parish, sir! To have our own founder, our own evangelist, to dwell here as patron of our kirk!'

'They've nothing like it in Lanark,' agreed the clerk, nodding again. 'Them and their wee bit of the True Cross!'

'Are you saying that's your saint that Rab Simson found, Sir John?' asked Patey. 'Never! It's no but a stinking bundle of rotted leather, and so Henry tellt all the folk standing in line in our stable-yard this morning.'

'No, surely, sir,' objected Alys, 'he has no tonsure, no trappings of a priest –'

'There's no sign on him at all,' agreed Gil.

'Did St Roch have the trappings of a priest, madam?' demanded Sir John eloquently, waving his hand towards the church. 'Did Our Lady wear a nun's garments? Besides,' he added in a more practical tone, 'you said yourself, maister, they'd have rotted down in the peat. We'll get him clad as befits him soon enough. Indeed.'

'Who's this coming, Maister Gil?' said Steenie, peering past the buff-coloured folds of Alys's skirts. Gil turned in the saddle, to see a rider in Cauldhope livery approaching fast, leading a spare horse.

'I must send to your lady mother to get all arranged,' warbled the priest. 'We'll have a great procession, wi' music and green branches, and –'

'Sir John!' said the newcomer urgently, reining in beside the group. Gil's horse shied restlessly, and Socrates hurried back from his inspection of the kirk-yard gate, hackles up. 'Thanks be to Our Lady I've found you, maister. I'm sent for you to Davy Fleming.'

'Oh!' said Alys, and caught Gil's eye.

'To Davy?' repeated Sir John in amazement. 'What's to do, Simmie? Is he in a bad way? I heard he was on his feet again.'

'He was,' said Gil. 'He was up at the Pow Burn yesterday.'

'Aye, but he sickened again yestreen after his supper,' said Simmie. 'And I'm seeking yourself and all, Maister Cunningham. Maister Michael said to ride on to Belstane for you, but since you're here I've no need. He's wanting a word wi' you, and it seems to be eating at him.'

'I will come too,' said Alys.

'Maister Michael wants a word?' asked Gil.

'Oh, I couldny say to that,' said the man confusingly, 'but it's for certain Davy Fleming wants you, for I heard him say as much to the maister. Mind you,' he added, 'I'm no so sure myself he's near death, for the way he shouted at Maister Michael this morning out of his bed, you never heard the like.'

'Just let me pack up what's needed,' said Sir John briskly, all professional concern. 'I'll need to bear an intinctured wafer wi' me, Jock, and I must borrow a horse –'

'You'll no need, I brought this beast in for you,' said Simmie.

'You'll be wanting the new box, then,' said the clerk to his master, with a significant look.

'Aye, indeed!' agreed Sir John. He grinned, and clapped his hands together. 'A good thought, Jock! Just wait here, Simmie, and I'll be right with you.'

Gil was shocked by the change in David Fleming, and recognized from the sudden stiffening of her back that Alys was equally dismayed. The man was huddled in the steward's chair in the little chamber off the hall,

244

bundled in rugs and racked by spells of shivering. The truth was self-evident of Alys's statement that he had his death on him; overnight his plump cheeks seemed to have fallen in, his eyes were sunken, dark-ringed and feverishly bright, and there was a sheen of sweat across his brow, darkening the limp, mousy hair which clung to it.

Alys went forward and began to feel her patient's forehead and neck with gentle fingers. He looked blankly at her, and then at Gil, then said to Michael where he stood in the doorway, 'I want a word wi' Maister Cunningham. It's right urgent, sir.'

'I'm here,' said Gil, wondering if the man could see clearly.

'There, now, my poor friend,' said Sir John in sympathy. He set his leather case down on a handy stool and began unbuckling the straps which secured it. 'We'll ha' a bowl and a jug of fresh well-water, maybe, Maister Michael? And I'll need a towel and basin and all. Indeed.'

Michael nodded and turned to the door of the steward's room. Over his directions to Simmie out in the screens passage Fleming said hoarsely, 'This first. I've something I must tell you, sir.'

'Now, now, man,' chided Sir John. 'What could be more urgent than your own confession and healing?'

'You should rest,' said Alys, 'and gather your strength.'

'Aye, well, I'm done for, mistress,' said Fleming, and licked dry lips, 'but this is important. I'll last long enough to set this in your hands, Maister Cunningham. You'll need to peruse this afore the quest on Thomas Murray, so you can tell the Provost all that's needful, all the evidence against the witch. One of them or the other – or maybe they're both in it,' he added. 'Aye, I wish I could ha' seen them took up for witchcraft and put to the test, but if that's no God's will for me, I must go without.'

'Tuts, man,' said Sir John, 'we'll no give up hope for you yet. We'll see to your spiritual needs, but then I've a remedy to try that I'll swear's sovereign against all wasting diseases, and who more deserving of it than yourself?'

'Set what in my hands?' asked Gil. 'Let me take it and get away, Sir David, and leave you to your spiritual duties.'

'The rent rolls,' said Fleming, catching at Alys's wrist. 'There they are on the desk waiting for your man, mistress, the rent rolls for the coal-heugh, the old one and the new one. You'll need to read it wi' care, maister, but it's all in there, all you need to know, you mind I told you of it last time you were in this chamber.'

'I hardly think Sir James would be pleased if I went off with his rent rolls,' objected Gil.

'Maister Michael will permit it,' suggested Fleming. Michael, reappearing in the doorway, nodded agreement. His face was thinned by anxiety, exaggerating the curved jaw and pointed chin.

'I could go through them too,' said Alys.

'No, no,' said Fleming, condescending even in his weakness, 'maybe you can read, lassie, but you've no the experience. It takes a man of law to discern these things –'

'Here's your basin, clerk,' announced Simmie, charging in past his master, 'and your water and all. Is it to be a wee Mass of healing? Or is it this new saint you've got? He should be a good help, seeing that Davy himself found him buried.'

'Ah, thank you, Simmie,' Sir John turned from the

leather case, 'and you can stay, indeed, and give me a hand wi' the censer.'

'New saint?' said Fleming, distracted from his preoccupation. 'What's this?'

'It's revealed to me,' said Sir John importantly, and kissed his stole before he set it over his shoulders, 'the corp from the peat-digging can be none other than St Malessock who first brought the gospel to this parish.' He bent to the leather case again, and produced a small linen bundle which he unfolded to reveal a leathery stick-like object. 'And here I have one of the holy man's fingers –'

'Oh, so Alan was right,' said Gil. Sir John gave him a look of blank innocence.

'You'll no dip that in the water, will you?' said Simmie, recoiling. 'I'd sooner the Lee Penny, myself. At least that's clean, considering how often it gets dipped.'

'Lockhart and his folk at the Lee won't be pleased if there's another source of healing in the district,' observed Michael. Sir John's jaw dropped. Clearly he had not thought of that.

'Who's Malessock?' demanded Fleming. 'It canny be any Malessock that came out the peat-digging, it's Thomas Murray.'

'No, it's no Murray,' said Simmie, 'for we found him by Bonnington yesterday, Davy, you mind Wat and I tellt you all.'

'I'll get away,' said Gil cravenly. Alys looked up and nodded, but Fleming's grip on her wrist tightened.

'The rolls, mistress. Yonder on the desk. Take the rolls, or you take them, sir.'

'Bring them out into the hall,' suggested Michael. Gil, in some relief, gathered up the two yellowing scrolls and stepped to the door. Alys disengaged her wrist from Fleming's grasp, and crossed herself.

'We'll leave you with Sir John,' she said. 'God speed the business.'

'Amen,' agreed Sir John.

'Read them wi' care, now,' admonished Fleming.

'He seemed well enough when I came home,' said Michael, 'though he was chastened once I'd done wi' him. Maister Gil would tell you about him being up at the Pow Burn . . .?'

Alys nodded. Across the hall where he had been ordered to wait, Socrates emitted a single indignant falsetto yip. Gil snapped his fingers, and the dog paced over to join them.

'You could sit here in the window, and get the light for the task,' Michael went on. 'No, he wasn't so good after supper last night, and this morning he took a wee sup of porridge, with honey in it after what you said about honey the other day, mistress, but it never helped, and then he called for Maister Gil and I thought we'd best get a priest to him and all, and set Simmie on to look for you.'

'Indeed, yes,' said Alys. 'You take that one, Gil, I take this, and then we can tell poor Fleming we've been through both. Has he been at the pear comfits again, Michael? I could smell them on his breath.'

'So did I,' Michael was striding up and down, 'but I've no notion where he's hid them.'

'He should fast now, with well-water to drink and not even bread to eat, till noon tomorrow, if you can manage it, and certainly none of the comfits.'

'I'll try, though the other men aye bring him food when he shouts for it.' Michael looked round as Sir John's voice rose in the familiar, comforting words from beyond the screens passage. 'Jackie Heriot's a powerful singer, isn't he? What's he about, anyway? What's that nasty thing he's brought wi' him?'

'He reckons our corp from the peat-digging is this Malessock he claims is in the parish records.' Gil had untied the tape on the older roll, and now spread out the end on his knee. Socrates sniffed at the edge of the parchment, then lay down with an ostentatious sigh, his head on Gil's foot.

'Could it be?' asked Michael uncertainly, pausing in his traverse. Gil grunted, but Alys looked up.

'I would not have said so either,' she said with regret. 'One thing to surmise that the corp might be someone from the days of the saints, or even from the time Our Lord was born, but another entirely to give him a name as if we had proof.'

Gil, aware of relief, nodded agreement.

'He came up out of the peat with nothing,' he said. 'All we know of him is the violent way he died. If Sir John wishes to give him a name and honour him, there's no harm, I suppose, but I'll believe he's a saint working miracles of healing when I witness one.'

'The Lee Penny works,' Michael argued.

'What is that?' Alys asked, finger on her place. 'Simmie mentioned it too.'

Gil immersed himself in the roll he held, only half hearing Michael's account of how a Lockhart, of the house by Carluke called the Lee, had brought back a mysterious coin from the Crusades, widely known to cure the pestilence and other serious illness if you drank water it had been dipped in. He was less convinced than Michael of its efficacy, though one heard tales.

'1481, *Lady Day, the fee paid*,' he read aloud as the tale ended. 'And Arbella Weir's signature to it. For all Fleming calls these rent rolls, it isn't strictly rent the coal-heugh pays, is it, Michael?'

'It's regular feu duty,' agreed Michael. 'And our share of the profits, as part of the conditions of the feu. There should be a note of those at the top of that roll, set out when old man Weir cut the first pit.' He stopped pacing to peer over Alys's shoulder. 'Davy's writing gets worse every time I look at it.'

'The man before him was no better,' said Gil.

'What does Fleming want us to look for?' asked Alys. She hitched up the skirt of her riding-dress to reach the purse which hung beneath it at her knee, and extracted her tablets.

'I'm not certain.' Gil paused, finger on an entry. 'He was babbling to me about the dates the Crombie men had died, from which he seemed to deduce witchcraft. If we find those, I suppose, and make a note of them, it should satisfy him. I'd not take the time, save to humour the man when he's in such a bad way.'

'He is,' Michael agreed, glancing at the screen again. Sir John had obviously anointed his penitent and was now chanting; his text seemed to be a life of the newly revealed saint, cobbled together from stock phrases. 'St Peter's bones, I think he's making that up as he goes along. What's Robert Blacader going to say about a new saint on his land?'

'I've been wondering the same thing.' Gil bent to the parchment again, and read the entry under his finger. '1477, *Lammas, the fee paid. Adam Crombie younger, his mark*, though it's a signature, not a mark, and *Adam Crombie elder obiit March last*. Then before that, in March, Arbella paid the fee, and at Candlemas before that it was Adam the elder. Their signatures are very different. But I see no great meaning in this.'

He copied the three entries carefully, and set the tablets aside.

'I have the death of Mistress Lithgo's man,' said Alys.

She turned her scroll so that Gil could read the entry. 'In March of 1484.'

Adam Crombie secundus obiit, ran the note. Two attempts at a Latin phrase had been scratched out, and *Undir a gret faling of the rokkes* written after it.

'Just as Phemie told me,' she added.

Aware of a lack of system, Gil re-rolled his document to begin at the beginning, and paused to study the original conditions of feu which Michael had mentioned. The steward of the time had copied them with care in a small clear hand; they were interesting, and he thought generous on both sides. The first coalmaster, Arbella Weir's father, had freedom to conduct the coalheugh as he wished, and in turn the Sir James Douglas concerned, likely Michael's grandsire he calculated, was to receive the regular feu duty, paid in person at Lady Day, and a fifth of the proceeds, paid quarterly.

'Not the profits,' he commented. Alys looked up, but did not speak.

'No,' agreed Michael, and grinned. 'The old man can tell you about that. He does a good mimic of my grandsire bargaining with old Weir.' He turned his head as the chanting from beyond the screen reached some kind of culmination, and water splashed. 'I hope they're careful wi' that basin. We don't want the records getting soaked.'

Gil bent to his task again, picking his way through the cramped lines of script. The year following the first payment a different name appeared. *Adam Crombie grieve pro Mats Weir*, stated the note beside it. Gil checked the date: August 1451. This must be when Arbella had been married. He frowned, made a note and carried on with his task. Year by year, quarter by quarter, the feu duty was paid, the share of the takings recorded, one man or the other signed the book.

'I suppose whoever was free would ride over here,' said Michael when he commented.

On Lady Day in 1465 Arbella had signed instead of her father, and thereafter her name appeared every spring. He frowned, and checked again, and located the brief comment appended to the Lammas entry: *Mataeus Were ob mart mcccclxv*. March 1465, indeed. He made a note, and went on.

The quarter-days came and went, Arbella or her husband signed the statements. Now and then a payment was missed, and a cryptic explanation accompanied the double amount next quarter. *Lammas 1470 Arbela Wyr from home last qr*, ran one. *Mart'mas 1474 yung crombis maridge last qr fee forgot*, was another. That must be when Mistress Lithgo came into the family. He grinned, thinking of the chaos and bustle that had surrounded their own wedding last November, even with Alys in charge.

'There's no entry for the last two quarter-days,' said Alys. He looked up, and saw her expression change to one of dismay. 'Of course, the fee was never paid this year.'

Beyond the screen, Sir John was still chanting. A waft of incense reached the hall, drifting blue in the light of the narrow windows, and making Socrates sneeze. Michael paused in his pacing to uncover his head and cross himself.

'That is all I can see,' said Alys, letting her scroll roll itself shut. 'I have noted anything out of the way, and who signed the book each time. Can I help you, Gil?' She stepped over the dog and came to sit at his side, studying his notes on the green wax of the tablets, glancing from that to the crabbed blocks of writing on the parchment. 'Michael, was there a new contract made out when Mistress Weir's father died?'

'Aye, and at my grandsire's death and all,' Michael agreed. 'The terms are still the same as the original, so the old man said. I'd wager neither side would think it worth the argument to change them.'

'What happened to old Weir, do you know?' Gil asked casually, finger on his place.

'No a notion.' Michael considered briefly, and shook his head. 'No, I think I never heard it spoken of. Could ha' been anything a collier might meet, including old age.'

'Not so many of them live to old age,' Gil said. 'And Mistress Weir's man? The first Adam Crombie that died at Elsrickle?'

'I was still in short coats,' protested Michael. 'I've no a notion what came to him.'

'Someone could ride to Elsrickle,' said Alys. Gil turned to smile at her, suddenly aware of her accent and the pains she had to take over the place-name.

'Why?' asked Michael. 'I thought we were finding who poisoned the man Murray.'

'To get the exact date of Adam Crombie's death,' Alys said, 'and if anyone remembers it, an account of how he died. Is there time to go today and be back in daylight?'

'I could,' said Gil with reluctance. 'You are right, we need to check that.'

'I don't see why,' said Michael. 'What will it prove anyway?'

'If he died in the same way as Murray,' said Alys carefully, 'it might mean that the same person poisoned them both.'

'If it was poison,' said Gil. 'It might only mean that the one learned from the other.'

'And if he didny? If it was a natural death?'

'Then I suppose,' said Alys reluctantly, 'this time it could have been anyone who handled the flask. For I

253

am very sure it was something in the flask, Gil, even if I can't identify it.'

'Who had it last?' Michael asked. 'The flask.'

'Joanna,' said Gil, more grimly than he intended.

'Only to put it in Murray's scrip,' Alys protested. He met her eye. 'Gil, no! Surely we can't –'

'We must suspect all of them,' he said, 'and she is the one to benefit most by his death.'

'It is not in her character!' she exclaimed, breaking into French. 'So gentle a girl, always ready to believe the best of everyone – Gil, I can't believe that she would do such a thing.'

'What, not kill? Alys, anyone can kill. One simply has to know how.'

'But there isn't a scrap of violence in her.'

'Poison works at a distance,' Gil reminded her, 'whoever administered it need not see its effects. No, I think all of them had the chance, and she had more than most, and benefited more than most as well. The emotional argument might do for the assize, but the truth –'

'But Gil, there are other reasons for killing Murray. All she did was handle the flask, by her account, she had no time to put anything into it without him seeing her do so –'

'What are you saying?' asked Michael, looking help-lessly from one to the other.

'I apologize, Michael,' said Alys in Scots, and sat upright away from Gil. 'We were – discussing whether Joanna might have –'

'Oh, surely not,' he said. 'Then again, I suppose it has to have been someone up there, if it wasny the man Syme, or Murray himself. What a fankle this is.'

'I'll go up to Elsrickle,' said Gil, bracing himself. Sixteen miles each way in the rain had little appeal.

'You go back to Belstane, Alys, and take the dog, and if Michael has fresh horses for Patey and me –'

'Well, that went right well,' announced Sir John, bustling into the hall with the pyx held reverently before him. Simmie followed, his arms full of the priest's gear, the smoking censer bumping his shins. 'Indeed. I'm sure our founder and patron will take notice of our petitions, after a celebration like that.'

'Davy's asleep, Maister Michael,' said Simmie in what he obviously intended to be a confidential tone. 'Dropped ower in the midst o' that last narration. Mind you, how anyone could sleep through Sir John here's singing I canny tell.'

'Aye, he's confessed and shriven, and heard the history of St Malessock and drank water that the relic's been immersed in, and it's brought him some peace of mind at last,' agreed the priest, divesting himself with care. 'Now, maister, he'll need to fast on well-water for a day and a night, and I'll be back the morn's morn to see him. Indeed. But you'll send to me any time if you're concerned for him.' He beamed round the awkward little group. 'I hope I've been of service the day. Is there any other task of my calling required while I'm here?'

Sir Billy Crichton, rector of Walston, was a long-faced, long-limbed Borderer with the gloomy expression natural to a man who spent most of his life in a high, remote parish at the further end of Lanarkshire. His kirk was in Walston itself, a huddle of cottages and two tower-houses on the dark side of a steep lump of hills; Gil surmised that the sun would not reach the thatch between October and March. When he found Sir Billy, following the directions of an ancient fellow at a doorway, the rector was working his glebe land below the

255

village on the flat ground by the River Medwin. More precisely, he was turning the black earth with a foot-plough, with a cloud of white gulls screaming over his head, and was very glad to stop for a word with the stranger he had seen approaching on the track in from Carnwath.

'Oh, aye, we heard about that,' he said, as the gulls swirled about, shrieking in discontent. 'Young Dandy Somerville was at his cousin's at Carlindean and brought back the tale. Found dead in a peat-heugh, was he no? And doing miracles now, so Young Dandy said.'

'That was someone else,' Gil said, marvelling at the way word spread about the countryside. He gave the tale of Thomas Murray's death, so far as he understood it, and Sir Billy listened attentively, leaning on the tall shaft of his plough in the rain and shaking his head. The gulls settled on the roof of the little kirk, laughing at one another.

'Terrible, terrible. I'm right glad to ken the truth of it,' said the priest at length. That's more than any of us knows, thought Gil, but did not smile. 'And dead unshriven, pysoned by an unkent hand, you say? Terrible, terrible. God rest their souls. But I'm at a loss to ken how I might help you, maister. I've no notion who these folk might be, having never set eye on a one of them, and what I might tell you to your purpose it's beyond me to say. I'm sorry you should ha' rid out here only for that.'

'He'd no reason to call here,' agreed Gil. 'No, sir, I've ridden here on another matter. Do you mind a man called Adam Crombie, a collier, who died in this parish a good few years back? I think it was over at Elsrickle.'

'Elgrighill,' repeated Sir Billy, giving the name a different twist. 'Crombie. Aye, maister, there's such a name in the parish records. I was looking in them only last month, when I buried Maggie Jardine's youngest. What was it you were wanting to hear of him?'

'Anything you know,' said Gil hopefully. 'How he came to die here, whose house he died in, where he's buried. The date of his burial, if you have it.'

'Oh, aye?' The priest looked dismayed. 'I'm thinking you're in the wrong place for all that, maister. Can his folk no enlighten you? For there's naught in the records but the day of his burial, that's for sure.'

'Could you show me that?' asked Gil, thinking that he seemed to spend more time than he wished foraging through old documents. A man of law dealt with such things as a matter of course, but somehow this other occupation seemed to gravitate naturally in the same direction.

'I could.' Sir Billy looked at the sky, and then at the strip of ploughed land he had achieved in the day. 'I need to get this turned, for all that. It's time the oats was in, or I'll ha' no meal next winter. I hope you'll can wait while I've daylight?'

'I've a long ride home,' Gil said. And a squabble to mend at the end of it, he thought ruefully. 'And I'd hope for a word with whoever witnessed the man's death afore I take the road. The quest on the two that were poisoned is for the morn's morn after Sext, I must be back in Lanark by then.'

'You're welcome to a bed in the kirk,' Sir Billy assured him. 'My loft's dry and snug, there's room for a pallet for you, and your man can lie in the town. Plenty time for the ride back to Lanark the morn, and you look like a man of sense, maister, you'll can catch us up wi' the way the world's turning as Young Dandy would never think to do.'

'I really –' Gil began, recalling the way Alys had refused his kiss when they parted before the gates of Cauldhope.

257

'No, no. Away you up the town, maister,' this appeared to mean the huddle of cottages on the hillside above the church, 'bid Joan Liddell give you a stoup of her twice-brewed, and I'll come for you when I'm done here.'

Sir Billy bent his back to the plough again, and Gil stepped reluctantly back from the claggy furrows, watching the man's expert thrust and heave with the simple device and the way the black soil turned and crumbled away as the culter tilted, the worms wriggling in the fresh tilth. The gulls swooped screaming from the kirk roof, and he turned and picked his way obediently up to the houses.

Patey was already established in Mistress Liddell's house, buried to the cheekbones in a wooden beaker. He emerged from it grinning as Gil ducked under the lintel, directed by the same ancient as before.

'Aye, maister,' he said, and licked the foam from his top lip. 'I doubt we'll no get back to Carluke this night. The light's going already.'

By the time he got the promised sight of the parish records, Gil felt he had paid dear for it. Mistress Liddell's twice-brewed was strong, but sour; he suspected there were nettles in the mash, and possibly other strange adjuncts, but knew better than to ask. He sat by her door, his feet tucked under the bench to avoid the steady dripping from the thatch, surrounded by an attentive audience who demanded news of the rest of the country, of King James, of the doings in Lanark and Carnwath. They had little interest in Edinburgh or Glasgow, but heard the latest tale of the embassies to English King Henry with judicious noddings. It was more taxing than his visit to Forth, reminding him strongly of the examinations which had earned him his two degrees. At least then he had not been interrupted by Patey, who had an opinion on everything.

Sir Billy came up from the glebe land in the midst of the interrogation, and drew a stool into the doorway as of right, stretching his boots out under the eaves-drip so that the last of the mud was washed off. Mistress Liddell, a small determined woman in a sacking apron, had already assured Gil that the priest aye sent strangers to sup her ale, and he was clearly as much at home under her roof as any of the assembly. As the light failed, the hearers slipped away to their suppers, but much to Gil's relief he and Patey were summoned within, seated with the priest and Mistress Liddell's man round the peat-fire in the centre of the floor, and served with hard, dark bread and broth in generous wooden bowls. The broth was savoury with roots and meat; when Gil commented, the man of the house, silent until then, said:

'Aye, the mistress keeps a good stewpot.'

'Joan and her man feed me for their tithe, ye see,' said Sir Billy, 'for I don't like to have charcoal in my loft. Too close to the thatch.'

'That's right handy,' said Patey, 'for a woman kens cooking and a priest kens priesting and why mix one wi' the other? It's right good, mistress, if you wereny spoke for a'ready I'd be looking to take you back to Belstane wi' me.'

'Och, you!' said Mistress Liddell, not displeased. 'Now you'd best be down the hill wi' your guest, Sir Billy, afore the light's all away. Will I draw you a jug of the good stuff to take along wi' you?'

'Aye, do that, Joan. Come away, then, Maister Cunningham, we'll get a look at the books.' Sir Billy rose to his considerable height, pronounced a blessing, received the promised jug, and made for the doorway, Gil following him. As the man of the house drew back the leather curtain which blocked it, rain rattled on the walls and blew through the aperture. Patey, dim in the glow of the peat-fire, raised his wooden beaker and settled lower on his creepy-stool.

'Good night to ye, Maister Gil,' he said, apparently without irony.

Chapter Twelve

Walking into Dalserf from the ferry at Crossford, Alys
had no trouble finding the kirk, long before Steenie's
helpful comment. It stood on the flat ground in a bend
of the Clyde, neatly built of dressed red stone, and had
a tall porch and two glazed windows in its south wall.
A dozen or so small cottages crouched round it, and a
track led to more perched among the trees in a cleft of
the steep valley side, woodsmoke rising through their
thatched roofs to mingle with the green haze of the
new leaves.

Sir Simon Watt, priest of Dalserf, a small wiry man
bundled in a worn budge gown, was delighted to
receive a bonnie young lady as a visitor. He said so, a
number of times, while he bustled about the low-
ceilinged chamber above the porch, setting a stool for
Alys, calling down to one of the old women in the
church for ale from the best brewster in the place, locat-
ing a box of sweetmeats someone had given him last
Yule. Finally he sat down opposite her, and surveyed
her appreciatively with sharp grey eyes.

'And what can we do for you in Dalserf, madam?
I take it you're no after pastoral counsel, seeing
Jackie Heriot's a deal closer to Belstane than we
are. You've never crossed the Clyde just to view our
wee kirk?'

'No,' admitted Alys, 'though it is a pretty kirk, and so well tended. It is mostly old work, I think? But the pulpit is new.'

'Aye, and Our Lady on the wall by the chancel arch.' Sir Simon's lean face split in a grin like Socrates'. 'The good women about the place were right put out when she was painted fresh,' he confided, offering the sweet-meats. 'They had to explain all their petitions to her again, they said, for she looked so different she must certainly be a different person.'

'But of course!' said Alys, sharing his amusement.

'And is it no Belstane where the man's been raised up out of the peat-digging, all uncorrupted? What's this I hear about him doing miracles?'

'Many people have come to view him, and now to make their petitions before him. I think Sir John is hopeful,' said Alys cautiously, 'but we have seen no miracles.'

'Well, the word's all across my parish the day, and there's a many folk crossed the Clyde seeking some benison or other. Though what Leezie Lockhart's look-ing for, and her past fifty and never wedded, is more than I can jalouse, and so I told her when she was through the place this noon bound for the crossing.'

'My groom said the ferry was more busy than usual,' said Alys. 'I hope they are not disappointed. The body seems to us a man like any other, slain long since and buried there. He's hardly uncorrupted, rather he's tanned with the peat like old leather, and he will fall into dust if we do not bury him soon.'

'Aye,' said Sir Simon, nodding sagely. He lifted a marchpane cherry from the box, and bit into it. 'I can see how that would be. Well, I canny prevent my flock running after such a thing, and if one or two finds peace of mind by it, well and good, it's a grace. So how can I help you, madam?'

262

Alys set her beaker down and folded her hands in her lap.

'I am a friend of Joanna Brownlie,' she said. 'I think you know her, and you'll know she has not to seek for her troubles.'

'Aye, I do. But I heard she'd taken a second husband. Is that not succeeding –?'

'That's the man who is missing from the coal-heugh. And now he is dead.'

'Never!' The priest crossed himself with the hand that held the cherry, and muttered briefly in Latin. They both said Amen, and he continued, bright-eyed, 'I'd heard about that, but I never knew it was Joanna's man, the poor lassie. Been gone for months, is that right?'

'Five weeks,' said Alys precisely. 'Since the morrow of St Patrick's day. And found dead only yesterday, though we think – my husband thinks,' she corrected scrupulously; she might still be annoyed with Gil but she would give him all credit, 'he has been dead since before Lady Day.' She smiled earnestly and the priest nodded again. 'Joanna needs the support of her kin, good though the folk at the coal-heugh are to her, and I hoped you might have some clearer idea than she does herself about where her brothers are.'

'Her brothers!' Sir Simon sat back, looking at her in some dismay. 'She'll get no support from them. Still, I suppose they should be given the chance. You never can tell, wi' kin.'

'They are not close, then?'

'Oh, they're not close. Never were. I suppose it's no wonder, two great laddies wi' the farm work to see to would take it ill out that their mother made such a pet of the wee thing, but they never took to her, as bonnie as she was, and then they both left home no long after I came to the benefice, and got set up for themselves.'

263

'Yes, I think Joanna was a late bairn. They would already be well grown when she was born. Mistress Lockhart must have missed her sons when they left,' said Alys, and got a sharp look at her use of the surname.

'She'd the lassie still at home. Told me once she'd always wanted a lassie to raise.'

'But then she died before Joanna was grown. Like my mother,' added Alys.

'It comes to many of us,' said Sir Simon in compassion. 'Aye, Marion died, poor woman, and grievous hard she found it to leave her daughter. Could hardly go to her rest, the poor soul, till she had her man swear in front of me that he'd cherish Joanna as his own ewe lamb.' He sighed, and shook his head. 'That's a deathbed I'll recall my life long. The lassie weeping, and her father sat by the pillow like a stone statue, and the two brothers summoned from their homes the one leaning on either bedpost,' he gestured with one hand and then the other, 'watching their mother as she failed. *Cherish her*, she kept repeating, *as your own ewe lamb. Swear it, Will*, she said. One of the sons said, *What need of him swearing, he's aye been doted on the wench*, and the other said, *Swear it, Father, and get this over*. But you've no need of hearing this, madam. What was it you were asking me? Where would the brothers have got to?'

'Yes. Yes, I hoped you might know more than Joanna.' Alys brought her thoughts to bear on the question. 'I'd heard they might be in Lesmahagow, but then –'

'Oh, no, they've both left there and all. One of them moved on a while back, I mind that, for he was nearly too late in returning when their father reached his end.'

'I wonder where they went,' said Alys hopefully.

'Ayrshire,' said Sir Simon with confidence. 'Sorn way. I'm from thereabouts myself, you understand, lassie, so it stuck in my mind when I heard. But where the other one – Glasgow? Ru'glen?'

'No matter,' said Alys without truth. 'What was it Maister Brownlie died of? I heard he took ill not long after Joanna's first husband died.'

'He did,' agreed Sir Simon, nodding. 'Poor soul, he'd a bad time of it. Two month of a wasting illness, wi' cramps to his belly and his legs, and pains in his wame to make him cry out. I visited often. He was wandering in his mind at the last,' he added, 'talking of owls on the bed-foot, and trying to make Joanna swear to have a care to Mistress Weir the same way he'd sworn to her mother, but he made a good end none the less, and made his confession and died at peace.'

'Our Lady be praised for that,' said Alys, and Sir Simon said Amen. 'What did they treat him with? It sounds like a sorry case.'

'Oh, there was a fellow over from the coal-heugh almost day by day wi' one receipt or another, a simple, a decoction, a tincture. Auld Mistress Weir and the other good-daughter both are herb-wise, maybe you've noticed that, and they kept sending anything they thought might ease him a wee bittie. But nothing helped.' The priest smiled ruefully. '*They all make me feel worse*, Will said to me one time.'

'Poor man,' said Alys. 'At least he saw all his children established in the world before he died. Rutherglen, you said?'

'Or Cambuslang. Or maybe it was Glasgow right enough.' Sir Simon lifted the box of sweetmeats and held it out to her. 'There's a strange thing, I've only the now thought of it. That was Hob that moved away down the Clyde, to Ru'glen or Glasgow, and I've heard them say the reason why he moved was, the place he had in Lesmahagow was full of owls.'

'Owls?' Alys repeated, since this seemed to be expected.

'Aye, owls. The story goes that they sat on the roof-tree and screeched all night, and stole the seed-corn out the meal kist, and he couldny take it longer and left the place. And there was his father as he lay dying talking of owls at the bed-foot, where, let me tell you, there was never an owl when I was there, poor soul.'

'How extraordinary!' said Alys. Do owls eat grain? she wondered. I thought they caught the mice and rats who would eat it. 'Are there a lot of owls in Lesmahagow?'

'I was never there,' admitted Sir Simon.

'And both the sons came back to the burial,' said Alys.

'Aye, and the displenishing, which is what brings most folk back to the old home,' said Sir Simon drily. 'It's seldom an edifying sight, the family after the funeral.'

'I hope the Brownlie funeral was harmonious.'

'No,' said Sir Simon. 'I wouldny say it was.' He shook his head, contemplating the past, and took another sweetmeat. 'I wouldny say it was,' he repeated.

'Did they disagree over the will?'

Another of those sharp looks.

'Aye, though it was clear enough. I scribed and wit-nessed it. All the outside gear to the sons, *to divide equably atween my sons Thomas and Robert Brownlie*, and the inside gear *to our dear Joanna that was born in the year of 1470*.'

'How odd,' said Alys. 'What a strange way to put it. As if there was another Joanna.'

'I thought that myself,' agreed Sir Simon, 'but there was never no more than the one lassie in the house-hold. But that was the way Will dictated it, and he'd no be shifted. Poor man,' he sighed, 'he doted on the

266

lassie, even though – Then the coin in his kist was to be split three ways after payment of his debts and a gift to the kirk. Straightforward, you'd think.' Alys nodded. 'Aye, you'd think, and you'd be wrong. What must they do but argue about what was inside gear, and discover a sum owing to Tammas that must be settled afore the coin was split. In the end, I'd say, Joanna got little more than half what was her due.'

'It's a strange thing, human nature,' said Alys. 'A great sum or a small one, neither is easy to share out.'

'Aye. Mind, she was still left to the good. A saving man, Will Brownlie, and did well from the property he held.' Sir Simon considered Alys. 'Is there aught else I can tell you, lassie? I'd aye a fondness for Joanna Brownlie myself, I'd be glad to help her in her difficulties.'

'They all made him feel worse,' repeated Lady Egidia. 'In what way, do you suppose?'

'I never asked,' said Alys with regret. 'He is a clever man, but I think with no medical knowledge. He might not have been able to tell me. But I think he found something odd about the man's deathbed, from the way he spoke.'

'Yes.' Lady Egidia stroked her cat thoughtfully. 'I like that hood better on you, with the narrow braid,' she observed. 'It becomes you more than the other one. You have good taste, my dear.'

From a woman presently clad in a patched kirtle and a loose budge gown of her late husband's this did not seem to be much of a compliment, but Alys had seen her mother-in-law dressed *en grande tenue* and took it at its proper valuation. Aware of her cheeks burning, she answered lightly, 'But of course. I chose Gil.'

'And he is making you happy?'

'He is,' Alys said, resolutely not biting her lip. Of course, the inquisition had to come, and a well-bred woman like this one would conduct it neither too early nor too late in the visit, and certainly in Gil's absence.

'You don't seem certain.' Lady Egidia raised one eyebrow, in an expression Alys had seen in Gil. Socrates, sprawled before the hearth, raised his head and stared at the hall door. 'Have you quarrelled? I heard your voices last night.'

What else did she hear? wondered Alys in alarm, her cheeks flaming again. 'No, no,' she said hastily. 'Gil had a dream that woke him, and we talked a while.'

'And then lay down again.' There was no hint of innuendo in the tone. 'So was it today you quarrelled?'

'We haven't –' Alys began, and the eyebrow rose again. 'It's a disagreement only. Nothing important – well, it is important, but not –' She caught herself up, took a deep breath, and explained briefly: 'He suspects all of the Crombie women, that is he suspects any one out of all of them, and I do not.'

'It seems to me he must be right – it must be one of them is the *bludy tung undir a fair presence*. Do you have good reason for excluding any of them?'

'I think so.'

Lady Egidia considered her for a moment, then smiled.

'He'll apologize,' she said. 'But don't let him always be the one to apologize. Even when he's wrong.'

'I know,' said Alys, answering more than the smile. Her mother-in-law stretched out a hand to her, over the sleeping cat, and was clearly about to speak when Socrates scrambled to his feet and they heard Alan Forrest's voice on the stairs.

'Mistress? It's Jackie Heriot here, about the corp in the feed-store. Will you see him?'

'Aye, send him up, Alan,' said Lady Egidia resignedly in Scots, and scooped the cat up. 'Come away in, Sir John. You'll stay to supper?'

'St Malessock,' Sir John corrected, sweeping over the threshold. 'Our martyred St Malessock, that brought the gospel to these parts and was cruelly slain for his faith.' He seemed to have gained in stature since the morning, Alys noticed, rising with her mother-in-law and bending the knee for his blessing. The ownership of a new and possibly important relic had done much for his self-esteem. 'I never meant to put your household out, madam,' he demurred, when the invitation was repeated. 'But it would be right welcome. Indeed. I've been up the Pow Burn wi' pastoral comfort and a Mass for them in their grief, and thought I'd come by this way to enquire when it would suit you to have us fetch our saint away, with a great procession and music and all.'

'Aye, St Malessock.' Lady Egidia sat down again, and the cat settled itself ostentatiously on her knee, glaring at Alys. 'I heard about that. Has he cured Davy Fleming?'

'Oh, too soon to say, too soon to say. We left the poor soul asleep, did we no, mistress,' he said with a nod at Alys, 'which at the least will do him some good, and if he can fast as I bade him and ask the saint's help, then I've great hopes. Great hopes,' he repeated, stroking Socrates' head.

'And how are they all up at the coaltown?' asked Lady Egidia.

Sir John shook his head compassionately. 'All at sixes and sevens, madam. The young widow – Mistress Brownlie – is overcome in her grief, and Mistress Weir is quite ill wi' concern for her.' Alys had difficulty in recognizing this picture. 'I said a Mass for them, though we had to make do with household candles to light it, the rats had eaten away all the ones in the box, even the wicks, indeed. Strange to think that the cause of their sadness is the source of our rejoicing, is it no? And tell me, mistress,' he turned to Alys. Trying to work out the logic of his last statement, she was taken by surprise. 'I think you were there when our saint came up out of the peat? Did you not see any portents? Was there no sign, no lights in the sky or flames hovering over his brow, nothing like that?'

'Nothing,' she said firmly, wishing Gil was present to share the moment. Sir John looked so cast down at this that she felt impelled to add, 'But I was not there when he was discovered, sir. When Maister Cunningham and I arrived he was already taken out of his burial-place and laid on a hurdle. You should ask the men of Thorn, who found him.'

'Thorn,' he said reflectively. 'Aye. Well, I can ask.'

'Best ask them separately,' said Lady Egidia on a sardonic note, 'if you want to get at any sort of truth there.'

'Oh, they would not lie to their priest,' Sir John responded, shocked.

'And the other folk at the coaltown?' pursued Lady Egidia. 'Mistress Lithgo and her daughters, young Crombie himself, how are they? I hardly think Crombie will be grieved for his grieve,' she pronounced, savouring the play on words, 'but the man was part of the household, so I've heard, and it stirs up the melancholy humours when death comes under your roof.'

'Indeed,' agreed Sir John, crossing himself. 'As you say, madam, young Crombie's hardly touched by it, save that he must be at the quest in Lanark the morn's morn. They were to ride out shortly after I came away, and lie in Lanark town tonight. The old lady was to go and all, though I tried to persuade her against it.'

'Mistress Weir?' exclaimed Alys involuntarily. Both of them looked at her, and she was annoyed to find herself blushing. 'But can she travel so far?'

'That was my concern, though I think her stronger than she looks. And spryer,' the priest added. 'These old women are often – indeed.'

'Indeed,' said Lady Egidia in the same sardonic tone as before.

'As for Mistress Lithgo and the two lassies, I scarcely saw them. The younger lassie was attending on her grandam, though I did wonder – and the older one and her mother were that busy about their stillroom, mixing and pouring this and that.' Alys glanced sharply at her mother-in-law and found her own sudden anxiety mirrored in the older woman's face. 'But I talked a while with Mistress Brownlie, brought her to a knowledge of God's goodness and grace, comforted her I hope. Indeed.' He crossed himself.

'I'm sure you were a comfort,' said Lady Egidia, sounding sincere.

'What were you going to say of Bel?' Alys asked. 'The younger lassie,' she added, as he looked blankly at her.

'Oh, the younger one. No, I wondered if she wished – och, it's a daft notion, poor lassie, she canny speak her needs, only that she knelt afore me as if she would ha' made some confession. But her grandam called her and told her not to take up my time. Certainly it takes a time to confess the poor lass. I'm sure Mistress Weir was right. Indeed.' He wound down as if his string had run out, and crossed himself again.

'I am sure you are right,' said Alys soothingly. Lady Egidia looked at her, but did not speak. 'Sir John, had you any acquaintance with the dead man – with Thomas Murray?'

271

'Wi' Murray?' Sir John looked from her to Lady Egidia. 'I did, indeed, a small acquaintance. A good enough fellow, but a good opinion of himself.'

Confession, thought Alys. He has confessed the man.

'Was he honest in his employment?' asked Lady Egidia, stroking the cat.

'He was. I can safely say that he was.' Sir John nodded judiciously.

The two women looked at one another again. One thing he cannot have confessed, thought Alys, and saw the same assumption in her mother-in-law's face.

'He died in mortal sin,' said Lady Egidia, as Alan Forrest entered the hall, followed by the women with responsibility for the linen and tableware. 'Ah, supper must be ready.'

'You asked me of his employment, madam,' said Sir John, 'and I say he was an honest workman.'

Alys's estimate of Sir John rose. It took a strong character to stand up to her mother-in-law.

Over supper, by unspoken agreement, they allowed the priest to soliloquize almost uninterrupted on the forthcoming translation of St Malessock. Alan Forrest listened from his place next him at the board, with a wary expression as if he was certain too much of the planned junketing would devolve on him.

'It'll be a longer procession than the opening of Parliament, Jackie,' he said at last. 'You should send to Lanark and get the carts from Corpus Christi, and save your feet –'

'No, no,' broke in Lady Egidia, in tones of innocence. 'I'm certain you should put the corp – the saint on the Meikles' cart, Sir John. They brought him here, after all.'

'The men of Thorn must have a part,' said Alys, keeping her face straight despite the image this conjured up. 'And if he should recover, so must Sir David.'

272

The meal was over, the long table cleared away, and the two women, Socrates and Sir John had retired to sit by the brazier in one of the smaller chambers before Alys accepted that Gil would not be home that night. The evening ahead of her suddenly seemed very long and empty, though the board had been set up for the game of tables, and she knew there was a piece of plain sewing waiting in their chamber. She sat smiling and nodding and caressing the dog as her elders conversed, wondering whether he had stayed away because she had argued with him, or because it was too late to come home. When the priest finally rose to take his leave, and extricated himself in a flurry of compliments and *Indeeds*, Lady Egidia looked wryly at her and said:

'My dear, if you're only now learning that love hurts, you have been fortunate.'

'Am I so obvious? I'm sorry, madame – I was better reared than that.'

'Not to our guest, I imagine, but I could tell you were elsewhere. Gil will put his duty first, you know that. He'll be home when he's done it.'

'I wouldn't have him otherwise,' Alys said firmly. Lady Egidia turned her head sharply as a step sounded in the hall, but Socrates had done no more than prick his ears, so Alys was not disappointed when it was Alan who appeared in the doorway, looking harassed.

'It's her from the Pow Burn at the yett, mistress,' he said. 'She'll not say what she wants, save it's for Maister Gil only. I've tellt her he's not here and won't be back this night, but she's saying she'll wait.'

'Which of them?' asked Alys with sudden anxiety. 'Is something wrong up there?'

Alan looked at his mistress, who nodded. And I was trying not to put myself forward, thought Alys.

'It's Mistress Lithgo. The one that does the healing. She was up at the yett as soon as I saw Jackie Heriot out to the road, just walked down from the coaltown. She'll not say what it is,' he repeated, 'only it's for Maister Gil.'

'See if she'll speak to one of us,' said Lady Egidia, regaining control.

Beatrice Lithgo was seated in the steward's room, still wrapped in a great blue plaid, her indoor cap covered by a veil of coarse black linen secured with a carved wooden pin. Her feet were propped on a brass box of charcoal, a cloth bundle and a jug of hot buttered ale beside them, and she held a cup in her hands. Her face was shadowed from the candlelight but she was as still and tense as a strung bow. As Alys stepped into the room and closed the door, she looked up and her mouth twitched in a small smile.

'M-my husband is not here,' Alys said. 'He went – he went on an errand. We think he may not come back till morning now.' Beatrice considered this, the expression of her eyes hidden. 'Is there some difficulty at the coalheugh? Can I help, or should we send someone with torches to Cauldhope?'

'No, Maister Michael's not who I need.' The other woman looked down at the cup of buttered ale, and up again. Her shadowed gaze met Alys's and slid aside. She looked higher still, at the broad boards stretched between the rafters, and took a breath. 'I want to ask Maister Cunningham who I should tell.'

'Tell what? Has something happened? Are your daughters safe? Is Joanna –?'

'They're well enough.' Again, the quick glance at the ceiling. Then, squaring her shoulders and looking Alys in the eye, she said, 'I need to ask your man who I should tell that I poisoned Thomas Murray.'

Alys put out a hand and steadied herself on the corner of the steward's desk. She became aware that her mouth had fallen open; closing it, she said very

274

carefully, 'You wish to confess to poisoning Thomas Murray?'

'You heard me right,' Beatrice assured her, with a faint flicker of her usual irony.

'Do – do you know what that will lead to? If you confess? If you are found guilty?'

'Drowning.'

The Scottish form of execution for a woman, thrust into a pit with the hands tied, held down by long poles. Probably better than hanging, if one had the choice. Alys stared at her, then turned away and poured herself a cup of the buttered ale, as much for something to do with her hands as anything else. She sat down, and sipped the fast-cooling brew, her mind still racing. After a moment she said, 'But what about your children?'

An infinitely small shrug was the only response.

'How.' She swallowed. 'How did you do it? What did you use? *Why* did you do it?'

This could not be happening. Gil should be here. Why had he not come home?

'I put the poison into the flask,' said Beatrice, patiently and very slowly. 'Seeing Arbella had tellt him to use it to mind her birthday.'

'When? When did you put it in the flask? And what did you use?'

'You keep asking me that. I should ha' thought you could work it out for yourself, lassie.'

'No, I think you have to tell us.' Alys frowned, trying to fit this into what she knew already. 'I don't understand why, either. Should we send after Sir John Heriot? Would you wish to confess to him?'

'No,' said Beatrice briefly. 'He was annoying my lassies, Thomas I mean. And Joanna,' she added as an afterthought.

'When did you put the poison in the flask?' Alys asked again.

'I got the chance while he made his farewells.'

'But where was the flask then?'

'In his scrip. In the hall. They were all in the window chamber, and nobody saw.'

It fits together, thought Alys. As I should have expected.

'And what was it? What did you use?'

'Work it out, lassie.' Beatrice sat back, her shoulders softening as if she had laid down a burden. 'Now, if your man's no looked for till the morn's morn, you'll have to keep me here,' she prompted. 'A dangerous felon like me's no safe to be running about the countryside in the dark. Will your good-mother be wanting to chain me?'

'I've no idea.' Alys found she was still staring at the older woman, unable to read her expression. 'Sir John cannot be far on his road – would you like me to send after him? Will you not confess to him?'

'Our Lady save you, my dear,' said Beatrice, with a flicker of amusement, 'I stood out there in the mirk getting chilled to the bone, waiting for him to take his leave. No, we'll not trouble Sir John. Your man can hear me when he comes home.'

'Won't they miss you at the coal-heugh? Your daughters will be worried.'

'Not them. I sent them off to bed, after Raffie left for Lanark wi' Arbella, and shut myself into the stillroom. They'll no ken till the morn that I'm no in there minding a triple-distillation.'

'What – what will happen to them? They can't . . .' Alys ran out of words, and Beatrice gave her another ironic smile.

'They'll can go wi' their brother. I've got him a good position as under-grieve wi' Russell at Laigh Quarter, over in Cadzow parish, though his grandam doesny know of it yet. Have no fears for them, lassie.'

There was another pause, while Alys's thoughts swirled and submerged like linen surging in a wash-tub. A fresh point surfaced, and she seized on it.

'What about the other man, the forester? Did you know about him? Did you know about Murray being –'

'No, I never discussed his tastes wi' the man. And I never knew about the other fellow. I'm right sorry about him,' Beatrice said. It sounded like the truth.

'Tell me again,' said Alys. 'You put the poison –'

'Into the flask, where it was in his scrip in the hall, afore he left. Because he was annoying my lassies and Joanna. That's the trouble wi' herbs,' she said sadly. 'They can heal, and they can kill, and once you've the knowledge in your hand, it's too easy to use it. Will you lock me in, lassie? I brought my night-cap, I can lie here as well as anywhere.'

As Alys stepped from the chamber, Alan Forrest, on the stair outside with a candle, said in an urgent whisper, 'Mistress – Mistress Alys – I heard all that.' He held out a substantial iron key. 'What are we to do wi' her? Maister Gil's no back yet, we'll no see him till the morn, what will we do?'

'We tell Lady Egidia first,' said Alys, turning the key in the lock and giving it back to him. 'She must direct where we put her or if she stays there. And we must get word to Gil as soon as may be in the morning.'

'Aye, but where is it he's gone? And there's the quest and all, I took it you and the mistress'd want to go down to Lanark first thing to witness that. And an owl out there screeching in the stable-yard, fit to deave every beast in the place,' he added, following her up the curling stair to the hall.

277

Lady Egidia was as astonished as Alys had been.

'Confessed to poisoning Murray?' she repeated. 'I canny believe it. It goes against everything I ever heard of her.'

'I heard her confess and all, mistress,' Alan assured her.

'She asked me to lock her in,' Alys said, 'but would you wish her to lie in the steward's chamber? Certainly it is warm and dry and we can give her a pallet and a blanket, but –'

'Aye, that's the best plan. You'll see to that, Alan. And no point in trying to find Gil till the morning.' Lady Egidia frowned. 'Will he come home, I wonder? If he's really gone so far as Elsrickle, it must be fifteen or sixteen mile from here, he may go straight to Lanark for the quest. Well, no sense in fretting over that just now.' She waved at the door. 'Go and see Mistress Lithgo comfortable, Alan, and maybe you would let the dog run in the yard a bit, and then you can get to your own rest.' She delivered a brisk blessing, and her steward departed reluctantly, towing an equally reluctant Socrates. 'A good man, Alan,' she said as their footfalls diminished down the stairs, 'but his ears are by far too long, and everything he hears gets to Eppie. Sit down, my dear, and we'll see if we can work this out between us.'

'My head is all in a whirl,' Alys confessed, obeying. 'I can make no sense of it. Why would Beatrice do such a thing? She is the one everyone calls a good woman.'

'A good healer,' agreed Lady Egidia. 'A wise woman, in all senses of the word. So if we assume there is some reason for her action, we'll get on better.'

'I can think of only one reason for such an action,' acknowledged Alys.

'But who? Who is she protecting?'

'Someone she loves? Someone important to her?'

'You've spent time with her lately. Who would you say is important enough for her to go willingly to execution for that person?'

Alys considered this, turning over her conversations with Beatrice Lithgo in her mind, but nothing seemed to offer itself. She shook her head.

'She is a woman of great reserve. Her daughters, of course, and her son if he was suspected, though I don't think Gil has even considered him –'

'He was in Glasgow at the time, I believe,' agreed her mother-in-law.

'– but as for Joanna and the old woman, I should say she was very fond of Joanna but held Mistress Weir in ... in ...' She paused, searching for a suitable word. 'Respect, I suppose, as one ought.' Their eyes met, and she saw amused acknowledgement of this in her mother-in-law's expression. 'No more than that. I've seen no sign that she dislikes her, but there is no liking.'

'I wonder why she stays there,' said Lady Egidia. 'Has she nowhere else to go?'

'If her portion is tied up in the business, it will be impossible for her to leave without unpleasantness,' said Alys. 'And the same must apply to Joanna, I suppose.'

'So we think Mistress Lithgo is protecting her daughters, or possibly Joanna. Do you suppose she thinks one of them poisoned Murray, or simply that one of them is suspected? I wonder what the younger girl wanted to confess?'

'Gil suspects all of them, including Mistress Lithgo herself,' observed Alys. 'I suppose he must have given away that much when he was last there.'

She drew her tablets out of her purse, and smoothed a list of dry stores off the second leaf, burnishing the last marks with the back of her fingernail. Socrates returned midway through this process, and had to be

279

reassured and ordered to lie down. That dealt with, she made a neat list of the five names, and after a moment's deliberation added Raffie at the end. Incising several columns beside the list, she said thoughtfully, 'We know some of them have the knowledge of simples and poisons, but how much knowledge does it take?'

'It has to be something which can be given in liquid,' supplied Lady Egidia, 'with a taste that can at least be disguised.'

'And a single dose must suffice.' She looked at her list. 'Much as I like her, I could not credit Joanna with so much sense, any more than a spring lamb, but perhaps I misjudge her. All the others could know that much from either Arbella or Beatrice.' She made a mark beside each name in the first column.

'What next?' asked Lady Egidia. Alys glanced up sharply at her enthralled tone, wary of mockery, but the older woman's expression matched her voice. 'Opportunity, or a reason for ministering poison?'

'Opportunity,' said Alys firmly. She tried to recall the several conversations about the silver flask, piecing them together as they came to her mind. 'Mistress Weir gave the flask to Bel to take to Murray before he and Joanna left their apartment. By Joanna's account, she put it straight in his scrip under his eye.'

'So Arbella and her granddaughter had the chance, but not Joanna. Raffie was in Glasgow, I suppose. What of the other two?'

'Phemie told us they all broke their fast together in the other chamber, all of them except Joanna and Murray. You know, Raffie could have given the stuff to one of his sisters to minister, perhaps without saying what it was.' She made a note at the foot of the leaf. 'I must ask Phemie, before she knows where her mother is and why she came here.'

'Ask her what?'

Alys looked up with an apologetic smile, realizing she had not finished the sentence.

'Whether she or her mother went out into the hall after Joanna came through, but before they all went to see the travellers off.' She looked at her list, and marked two names off in the second column.

'And we come to the reason,' said Lady Egidia. 'If there can be said to be a reason for killing another Christian.' Or anyone else, thought Alys, but did not say so. 'Did you tell me the lassie Brownlie was afraid of her man?'

'I thought she was,' agreed Alys. 'Beatrice thought she was. Joanna herself will say nothing against him.'

'Hmm. A well-reared lassie. And the younger girls?'

'Murray made fun of Bel and her lack of speech. He had slighted Phemie, who thought he would have married her until Joanna's portion became known –'

'Aye, Joanna's portion. That's a strange matter. Why – no, we must think this through first. What about the older women?'

'Mistress Weir and Murray were at odds over the running of the business.' Alys looked down at her list again. 'She only said that she was disappointed in him, but Phemie told me, and her brother told Gil, that the man had ideas of his own which did not suit the old lady. There was shouting, Phemie said.'

'That might be enough. Money does strange things to people. As for our penitent down in Alan's chamber, did she give a reason, or were you to work that out as well?'

'She said Murray was annoying her lassies, and Joanna.'

'No,' said Lady Egidia after a moment. 'She is a rational woman, and a healer. That makes no sense.'

'No. I think we are agreed, Beatrice Lithgo may have confessed, but she is probably not the poisoner.'

'So who is she protecting?'

'We come back to that,' agreed Alys.

'And today,' said her mother-in-law, with an abrupt change of direction, 'you went to Dalserf. What's your interest in Joanna Brownlie?'

'I heard a lot about the family,' Alys said. 'Particularly about her father's deathbed. And his will was very interesting.'

'What, you think the man Brownlie was poisoned and all?'

'Well, I wonder,' she said earnestly. 'His death was different from Murray's, but it sounds very like the way Matt Crombie died.'

Lady Egidia studied her for a time, her long-chinned face solemn in the candlelight.

'How many?' she said eventually.

'Four of the family, I think,' said Alys. 'And also Joanna's father. Five all told, I suppose, though not all by poison.' Her mother-in-law counted on her fingers, frowning, and finally nodded. 'But what worries me is why there has been an extra death this year.'

Lady Egidia looked at her, pursed up her long mouth, and finally said, 'And then there is this errand that has taken Gil to Elsrickle. It's a long ride for something that won't prove anything whatever the answer might be.'

'It won't prove it, but it adds to the picture,' Alys began, and was interrupted. Socrates raised his head, and suddenly scrabbled to his feet, claws scraping on the tiled floor, and rushed out into the hall. There was a furious hiss, a flurry of movement, a yelp from the dog almost drowned by the clatter and crash of pewter dishes, and a long-drawn-out yowling.

The two women collided in the doorway, the streaming flame from the branch of candles just missing Alys's velvet hood. Out in the hall, the light growing as Lady Egidia hurried the length of the chamber, they found the dog abased below the plate-cupboard amid the debris of the display, while the grey cat, all standing fur and round furious eyes, swore at him from the top shelf, tail lashing.

'Socrates!' exclaimed Alys. 'What a bad dog!'

'Silky has been teasing him,' said Lady Egidia, magnanimous in her pet's victory. 'I dare say she taunted him from out here just now. Has she clawed him?'

'He seems unhurt. Oh, no, here is a scratch on his nose.' Alys dabbed at it with her handkerchief, while the dog rolled his eyes at her and at the cat. 'Bad dog. Look at all the dishes you have brought down!'

She lifted the nearest, and stacked them up on the shelves. Lady Egidia set down the candles and joined her in the task, remarking, 'I'm surprised they aren't up from the kitchen to see what the noise was. It sounded like the clap of Doom. What's this? Oh, that piece of stone Gil had in his purse. Will you take it? If you're going up to the coal-heugh tomorrow you could give it back to the lassie.' She retrieved a round dish which had rolled into the hearth, and blew the ashes from it. 'And take both Steenie and Henry with you, my dear. Silky, you are a naughty cat.'

Chapter Thirteen

'I've no recollection,' said Phemie. 'You'll no tell me, Alys, that you rode all the way up here, and two of your good-mother's men at your back, just to ask me did anyone go into the hall alone that day?'

They were seated in the room she called the window-chamber, before the great glass window, Phemie and her sister side by side on the cushioned bench and Alys on one of the backstools with Socrates' head on her lap while he watched the girls intently.

'No, no,' said Alys hastily, 'I have more reason than that. But Phemie, you must see, the quest will most likely find that someone here gave the poison to Thomas Murray, and you need to be ready with the right answers when they come to ask them.'

'Oh.' Phemie glowered at her, lower lip stuck out, in an expression which reminded Alys again of the younger Morison girl. Apparently she had not thought about this until now. 'I've no recollection,' she said again. 'I was here, eating my porridge. What about you, Bel? You were here too, were you no?'

Her sister nodded, and pointed emphatically at the floor of the chamber where they sat.

'And the others? Joanna, your mother?' asked Alys innocently. 'Where is Joanna just now? How is she today?'

'My mother's been called out, I suppose, or she could

284

tell you herself and Joanna's laid down on her bed again. I'll go to her directly. No, she never came through till Murray did.' Phemie's tone was still disparaging when she referred to the man. 'My mother was in here dishing out the porridge. The kitchen brings it in and sets it up there,' she indicated the pale oak court-cupboard, 'and we serve ourselves. Or my mother sees to it.'

'And you all stayed in here till you went out to see them off.'

'That's right. What does it matter, anyway?'

'We need to find out all we can about how the man died,' Alys supplied. Bel turned wide blue eyes on her, considering her carefully, but gave no other sign. 'I should like to look in your mother's herbal, that she keeps in the stillroom. I wondered, too, if you would let me look at the great account book, the one your grandam showed me the first day we were here.'

'It's in her chamber,' said Phemie. 'Why? What will that tell you, just columns of numbers and names like that?'

Oh, my dear girl, thought Alys, and you a merchant's daughter too. Aloud she said only, 'It will tell me if Murray was an honest workman, as everyone says he was. If he was stealing from the business,' she amplified, in answer to Phemie's puzzled look, 'it should show in the accounts, though it might be far to seek. How long was he here?'

'Five year, maybe. If he was stealing coin, Arbella would notice,' said Phemie. 'Have you not seen yet that nothing happens up here by the Pow Burn that she doesny know of, one way or another?'

And that was not what you said before, thought Alys.

Bel stood up abruptly, gestured for Alys to follow, and led her out into the hall. Socrates' claws clicked on the flagstones as they went the length of the wide space and through a doorway at the back, into another pair of chambers. This was, quite plainly, Arbella's apartment. Alys looked about her curiously.

The chamber nearest the hall was panelled and painted, with several figures of saints on the wall by the fireplace and a garland of flowers round under the rafters. A curtained bed took up most of the floor, with a clothes-kist at its foot. There was a musty smell which made Alys wrinkle her nose. Socrates, pressed close against her thigh, raised his head, sniffing, and the hair lifted on his narrow back. Bel glanced at the bed, with its neatly bagged-up curtains of verdure tapestry, almost as if she expected to see it occupied, but went round it to the further door and opened that.

The inner chamber was small and gloomy. A bench at one end held a fortune in glassware, the delicate blown shapes reflecting light from the high tiny window. Alys identified flasks, two alembics and several curving tubes whose use she could only imagine. There was red wax to stop the joints with, and a stand below which one could place a small charcoal burner. This was more than a stillroom, she thought, recalling Mère Isabelle's working quarters.

The musty smell was stronger here, with a foxy overtone which made her gag, and a definite recollection of a mews she had once been shown. She was unsurprised when Bel pulled open one of the drawers beneath the bench to see it crammed with rustling linen bags, each neatly labelled in the same beautiful hand as in the account book. Arbella's herb collection also rivalled Mère Isabelle's.

'Did you gather all these?' she asked, bending to look at the labels, but Bel gave her a pitying look, closed the drawer by bumping it with her hip and reached to open another. Over their heads feathers ruffled, and both girls looked up; following Bel's gaze Alys found she was being watched by round pale eyes, peering from the shadows above the window. 'An owl?' she exclaimed. 'Can it be an owl, here in the house?'

Bel nodded, glowered at the creature, and with some ingenuity extracted something large and rectangular from the drawer she had touched, using her skirt to shield it from – yes, certainly from the owl's gaze.

'They are everywhere,' Alys said. Bel nodded again, clutching her prize under the folds of blue wool, and jerked her head to summon Alys into the outer room. Kicking the door shut behind them, she set the great account book carefully on a little prayer-desk by the head of the bed, then smoothed down her skirt and mimed someone holding a bird, stroking its feathers, simpering with affection. 'It's your grandam's pet?' Alys guessed. Bel nodded, but turned to the book. Opening the leather-bound boards, she leafed through the pages until she found the most recent entries, and stood back in triumph.

The accounts were very clear, and gradually drew Alys's thoughts away from the presence of the owl. The movement of coin, in and out of the coaltown, was meticulously itemized. The coal was tracked with equal precision. The numbers added up, marching down the pages, each line a distillation of some man's labour in the dirty, sweaty dark of the mine. I am fanciful, Alys told herself, turning back leaf by clearly inscribed leaf. It must be the effect of kneeling before the book like this, as if it was a prayer-book. The dog sat tall beside her, his chin on her arm, almost as if he too was reading the elegant writing.

Bel touched her hand to get her attention, and when she looked up sketched Arbella's wired headdress and upright stance, then folded her hands as if in prayer.

'She prays over the book?' Alys guessed. Then she thought, how silly, it is such an illogical fancy, but Bel nodded, unsmiling. How did she guess what was in my head? she wondered.

Two years back, in '91, a flurry of extra work was recorded. A winding-shaft and its shelter, *yhe new over wyndhous*, was carefully accounted for, along with the wood to build the gear and a heavy hemp rope. Joanna's dowry and inheritance being put to the good, thought Alys, and yet they don't seem to use the shaft. There was no mention of Matt's death. She turned further back, and became aware that the figures were changing. Comparing the Lady Day accounting year by year, when the returns on the winter's coal would have come in, she could see that the profits were not so good in recent entries as the earlier ones. She detected no abrupt change when Murray came to the coaltown, nor when he was promoted to grieve, though both these events were noted.

She turned more pages. The death of the younger Adam Crombie, Beatrice's husband, was signalled only by a record of the extra work needed in 1484 to clear the roof-fall. Studying the numbers which lay on the page before and after it, she came to the reluctant conclusion that business improved after his death, and then slowly deteriorated to the present figures.

Why should that be so? she wondered. Was it a question of the control of the business, or of who had a say in where the money went? What difference had it made when the younger Adam died? She heard Beatrice's voice in her head – *My man never liked to have much to do wi' the pit, Our Lady succour him.* Presumably matters went better when Arbella had sole control.

She turned back through the book, considering the implications of this. But even if her suspicions were correct, there was no need to poison Thomas Murray. Unless he had uncovered the same facts that she had recognized. Murray had questioned Isa in the kirk in

Carluke, she recalled. But Sir Simon at Dalserf had no knowledge of him, had presumably never met him.

'Does anyone else look at these accounts?' she asked Bel, who was still watching her intently. The other girl shook her head, and pointed firmly in the direction of the drawer where the book had been stowed. 'Not Thomas, not anyone else?' Another shake of the head. She turned a leaf, and registered the same change in the figures in March of 1477. The year Arbella's own husband, the older Adam, had died. And what has Gil discovered? she wondered. How did the man die, sixteen miles from here, too far to bring the body home? I would bring Gil back if he died in – in – in Paris, she thought.

Bel was becoming restless. She put a hand out as if to redirect Alys's attention to the most recent accounts, but did not touch the book.

'I will not be long,' Alys assured her. 'I have seen nearly enough.' She turned more pages back with care, one and then several together, and there it was, the information she was sure she would find, laid out on the page in complex looping letters. 'Bel,' she said slowly, 'do you know whose hand this is? There's half a year in a different writing.'

Bel shrugged, and pointed to the date: mcccclxx. Alys nodded.

'1470. Before you were born,' she agreed. 'Or I. No reason you should know. I wonder where your grandam was, that she couldn't keep the accounts herself.' She looked closer at the slanting columns crawling down the page. 'It was someone who could scarcely add up, whoever it was.'

Bel peered over her arm at the loops of writing, and put out a pointing finger at the same moment as Alys recognized that the curling scroll near the foot of the page was in fact a name. Under it a double line had been ruled, with a chilling finality.

'Gulielmus,' she made out. 'That is William.' Bel gave her a withering look. 'And the surname is – is – Fleming. William Fleming. Was that David Fleming's father, I wonder? I know he worked here.'

Bel shrugged, then turned her head sharply as voices sounded in the hall, and footsteps approached rapidly. Socrates got to his feet, head down, staring.

'Alys? There's a laddie out here asking for you.' Phemie halted in the doorway. 'Says he's got a word from your man.'

'From Gil?' Alys jumped up and came round the end of the bed. 'Is he safe? Who – is it Patey?' Behind her Bel was closing up the book and lifting it off the prayer-desk, and a faint annoyance crossed her mind – I wanted more time at that – but word from Gil took precedence.

It was indeed Patey out in the dim hall, hung over and disgruntled at being sent on again from Belstane, ducking in a graceless bow and pushing Gil's own set of tablets at her. The dog's nose twitched as he identified the familiar scent.

'Oh, he's taken no harm,' Patey agreed, 'other than by sleeping snug in the kirk loft in Walston, while I lay wi' the rats in a alehouse where I wouldny keep pigs, however good her ale might be. So he would have me ride on home and then they sent me up here to seek you, so you might as well look at what he's sent and I hope it was worth it, mistress.'

Alys was already moving to the open door, drawing the tablets from their soft leather pouch, turning the thin wooden leaves to find the message intended for her. Here it was, in French, in his clear, neat letter-hand.

My dearest, she read, and her stomach swooped at the words, *the man we sought died on the twentieth of March*

290

*in the year we knew of. He ate dinner with others, and drank
alone from a flask he had with him. Later he fell from his
horse in a swoon and struck his head, and died without
speaking again.*

She gazed at the writing, suddenly aware of two layers of thought in her head. One was competently
assessing this news and concluding that it only added
to their suppositions rather than confirming anything.
The other was studying the salutation, over and over,
while her heart sang. *My dearest*, he had written. *Ma
plus chère.* She knew well that she was loved, but here
it was in writing.

'Is it a billy-doo from your man?' asked Phemie in
envy, and she realized that yes, indeed, it was a billet-
doux, the first he had ever sent her.

'In a sense,' she said, and put the tablets away, stow-
ing the brocade pouch in her purse and straightening
her skirt over it. 'Where did you leave Maister Gil,
Patey?'

'He went straight down to Lanark for the quest,' said
Patey resentfully, 'which I wanted to hear and all, and
I'd ha' thought you'd be down there yourself, mistress.
And the mistress has went,' he added, 'all in her good
gown to take him the word of the woman Lithgo and
her –'

'What about my mother?' said Phemie sharply.

Alys, suppressing annoyance, said, 'She is at Belstane, and perfectly well. Patey, go see your horse
attended to, and find out if Mistress Weir's kitchen can
give you some refreshment.'

'Why is she at Belstane?' demanded Phemie, as the
man took himself reluctantly out of the house door.
'When did she go there? I've not seen her since
yestreen.'

'She fetched up at my good-mother's yett last night
just before dark,' said Alys guardedly.

291

Phemie stared at her. 'So why's she no come home this morning? Is she still there?' Then, her suspicions growing, 'It's no a call on her healing, is it, Alys. What are you no telling us?'

'She's locked in the steward's chamber at Belstane, that's where she is,' said Patey, still standing just outside the door.

'Patey!' said Alys, furious.

'What?' said Phemie.

'And chained and all, they're saying, seeing she's confessed to slaying the man Murray wi' strong poison.'

'Patey!' exclaimed Alys again, but her voice was drowned by Bel's sudden sharp cry, and that by a heartbroken wailing from the doorway to Joanna's chamber.

'She's done what?' demanded Phemie, as Joanna herself tottered out into the hall, arms outstretched, her bedgown falling away from her slender kirtled figure, and collapsed on the swept stone floor at Bel's feet. 'Alys, what has my mother done?'

She kept repeating this while the three of them contrived to get Joanna on to her feet and supported back to her own bed. Alys, chafing at one of the widow's limp hands, finally had no option but to reply.

'She has confessed, as Patey said, to poisoning Thomas Murray.' The hand she clasped tightened convulsively. 'I do not think she did it.'

'Then why has she –? And why did you no tell us when you came up here? What are you at here? Whose side are you on, anyway?'

'My husband's,' said Alys, as the first answer that came to her.

'Aye, I suppose,' said Phemie sourly. 'And here I thought you were my friend.'

'I hope I am,' said Alys, flinching from this blow. 'And Joanna's, and Bel's.'

'Then why –?' She stopped, and stared at Alys from the foot of Joanna's bed. 'You're saying you don't believe her? Why not? Why's she still locked in chains if you don't think it was her doing?'

'She isn't in chains, believe me. Do you think it?' Alys countered.

'No, but . . .' Phemie stopped to consider this. Alys watched with interest, despite the awkwardness of the situation, recognizing that the other girl was putting her undoubted intelligence to work perhaps for the first time. 'She's my mother. I ken her mind, her way o' working. I could never see her using her craft for that kind of purpose. You're no family, you must have a reason for no thinking it.'

Bel crossed the chamber with a small cup in her hand, and offered it to Alys for Joanna. It held the familiar brown sticky cordial, with its scent of cough-syrup. Alys glanced across at the cupboard, to see the yellow-glazed pipkin she had encountered before sitting there with its cover askew. She sniffed the cordial again, trying to compare the smell with that on the flask Gil had brought home.

'It's her own store of the stuff,' said Phemie roughly. 'You've no need of suspecting Bel of trying to poison her.'

'I know that.' Alys raised Joanna's head, and gave her a few sips of the stuff. 'It was a good thought. Joanna, do you feel better now? Can you talk?'

Joanna pulled herself to a sitting position, but shook her head, putting one hand to her brow. Phemie watched her, frowning, and then said, 'Why would my mother confess to something she'd no done?'

Bel turned to look at her sister, but made no sign. Alys waited for a moment, and said, 'For a good reason, I'd assume.'

293

'She was asking at me yestreen,' said Joanna faintly. 'After the others left for Lanark.' She put her hand over her mouth, staring wide-eyed at the coverlet. 'She asked me how the poison might ha' got into Thomas's flask, and I said I had no notion. Oh, say she never did it!'

'Had you talked about it at all before that?' Alys asked.

'The old witch wouldny have it discussed,' said Phemie. Bel tossed her head in disagreement, and Phemie added, 'No that that stopped Raffie, o' course, but Joanna was in here most of the time, so she never heard him, did you?'

'No, I never,' agreed Joanna wearily. 'I tellt your mother how Bel brought us the flask that morning and how I put it in his scrip and never saw it again. Nor I never want to see it again neither,' she added, with a flicker of that spirit she had shown before. 'I'll sell it and give the money to the poor. He was never an easy man, but he was my man, I never wanted him dead.'

'Did she believe you?' demanded Phemie.

'I've no notion.'

This is getting me nowhere, thought Alys. She was about to ask another question when the shouting began outside. Socrates scrambled to his feet and put his paws up on the windowsill.

'No again!' said Phemie. 'Is it another fight? They shouldny be up on the surface the now anyway.' She strode across to the window as she spoke, and drew an indignant breath. 'Would you believe it? There's that fool Fleming in the place again, after Arbella told him no to come back here!'

'Fleming?' said Joanna apprehensively. 'What's he here for? Don't let him —'

'Fleming?' repeated Alys, hurrying to look. 'I had thought him dead by now!'

'Never you worry,' said Phemie. 'Jamesie has him in hand. That's what the shouting's all about.' She looked at her sister, and then at Joanna. 'I'll get a word wi' Jamesie. You stay here,' she instructed, and left the room, without glancing at Alys.

There was a knot of men by the small building Phemie had identified as the office. Several were colliers or surfacemen, caked with silvery mud and brandishing their tools. In their midst, Jamesie Meikle and David Fleming stood face to face, the man Simmie nodding at the priest's back while Fleming shouted incoherently at the collier, pointing wildly at the office, at the little chapel, up at the house. As Alys watched through the window Phemie came into sight, clumping purposefully over the cobbles on her wooden soles, but the men seemed not to notice her.

There was a tugging at her sleeve, and Alys turned to find Bel at her elbow, gesturing urgently towards the door.

'You want me to go too?' she asked. The girl nodded, and indicated by more gestures that she would stay with Joanna.

'You'll likely can stop them getting to blows,' said Joanna, with a confidence which Alys found touching, and craned unsteadily to see out of the window. 'Oh, my, what's Jamesie – oh, what will he do? Please, will you go and stop them?'

Jamesie Meikle was still trying to be reasonable. As Alys approached, he was saying, 'Our mistress forbade you these policies last time you were here. You shouldny be on her land at all, let alone trying to search the office where the tallies and the accounts are kept. We'd be well within our duties to fling you in the burn and leave you –'

'The law will support me,' declared Fleming feverishly, 'I'll take the evidence to the Sheriff straight way, and he'll see the right o' my actions! I ha' proof positive now of the witchcraft that's being worked here, and one or all of these wicked women will –'

'We'll ha' no more of that,' said one of the colliers, hefting his mell.

'And as for you, Simmie Wilson,' continued Jamesie, 'I'd ha' thought you'd more sense than turn up here poking your nose where this glaikit sumph tells you.'

'Sumph, is it?' howled Fleming. Alys studied him anxiously; she was astonished to see him on his feet, but it was clear his recovery was anything but complete. The man was trembling and sweating, hollow-eyed and hollow-cheeked, his clothes hanging from him as if he had lost half his weight. She could smell the pear comfits from where she stood.

'Aye,' Simmie was saying, 'but I found what he said I'd find, which is proof o' witchcraft, Jamesie Meikle, so what do you think of that?'

'Proof? Aye, proof of your own soft-headedness,' said someone.

'There's all the candles gone from the chapel,' protested Simmie, 'just as Davy here said I'd find, though he put new ones just the other week –'

'Is that what Agnes Brewster's been burning?' said another voice, to laughter.

'Well, what d'you call this?' said Simmie, goaded. He fetched a bundle out of the breast of his doublet and opened it out into an appalled spreading silence. Between the coal-blackened shoulders Alys saw as clearly as any of them what lay within the sacking. Four little mommets, clumsily modelled of white wax, clad in scraps of cloth and pierced with thorns through heart or head, three with bare crumbling waxen legs, the fourth in petticoats. Her heart sank. This was definite proof of witchcraft. But who – which of the people here – had made and hidden these?

For perhaps five breaths the silence hung, and then incongruously a lark burst into song over their heads. As if it was a signal, the man nearest to Simmie struck out, knocked the little figures to the ground, and stamped on them with a muddy boot, saying savagely, 'Where's yer proof now, Simmie Wilson? Show that to the Sheriff, won't ye?'

The other men began shouting round him. Fleming threw himself forward with a cry of rage, scrabbling in the dirt for the fragments of wax, and Phemie, white and trembling, seized Jamesie Meikle's elbow saying under the noise, 'He made that up! Surely he made that up, he must ha' made those things himself!'

Meikle turned to look at her, as some of the men laid large rough hands on Fleming, and Simmie held the sacking wrapper up above the mêlée saying indignantly, 'No I never, I found them, they were up yonder hid in the thatch!'

'Up where?' demanded Phemie, but Alys, who had seen where he pointed, stepped back away from the group and set off round the end of the house and up the hill, the dog at her heels. One for Thomas Murray, she was thinking, one for David Fleming. And the others must be – yes, they must represent Gil and herself, newly constructed, the immediate reason for the absence of candles in the little chapel. And Gil had that terrifying dream. She shivered, crossed herself, and turned uphill, making for the *new over wyndhous* which Arbella had accounted for so meticulously. For the first time, she had begun to consider that there might be some foundation for Fleming's persistent ideas, and it was an unpleasant thought.

Halfway up the slope, she found the two men who had accompanied her from Belstane were beside her.

'What's ado, mem?' asked Steenie, still wiping ale from his mouth. He acknowledged Socrates' greeting and added, 'Davy Fleming was like to die yesterday, and now he's up here shouting at the colliers, is it a miracle right enough?'

'More like the fasting has helped him,' said Alys, pausing to look over her shoulder at the group in the yard. As she watched Phemie spoke, distracting the men, and Fleming seized the chance and ducked away from the grasping hands round him, slipped into the colliery office and slammed the door. By the time the sound floated up to them Jamesie Meikle had already deployed three men to guard the little building, and was confronting a belligerent Simmie.

'And what's the stushie about?' asked Henry at her other elbow.

'Fleming has been searching the place for signs of witchcraft,' said Alys.

'Witchcraft?' said Henry in alarm. 'Here, if Beatrice Lithgo's taken up for a witch, where am I to get supplies for dosing the horses?'

'Embro?' suggested Steenie. 'Where are we going, mem?'

'Here,' said Alys, pausing before the wide, low structure of the upper shaft-house. 'Simmie said he found something here, hidden in the thatch, and I wondered if there was anything else to find.'

'Proof?' asked Henry sharply. 'Simmie Wilson wouldny ken proof if it bit him on the bum, any more than our Patey. Who I've sent back to Belstane, by the way, mistress.'

'This could have been proof,' admitted Alys, 'but one of the colliers destroyed it.' She shivered. Her skin was still crawling at the sight of the little figures, brief as it had been, with their tatters of clothing and their pierced bodies.

'Colliers is odd folk,' pronounced Steenie. 'But who's he naming for the witch? Who'd hide something up

298

here as far from the house? What are we seeking anyways?'

'I don't know,' said Alys. 'I want to look for a hiding-place, but there may not be anything left in it, if Simmie found it.'

Both men looked at her a little oddly, but they began to inspect the thatch obligingly enough, looking under the eaves at the bundled ends of the heather-stems and prodding as far up the roof as either could reach. Alys ordered the dog to sit at the doorway, stepped inside and peered up into the shadows at the purlins which supported the thatch, trying to ignore the shaft gaping blackly at the centre of the hut. There seemed to be nowhere to hide anything; the clay-daubed hurdles rose to meet the roof-frame, with no ledge or wall-plate at the top, and she could see nothing like a shelf or niche under the thatch. Up in the crown of the roof there was the ruffling sound she had heard before, exactly like feathers, like a bird settling its plumage. She turned towards the winding-gear, and something fell from the rafters in silence and swooped at her face, missing her as she ducked and exclaimed in terror, sailed on out of the doorway and up over the hillside, the dog in delighted pursuit.

'What's up?' demanded Henry, arriving with Steenie as she straightened up. 'What made ye squeal, lassie? Mistress,' he corrected himself. 'What was yon?'

'It was a owl,' said Steenie, looking back over his shoulder. 'Did it hurt ye, mem?'

'No,' she said shakily, her heart hammering, 'no, it gave me a fright, that's all. It came down from nowhere, out of the roof.' Yet another of the creatures. And no wonder Gil had a bad dream, she thought, after the same thing happened to him.

'Out of the roof? Where was it perching?' asked Steenie.

Henry nodded. 'A good thought, Steenie lad. What was it standing on?' He swung himself up on to the frame of the winding-gear and peered along under the roof-tree. 'I see it – there's a cross-beam. Now can I reach it?'

'Have a care!' said Alys involuntarily, as he stretched out an arm, but he drew back, with a wary look at the rope disappearing down the shaft, swung himself on to the ground and tried again from the other side of the structure.

'Aye,' he said, groping along the beam. 'I'd say it roosts here. Foot of the shaft must be littered wi' its pellets. And what's this? Cloth?' He came down again, holding his find by one corner, and looked at Alys. 'We'll take it into the light, mistress, but are ye for opening it up?'

'Oh, yes.' She took the thing from him, and stepped out into the daylight to inspect it. Socrates returned from his pursuit of the owl and sat down, tongue hanging out, as she did so. The cloth bag was as big as the palm of her hand, very dirty though not troubled by owl droppings, and seemed to be of silk damask as if it contained a relic. She untied the cord and drew out a swaddled bundle; both men were watching intently, and Steenie crossed himself as she began to unfold the brown linen wrappings.

The object at their centre was not readily recognizable. It was longer and thicker than Alys's thumb, yellowish, wrinkled and waxy. She stared at it for a moment, and said, 'Is it a root of some herb? A mandrake, perhaps? I never saw one.'

'Nor did I, mistress,' said Henry drily, 'but I never heard that a mandrake had a fingernail. See, this side.' He indicated one end of the thing. She tipped it over on her palm, and saw the nail, thick and cracked, as yellow as the rest of the finger. She jerked the object away from her in a sudden convulsion of horror, and it flew between the two men and landed in a clump of heather.

Socrates pounced, and came up grinning, the hideous thing clutched in his teeth. Alys lunged at him, but he bounded away, tail waving.

'Give!' she ordered. 'Leave it! *Leave!*'

'What is it, anyway?' demanded Steenie, crossing himself again.

'A thumb,' said Henry grimly. Alys drew a deep breath, and forced herself to stand still and consider matters.

'It could be a relic of some sort,' she said, 'all wrapped up like that, but there was no paper with it to name it, as a relic should have. I don't –' A crunching sound alerted her, and she flung herself at the dog again. 'Socrates! Give, you dreadful dog, give!' This time, despite Steenie's attempt to help, she managed to get the animal by the collar, and prised his narrow, powerful jaws open with difficulty. The fragments of bone and dried flesh which emerged were bonded with saliva; she caught them in the linen binding and pushed the dog away, holding the unpleasant bundle out of his reach.

'What do we do wi' it, mistress?' asked Henry, scratching the back of his head. 'If it's a relic it'll no do to let on the dog got it –'

'It's no relic,' said Steenie scornfully. 'Hid in a filthy place like that? I say we put it in the bag and drop it down the shaft, mem, and nobody's to ken how it got there if it's ever found.'

'It is a proof of witchcraft,' said Alys, stuffing the bundled linen back into the bag. Socrates pushed at her hand with his long nose, hoping to get his new toy back, and she tapped his muzzle with her finger. 'No! No, I think I must show it to Gil at least, though I do

301

not like taking it with me.' She pulled up her skirt to reach her purse, and after a moment's thought wound her beads round the damask as some protection, before she stowed it beside Gil's tablets. 'Did you find anything in the thatch?'

'Only the hole where Simmie Wilson pulled out whatever he got,' said Henry. 'Mistress, is that the family coming home? There's a deal o' ponies coming across the hill yonder.'

'Your brother stayed behind,' said Arbella in a faint voice, 'to see to the coffining and arrange a burial. But Maister Michael here, seeing how weary I was, offered to bring me away.' She accepted a glass of the omnipresent cordial from Bel, sipped at it, and gave Joanna a smile of infinite sympathy.

'It went well enough,' reported Michael, nodding at her words. 'The assize brought it in as murder, and directed Maister Gil to search out who was the guilty one.'

'He was there in time, then?' said Alys. She moved her feet to allow the offended dog to lie down under her backstool, and her purse bumped against her leg.

'Oh, never doubt it, my dear,' said Arbella. 'So all will be well. I'm certain he'll get that settled in good order. And what brings you up here? Did I see you at the over windhouse the now?'

She has eyes like – like an owl, thought Alys.

'Davy Fleming's on the policies,' burst out Phemie before she could speak, 'and searching the place for evidence of witchcraft so he says. Cauldhope's man Simmie found something up at the windhouse, so he said, and she went up for another look at it. Did you find aught, Alys?'

302

'We found the hole in the thatch where Simmie got the bundle he had,' said Alys truthfully, though the object in her purse seemed to burn her shin through kirtle and shift.

'Fleming?' said Arbella, her voice suddenly much stronger. 'I thought he was dying!'

'So did I,' said Michael. 'Mistress Weir, I'm right sorry if he's up here again making a nuisance of himself —'

'He's barred himself into the office,' said Phemie, 'wi' the great desk across the door, and Jamesie set three of the men to have an eye to the place in case he got out. They'd found — Simmie found —' She halted, and looked at Alys.

'Wax figures,' said Joanna into the hesitation, and shivered. 'Jamesie told me. Little mommets, all clothed and stabbed through wi' thorns. Who would make such things here, Mother? Is it all true, then? Mother, I canny believe it, that one of this household —'

'I'll not believe it,' said Arbella, and slammed her stick on the floorboards. 'There's none in my household would practise such a thing. Fleming has made them himself, to cast suspicion on us!'

Alys preserved her countenance, aware of Michael looking at her.

'Where is Gil?' she asked him quietly.

'He went back to Belstane with Lady Cunningham. I think he expected to find you there, and he wanted a word with Mistress Lithgo.'

'Aye, where is my good-daughter?' asked Arbella, catching the name. 'Phemie, my pet, where is your mother? Not in her stillroom yet, surely?'

'She's at Belstane,' said Phemie, 'locked up they tell us, seeing she went there to confess to poisoning Thomas.' She watched with evident satisfaction as Arbella stared at her. The old woman's mouth fell open, her pale clear skin went an unpleasant blotchy yellow, and it was suddenly obvious that she painted her face.

'Beatrice?' she said sharply, making some recovery. 'Beatrice has confessed to –'

'She spoke to me last night,' said Alys. 'I do not believe it, madame.'

Arbella studied her narrowly, then said much as Phemie had done, 'Why no?'

To Alys's relief, she was spared the need to answer this. Yet again, shouting broke out in the colliery yard below the house. Phemie craned to see down the hill, and sprang to her feet with an exclamation.

'He's out! Fleming's out! He must ha' slipped by the watch. Where's he making for?'

Alys jumped up to look, and through the writhing glass saw the running figures, the pursuit, the staggering quarry. He reeled down the hillside between the scatter of huts as though he was drunk, the colliers slithering after him through the grey mud, and suddenly changed direction and dived into the doorway of another low wide building like the upper shaft-house. Two men reached it almost immediately, and Alys waited for them to follow him in and drag him out into the light, but they checked in the doorway as if frozen where they stood. Another reached them, and two more, and all stood staring into the little building in what seemed to be dismay.

'What has happened?' Alys said in alarm.

'He'll have gone down the shaft,' said Phemie. 'That's the low shaft-house. He'll ha' fell in, the state he was in.'

'Just like his father,' said Arbella slowly, with a strange emphasis. She bent her head, crossing herself. 'What an end.'

* * *

Alys hurried forward into the dark, half crouched, thinking that this was less of a treat than she had imagined it would be a week ago.

'He still lives,' said Arbella ahead of her. 'Mind how you go, mistress.'

Alys nodded, then realized the movement would not be seen.

'I am minding,' she said, stooping lower where the candle lit a low curve in the roof.

The mine stank. She had not expected this. Brought up with stone, she knew the scents of damp rock, of the blood-red, rusty water and strange colourless plants which one found in dark places, but she had not been prepared for the distant smell of human ordure and rotted food. And rats, which scrabbled in the dark. Ahead of her Arbella picked her way up the slope, moving freely and confidently like a fish in water.

'I take it right kind in you,' the old woman continued, 'to agree to come below ground with me. If she'd been here I'd ha' brought my good-daughter, you understand, but you're near as herb-wise so she tells me, and by what Jamesie said the man still lives.'

He could be heard groaning, Jamesie Meikle had said, the shaft being no more than five fathom deep. This had earned a sharp response from Arbella, along the lines that she had watched them sink it before he was born or thought of. Ignoring this, he had declared that he would not risk sending a man down by the shaft, because the winding-gear was old and needed to be repaired. He would need to get someone to go in with him from the mid ingo. Alys understood this to mean the middle of the three entries, the one not in current use. At this his mistress had announced that she would go, commandeered Alys's help, and ordered Jamesie to assemble what was needful to get the man out, alive or dead, and follow them in.

So now, her riding-dress and hat left in the office, the skirts of her kirtle belted up, and one of the miners' hooded leather sarks over all to protect her from falling stones, Alys was groping her way up the surprisingly steep slope behind a similarly clad Arbella, wondering how wise this had been, errand of mercy or no. Whatever Gil resolved about the death of Thomas Murray, it seemed likely to inconvenience the Pow Burn household, and she was uncertain how much Arbella knew she had discovered. Quite apart from Bel's message on the slate, she reflected. Her purse, with the gruesome find from the upper shaft-house, was in the office with her riding-dress, and though she might feel as if it was outlined in red ink nobody else had reason to notice it, which was a small comfort.

'I'll not have Will Fleming's son fall to his death in my coal-heugh,' said Arbella suddenly, as if there had been an argument, 'and let folk say I did nothing about it. If this one is no more than half the man the father was.'

Alys made some mechanical answer. She was staring about her, moving cautiously. The candle flame leaped and flickered in surprising draughts, but showed gaping dark places to right and left, perhaps the rooms Phemie had described, which meant that the massive pillars of living rock between them were the stoops. The roof was uneven, but seemed to be the lower surface of a bed of sandstone, the flame striking tiny sparks in the grains of sand in its matrix. The tunnel walls were black, but only a section at knee height was coal. There were sounds – dripping water, the rattle of an occasional falling stone, a faint creaking now and then. A shout, presumably from the surface, which resounded eerily in the tunnels and spaces. And it was dark, darker than she would have believed possible, outside the patches of candlelight.

At least, she reflected, there were likely to be no owls underground.

There was a groan which echoed along the tunnel, and faint voices, sounding oddly flat. Of course, if we are close, she thought, we must hear the men at the top of the shaft even when they don't shout.

'Here he is,' said Arbella. She had halted, and was holding the candle over a sprawled shape on the tunnel floor. 'Bring your light, lassie, and we'll see what ails him.'

The tunnel was wider here, and there were various items strewn about, a broken basket full of spare tools, a couple of coils of rope, two wooden buckets big enough to hold a ten-year-old child. A bundle of timbers lay just to one side of the patch of stones and earth which had come down the shaft, and on it, back ominously reflexed, lay Fleming. Alys came forward, turned up one of the buckets and fixed both candles on its base by dripping wax to secure them.

'It does not look good,' she said.

'Aye, he's about ready for the priest, I fear,' agreed the old woman. She bent and patted Fleming's face. 'Davy! Davy Fleming! Can you hear me?'

There was a pause; then the man's eyes opened.

'Who –?' he croaked.

'That's me, Davy. Arbella Weir. I'm sorry to find you like this, Davy. Death unshriven's no what I'd ha' wished on your father's son.'

'I am shriven,' he croaked.

'Where does it hurt?' Alys asked, taking his hand. His eyes rolled towards her, and in the light of the two candles he knew her. A wisp of his ingratiating smile crossed his face, and he drew a harsh breath.

'Mistress,' he whispered. 'Doesny hurt. Thanks be – Our Lady. Did you read –?'

'I read it,' she said. And keep quiet, man, she thought. 'Save your strength, Sir David. We'll get you out of here and made comfortable as soon as maybe.'

'I willny – last so long.'

'Aye, well, you meddled in things that wereny your concern,' said Arbella, her face in shadow, 'and it's brought you to this end, the same as your father. I'm right sorry, man.'

'I've learned,' Fleming whispered. 'I know. I know what you've been –'

Arbella sat back, and knocked the bucket which supported the candles. They fell over, rolling across the flat wooden base, sending shadows leaping wildly round the three of them, then on to the floor of the tunnel. One went out. Arbella twisted awkwardly in pursuit of the other, and put her hand on it.

Alys exclaimed as darkness complete enveloped them.

'Never fear, lassie,' said Arbella's voice. Alys could hear movement close to her, the rustle of clothing, a creak from the thick leather of the collier's sark Arbella wore. Fleming drew another harsh breath, and breathed out, and made a short choking noise. In sudden alarm she crouched there in the dark, waiting for his next breath.

It never came.

Chapter Fourteen

Gil gazed in exasperation at Beatrice Lithgo.

'I'll not believe you,' he said. 'I don't accept this confession.'

She shrugged, suddenly looking very like her older daughter. 'I'll not retract it.'

'Who are you protecting?'

'Protecting?' She raised her eyebrows.

'Then what about the other deaths?'

'The forester?' She crossed herself. 'I'm right sorry he died, Our Lady bring him to grace. I never intended that.'

'I meant,' said Gil, and counted them off, 'Matt Crombie, Will Brownlie, your own man, your good-father. Did you kill them too?'

'No,' she said blankly. 'Why would I kill any of them?' There was a pause in which she seemed to be thinking over the list. 'No, I'd no reason to poison them. They wereny poisoned,' she added hastily.

'You're certain?' said Gil. She raised her eyebrows. 'I've just come back from Walston.'

'From where? Oh, aye. The parish where Auld Adam died. And what did you find there, maister?' she asked in conversational tones. 'I was never there myself.'

'You've not missed much,' Gil admitted, 'it's two villages and a high hill, but I'd a read of the parish records, kept by Sir Billy Crichton in very good order, and this morning at first light I got a word with the folk that took Adam Crombie in when he fell from his horse.' She watched him, still giving nothing away. 'It seems he ate his dinner in the High House at Elsrickle, along with his two men, and drank a toast to Arbella's birthday from a silver flask he had with him, which he didn't share. He set out to ride on to the next house on his round.' She nodded. 'A mile or so down the road he seemed dazed, as if he was unsure of where he was, and fell from his horse in a swoon, and struck his head. He was carried into the nearest house, and there he died without speaking again.'

'Was his belly afflicted?' she asked, frowning.

'No. I asked about that particularly, after what you said the other day, and he had neither vomited nor purged. I spoke with the woman of the house,' he added, 'she'd be like to know.'

She nodded again, accepting this. He waited, but when there was no further reaction said, 'It seems very like whatever slew Murray and the forester. But of course you'd know that, wouldn't you?'

Another long look, but no words. This was hard work.

'My mother has suggested it was orpiment slew your good-brother and Will Brownlie. Does that sound right?'

She nodded again, very slowly, and closed her eyes. 'Orpiment. Arsenical salts. Of course, it fits, of course. And the collier's bairns and all, that were took ill the same summer. But why? Who would want to kill Matt, the bonnie lad? And what had the man Brownlie done, save father Joanna?'

'That's what I'm trying to find out,' he said patiently. 'You could help me, if you weren't wasting my time trying to confess to all sorts of wickedness. *The falshede of the woman is wonder merveyllous.*'

Her eyes flew open, and she gave him another long

look. But he had lost her again, he could see that. He would get no further co-operation.

He paused on the stairs down from the steward's room, looking from one of the slit windows out over the grazing-land towards the peat-digging and the track which led to the coaltown. He had dreamed again before dawn, and it was still with him; this time he had stood on a bare hillside, looking across this same land-scape. Someone stood beside him; when he turned to see, it was a man, a stranger, naked but for a leather cap and a russet fox-skin belt. Smiling at Gil, he had held out in one hand a dull black stone with a little fish drawn on it, in the other a sprig of yew, the green needles and waxy red berries vividly identifiable. *Thank you*, the stranger said. *You need these.* Then Sir Billy had roused him for the ride over to Elsrickle.

It felt important, but it seemed to mean nothing.

His mother, restored to her working clothes, was in the stable-yard inspecting her horses, and looked round as he came down from the house.

'Are you for the Pow Burn, dear? Here's Patey just come in – Alys has your message.'

'Is all well up there?' he asked the man.

'Oh, aye. Well, they're all to sixes and sevens, but apart from that. And the auld wife away, and Davy Fleming playing merry-ma-tanzie about the yard, and –'

'Fleming?' said Gil sharply.

'Michael said he left the man abed,' said Lady Egidia in surprise, 'and dying, he thought.'

'He was dying,' said Gil.

'Well, he was up at the Pow Burn the now,' said Patey sulkily, 'and making Simmie Wilson and me hunt all about the place for proofs of some sort, whatever he meant by that. No candles in the chapel, and Jamesie Meikle shouting, I went back to their kitchen, you can believe it. Only but Henry sent me home, and I've had no dinner yet.'

'We left Michael and Mistress Weir at the road-end, how long since?' said Gil to his mother. 'She must be home by now. Alys will need help.'

'Take the bay with the white blaze,' said Lady Egidia, 'he's fresh and he's fast.'

The coaltown was in greater disarray even than Patey had said. Gil could see this as soon as he came over the shoulder of the hill. There was no work going on, and many of the colliers were standing about in the yard in twos and threes, staring grimly up the hillside. The women had come down from the row of dwellings and were also waiting in silence near the topmost ingo, plaids drawn round them, the children in their midst. Nothing seemed to be happening, but as he neared the house, two men emerged from the black entry of the mine, supporting a third one; a woman screamed, and hurried forward, and another fell to her knees wailing.

Michael emerged from another outbuilding as Gil dismounted. He cast an anxious glance up the hill, and said, 'I'm right glad to see you, Maister Gil. All's to do here!'

'Where's Alys?' demanded Gil. 'And where's Fleming?'

'Underground,' said Michael. Horror-struck, Gil looked from him to the group at the ingo and the screaming woman. 'No, no, it's no that bad. At least, it is, but that's no where she is.' He drew a breath, and explained more clearly. 'Fleming ran in there and fell, went five fathom down that shaft yonder.' He pointed to the low building from which he had emerged. 'He's lying injured at its foot, and Mistress Weir went in by the mid ingo to see to him and took Mistress Mason along wi' her.' Gil stared at him, his stomach suddenly churning. 'Jamesie was to get men and hurdles together and follow her to bear him out, but the two of them had barely gone underground when someone came out at the top ingo shouting that there was a roof-fall in there, and men trapped, and he dropped all to clear it. They'll be a good while longer, I'd say, that's only the first one come out now.'

'And Alys is below ground with Mistress Weir,' said Gil grimly, tethering his horse. 'How came you to let her –' He bit that off. Michael had no authority over his wife. 'Fleming fell down a shaft, you said? Which one?'

'Yonder. Where Henry is.' Michael followed him towards the wide low structure. 'I tried to call down to them, but the echoes are too strong, you canny hear a word.'

'I've tried and all,' said Henry, without looking up from his task. 'Steenie, can ye wedge that balk there – no, that one – under here?'

Steenie gazed uncertainly at the choice of timbers available, but Michael lifted the length indicated and fitted it into position. Henry looked up, nodded, and handed him another piece.

'Brace that there,' he said, pointing. 'I'm fixing the winding-gear, Maister Gil. Aye, that's right, it goes there. I've no notion how we'd get in by the tunnel, but if we can get this sorted we can send a man down on a stick.'

'I'll go,' said Gil, over the churning of his stomach.

'Better be me,' said Michael, now almost standing on his head at one corner of the wooden structure. 'I'm half your size.'

'That's my wife down there,' said Gil. He leaned over the shaft and peered down it. 'How long a walk in from the ingo would it be? There's no light down there yet.'

'There was,' said Henry. 'It went out a while ago. Jamesie Meikle said it would be half a mile. Near half an hour's walking, I'd say, all in the dark like that.'

'And where's the dog?' Gil asked. 'Did he go with Alys?'

'He was somewhere about,' said Michael. He straightened up. 'That's it, Henry.'

'Why has the light gone out?' Gil fretted. 'Have they left to come out again? Surely not. What would – if the man fell down this shaft, five fathom, he's not fit to walk away and two women would hardly carry him. I don't like this. Are we ready, Henry?'

'Near it,' said Henry, with maddening calm. He looked up at Gil. 'I'm no going to go home and tell the mistress I dropped you down a winding-shaft, now am I, Maister Gil? She'd have my head up on the gate to fright the horses.'

'Can we lower a light to them on a rope?'

'Not a good idea,' said Michael. 'See, the light causes an updraught, and the draught makes the light to burn stronger, and either it's all consumed afore it reaches the bottom, or it blows out, or it burns through the rope.'

Light, faintly yellow, flowered at the bottom of the shaft. There was movement, but it might have been the shadows flickering. Socrates barked somewhere, and it resonated with a sound like the Questing Beast. Gil stared downwards in alarm, and called Alys's name. The word echoed and rebounded and returned, and with it like a bird's cry her voice, his name.

'Ready,' said Henry. He dragged the rope's end towards him, and inspected it carefully. 'Aye, it's lasting well enough. Just don't swing about, Maister Gil.' He lifted another piece of timber and proceeded to knot the rope competently about the groove in its centre. Once he was certain it would hold he handed the assembly to Gil. 'Right you are,' he said. 'Steenie, Maister Michael, we'll all three man the beam.'

'He's dead, isn't he?' said Alys into the dark.

'Aye,' said Arbella. 'He's no breathing. *Sancta Maria mater dei, ora pro eo.* It was a long drop, and likely his back was broke wi' landing on these timbers.'

'Yes,' said Alys, trying to keep the doubts she felt from her voice.

'He'd no ha' lasted much longer, even without the fall,' continued Arbella. 'You saw it too, lassie, didn't you? Beatrice tellt me what ailed him. It's better this way.'

'What, dying underground, filthy and in pain?'

'Better men than him has died underground!' said Arbella sharply. 'Coal comes out the earth, but it aye takes blood in exchange.'

'How much blood?' asked Alys softly.

'More than you'd think. But men come and go, lassie. Mind that. Never grieve for one, for you'll aye get another.'

Impossible, thought Alys. There is no other like Gil.

'Like Joanna,' she suggested aloud. 'I think she might take the man Meikle, when she has done mourning Murray.'

'She could do worse,' admitted the other voice.

'She has no notion to your grandson?'

'No,' said Arbella curtly. Then, after a moment, 'They're too close kin. Raffie is her nephew. She was married on his uncle, after all.'

'I forgot that.' Alys was groping about her. 'Did one of the candles fall this way?' She could feel more lengths of wood, smaller timbers than the ones Fleming had landed on, and some flat pieces of metal whose purpose was not clear, and lumps of stone of every size, but not the candle. The top of the shaft showed faintly less dark in the blackness, but no light came down it.

'No, they went to my other side.'

The conversation at the top of the shaft continued, and in its silences the sounds of the mine grew. Water dripped, there was a distant tapping, stone creaked again. Alys began to be aware of just how much stone lay above her head.

'What led your man to find Thomas Murray?' asked Arbella suddenly.

'He found the place in Lanark where the man went drinking,' said Alys, 'and they told him who his friend was. When he knew also that the friend had not been seen for as long as Murray, he went to his house to see what could be learned, and so found them.'

'Aye.' Another pause. 'Mind, I never knew that about Thomas. If I'd ha' known –'

'There was an owl in the trees by the cottage,' said Alys, as if it was to the point.

'It wasny within the place,' said Arbella, as if that answered her.

'Will you not search for the candles, madam?' asked Alys. But my flint and tinder are in my purse, she realized.

'Feart for the dark, are you, lassie?'

'It doesn't trouble you, does it – being in the dark, I mean?'

'It's never troubled me. You sit here quiet, you'll hear the voice of the coal. And your man thinks Thomas was poisoned. What makes him so certain?'

'We tested the dregs of the flask,' said Alys cautiously. Was that a movement she could hear, along the tunnel they had climbed to reach this place?

'Oh, aye? The flask. Had they both drunk from the one source, then?'

'Both are dead,' Alys said.

'And they died how? It wasny right clear at the quest.'

I have heard Gil give evidence before, thought Alys, he would have made it very clear. Aloud she said, 'It seems as if they felt no signs until they were abed, and then perhaps they were dizzy and became unconscious, and so died. There was no other sign to be found, as he told Mistress Lithgo two days since, no effect on their bellies.'

'Aye,' said the other voice in the darkness. 'That would be right. And has your wisdom discerned yet what it was they took?'

'Not yet.' Well, she thought, I am not certain yet. She turned her head to listen; there was definitely movement, stones shifting under a footfall. What was the voice of the coal, anyway? Closer at hand Arbella's leather sark creaked.

'You're slow, for one that claims to be herb-wise. And what will your man do next to find who is to blame?'

'He will ask more questions.'

'Aye, he's good at that,' said Arbella. It was clearly not a compliment. 'Did my good-daughter talk to you yestreen?'

'Mistress Lithgo?' There was a thumping overhead, as if someone was hammering timbers, but there was also certainly movement close to her, on both sides. Arbella was stirring, the little sounds of leather and stone suggesting that she was indeed searching for the candle, and from down the sloping tunnel came the footfalls again. Something was approaching slowly through the dark. She stretched her ears, trying to hear the tiny noises. Not booted feet, surely? 'Yes, I spoke to her. She said she poisoned Thomas Murray, because he was annoying her daughters and Joanna.'

'She never did such a thing.'

'No, I think not,' agreed Alys.

'You said that afore. Why d'you think not?'

317

'I think she is protecting her daughters.'

'You think one of my lassies poisoned Thomas?'

'I think Mistress Lithgo fears it, or fears my husband might think it.'

Close beside her, something large moved, a waft of hot fishy breath reached her. She recognized it just as the cold wet touch came on her cheek.

Socrates.

Stifling laughter, she put an arm across his reassuring narrow back, and he licked her face as Arbella said, 'But not you. Why not?'

Where are Jamesie and his men? she wondered. What is happening overhead? I do not know how long I can hold off this inquisition, and what if she becomes angry?

'Why not?' repeated Arbella. 'What does your man think?'

'We haven't spoken of it since yesterday,' she parried.

The scrape of flint and steel alerted her. Almost automatically she turned her head away and closed her eyes, and light flared beyond her eyelids. Beside her the dog tensed, and she felt him growl. Her free hand closed on one of the lengths of wood which lay beside her, and she opened her eyes, to find the space where she sat lit by one candle, in brilliant contrast to the total darkness. David Fleming lay on the heap of timbers staring blankly at the stone roof, and Arbella was on her feet, lunging towards her, knife in one hand and a lump of rock in the other.

Scrambling up and swinging the balk of wood she struck the knife, and it flew glittering into the tunnel and rattled down the slope. She hefted the stave, twisted it, swung it back, realized she had grasped it in the hold which Gil had shown her – how many days ago? – and struck Arbella's wrist. The woman cried out, and recoiled. The dog bounded snarling round them, threatening to upset the candle again, and wonder of wonders Gil's voice echoed down the shaft, booming and resounding but heart-warmingly familiar.

'Gil!' she shrieked. Wood creaked high up, and stones rattled down the shaft and fell on her leather hood. Her opponent hissed, and lunged again, and Socrates leapt to seize the old woman's arm. Arbella struck at the soft of his nose with the stone, breaking his grip, and flung herself forward. Alys swung her wooden stave again, *across, and twist the blade, and back*, stepped backwards to avoid the reaching hands, and went down as her foot turned on a stone, writhing round to land on one knee. Using the stave to hold off her attacker, she scrambled to her feet, and the dog leapt past her, snarling hideously, struck Arbella at shoulder height with his forepaws, and brought her down.

More stones rattled down the shaft, and Gil shouted urgently to her, but she was panting too hard to answer him. The dog was standing over Arbella, his teeth at her throat. Blood dripped on her from his muzzle. Rope creaked and twanged, and suddenly Gil arrived beside her with a rush and a clatter of wood, blinking in the light, whinger in hand.

One breath, and he took in the situation.

'You picked a strange place to practise,' he said. 'I told you to keep the point up.'

'I was distracted,' she said. 'Gil, she killed Fleming, before he could tell me what he knew.'

'He was next thing to dead already,' said the woman on the ground. Socrates growled. 'I gave him his quietus, no more. Call your dog off me, Maister Cunningham, if you would, and you'll need to have a care to your wife, for I think her mind's turned wi' the dark. It does that to folks.'

'Does it?' said Gil politely.

319

'And she poisoned Thomas Murray,' said Alys.

'It could be nobody else,' he agreed.

'You've no even worked out what slew him,' said Arbella, though the dog growled again. 'How can you tell who it was?'

'I know very well what slew him. Where is the yew tree, madam?' asked Alys. Gil looked down at her, and smiled in the candlelight.

'Of course,' he said.

'Your mind's turned, lassie,' said Arbella again. Socrates' snarl grew louder. 'Call this brute off me, maister, I'm an old woman and it's no right to keep me here on the cold ground wi' a savage beast standing ower me –'

'Was it right to kill Murray and an innocent bystander?' Gil asked. He handed Alys his whinger, and lifted the stick which had fallen the last few feet of the shaft with him, measured the broken end of the rope which was tied to it, and began to unravel the knots about the stick. Arbella shrank away from the dog's teeth, the hood of her leather sark falling back. Her linen undercap had come askew, and her white hair straggled loose, the blood from the dog's nose darkening it in the candlelight.

'None so innocent, was he?' she retorted. 'Filthy catamite!'

'He had done you no harm, and he should have had his chance at repentance. But those were only the most recent, I think. What about the others?'

'What others?' said Arbella scornfully. 'You're raving, the pair of you.'

'Your husband,' said Gil. 'Your son Adam, seven years after him –'

'Attie went under a roof-fall, ten fathom that way.' She jerked her head sideways, and the dog growled deep in his chest.

'Like the one today?' said Gil. Alys glanced at him in the dim light, then hastily back at her target. 'So you admit to poisoning your husband?'

'I said no such thing.'

'And there was your other son, seven years after Adam.'

'You're reading a strange lot into our ill fortune, sir.' Arbella stirred, and the dog snarled in her face. 'Free me of this monstrous brute, afore the roof falls here –'

'Is that a threat?' Gil was still working on the knots. The light could be no help, thought Alys, glancing at him again. He must be working by touch alone. 'Why did you kill Murray?'

'Have I said I did?'

'I know you did, and I've a good guess at why. I just want to know which reason you'll give me.'

'No, maister, you tell me. Why should anyone kill Thomas Murray?'

'He asked too many questions, didn't he?' said Alys, still holding the sword ready. 'He had got too close to the secret.'

'Secret!' scoffed Arbella from her prone position. 'What secret?'

'Give me the sword,' said Gil, 'and you tie her arms.'

Alys obeyed, the dog was persuaded with difficulty to stand back, and Arbella sat up, still scoffing. Alys bound her arms at elbow level, and said quietly, in the old woman's ear, 'Did he know who her father was?'

The spare body between her hands jerked convulsively at the words, but what Arbella said was, 'Whose father? All the fathers in the place is dead.'

'That's true,' agreed Alys. And whose doing is that, madam? she thought. 'But had he guessed it?'

Arbella threw her a glance of acute dislike, but did not answer. Gil watched carefully, saying nothing. Alys sat back on her heels and went on.

321

'As grieve, he had access to the accounts. There's a lot to be learned from well-kept accounts, Mistress Weir, and yours are very well kept. I think Murray had come too close to – to a thing you would rather he didn't spread about. So first of all you wedded him to Joanna, but that was hardly a success, was it?' Arbella said nothing. 'Then when he began to ask for more favours, he had to go. What had he asked for? Money? Control of Joanna's portion?' Still there was no answer. 'And you have killed before, madam, haven't you, many times, as my husband says? But that was different. That was for the coal.'

'For the coal?' Gil repeated.

'Coal takes blood in exchange, she told me.' Alys leaned closer to Arbella again. 'If I swear,' she said coaxingly, 'to do my best to make sure she never learns, will you confess to poisoning Thomas Murray?'

There was a pause. Bruised, dishevelled, sticky with blood which was not hers, Arbella turned her head to stare at Alys.

'Now why would I do that?'

'Because you love her,' said Alys. 'You use your grandchildren, don't you? Raffie to be a learned man, Bel to fetch your herbs home, Phemie to gather intelligence. But you don't use her, you indulge her and pet her. You love her.'

There were voices, away down the tunnel. A light glimmered on the rock faces. Arbella turned her head to look down that way, and drew a deep breath and released it.

'What will you swear by?' she asked harshly.

'Yew,' said Lady Egidia. 'Yes, of course.'

'That was what Bel told me,' said Gil, tightening his clasp on Alys. He was beginning to feel warm again. 'I misinterpreted what she wrote. *Arbella poison yew.*'

322

'How effective a poison is it?' asked Michael Douglas, across the hearth.

'Very,' said Alys. 'It will kill a horse that eats some of the leaves.'

'A brew of the bark or the needles would do it,' said Lady Egidia. 'Bitter, I expect, but the cordial tastes strongly enough, by what you say, no doubt it would be disguised.'

Gil nodded, and stretched his feet nearer the fire, beside the sleeping dog. Alys moved closer against his side, and smiled up at him.

When he and Alys had reached the gates of Belstane in the middle of the afternoon, chilled to the bone and caked in the mud of the coal-heugh, Lady Egidia had taken one look at them and ordered the fire lit in the washhouse. They had scandalized Alan Forrest and deeply amused his mistress and her waiting-woman by sharing the resulting hot tub, and were now clean and relaxed. Alys's hair was still lying loose on her shoulders and shining in the candlelight, to Gil's quiet pleasure. Even when Michael had arrived to report Arbella's safe incarceration in Lanark jail, she had not covered it again, but only bound it back with a linen fillet, quite as if the young man was a member of their close family.

'And was Fleming right about the witchcraft?' asked Lady Egidia now.

'Yes and no,' said Alys. 'There was – there was certainly evidence. He showed us several wax mommets, all stuck with thorns and pins, and Henry and I found – ugh!' She shivered. Gil tightened his arm about her again, thinking of the way the little brocade bag had flared yellow smoke and made a great stink when they thrust it into the remains of the washhouse fire. 'But I think the witchcraft was Arbella's work, not any of the others. They were as horrified as the men to see it.'

'You haven't got her to confess?'

'Not to that,'said Michael, 'and no need for it, that I see.'

'I agree,' said Gil, 'though the Sheriff may think otherwise. The charge of murder is enough.'

'But will that go through?'

'It should, though it's only the one charge. I'd dearly like to see her tried for the other three or four, but they're too long ago, the evidence is too circumstantial. She'll drown for Murray at any rate, and well served.'

'Aye, and why was she busy killing all the men round the coal-heugh?' demanded Michael.

'I'd like to know and all. It seems an odd way to behave,' pronounced Lady Egidia.

'I think you got an answer to that, sweetheart?' Gil asked, looking at Alys.

'Not clearly. I wonder if she is a little mad? She told me that the heugh demands blood, that the coal is paid for in blood.'

'But colliers get killed anyway,' said Michael. 'It's a dangerous trade.'

'Like horse-breaking,' agreed Lady Egidia.

'I think she made sure of a death regularly,' said Alys. 'What is worse,' she added, eyes round with distress, 'is that it seemed to me as if the profits did improve after each one. She must have reckoned that it worked.'

Michael shook his head.

'One thing to get killed in an accident, or in preventing a worse accident,' he said, 'the colliers all know that happens. It's part of the trade, as I said. But to be slain deliberately, without warning or mercy, only for the profits – what a fate for a Christian soul!'

'Her husband and her own sons,' said Gil's mother in distaste.

'And David Fleming's father,' said Alys quietly.

'A vicious woman. There is no end to human wickedness.' Lady Egidia looked at the sprawled dog. 'And you and Socrates took her captive between you, Alys?'

'They did,' agreed Gil, looking down at his wife with pride. 'I arrived like a god from the skies thanks to Henry and Michael, and praise be to St Giles the rope only broke when I was at the foot of the shaft, and there I found the two of them standing over Arbella Weir, and David Fleming lying dead.'

'But what possessed you to go underground alone with such a woman, my dear?'

Alys moved uneasily in Gil's clasp, and he caught her sidelong look. They had already had that out as they rode across the hill, the two grooms at a tactful distance once they had assured themselves that neither had taken any hurt.

'I couldn't find a way to refuse,' she said, as she had said then, 'without making her suspicious. I've learned a lesson,' she added. 'I have never been so frightened in my life. And I was protected, of that I am certain.' She felt under the folds her skirt, and drew something from her pocket. 'Gil, I have not shown you this. I turned my heel on it when Arbella attacked me, and so I fell and she missed me. Look what it is.'

It was a fragment of black stone, dull and heavy. On one flat surface, clear in the light from the stand of candles beside them, in delicate, perfect detail, was a fish.

'You can even see the rays in its tail,' he said, marvelling. 'Oh, I agree, Alys, this is no work of human hand. It must be God's work indeed, set in the stone. But how do you know it was this stone that tripped you?'

'It was in the right place,' she said simply, 'and you can see the mark of my shoe. See on the other side?'

He turned the thing over, and nodded at the scrape on the underside. He was not convinced it was the stone which had tripped her, but it did look like the stone which the man in his dream had given him.

'You wanted one of these,' he said.

'And now I have one,' she said, and rose to show it to Lady Egidia, who inspected the fish in wonder, but passed it to Michael and returned to the point at discussion.

'But was Mistress Weir already suspicious? Is that why she demanded you accompany her?'

'I think she feared Gil was close to her,' Alys admitted. She returned to her place at his side, and he put his arm round her again, still grateful for the reassurance of her safe, solid presence within his clasp. 'But she had been less clever than she thought. None of the men was surprised to see her bound, were they, Gil? And I think her granddaughters were more relieved than anything else. Bel in particular must have known a lot of what she was about.'

'It was only Joanna who made an outcry,' said Michael ruefully.

'That was difficult.' Gil pulled a face, recalling the scene, with Joanna in a hurriedly laced gown, her kerchief half unpinned, first trying to free Arbella and then, as she realized why the old woman was being held, shrinking back in horror.

'If Arbella truly made a pact with the Devil, as witches are said to do,' said Alys seriously, 'I think that was when it came home to her what she has lost by it.'

'But she has confessed to killing Murray,' said Lady Egidia. Her grey cat came into the hall, and she made room on her knee.

'She has confessed,' agreed Michael, 'and repeated it just now before witnesses, down in Lanark.'

'Aye, and what did you use to bargain with her, sweetheart?' Gil asked. 'I'm not sure what we've agreed to keep secret. It was obvious it was the only

326

way we would get a confession, and we'd no grounds for holding her without one, but I still don't see what we were swearing to conceal.'

The cat strolled past its mistress and paused, one paw in the air, glaring at the somnolent dog. Alys watched the animals, biting her lip.

'The real reason she killed Thomas Murray,' she said at length. 'That's what I've been seeking out, talking to the folk who knew Will Brownlie and his wife. It wasn't the question of control of the heugh, though that may have been the demand that tipped the balance. He had guessed something she didn't want known.'

'You said that,' Gil said patiently. The cat stepped forward and sniffed delicately at Socrates' injured nose. The dog opened an apprehensive eye but made no other move, and the cat put out a small pink tongue and began to wash the bruised and swollen tissue.

'She isn't Will Brownlie's daughter, of course,' said Lady Egidia. Alys nodded. Gil looked from one to the other of his womenfolk, assailed yet again by a feeling that they could communicate in a way that was closed to him.

'Who isn't?' said Michael. 'Do you mean Joanna? So whose daughter is she?'

'Who else?' said Alys seriously. 'I think her father may have been David Fleming's father. There is a William Fleming in the coal-heugh accounts about the time she was born, and Arbella was clearly absent for a time.'

'And her mother is – ah!' Gil stared at her, open-mouthed. 'You mean she sacrificed her lover as well as – sweet St Giles! No wonder she doesn't want Joanna to know.' And how had his young, gently reared wife recognized that so quickly, he asked himself. *From helle to Heven and sonne to see, nis non so wys.*

327

'No wonder,' agreed Alys. 'It never happens in the romances,' she added, 'only in the ballads. I suppose it shortens the tale quite painfully, to have hero and heroine realize too late they are brother and sister.'

'Brother and – oh, no!' exclaimed Michael in horror. 'Oh, the poor souls. What wickedness! To let them meet, and fall in love, and never know –'

'And so Matt had to go,' said Gil, working it out, 'and Will Brownlie. In case the secret came out.'

'The man Brownlie can't have known Joanna's parentage,' Alys said. 'If his wife had still been alive she would have prevented the marriage.'

'But is it right to keep it secret?' Michael objected. 'Such a great sin should be confessed and penance assigned, for the sake of her soul –'

'Why?' said Gil. Michael stopped, staring at him. 'What benefit? We have no proof of Joanna's parentage, Michael, only strong supposition. Apart from Arbella, everyone who might have known is dead.'

'She saw to that, I think,' said Alys.

'If there is a sin it was committed in all innocence, it's hardly mortal. Why add to the poor woman's unhappiness?'

'But –' the younger man began. 'Someone should – someone should –'

'Talk to your confessor when you get back to Glasgow, if it troubles you,' advised Lady Egidia. 'Without naming names, perhaps. But I can assure you now, you and Tib are not blood kin in any degree that matters.'

There was a short pause, in which Michael slowly went first dark in the firelight, then quite pale. He turned to his godmother with his mouth wide open, and she put out an elegant, weather-roughened hand and pushed his chin up.

'You look like a carp in a pond,' she said. 'There is the spiritual relationship to deal with yet, but if you're still of one mind, the two of you, I'll talk to your father about it next time he comes home. Likely, between the two households, we can afford a dispensation.'

'Perhaps Gil can help,' said Alys diffidently, 'as head of the family.'

'I've no doubt of it,' said Gil, recognizing the code in this statement. Michael, apparently quite unable to speak, looked from one to another of them and a grin spread over his face.

'And if you wait a few days,' prompted Lady Egidia, 'you'll be able to give thanks to our new saint down in St Andrew's in Carluke town. You realize none of this would have come to light if he hadny come up out of the peat-digging so that you all began asking questions.'

'Possibly not,' said Gil.

'The procession is to be tomorrow,' his mother went on, 'with singers and garlands and I don't know all what. I wonder what the man himself would have made of it, whoever he is? Would he have been grateful?'

'I think he is,' said Gil, thinking suddenly of his dream. 'I think he is.'

The grey cat, satisfied that Socrates was clean enough, surveyed the fire and the dog's sprawled shaggy limbs. Selecting a spot in the crook of one long foreleg, it curled up, its back against the new draught-stop, blinked once at its mistress, and tucked a paw over its ear.

Socrates licked his nose, sighed, and went back to sleep.